BEHIND THE PLATE

THE BOYS OF BASEBALL #2

by

J. Sterling

BEHIND THE PLATE

Edited by:
Jovana Shirley
Unforeseen Editing
www.unforeseenediting.com

Cover Photographer:
Kim Komnenic
IG: @Kim_ic

Cover Model:
Alex Koch
IG: @lx_koch

Cover Design by:
Michelle Preast
www.Michelle-Preast.com
facebook.com/IndieBookCovers

ISBN-13: 978-1-945042-28-7

Please visit the author's website
www.j-sterling.com
to find out where additional versions might be purchased.

Other Books by J. Sterling

Bitter Rivals—an enemies to lovers romance
Dear Heart, I Hate You
10 Years Later—A Second Chance Romance
In Dreams—a new adult college romance
Chance Encounters—a coming of age story

The Game Series:
The Perfect Game—Book One
The Game Changer—Book Two
The Sweetest Game—Book Three
The Other Game (Dean Carter)—Book Four

The Playboy Serial:
Avoiding the Playboy—Episode #1
Resisting the Playboy—Episode #2
Wanting the Playboy—Episode #3

The Celebrity Series:
Seeing Stars—Madison & Walker
Breaking Stars—Paige & Tatum
Losing Stars—Quinn & Ryson

The Fisher Brothers Series:
No Bad Days—a New Adult, Second Chance Romance
Guy Hater—an Emotional Love Story
Adios Pantalones—a Single Mom Romance
Happy Ending

THE BOYS OF BASEBALL
(THE NEXT GENERATION OF FULLTON STATE BASEBALL PLAYERS):

The Ninth Inning—Cole Anders

Behind the Plate—Chance Carter

Safe at First—Mac Davies

About the Author

Jenn Sterling is a Southern California native who loves writing stories from the heart. Every story she tells has pieces of her truth in it, as well as her life experience. She has her bachelor's degree in Radio/TV/Film and has worked in the entertainment industry the majority of her life.

Jenn loves hearing from her readers and can be found online at:

Blog & Website:
www.j-sterling.com

Twitter:
twitter.com/AuthorJSterling

Facebook:
facebook.com/AuthorJSterling

Private Facebook Reader Group:
facebook.com/groups/ThePerfectGameChangerGroup

Instagram:
instagram.com/AuthorJSterling

Follow Me on These Book Loving Sites:

Amazon
BookBub
Goodreads

Dedication

This story is for every person who fell for our loveable screw-up, Jack F'n Carter and the love of his life, Cassie Andrews. Chance's book is for all of you. I know you've been waiting. I'm so excited he's finally here!

Prologue

The Summer Before Junior Year of College

Chance

THE AIRPORT WAS too bright, light filtering in from every direction as I looked around at the sheer amount of people rushing in and out, avoiding touching each other like they had the plague. Why was everyone always in such a hurry?

My phone buzzed in my hand, and I looked down, seeing a text from Cole Anders, wishing me good luck. I was surprised that he remembered I was leaving today.

Cole was my teammate at Fullton State, and he had just gotten drafted for Houston. I couldn't have been happier for him for getting the chance to pursue his professional dreams, especially after all the shit he'd gone through last season in order to get there.

I typed out a quick reply, telling him the same thing back, and shoved my phone in my pocket when it buzzed again.

I pulled it out, pressed on the screen, and saw a picture of Mac's face zoomed in way too close. Mac Davies was another teammate of mine, but he was also my closest friend. He was currently driving to Washington state to play baseball for the summer there, and I knew he was bored traveling by himself. I sent him a picture of me flipping him off, and my mom swatted my hand.

"Really?" she pretended to scold me, but I knew she didn't really care.

"It's just Mac," I said, like that should excuse my behavior.

"I like Mac. Don't be mean to him," she chastised, and I rolled my eyes, apparently a trait I'd gotten from her since my dad brought it up each and every time I did it.

"I like him too. That's why I'm mean to him." I smiled, and she shook her head, her eyes starting to water.

"Mom, no." I stood in the airport with my baseball bag slung over my shoulder as I watched my mom's bright green eyes fill with more tears. "Please don't cry. Dad, help!" I turned to look for my dad, willing him to come and get my mom, but he was preoccupied with my little sister, Jacey, who wasn't so little anymore.

My mom wiped under her eyes and smiled. "I'm fine. I'm sorry. It's just always emotional when you leave for the whole summer."

"I've been doing this every year since I was a freshman," I reminded her, but it was no use.

I'd been invited to the most exclusive baseball programs each summer since I started playing college ball. I knew how lucky I was to have this chance and how most other guys would kill to be in my position, but I also knew how hard I'd worked for it. Invitations like this didn't get handed to guys who couldn't play the game, no matter what your last name was. I'd earned the right to be on that field with the best of the best, but some players never saw it that way. To some guys, I'd always be riding my dad's coattails, and nothing I did could change their minds.

"I know. It's still hard though. Wait until you're a parent. You'll see," she said before her expression changed, and she swallowed. "No. I mean, do not be a parent. Just say no. Not yet. No kids for you. You're still a kid."

She kept saying all the things she'd told me a million times before, and my dad finally decided to walk over and save me from the lecture starting that was *all his fault, it was about to happen* anyway because of his past.

My mom tended to absolutely freak out whenever the thought of baseball groupies going after her only son shot into her mind. It was like she was catapulted back in time, her face twisting, eyes narrowing, heart breaking. I knew far too much about my parents' dating history and the things that they had gone through when they were my age. But I wasn't my dad. At least, that was what I'd been told a thousand times by everyone who had grown up with him. Apparently, not sleeping with the entire female population made me nothing like my old man.

I'd started keeping girls out of my life once I realized that some of them were exactly like the ones my parents had always warned me about. I'd grown up hearing stories about females with malicious intent, but it never really sank in until it started happening to me in high school. It scared the living shit out of me to realize the things that girls were capable of doing and saying, the lies they were willing to spread just to escape their reality and hopefully gain a part of mine.

There was a time when I was stupid and naive and believed that people meant the things that they said, but I learned that wasn't true time and time again after getting burned by females I'd genuinely liked and thought they liked me back. They didn't. At least, not really. They liked the idea of me being a famous baseball player with a lot of money. They wanted a part of that, and I wanted none of them So, I had become untrusting and closed off. All I wanted to do was play professional baseball, and I did not want my future derailed in any way.

My dad was Jack Carter, former Major League Baseball player—on and off the field—and all-around legend at Fullton State. He cast a long and wide shadow, but to be honest, I never felt like I lived in it. Where Jack Carter was one of the best left-handed pitchers anyone had seen in years, I was one of the best catchers on the field. You tried to steal on me, and it was to your detriment. Take too big of a lead at first base, and I was going to throw your ass out before your fingers even reached back for the bag. I had a cannon for an arm, and I wasn't afraid to use it.

My dad wrapped his arms around my mom and planted a kiss against her head. "What's this about Chance having kids?" He gave me an all-knowing look, clearly getting joy from riling my mom up. It was one of his favorite pastimes, teasing her.

"I was just reminding him that he's not allowed to have

any," my mom spoke up, and Jacey laughed.

"Ever. I'm not allowed to have any ever, apparently," I added, not that I had a problem with that, to be honest. I couldn't even imagine finding someone who looked at me and didn't get dollar signs in their eyes.

My dad stepped away from my mom and toward me, putting his hand on my shoulder. "You know she just worries."

"I know." I narrowed my eyes. "Because of you."

"Well, I wasn't as smart as you are," he offered with a shrug, and Jacey busted out laughing again.

"What are you laughing at, Squirt?" I turned to face her and rubbed my fist on top of her head, messing up her hair.

She used to let me do it when she was younger, but now that she was fifteen, she hated it.

"He called you smart. We both know that's a lie." She maneuvered herself out of my grip and started straightening her blonde hair.

"What do you know about it?"

My little sister was far too fluent in sarcasm and being a smart-ass. I wanted to get pissed at her for it, but it usually made me laugh. My sister and I had a great relationship. I wasn't sure if it was the six-year age difference or just our personalities, but we always got along. Except for when she started crushing and flirting with my friends. I wanted to lock her in her bedroom and never let her out.

"I know you can't pass math." She stuck her tongue out and ran a few steps away, so I couldn't reach her. "Sucks to be dumb!"

I swiveled my head toward my parents, knowing that they had ratted me out to her. What she had said was the truth, but still. I'd delayed retaking this math class for as long as I could, and I couldn't put it off anymore. If I didn't pass this class this coming fall semester, I wasn't going to be eligible to play … *in my freaking draft year.*

The worst part was that I'd gotten drafted right out of high school, but after a long talk with my dad, I decided that I wasn't ready. I elected to go to Fullton State on a full-ride athletic scholarship, and my dad also got offered a coaching position with the team. The goal was for me to improve my game, see better competition, and honestly, take a little time to grow up. Everyone had thought I was crazy to not accept the offer, but it had never once felt like a mistake to turn it down—until now, when things were starting to feel more out of my control.

I wished I were a genius when it came to school and could pass my classes with ease like Mac and some of the others, but I wasn't. And while I knew that an education was important, I really was only at Fullton State to play baseball, not to learn about things I'd never use later on in life.

"Really, you guys? You have to tell her all my personal business?" I asked both of them, not knowing who was to blame.

"She overhears everything," my mom whispered toward me.

"I heard that," Jacey announced from ten feet away.

"See?" My mom's green eyes were wide. "It's not natural."

"Heard that too," Jacey said in a singsong tone.

Shaking my head, I looked up toward the large clock in the terminal and glanced toward the line at security. "I need to get going," I said, my tone sadder than I had intended. The last thing I wanted to do was upset my mom again and have her start crying.

"Did you hear about Coby?" my dad asked, almost hesitant, and I nodded.

"Yeah. Uncle Dean called me."

Uncle Dean was my dad's brother and my unofficial sports agent. Even though we weren't allowed to sign any paperwork until after the season ended, it went without saying that he would be representing me. There was no way that I'd let anyone else handle my career. Not just because he was family, but also because he was respected across the industry and great at his job. I trusted my baseball future in his hands.

"And I talked to Coby this morning."

My cousin, Coby, Uncle Dean's son, was a baseball player too.

We had always talked about going to Fullton State together and playing on the same team in college. I thought it was our shared dream to continue some sort of Carter legacy, but instead of coming to school with me, he decided to play baseball out of state.

I was hurt at first when I found out, but after talking to Coby, I understood his reasoning. He knew that if he came to Fullton, he most likely wouldn't be a starter for a couple years, if at all. He played infield and ours was already stacked. Coby's best chance at actually playing and having a future in baseball was to go play somewhere else. I knew how hard the decision must have been for him to make, and I supported him a hundred percent. He'd sounded relieved when I congratulated him.

"I was really sad about it at first but mostly for selfish reasons. But I think it might be the best decision for him," my mom said, always the logical one.

"It is. He's doing the right thing," I agreed as I sucked in a breath. "I really need to go," I urged, hoping they'd let me walk away this time.

"Have a great season. We'll come out soon," my dad said with a grin, and I felt a little lighter.

I genuinely loved whenever they came to watch me play in the summer. It made baseball feel even more right, knowing they were all there, cheering me on.

There wasn't a time when I remembered even playing baseball without my dad around, so summers always felt a little weird without him. You would think most kids would love the freedom, but I loved having my dad's opinion, feedback, and help. He made me a better ball player.

My mom reached for me and hugged me hard. "You're my favorite son."

"I'm your only son."

"So? You're still my favorite," she said with a small laugh.

"I'll take it," I said. Right when she was about to speak, I interrupted, already knowing what was coming next, "I know, Mom. Stay away from the girls who think I'm their meal ticket out of town."

She shrugged. "You can't blame me for being concerned."

I could.

But I don't.

She wasn't wrong when it came to the way some of the girls acted. It seemed like not much had changed between my dad's time playing baseball and mine. Girls chased me. They left their cell phone numbers on my Bronco windshield, stalked my social media profiles, sent me a million and one direct messages, pretended to run into me on campus, hung out with my teammates to get closer to me, befriended my little sister to get to me—that one pissed me off the most—and showed up at my place, uninvited.

One girl had even broken into my dorm room and waited naked for me in my bed until I got home from an away game my freshman year. All this shit sounded completely made up, and I wouldn't have believed it if it hadn't happened to me. My dad had probably welcomed it back in his day, but I hated it. And my teammates couldn't understand why.

They'd ask, "What kind of guy complains about getting naked pictures from hot chicks all the time?"

What they didn't know was that I'd been dealing with that kind of thing my entire life. None of those girls really wanted *me*. They wanted what they thought being with me meant. Girls wanted Chance Carter, but they didn't even know me Being wanted for all the wrong reasons wasn't a turn-on. I'd stopped trusting girls years ago, and I didn't see that changing anytime soon.

I didn't want to change.

And I didn't know how.

"Come on, Kitten. Tell Chance bye, and let's go home." My dad called my mom by her pet name, and she rolled her eyes, pretending to hate it even though she loved it and wasn't fooling anyone, least of all my father.

"I'll text you when I land," I said as I started to slowly walk away toward the security line in the distance.

My little sister ran up to me and gave me a hug. "I hate that you're gone all the time. Especially in the summer."

"At least you have the twins," I said, reminding her about our twin cousins, Sadie and Sami, who were also her best friends.

"But it's not as fun without you," she admitted, and I gave her one last squeeze.

"I'll miss you too," I said with a grin before I started worrying. "Don't block me on social media," I warned, giving her a pointed look, knowing that I could recruit Sadie and Sami or their brother, Coby, if I needed to get the dirt.

Jacey was always posting things online that drove me crazy, and she knew it. Half the time, I thought she had done it on purpose just to mess with me or get a reaction since I no longer lived at home and couldn't do anything about it. It was her way of getting my attention.

Have you seen the way teenage girls dress these days? I mean, come on.

"Then, don't go all psycho older brother on me, and I won't." She raised her eyebrows, challenging me.

She was always challenging me. No one told Jacey what

to do, and she made sure everyone around her knew it.

"That's my job," I said, reminding her that, as her older brother, I was here to protect her.

"No, it's not. I already have him." She nodded her head toward our dad, who was currently holding our mom in his arms and kissing her like there wasn't anyone else around.

"You can sweet-talk him though," I complained because she'd had our dad wrapped around her little finger the minute she was born.

She gave me a little curtsy because she knew it too. It was embarrassing, watching the way he caved whenever it came to her.

"Not my fault he loves me more than he loves you," she said, and I groaned.

"Try not to break any hearts while I'm gone."

She shrugged. "No promises."

It was official. My sister was more like our dad than I'd ever be.

"I'll miss you. Even though you suck at math," she said before running away.

Little shit. But she wasn't wrong. I really did suck at math.

Coming Home

Fall Semester

Chance

I FLEW BACK home to Southern California the morning after summer ball ended. My dad picked me up at the airport, sunglasses covering his eyes and a grin on his face, and I looked around him for my mom or sister. I noticed a few people eyeing him like they recognized him but weren't sure from where. They snapped photos on their cell phones to analyze later, I assumed.

"Just you?" I asked, still not believing it as he pulled me into a bear hug and reached for my.

I half-expected my mom to hop out from behind a pole or something.

"I told your mom I needed to do some things at the field after I dropped you off," he said, letting me know that if he hadn't said that, the whole family would have shown up at the airport for my arrival and expected me to go home with them instead of heading to the baseball house.

"Thanks," I said, feeling relieved. It was shitty of me to

react that way, but I was exhausted.

School started in two days, and I needed to unwind. Alone.

"I figured you didn't need the fanfare."

"Not today," I agreed, fighting off a yawn.

I'd slept for most of the flight, but I was still tired. Nonstop baseball with only three days off the whole summer would do that to a person.

"Let's get your shit and get you to your new house," my dad directed as he slung an arm over my shoulders and walked us toward baggage claim.

WE PULLED INTO the driveway of the baseball house like we'd done it a thousand times before even though this was the first time we'd driven here together.

"I parked The Beast over there," he said, pointing at the old Bronco.

It was my dad's old car, and I fucking loved it. My mom had said there used to be a hole in the passenger floorboard or something like that, but my dad had had it fully restored at some point during my childhood after I told him I wanted it when I was bigger. I never remembered saying that, but I must have because he had given it to me on my sixteenth birthday, and I'd been driving it ever since. I loved that damn car.

"I've missed driving it." I opened the passenger door, stepped out, and stretched, reaching my arms high into the air.

My dad popped the trunk before leaning out the driver's window. "Come home for dinner soon. Before things get too crazy here."

"I will," I promised.

When I'd first moved out freshman year, we had tried to have family dinner with everyone once a week. I learned quickly that I wouldn't be able to realistically make that happen. School and baseball were too time-consuming, so we had switched it to once a month. Sometimes, I made it, but most of the time, they happened without me, much to my mom's disappointment. I hated making her sad, but I could only do so much.

"Now that Coby's gone, me and your uncle are outnumbered," he said with a shake of his head. "There're five of them, Chance. Five!" he added, and I laughed before realizing that he was right.

The two Carter households had officially been taken over by females … not that they hadn't always run the show in the first place.

"Maybe I'll just stay here," I teased, and my dad growled. He literally fucking growled.

"Just get your ass home. And call your mother," he demanded, and I gave him a head nod as he drove away.

I pulled my travel baseball bag across the driveway toward the front door. Nudging it open, I was immediately hit with a rush of air, and I realized that the sliding back door must be open. Laughter and cheers filled the otherwise quiet space, and I knew that whoever was here was out in the backyard. I tried my best to sneak into my room without anyone noticing.

Cole had made sure that I got his old bedroom before he moved out last year. It had its own bathroom and a lock on the door. Two things I desperately needed if I wanted to ensure any kind of privacy. Which I did.

It was my draft year, and it was hard enough in general to keep the girls away, but living in the baseball house was going to be even more challenging. Cole had known that, and that was why he made sure that I was the one who got this particular room, even when a senior on the team said it should be his simply based on seniority. He was one hundred percent right, but he thankfully backed down once he heard the reasons why I wanted it, and it didn't cause a problem between us. The last thing I'd needed was to fight with a guy on my team over a fucking room.

"Hey, man," Mac's voice rang out as he walked through my door, a big grin on his face.

I stopped pulling things from my bags long enough to greet him.

"Hey. Good to see you," I said as we clapped each other on the backs. "I was just wondering if you were here or not."

"Everyone's out back. I just got in," Mac said. He was from Arizona and was one of the few guys on the team from out of state. "How was your summer? I saw your stats. You were on fire." He grinned like he was so full of pride that he might burst.

I'd had a great summer at the plate and behind it. "Yeah. Aside from the usual bullshit, it was really good."

Mac plopped down on my bed and bit into an apple I hadn't even seen him holding. I wondered for a second if he'd pulled it out of his pocket or where the hell it had come from when he asked, "What kind of bullshit?"

"The *Jack Carter's your dad*, *egotistical asshole teammates*, and *girls who don't take no for an answer* kind," I said with a tired voice and a nod.

It wasn't anything Mac hadn't heard or witnessed before. We'd been friends since we were freshmen, playing together for just as long. He always said that my loss was his gain. I needed the girls to stay the hell away from me, and Mac wanted them all, especially after he'd gotten his heart broken one time after a game. We were complete opposites when it came to females, but there wasn't anyone I trusted more than him to have my back.

"Standard Carter shit," he said as he took another bite into the fruit, the juice spraying everywhere.

"Pretty much."

"Tell me about it though. I want to hear details, man. My summer team blew. I did all right, but the competition was weak," he said as I continued to hang up my clothes in the closet and toss shit into my dresser without folding them.

Mac had gone to play at a lower league than I had played in, but it was still one of the best in the country. I was actually surprised to hear that he hadn't had a good time. The whole point of playing during the summer was to be seen by scouts and to face competition we wouldn't otherwise.

Summer ball was supposed to give us the chance to get more exposure.

"Your team wasn't good?"

He shook his head. "Not like I was expecting. Every team we played was like playing here. I think I wanted more. A chance to get better, you know? To play against guys who would push me to push myself."

"I completely understand," I said because that was the whole reason I'd gone to college instead of playing professional baseball straight out of high school. I wanted to get better first. "I'm sorry your team sucked though."

"Just sorta felt like a waste of time, you know?"

"Yeah, but it wasn't. Trust me." I stopped putting shit away to look at him. "I guarantee that scouts who didn't know you before saw you, and now, they'll be watching you. Playing there will be a good thing in the long run."

"Always seeing the positive," he said, finishing off the apple and tossing the core into a trash can I hadn't even known was sitting next to the desk. "Tell me something, Carter." He didn't finish his thought, so I gave him a look, and he continued, "The guys on your team really gave you shit about being there?"

"Just one," I said as I thought back to the last few months on the East Coast.

"How does anyone play with you for a single inning and think you got there because of your dad?"

"I don't know." I shrugged. "But I'm used to it by now. I've heard it my whole life. I know it's bullshit," I said with a bored look as my mind started replaying the night it had all exploded.

The first thing I'd learned since stepping onto the field this summer was that Dylan Breakers was an asshole. He played right field, and God had blessed him with an arm from the heavens. That kid could throw someone out at home from two hundred feet away without breaking a sweat. But like I'd already said, he was an asshole. I'd even heard rumors that his teammates back home couldn't stand to be around him. It was hard, competing with an ego that choked all the air out of a room.

"At least we'll be getting drafted off of our skills and not our daddy's last name," Dylan said one night during a group dinner out.

I hit the top of the table, making a glass of water spill and silverware clatter. The rest of the team stopped moving, even their mouths stopped chewing. To be honest, I thought everyone was holding their breath.

It wasn't the first time I'd been accused of riding my dad's coattails, and I knew it wouldn't be the last, but I'd had enough of Dylan's piss-poor attitude today. He'd thrown a hissy fit during the game when he got called out on strikes during two of his three at bats. He had kicked the dirt, yelled at the umpire, and thrown his helmet in the dugout, narrowly missing a teammate. Dylan was a fucking virus who had the ability to infect a whole team, and I hated him for it.

His fiery eyes met mine, daring me to make a move. "Got something to say, Carter? Say it!" he screamed, creating even more of a scene than I'd just done.

I didn't even have to look around to know the entire bar was watching us and most likely filming on their phones whatever altercation was about to take place.

My teammate Jason's arm splayed across my chest, holding me in place. "He's not worth it, man."

"What'd you say?" Dylan's chair screeched as he pushed it back to stand, tossing the girl from his lap, who yelped in response as she struggled to stay upright.

"I said, you're not worth it," Jason responded, his tone bored. He reached for another fry, put it in his mouth, and chewed it slowly.

"I'll be worth more than your life after the draft next year," Dylan said in such a convincing way that I thought he actually believed it.

I started laughing and couldn't stop.

My laughter continued as the sound of patrons getting back to their food made its way to my ears. I was grateful they had stopped fixating on us. The last thing I wanted to do was get in an actual fight with a teammate in front of the whole town, but this summer had the potential to be explosive. There were too many egos, too close to draft season. Every guy on the team thought they were better than the next. Shit was bound to hit the fan at some point.

"What the hell are you laughing at?" Dylan asked as his face flamed with color.

"You," I said, staring right at him. "You're a joke. A delusional fucking joke." I pushed my chair back, stood tall, and leaned over the table to make sure he could hear me without my having to shout. "You'll be lucky to get drafted at all with your attitude. Do any of your teammates back home even like you?" It was a low blow, and I knew it, but

sometimes, I had a bit of a temper.

It was the one thing I knew I'd gotten from my dad, and I wasn't sorry about it. That Carter fire came in handy when guys underestimated me. They thought I was chill and laid-back and could use me as a verbal punching bag. But push me too far, and all kindness disappeared.

I distinctly remembered two times when my dad had lost his temper.

The first was when someone had disrespected my mom at dinner. He hit on her when she went to the restroom, waited for her to come out, and then tried his luck again.

My dad had a bit of a possessive streak when it came to my mom, and after hearing all the things they'd been through as a couple, I honestly couldn't blame him. And even I had to admit that it was nice to see my parents still so in love even if they grossed me out half the time.

When the offending guy stood up at exactly the same time as we did to leave the restaurant, his eyes firmly attached to my mom's ass, my dad didn't give him a chance to apologize before he punched him in the jaw and told him to never look at his wife again.

"Breathe in her direction, and it will be the last thing you do. Push me on this. I fucking dare you."

It was scary as hell, seeing my dad so angry, but I also remembered feeling weirdly proud. My dad was a badass, and my mom loved it. She hung all over him, draping kisses on his cheek as we left, and could barely stay in the passenger seat on the entire drive back home. I'd learned in that moment that the right woman would want you to go to bat for her, so to speak. Or maybe it was just my mom?

The second time my dad had come unglued, his temper like a wild beast, was when a pissant, stupid kid tried dating my sister just because she was Jack Carter's daughter. My dad overheard him in the pool one day, asking Jacey where her dad was and asking when he could meet him and if she thought he would sign a couple of baseballs for him and his friends. When Jacey asked why he cared so much about her dad and not her, he admitted that his friends were huge fans and that was why he had asked her out in the first place.

My dad stormed outside and practically dragged the kid from the pool by his hair before threatening his life—a twelve-year-old boy with braces. He told him he'd rip the braces off his teeth with his bare hands if he ever talked to Jacey or pretended to like her because of who her father was. Needless to say, that kid was never seen at our house again, and after Jacey was done having a meltdown of epic proportions, she had thanked our dad for sticking up for her.

My dad was fiercely protective over our family, and I respected it.

"Like I said, Carter, you're only here because of your last name," he spat.

I shook my head before sitting back down. That was literally all he had to say to me, and we both knew it was bullshit.

"Chance is here because he's the best catcher I've ever seen behind the plate. You know it. I know it. Coach knows it. Hell, all the scouts know it too. You're only here because your last name is played out, and frankly, it's fucking

stupid."

"Fuck you, McAllister," Dylan said to our best pitcher, Cayden, before sitting down and pulling the girl back onto his lap.

She squealed in delight, and before I knew it, they were making out, all conversations stopped.

"Thanks." I gave a nod to Cayden.

"It's all true," he said, "but you're welcome anyway."

"Chance?" Mac's voice dragged me back into the present. "You good?"

"Yeah, man. Sorry. Just got lost there for a second." I went back to unpacking.

"So"—Mac grinned at me, and it was the kind of grin that told me I was going to hate whatever he said next—"end-of-summer party before school starts?"

"Are you asking me?" I cocked my head toward him because it had sounded like a question.

"I'm not asking, dude. It's happening." He wiggled his brows, and I realized that even though he was legit the most girl-crazed guy I'd ever met in my life, I'd missed hanging out with him.

"When?" I wasn't in the mood at all to have a party at the house, but I knew I'd be in the minority.

The guys loved having people over. Correction: the guys loved having *girls* over. And girls were the last thing I wanted. If it were up to me, we'd never host any parties or have any single females here.

"Later."

"Tonight?" I blew out an exasperated breath. All I wanted to do was sleep. I was exhausted.

"Yep. And don't even think about staying in this room all night, or I'll fill it with pussy. And I don't mean cats."

"Get out." I pointed at my door with a laugh, and he stood up and walked backward, his hands in the air, still whispering under his breath.

After looking around at the things I still had left to organize, I fell backward onto my bed, knowing that Mac would follow through with his threat if I tried to hide in here without at least making an appearance.

Guess I have a party to get ready for.

Pre-Fall Party

Danika

"THE GUYS ARE throwing a party tonight," my roommate announced as she bounced into our tiny living room, where I had been sitting and reading a book quietly just moments before.

She was always ridiculously happy. I guessed that was what happened when you had a name like Sunny. You had to live up to it.

"What guys?" I asked because there were thousands of guys on campus, and without being more specific, I had no idea who she meant.

"The baseball team!" she exclaimed, and her smile grew even wider.

Like I'd said, Sunny was the epitome of her name.

If there were an opposite to her light, it would be me. Sunny was all blonde hair and fair-skinned, where I was dark-haired and olive-toned. She had been born and raised in the suburbs of Southern California, and I had been born and raised in the city of Manhattan. We were as different as night and day, but somehow, our friendship worked. What I liked most about Sunny was that she was genuine and honest—two things that I respected more than anything else when it came to girls who were my friends … or when it came to anyone actually.

"Okay. And your point is?" I folded my book, my hand tucked between the pages to hold my place as I waited for her reply. I couldn't have cared less that the baseball team was throwing anything, much less a party.

Don't they celebrate themselves enough?

It wasn't that I didn't like to go to parties on campus because I absolutely did. I loved the freedom that being away from home gave me, and I intended to enjoy it for as long as I was still living in California—away from the watchful eye of my father. My dad wasn't a bad guy by any means, but he worried about his only child—me. And after my mom had died the summer before my senior year of high school, his worry had turned into a serious bout of overprotectiveness. One I needed to escape before it suffocated the life out of me completely.

"My point is that it's the baseball team! Make an exception this one time. For my sake? Please," Sunny begged, her pretty smile now turned into a full-on pout. "Jared isn't back from New York yet, and we never go to the baseball parties when he's here."

She wasn't wrong. I usually avoided the athletic parties and only went to fraternity-hosted ones … with my boyfriend, Jared, by my side. For whatever reason, guys in frats seemed easier for me to handle. I wasn't sure why because fraternity guys were in a class of their own, especially when they were drunk, but they felt like pieces of cake to deal with when I compared them to the athletes at Fullton State.

Maybe it was because the athletes on this campus tended to be arrogant pricks who were above the law. Even worse, they all knew it. I didn't trust them. So, I pretended like they didn't exist—unlike every other female on campus. Where most girls chased the players here, I walked the other direction, hoping like hell they didn't follow.

I'd been dating Jared since high school. We moved here from New York together after Jared suggested we go together on a whim one night during dinner. I wasn't sure if he'd even thought it through or not, but the way my dad's face had relaxed, like the idea was the only thing in the world that gave him any semblance of peace about my wanting to move across the country for school, made me unable to say no.

Plus, the idea of my boyfriend and me moving across the country without anyone else was exciting. My only stipulation was that we didn't live together even though Jared had mentioned it once. I thought we were way too young to really start playing house. Moving to attend the same college was one thing, but living together was another thing entirely. Thankfully, my dad and Jared's parents had all agreed. Our two families had been friends for as long as I could remember. Even though I would have sworn up and down that I didn't need anyone to go to California with me, it was comforting, having Jared here. He was a piece of home who always understood me when it felt like no one else did.

I'd been lost in my own thoughts as Sunny continued her pitch, "I want to hang out with the team so bad. Maybe make out with one of the players. Or two. I will go alone because that's how much I want to go, but I really don't want to go by myself. Come onnnnn," she whined.

I removed my hand from inside my book and placed it on the coffee table. I was obviously done reading for the day.

"I'll think about it," I said, and she jumped up and down like a grand-prize winner on the *Wheel of Fortune.*

"That means yes." She did a little dance, her hands waving in the air. "Thank you, Danika. Thank you, thank you, thank you. You won't be sorry."

Even as she said the words, I knew they were a lie. I would end up regretting this. And that wasn't me being pessimistic even though Jared and Sunny both constantly tried to tell me that I was. I was a realist. And realistically, this party was going to suck because the athletes at this school were total assholes, and I was sure the baseball team was no different. Matter of fact, they were probably the worst.

I WAS HATING this already. Sunny was dressed to impress. Well, as much as it took to impress a college guy, that was. The rule was basically this: show as much skin as possible. The end. She was in a tiny crop top that barely covered her girls and painted-on skinny jeans full of rips and tears. I wore my usual ensemble of black leggings with shit-kicking combat boots and an off-the-shoulder black cropped sweater. You could take the girl out of New York, but you couldn't take New York out of the girl.

We pushed through the front door and were greeted by a ridiculous amount of people. All the lights in the house were on, and from a quick sweep of the room, I could see there seemed to be an equal ratio of guys to girls, which was surprising. Usually, at any party, one gender outnumbered the other by a significant amount.

"Woohoo! I can't believe we're actually here," Sunny shouted over the noise in my direction.

I hated that she was so starstruck over these guys.

"It's a college party. We're in college." I leveled her with a hard stare. "Where else would we be?"

"But it's the baseball team. I mean, Mac Davies and Chance Carter are somewhere in this house right now! So are Colin Anderson and Dayton Mawlry. Hello! How are you not excited?"

She waved a hand in front of my face, but I refused to blink and pretended to be bored.

I wished I'd had no idea what those names meant or who she was talking about, but I did. I'd recognized every single one as she rattled them off. I could have blamed the fact that I'd worked in sports tutoring for the last three years before I stopped, but it was more than that. There was no way that someone could go to school here and not eventually learn the names of the athletes who were likely to go pro. It was literally unavoidable, no matter how hard you tried.

Posters of the teams littered the campus walls at every turn, changing out, depending on the season. But in the meantime, they were everywhere—on the buildings, in the girls' restroom, wrapped around light poles. The art department spray-painted graffiti depicting certain players outside their halls. Even the campus bookstore had their walls strewn with the faces and names of various athletes. And they sold postcards of the teams that you could buy and mail out. *Postcards!* For mailing! Who the hell wanted a postcard of a bunch of guys they didn't know?

"Ladies." The voice pulled both of our attention.

Mac Davies. I knew who he was the second my eyes followed his voice. He was actually adorable—as far as surfer-looking, light-haired guys went. But he wasn't my type. I liked my guys tall and dark. Not that I was looking since I had a boyfriend and all that.

"I'm Mac. Your host for this evening." He winked, and before he could say another word, I started to leave, accidentally ramming into his shoulder on my way out. He grabbed me, most likely to help steady me on my feet, but I didn't like it.

"I'm not interested," I said before maneuvering out of his grip. "But she probably is." I thumbed toward Sunny, who was standing there, blushing like a schoolgirl with a major crush.

I knew I came across abrasive to some people, but I honestly never really meant to. It was just that the attitude here was so different from back home. No one was ever offended by my remarks or opinions in New York. But out here, they acted like I'd slighted them somehow or hurt their feelings when I was just being honest. I wasn't the type to beat around the bush or act fake, and that seemed to be what Californians had been raised on. Sunny always encouraged me to deliver my words in a softer tone, but I didn't know how.

Walking away from Sunny and Mac, I looked around the space, wondering where the best place to escape might be. I knew I couldn't hide in a bathroom all night even if the idea sounded good. Someone would eventually need to get in there, and I didn't want to be lounging in the tub, reading a book, while they broke the door down to get in. After seeing how crowded the kitchen and the living room were, I decided to wander into the backyard, hoping for a dark corner. I wasn't trying to be antisocial, but I usually went to parties with Jared, and whenever he wasn't around, it looked like I was single and ready to mingle. Some guys didn't take no for an answer very well, especially when you added alcohol and egos into the mix.

The backyard had little twinkling lights hanging all around, and instead of being annoyed by the cheesiness of it, I found it endearing and almost calming. A small group of people were standing around a keg, but a knee-high concrete wall ran the length of the yard, away from the lights. I made my way over toward it and sat down, hoping to blend in with the bricks or the dark night sky.

"You purposely sit here?"

I turned to my right and jumped. *How hadn't I seen the*

guy sitting less than ten feet from me? He wasn't even dressed in all black, like I was, but he seemed to want to hide even more than I did.

"Shit. You scared me."

"I scared you?" he huffed out an annoyed laugh. "You didn't see me here?" he asked with disbelief in his voice.

He obviously assumed that I had sought him out on purpose, hoping to be near him. Arrogant prick of a baseball player.

"I actually didn't, or I would have sat somewhere else," I bit back, trying to make it crystal clear that my being anywhere near him had been purely accidental.

"Parties not your thing?"

"Baseball players aren't my thing."

"Then, you're in the wrong place," he added, actually sounding a little amused.

"Trust me, I'm aware. This wasn't my idea." I angled my body away from his, not that I could see him that well anyway and he wasn't making any moves to change that fact.

He sat perfectly still in the dark, and to be honest, I was okay with it.

"Let me guess. Overenthusiastic roommate who didn't want to come alone?" He had nailed my situation far too easily.

"How'd you know?" A small laugh escaped from my lips as I realized that he was way too familiar with how we girls worked.

"I've heard that excuse once or twice before," he said.

I wasn't sure if he was trying to be insulting or not. *Did he think I was making things up just to get close to him?* He probably did. He was a baseball player after all.

"You think I'm lying?"

"I don't know you, so I don't think anything."

"You know, you're kind of a dick," I said, my accent growing as thick as my irritation. It always came out stronger whenever I started to get fired up.

He laughed, his voice throaty and gruff. I hated that I liked the way it sounded when I was supposed to be irked by his very existence.

"What's your name?" he asked, and I took it as my cue to stop whatever this was before it started.

"I have a boyfriend," I said before pushing up from the wall and heading back inside toward the chaos, leaving Shadow Guy in the dark.

Sunny was still with Mac, his hand on her waist. I figured she didn't need me around anymore and wouldn't care if I went home to finish reading my book. Which was exactly what I planned on doing after I made sure she was cool with it. Why? Because the boys in books were way better than any guy at this party could ever be.

Meetings

Chance

I WATCHED MISS I Have a Boyfriend walk away from me and laughed to myself. She was feisty and had an attitude and an accent that had instantly pulled at something in me.

My family had spent a lot of time in New York when I was growing up, so I'd always had a soft spot for it. The people there were so different from the people here. They were more direct, honest, straightforward, and forthcoming. At least they always seemed to be. LA was filled with fake people trying to use you, and they would do anything to anyone in order to get ahead. New Yorkers might have had that kind of attitude in their blood, too, but I was fairly confident that they'd stab you in the stomach to make sure you saw it coming, as opposed to stabbing you in the back, like they did out here.

The girl never looked at me again as she stormed across the yard, her long, dark hair moving with each step. When she'd first sat down, I could have sworn that she'd seen me here and done it on purpose. Most girls did. But when I said something to her, she practically jumped out of her fucking skin, and I knew I was wrong. I'd actually scared her. And what did I do? I'd acted like a jerk instead of apologizing.

My mom would have kicked my ass if she'd heard me just then. She was always telling me to stop being so closed off and that I needed to learn how to trust girls and let them in. The problem was, she'd also raised me to keep my wits about me, to think with the brain in my head and not to trust too easily, so the lessons were contradictory at best.

Pushing up from the wall, I wondered why I was still hiding in the dark when I could be in my room. Mac had threatened me earlier, but he'd be distracted with girls by now, and he wouldn't care where I was or what I was doing. I needed to catch up on sleep before school and six a.m. workouts started, so I planned on spending the rest of the party alone, in my room, doing exactly that.

When I stepped inside the crowded party, I found myself searching for the girl from outside. *Why do I care where she is?*

Before I could question myself any more, I spotted her, talking to a blonde girl attached to Mac's hip. She scowled, her face animated as she gave Blondie a quick hug before heading out the front door.

She's really leaving?

I didn't want to care or be intrigued that she was leaving a baseball party alone, but I felt a little of both.

I unlocked my bedroom door and quickly closed it behind me before checking around to make sure no one had gotten in while I left it empty. Poking my head under my bed, behind my shower curtain, and inside of my closet, I blew out a relieved breath when the coast was clear. It sounded ridiculous, but girls sneaking into my room had happened more than once. Grateful that the lock had done what it was supposed to, I fell back onto my bed. My head hitting the pillows was the last thing I remembered.

I WOKE UP the next morning, once again grateful for the lock on my door and the fact that I'd turned off my phone alarm for practically the first time in my life. My body felt like I'd slept more in one night than I'd slept in months. To be honest, I probably had.

Reaching my arms over my head, I stretched before adjusting my erection and heading into the bathroom for a quick shower. Every guy on the team had a meeting scheduled with Coach Jackson today, and I needed to get ready for mine.

I WALKED THROUGH the locker room and headed toward Coach's office. He was waiting for me, and the second his eyes met mine, he motioned for me to close the door and sit down. Up until that point, I hadn't been nervous at all, but looking at the expression on his face now changed all that.

"Coach?" I said with a question in my voice.

He didn't look happy, and I had no idea what I'd done wrong.

"How was your summer?" he asked even though we both knew that he already had the answer to that question.

There was no way in hell that Coach hadn't stalked my stats all season long and read the write-ups online. He'd kept in contact with my summer ball coaches every year since I started playing for him.

"Great. I felt really good out there," I said, feeling a little more confident. If there was one thing I never questioned, it was my ability to play this sport.

"You looked good. So"—his tone changed, and I shifted in my chair, unable to sit still—"math."

One word, and my stomach twisted. "I know." I squeezed my eyes shut with a groan, embarrassed that it had come to this.

"Do you? Because if you don't get a C or higher, you won't pass the class. And if you don't pass the class, you won't have enough qualifying credits to play."

I swallowed around the lump in my throat. No matter how well I'd played this past summer or how good of a player I was right now, it didn't mean shit if I couldn't play this upcoming season.

"I know, Coach. I'll—" I started to say before he cut me off.

"I've arranged for tutoring," he insisted, almost like he'd planned on me arguing. "I can't risk you failing. You can't either."

"Of course. That's fine. I'll do whatever it takes," I said because I meant it. There was no fucking way I wasn't going to play in my draft year because I couldn't pass a stupid math class. I'd do whatever I needed to make sure I passed.

"You start tomorrow," he said before looking back down at some papers on his desk and shuffling them around.

Being a Division One athlete and passing all of my classes was a juggling act that I sometimes struggled with. Baseball required all of my time and attention. If I wasn't on the field, working on my throws from home or in the cages, practicing my swing, I was in the gym to make sure my body stayed healthy or in yoga classes to keep my knees strong and limber from the inside out. Baseball was my passion and the only thing I saw in my future. It felt like there was little room for anything else during each day, especially school and all of its separate demands.

The ironic part was that unless I passed all of my classes, I couldn't even play in the first place. No one cared that Algebra had nothing to do with baseball. All they cared about was that I played for a top-notch university and in a program that required athletes to take and pass classes each semester with a two-point-five grade point average or above. Which was how I'd found myself in my current predicament.

"Can I ask something?" I asked quietly.

Coach didn't seem to be in a chatty mood.

"What is it?" He looked up at me, the large bags under his eyes telling me that he hadn't been sleeping much.

He looked stressed, and I knew that my math problem

had most likely added to it.

"I need a guy tutor. It can't be a girl." I was about to launch into some long-winded explanation about why I couldn't have a female tutor when Coach simply agreed with me.

"I know that, Carter."

"Cool. Thanks. Is that all, Coach?" I asked, hesitating to stand until he excused me.

"Yeah. But keep me updated if you aren't going to pass. Any trouble or if the tutor isn't working out, I need to know in enough time to turn it around. You hear me?"

"Of course."

"Get out," he said, and an uncomfortable laugh escaped me as I exited his office and prayed like hell I'd get a tutor who could actually help me.

SCANNING MY SCHEDULE one last time, I breathed out a sigh of relief. Every other class I had this semester wasn't going to be an issue. For whatever reason, I'd been gifted with the ability to bullshit with the best of them. When it came to things like writing papers, public speaking, or anything else related to my speech communications major, I handled it like a pro.

But when it came to math, nothing seemed to stick. It was like my brain couldn't make sense of whatever was needed to learn how it worked. It was hard. And I didn't understand it. Whose idea was it to make letters stand for numbers anyway?

Walking into study hall with the rest of the team, I made my way over to one of the private rooms and walked inside to see my athletic counselor sitting there, waiting for me. Next to him was a girl dressed in all black who was too damn attractive for her own good—and probably mine. I hated that I'd even noticed.

"Chance, meet your tutor, Danika Marchetti."

I frowned because I could not have a female tutor and Coach knew it. My counselor knew it. Hell, everyone fucking knew it. How was I supposed to trust that this girl genuinely gave a shit about helping me pass instead of just trying to get in my pants? I knew it sounded like an arrogant thing to say, but it happened all the time. And not just to me. Girls volunteered to tutor athletes, but they weren't really there to help the guys at all. They used it as their chance to get close. It was an opportunity too good for them to pass up. They wanted a "ring by spring." Swear to God. I'd heard them say that phrase to each other on more than one occasion. It was even a hashtag on social media.

Girls like that scared the hell out of me.

"Danika," I repeated her name as I stared at her, trying to figure her out just by looking.

The all-black attire seemed to suit her.

"I'm sorry, do we know each other or something?" Danika asked, her attitude and New York accent permeating throughout the small space.

Her voice hit me like a slap to the face. It was her. The girl from the party. Little Miss I Have a Boyfriend.

"No. You're just unexpected, is all." I tried to come off uninterested, but I'd be lying if I said I wasn't the least bit intrigued.

And her name, it fit her the same way her outfit did. It sounded like fire and strength, and that was all she'd been since the minute we met. Danika, the little spitfire.

Her head cocked to one side as she tried to size me up in response, and I wondered if she knew who I was or not.

Did she remember me from the other night? Did she know who she was going to tutor before she agreed to do it?

"I was unexpected? What does that even mean? You signed up for a tutor, did you not? Am I wasting my time here?" Her accent grew stronger, and I knew she was agitated as she directed the last question at my counselor, Bryant.

"We signed up for this. You're not wasting your time. Everyone, just calm down." Bryant tried to make peace, but the two of us were suddenly straddling an imaginary line, preparing for a battle no one else could see coming.

No matter how I felt, it was vital that someone fucking help me with this class and not give me attitude about it the whole time.

"I didn't expect a chick, is all I meant," I explained and instantly knew that I'd said something wrong.

She tossed her long, dark ponytail from her shoulder as she squared off to face me, her hazel eyes ablaze. "First of all, girls don't like being called chicks. Second, you can get a new tutor if you want, but you'll have to wait. Everyone's already paired up for the semester. I was a last-minute add, and they *begged* me to help you," she said, emphasizing the word.

"Why would they beg you to help me?" I asked, not believing her.

"Because I'm the best math tutor they have on campus, and they know it. And apparently, you need me."

"Ha! Need you," the words escaped from my lips in defiance. I definitely needed the help, but I didn't need her.

"I don't have to be here," she argued back, smacking a piece of gum between her lips before reaching for her bag.

"Dammit." Bryant sounded exasperated. "Will you two just calm down?" he demanded.

I stopped fidgeting, and Danika put her bag down on top of the table.

"Danika, we do need you," he said first, and she looked at me with a shit-eating grin, like she'd won this round. "And, Chance, we're out of time. There isn't anyone else, and we've put this class off for as long as we can." He looked desperate, and it's because we were.

Waiting wasn't an option. If I didn't pass the class this semester, I could kiss my entire junior season good-bye. "He's right. I can't wait."

"Then, I guess you're stuck with me, Hotshot." Her gum snapped again, drawing my eyes to her mouth.

"Hotshot?" I guessed that answered my question from earlier; she knew who I was even if she didn't act like it.

That was why girls couldn't be trusted. They were too good at pretending to be innocent.

"Don't get all worked up over it. I'm not flirting with you." She serious, and I would have believed her if her eyes hadn't given her away. No matter how hard Danika tried to hide it, she was attracted to me.

Bryant cleared his throat. I'd almost forgotten he was even in the room. "Now that that's settled"—he sounded uncomfortable—"can I trust that you two won't kill each other if I leave you alone?"

"No promises." Danika batted her eyes in his direction quickly, and he looked like he couldn't wait to get away from us.

"Chance?" he asked, apparently needing my verbal confirmation that I wouldn't kill my tutor before he could actually leave the room.

"Give me a break," I said, slightly annoyed. "Little Spitfire and I will be fine."

Danika huffed out a noise in response to the nickname, and Bryant attempted to ignore it altogether.

"Okay. Good. Great. Just let me know if you have any issues." He moved to exit the room before stopping and turning back around to face us both. "But don't"—he held up a finger—"have any issues. I mean it. You two need to make this work. It's this or nothing."

"I get it," I said, my tone forceful. "I understand."

"Little Spitfire?" Danika fired at me the second the door shut and we were alone.

"Hotshot?" I fired back, and she grinned.

"I'm not little," she argued, and I found myself laughing.

"That's the part you didn't like?"

Her hazel eyes narrowed, and she refused to answer, cutting off whatever briefly peaceful moment we had allowed ourselves to have. "Anyway, is your counselor guy always that rattled?" she asked, and I shrugged.

"I think he's just nervous about the whole situation," I said, as if that explanation told her everything she needed to know.

"What situation exactly?" She was confused. "Us working together?" She wagged a finger between our two bodies.

"I just wasn't supposed to have a girl tutor, is all."

"I gathered that much. If it makes you feel any better, I have a boyfriend. And even if I didn't, I'm not interested."

"Oh yeah? Never heard that one before." I rolled my eyes.

She shook her head, taking two small steps toward me. Even with her "not little" height of five foot six, I still towered over her.

"You're infuriating, you know that? And full of yourself. And you don't listen." She stopped walking, her temper flaring as she glared up at me. "I. Have. A. Boyfriend," she enunciated each word slowly, as if it reinforced her point somehow. As if it mattered. "And even if I didn't, you. Are. Not. My. Type." Her finger poked my chest with each word.

Her eyes betrayed her yet again. The attraction that simmered behind them flared to life.

"You're not mine either," I lied because she was fucking gorgeous and mouthy, and if I had a type, she might be exactly it. "What's with the all black?"

"It matches my soul," she spouted, and I could tell that my question had annoyed her.

I truly hadn't meant to come off like such a dick, but I couldn't help it. She pushed all the buttons I hadn't even known I had, and this verbal battle only served to fuel whatever else it was that existed between us. It sparked in the air, creating little bursts of energy that I felt like I could reach out to touch and put in my pocket to keep for later.

"Your boyfriend's one lucky guy."

"He knows." She shot me a look as she tried to fight back a grin.

I could deal with her being attracted to me. I was used to that from girls. But I couldn't deal with the fact that *I* was attracted to her. That, I wasn't used to. I wanted to grab Danika by the back of her neck and shut her little sassy mouth up. I wanted her lips on mine, so I could do whatever I wanted to them. I wanted to taste her tongue, to feel it everywhere.

I wanted all of her soft parts pressed against all of my hard ones. Her long ponytail was practically begging to be wrapped around my hand until she stopped thinking that she was the one in control here. I wanted Danika whimpering my fucking name as I drove myself inside her and made her see stars until we both collapsed, sweaty and thoroughly fucked.

And I'd never in my life, up until this exact moment, wanted to do any of those things the way I wanted to do them to her.

This was going to be a problem.

A big fucking problem.

And it was only day one.

Tutoring Athletes

Danika

TUTORING MALE ATHLETES had become my least favorite thing to do. Which was why I'd stopped doing it last year after a certain football player wouldn't take no for an answer. He actually thought my signing up to help was some sort of ruse … that I secretly wanted to get closer to him because he had a good shot at the NFL draft later that year. When I told him that I didn't care about any of that, he didn't believe me and suggested we go study somewhere more private—his bedroom. It took everything in me to not lose my temper and do something stupid.

My having a boyfriend didn't deter him. Nothing I did or said made him stop his advances. It was like he didn't understand how any girl in her right mind could not want to date him, no matter her personal situation, preference, or taste. The guy harassed me online, waited outside of my classes when they ended, and even showed up at my apartment twice. I threatened to go to the athletic director and the Compliance Department about his behavior if he didn't stop.

Screw the cops. Going straight to the top of the university scared him more than anything else ever could have. I had grown up learning that money talked more than sense, so if someone could be paid off, they usually would be. I also knew that this guy could most likely talk his way out of a situation with the police or at least have someone of authority do it for him, and the last thing I wanted was to end up in some *he said, she said* situation that spun out of control and turned ugly.

I knew that if I filed a formal complaint with the head of Compliance, they were required to report it, and bigger institutions got involved, like the national committee for sports. He obviously knew it too. That was why he finally stopped trying to contact me and disappeared from my life like he'd never existed in the first place. And I'd stopped tutoring male athletes, only offering my services to females, from there on out.

It wasn't like I needed the money from the tutoring gig, so I could have quit it altogether, but I liked the challenge. I hadn't failed an athlete yet. I was the only tutor with a one hundred percent success rate going into my senior year. My boyfriend, Jared, never understood why I had even started doing it in the first place, but maybe that was part of the exact reason why I had.

When my freshman math professor had asked me to help out a basketball player in class, Jared hadn't liked it one bit and told me as much. Apparently, his disapproval spurred my rebellious nature, and I said yes, partially out of spite.

That single tutoring job spiraled into one that paid. Word

of mouth took off, and before I knew it, I was being requested by name. It felt good to get something on my own, with my own skill and talent, instead of my last name or my dad's help. And the ironic thing was, I'd had no idea up until that point that I could even be a good teacher. Or that I'd like it as much as I did. People my age generally tended to annoy me and get on my nerves but not in this student-teacher scenario. I'd found myself genuinely enjoying helping someone understand a concept that had seemed completely foreign to them before I came along. It felt satisfying to know that I had a hand in a person passing their class so that they could continue to chase their dreams. I knew that I made a difference in someone's life even if it was only for a brief moment.

So, when I'd gotten the call this morning, basically begging me to help one last male athlete, I'd almost said no without another thought and hung up. When they told me who it was for, I pretended not to care or be fazed, but Chance Carter was a legend on campus, whether he wanted to be or not. I assumed he wanted to be. Allegedly, without my help, he wasn't going to be able to play this season. Not a single game.

"His draft year," they had added.

As much as I hated to admit it, I did not want to be the reason that he couldn't play. Not when I knew that with my tutoring, he'd be able to.

I stupidly cared about his eligibility and wanted to help. A perfect stranger who meant nothing to me. A stranger who I currently couldn't stand. He was so arrogant and typical, thinking I wanted him the same way that idiot football player had once before.

I'd tried to convince Chance that he wasn't my type, but I wasn't sure he'd bought it. Which wouldn't surprise me, considering the fact that it was a bald-faced lie. Chance Carter was definitely my type in the looks department—all dark-haired and green eyes that saw way too much and that I swore looked right through me. He was tall with broad, muscular shoulders and thick thighs. He was a freaking god, and I was certain he was more than aware of that fact.

But none of that mattered because I wasn't available. And even if I were, dating an athlete sounded like the worst idea on the planet. Most of them couldn't keep their dicks in their pants, and the last thing I needed was some cheating asshole in my life.

No, thank you.

I wish someone would tell my body that we aren't interested because it clearly hasn't gotten the memo. No, we can't touch him! No, we can't sit on his lap and talk about the first thing that pops up! No, you cannot kiss those luscious-looking lips.

Chance was staring at me from his seat next to mine at the worktable, those ridiculous green eyes boring right through me. Staring. And not saying a word.

"What?" I asked in my most annoyed tone.

"Nothing," he said in response.

Even though I couldn't read his mind, I knew he was definitely thinking about something. I wished I knew what.

"I want to get this out of the way before we start," I

admitted before I could freaking stop my mouth from spilling stupid secrets. I wasn't sure why I felt the need to confess this to him anyway, but it was too late to take it back now.

"Get what out of the way?" He actually looked amused as he pulled some papers and pencils from his bag and placed them on the table.

"My dad's a big fan of your dad."

Chance laughed. "Really? He is?" He sounded honestly shocked.

"Is that so surprising?"

He shrugged. "Well, you are from New York. At least, I'm assuming you are with that accent and all."

"He's a genius, ladies and gentlemen."

He rolled his eyes before continuing, "Most New Yorkers I know are Yankees fans."

"I never said my dad wasn't a Yankees fan," I argued. All I seemed to do was argue with this guy. It was like I couldn't stop myself.

"So, he's a Yankees fan with a sweet spot for my dad?"

"Something like that. I guess they met at one point, and my dad really liked him. Always rooted for him," I added with a smile as I thought about how much my dad liked Jack Carter. He even had a framed signed jersey on the wall of his office. "Even when the Mets were playing the Yanks."

Chance matched my smile with a grin of his own, and a single dimple appeared.

How have I never noticed that adorable thing before this moment? Down, girl.

"Your dad sounds rebellious. I like him already."

I laughed out loud because I'd never thought of my dad as a rebel, but maybe Chance was on to something.

Ralph Marchetti was a big-time real estate mogul who had built his business from nothing but hopes and dreams and eventually a few investors. He'd started from the bottom and worked his way into becoming one of the most respected guys in Manhattan real estate.

"Let me ask you something," Chance said as he shoved his papers and pencils to the side, leaning his body on the table.

I grew nervous, wondering what he possibly wanted to know. "What?"

"Do you really have a boyfriend?" he asked, his eyebrows rising in question as he waited.

My jaw dropped open slightly before I narrowed my eyes. "You think I'd lie about that?"

He shrugged, all nonchalant, and I wanted to hit him.

"Yes, I really have a boyfriend, you arrogant ass."

Chance arched back in his chair and huffed, "You call me a lot of names."

"Well, you act like a lot of things," I fired back.

For every thought he had, I had one in response. It was like a verbal chess match, and I planned on winning.

"Who is he?"

"Who's who?" I asked before putting it together that he meant Jared. "Oh, my boyfriend?"

Chance nodded.

"His name's Jared."

"How long have you been together?"

"Why does it matter?"

"Are you always this closed off?"

"Me?" I let out a brisk laugh because Chance Carter apparently had a reputation for being as hard to get to know as a bank vault locked up after hours.

He was supposedly unbreakable, his innermost thoughts hidden behind a fortress of impenetrable walls, and I hated that I knew that about him. I blamed Sunny for all of my additional Chance Carter knowledge. She had heard me on the phone this morning and put two and two together, and as soon as I hung up, she'd launched into a sixty-second diatribe, detailing everything she had heard about him over the years, including the rumor that he hadn't gone on a single date since coming to school here.

"We aren't here to be friends, Hotshot. We're here to work, remember?" *God, why am I like this with him?*

Chance's face twisted into an unreadable expression before he reached for the papers he'd pushed aside earlier and pretended to sort them.

I found myself apologizing. "I'm sorry. You bring out the worst in me for some reason."

Green eyes met mine as he held my gaze. "I noticed," he agreed before adding, "But you're right. We're not here to be friends."

Six words that kicked me right in the gut. It was irrational, considering the fact that I had been the one to say them in the first place, but they sounded harsher, coming from his lips. I wanted to reach back in time, tear the words from my throat, and shove them into a grinder, where they could disappear forever instead of coming out and crash-landing between us.

"Do you even have friends who are girls?"

"No," he answered without even taking a breath.

I was curious about what made a guy like Chance Carter tick. I wasn't sure that I'd ever met anyone who didn't have at least one friend of the opposite sex. It was possible to be just friends, no matter what people said.

"Have you ever?"

He cocked his head to the side and studied me before responding, "I have a hard time finding girls who just want to be friends with me."

Ten seconds ago, I would have launched another grenade in our verbal war, but I suddenly didn't want to anymore. I believed that Chance wasn't trying to sound arrogant or come off like a typical jock. Somewhere deep inside me, I knew that he was telling the truth. I remembered seeing it on campus—the way girls followed him around or watched him while he ate in the commissary. And even though I didn't follow Chance on any social media platforms, I had come across his pictures before and had gotten lost in the sea of flirtatious and downright scandalous comments that had been left for him.

Without thinking further, I extended my hand toward him. He stared at it a beat before gripping it, his palm pressing against my own. A multitude of fireworks exploded inside my body with that single touch, but I fought them back, pretending that I felt nothing.

"Then, I'll be your first," I said with a grin, and he

cocked an eyebrow.

"My first what?"

"Girl who's a friend." I gave his hand one hard shake before dropping it, breaking our contact and hoping like hell I wasn't sweating. I felt hot and flushed all over.

"Now, you want to be friends? You just told me a minute ago that we were here to work."

He started to jump into whatever else he was going to say next, but I interrupted him, "I know, but I think you need one. You can't just have guy friends your whole life. You need at least one girl who won't lie to you. Who can give you a female perspective on stuff."

"I have a sister for that."

"I'm sure you have a mom too. Neither one of them can ever be impartial. Oh my gosh, why are you making this so hard?"

He laughed. "I don't know. You're like an emotional tornado, whipping things up, changing them all around, and then expecting me to like the chaos."

A tornado, huh? I'd never been called that before. At least, not to my face. "You do like it." The verbal jousting was back on.

"Is this what being friends with a girl is like? I'm exhausted already, and I need a nap."

It was my turn to laugh. "I think it's what being friends with me is like. So, are you in or what?"

He shifted in his seat and ended up leaning closer to mine. "What's expected of me in this 'friendship'?" He used air quotes around the word.

"I-I don't know," I stuttered because I hadn't thought that far ahead, and I didn't usually have to plan out requirements for people I wanted to be friends with. You just decided to be friends, and then you were. "Normal stuff, I guess?"

"Like what? Braiding hair and shit?"

I jerked my head back and gave him a look. "Chance Carter, do you know how to braid?"

His cheeks started to color, and all I wanted to do was tease him more about it, but I stopped myself when he answered, "I told you, I have a sister."

"That's actually kind of adorable." I felt myself softening. All of this internal melting was happening too quickly; it was too unexpected and far too unlike me. I cleared my throat and sat up straighter. "I think being friends for us means that we can talk about things other than math."

"Like baseball?" he asked, and I wasn't sure if he was being a smart-ass or being serious.

I shrugged. "I mean, sure. Yeah. If you want to talk about baseball, we can. Or girls. Or guys on the team pissing you off. Whatever."

"And in return, you'll talk to me about what? Your boyfriend and how romantic he is?" He sounded unhappy at the mention of Jared.

And that shouldn't have excited me. It shouldn't have made me feel any type of way, but here I was, sitting in this small tutor cubicle, next to Fullton State's living god, feeling all kinds of ways.

"I guess sometimes. But just for the record"—I held up a single finger—"girls usually talk about their relationships when they're upset. So, if I did talk to you about Jared, it would most likely be because I was mad at him, not because I was happy with him."

"Is that true? You'd only talk about your boyfriend if you were pissed at him?"

"Most likely," I said with a slight laugh. "Girls need to vent. Venting is like breathing for us. We do it to stay alive and to stop ourselves from killing the people who make us mad."

He leaned back in his chair, balancing it on two legs. "Kinda fucked up, don't you think?"

"What do you mean?"

"That you'd only talk about the bad things and not the good." His chair came down with a slam.

"It's not that." I tried to figure out exactly how to explain this to him. "It's just that we need to talk out the bad stuff. We want to feel validated in our feelings. We're not usually looking for a solution as much as we like someone to tell us that they get it. That they understand. And that they'd feel the same way too."

Chance nodded his head slowly, like the words were sinking into his skin and becoming a part of him. "I guess that makes sense. Totally reminds me of my parents."

"How?" I perked up because this—*this*—was what friends did.

"Whenever my mom gets riled up and is about to tell some story, my dad always asks her if she wants him to fix it or just listen. Then, he reacts accordingly."

Clapping my hands together, I couldn't stop grinning.

"Brilliant. Your dad's literally a genius. Do you know how many fights that question alone probably stops them from having?"

"I didn't before, but I kind of get it now."

"So then"—I extended my hand one last time—"friends?"

"What the hell?" He relented before shaking on it, and I pretended, once again, that I felt nothing when he touched me.

I was officially Chance Carter's first female friend. This was going to be interesting, to say the least.

The Boyfriend

Danika

CHANCE AND I called it a day shortly after our friend agreement. There wasn't much to do until his class met a few more times and we had actual problems to work on. With both of our proverbial walls bearing cracks, we parted ways without exchanging any additional information to get in contact. I decided that was for the best as I pulled out my phone to text my boyfriend that I was on my way over when I noticed that I'd missed a few calls from him.

Thankfully, Jared lived only a few blocks from campus, so I started walking. Being from New York, neither one of us had a car. I didn't even have my driver's license. I never needed it in the city. It was weird, being in a place where not having a car meant that you struggled to get almost anywhere. Ride-sharing was one thing, but if I wanted to go more than an hour away, I could forget about it.

Los Angeles was so different from Manhattan. LA was spread out, wide and vast, where Manhattan was compact, everything stuffed incredibly close together. But that was also what made it so exciting. There was more life packed into Manhattan than most other states had in their entirety.

The energy in the air here was different too. New York buzzed with life that you could feel when you walked the streets, but California didn't buzz in the same way. It zinged underneath the surface … a constant fizzle of energy waiting to explode at just the right time. New York was always exploding.

When I rounded the corner of Jared's street, I spotted his fraternity house immediately, the expansive lawn all brown and dead, trash littered on top of it. I knew the neighbors hated having a frat house so close by, and looking at it in the blaring light of day, I couldn't say I blamed them. I reached the front door and turned the knob, knowing it would be unlocked. The guys never locked their door, which seemed absolutely insane to me.

Unlocked front doors in New York? No. Just no.

"Where have you been?" Jared's voice hit me the second I stepped inside and shut the door behind me.

The living room was dark, the curtains closed to keep out the light as a group of guys sat on couches, playing video games. All of them mumbled their hellos to me without breaking eye contact with the giant screen, and I said hi back as I maneuvered around them, not wanting to interrupt their combat play. Heaven forbid I was the reason one of them *died* during their mission.

"Hello to you too," I said as I reached Jared.

He leaned down and planted a quick peck on my lips. The kiss was over as soon as it had begun. Long gone were the days of passionate, tongue-filled greetings that neither one of us could seem to get enough of. What had replaced them were now routine, almost-obligatory actions. Sunny had said that we acted like an old married couple before reminding me that she hadn't meant it as a compliment. She said we'd lost our spark, not that she was convinced we'd ever had one in the first place. I'd tried to reassure her that we did—or at least, we used to—but she never believed me.

Jared reached for my hand and pulled me down the long hallway toward his bedroom. He opened his door before closing and locking it behind us. "Where were you?" he asked again, sounding either irritated or worried—I couldn't tell which.

"Tutoring," I answered with a little bit of attitude because I wasn't sure I liked his tone.

"You said you didn't have anyone today." He gave me an inquisitive look as he moved to the bed, sat down, and patted the empty spot next to him.

I sat down, and he threw his arm around me, pulling my head against his shoulder.

"I didn't. But they called me this morning, begging for my help."

"That doesn't surprise me," he said, kissing the top of my head, his demeanor softening. "Who's it for?"

"Chance Carter," I tried to say his name with no emotional attachment whatsoever, but my body betrayed me. Just saying his name out loud made it spring to life.

Jared pulled away, so he could look me in the eyes. "The baseball player?" He was not happy.

"Yeah." *Is there any other?* I thought to myself but didn't dare say it out loud.

"No."

"Excuse me?" I argued, my defensive nature prickling. I did not like being told what to do. By anyone.

"I thought you were done tutoring guys. I don't want you to tutor him."

"Well, it's not really up to you."

"Are you joking, Danika? Don't you remember what happened before?" he asked, his voice breaking slightly.

I immediately felt bad when I realized that he was concerned for my safety after the whole football-player incident.

Jared had been pissed when I finally confessed what had been going on. I had tried to keep it all to myself, not wanting to create any more of a scene or involve anyone in the drama I'd wrongfully assumed I could handle on my own. When I realized that I couldn't, I told Jared everything, and I wasn't sure if he was angrier with the actual player or with himself for not being able to protect me and keep me safe. But the worst part of all was that Jared called my father.

Things between Jared and I changed after that. A part of me stopped trusting him in a way. And maybe it was immature of me to punish him for doing what he'd believed was the right thing, but I felt betrayed by his decision. I'd specifically asked him not to bring my dad into it, and he had done it anyway. Jared knew that telling him about the footballer stalking would only make him flip out.

And it did. I was forced to convince my father to let me stay and finish school here at Fullton State when he was ready to put a mob hit out on the player and drag my ass home to the "proper" coast before anyone could even notice the guy was missing. His words, not mine.

Jared changed after the incident too. He started acting differently. Like more of a bodyguard and less of a boyfriend. To be honest, I thought it was kind of hot at first, the way he wanted to protect me like some alpha Manhattan knight in shining armor, but my feelings eventually shifted. He grew too overprotective and started treating me like I was his job, his responsibility … his property. And I felt like a prisoner.

We had eventually found common ground, but things between us never truly got back on track. Not the way they used to be. I compared it in my mind to being on a waterslide: we were on the ride, but a little too much friction or a little too much water, and there was a good chance we were going to fly right off the side and pummel toward the ground.

"Chance isn't like that. He was pissed that I was a girl in the first place. You have nothing to worry about."

His body tensed. "Why was he pissed?"

"Because girls are crazy when it comes to him. I don't know. He didn't even want me there." I pushed to a stand and started pacing before stopping.

"But now, he does? Now, he wants you there?" Jared's dark brown eyes watched me, measuring my words against whatever was going on in his mind.

"Well, we came to an agreement," I admitted with hesitation. "I was his only choice, and he needs to pass the class."

Jared shook his head, his black hair flopping into his eyes. He really needed a haircut. "I don't like it."

"He knows I have a boyfriend." I hoped my words would reassure him that he had nothing to worry about. "And he's only interested in passing the class."

"That's what they all say." He lay back on his bed and pulled a pillow over his face.

I'd just gotten over here, but I already wanted to leave. I pulled out my phone from my back pocket and started texting Sunny, asking if she could come get me, right as Jared's hand gripped my wrist, the pillow that had been covering his face now falling to the floor.

"Stay." He gave me a look that spelled out exactly what would happen next if I did as he'd asked.

We'd kiss, he'd grab my hand and move it toward the bulge in his pants—*why do guys do that, by the way?*—we'd eventually wind up naked, and then it would end … with only one of us satisfied, exclaiming how amazing it was or how badly they'd needed that.

Hint: that person was not usually me.

"I have a lot of stuff to go over and prep for. I should go home, so I can get started," I lied, bracing for at least some sort of argument from Jared. Not only because he had been raised in the same place I was and we didn't give in without a fight, but also because I could stay and do my work here. I didn't need to leave, and we both knew it.

"Fine. Go home then." He flicked his wrist in a wave before staring up at his ceiling.

I stood there, momentarily shocked, as I fought back the sick laugh lodged in my throat. Jared had just dismissed me like I was an annoyance. And instead of feeling angry about it, I actually felt relieved.

That can't be a good sign.

Tutor Girl

Chance

MY "NEW FRIEND" had left the tutoring center before I could even ask for her number. That was what friends did, right? They exchanged phone numbers and sent each other text messages of kittens doing funny stuff and shit. Part of me thought she had done it on purpose—escaped before I gave her a reason to stay. Any reason. She had done us both a favor by leaving. The last thing I needed was to start thinking about her the way I already was.

Thank God she has a boyfriend.

That fact alone made it easier for me to keep my distance. I wasn't the type of guy who poached on someone else's girl. Hell, I wasn't the kind of guy who poached on any fucking girl, but here I was, thanking God she was taken so I could put the possibility of having her out of my mind. At least, that was what I tried to convince myself of as I loaded up my bag and drove back home.

I parked my Bronco in the driveway and headed toward the door of the baseball house before noticing Mac sitting on the front step, drinking something out of a glass bottle.

"Are you waiting for me?"

"Maybe." He looked up and winked.

"Stop being weird," I complained before sitting down next to him and taking the bottle out of his hand. I almost took a swig but stopped myself before studying the label. Thankful I'd looked at it first. "Kombucha. Really? Ugh."

"Don't talk shit about my kombucha. It's delicious."

I rolled my eyes before shoving the bottle back into his hand, wanting it as far away from me as possible. "It tastes awful."

"It does not. I love it," he whined, almost offended, like he'd personally invented the nasty stuff.

"Shit almost killed me the first time I tried it," I said, sounding like a complete pussy, but I had taken a giant gulp my first time and thought I was going to immediately puke in my car. I was lucky the stuff hadn't sent me to the hospital for poisoning or something.

"Not my fault you can't handle the 'bucha."

"Jesus. You did not just give it a nickname." I stared at him, my head shaking. "I'm sure whatever chick you hook up with next will love it. You two can share all the 'bucha together."

"Speaking of chicks to hook up with." He wagged his eyebrows before sitting there, staring at me, not finishing the rest of his sentence or thought.

"Um …" I cocked my head back and gave him a look. "What are you talking about?"

He started laughing. "Dude, your tutor girl! She's hot! Even with the all-black getup. Still hot."

The hair on the back of my neck instantly bristled, and I hoped like hell it didn't show. I'd been so preoccupied with Danika being a girl and all that I'd forgotten that the rest of my teammates were in the same room at the same time with their own tutors. I tried to play it cool and pretend like I wasn't affected by the mere mention of her, but having Mac bring her up rubbed me in all the wrong ways. "Is she? I didn't notice."

He laughed out loud. "You can't possibly be that blind, Chance. I don't care if you're not into chicks or dating or whatever, but you have eyes!"

"You're right. I do have eyes," I agreed in my most neutral tone.

He took a drink of his shit tea and shook his head. "At least admit she's good-looking."

"Why?"

"Because I need to hear you say it. Tell me you think your tutor is hot."

He pushed and pushed, and on any other day, I wouldn't have been rattled, but apparently, today was not like every other day because I. Was. Fucking. Rattled.

"You think everyone's hot," I argued, trying to steer us away from this topic.

He gave a noncommittal shrug. "We both know that's not true. But even if I did, Tutor Girl is on another level. Admit that you noticed."

Why is he pushing?

I was trying not to think about her, not to do anything when it came to her, and Mac was making it damn near impossible.

When I refused to answer, he continued his verbal vomit, “Oh shit. Did she flirt with you? Is she a cleat chaser? Is that why you don’t like her?”

He knew damn well that Danika wasn’t a cleat chaser. The girls who liked baseball players made it overly obvious. They showed up to every game and party, wearing practically nothing as they threw themselves at any player who would entertain their advances. Cleat chasers wanted to screw a player and weren’t at all particular about who they did it with as long as the guy was on the team. The hope was that one of them would stick and turn into boyfriend material. But that rarely, if ever, happened.

Listen, ladies, once you start sleeping around with multiple players on the same team, all hopes of becoming a girlfriend are off. Whatever guy takes that risk will get ridiculed to no end. Not to mention the fact that he’ll have to look his teammates in the eye every day, knowing that they fucked his girl. Not happening.

“Dude, she has a boyfriend,” I finally said, hoping he’d take the hint and shut the hell up already.

“So what?”

“Mac,” I growled.

“Maybe I’ll ask for her number then. I mean, if you’re not interested,” he said, and I wanted to explode.

My body buzzed with something foreign. Jealousy maybe? I couldn’t be sure because I’d never been jealous before. Not over a girl anyway. Baseball was another story.

“She might not be happy in her relationship. I feel like

it's my civic duty to at least find out," Mac said with a smirk, and I got the impression that he knew he was pushing my buttons.

There was zero chance I'd be letting him anywhere near Danika without me around. He would not be adding her to the list of chicks he'd hooked up with at this school. I must have made some sort of pissed off face because Mac put his free hand in the air.

"Fine, okay. I won't go near her. But don't get upset if she comes near me. I can't control how the ladies react to all this." He waved a hand around his body.

I pushed up from the ground and looked down at him. "Stay away from my tutor. I don't need you fucking this up or making it harder than it already is. I wasn't supposed to have a female tutor in the first place," I practically spat before storming inside the house and slamming the front door.

Dammit.

I'd just done the worst thing I could possibly do. I'd lost my cool for no good reason at all. This girl was already embedded in my head and screwing me up, and now, Mac knew it too. I'd all but confirmed it for him.

I'D SLEPT LIKE shit. Tossed and turned all night, Danika's hazel eyes showing up in my dreams whenever I was blessed enough to fall asleep. She haunted me. I'd known her less than twenty-four hours, and she was already fucking with my peace. Mac saying that she might not be happy in her relationship was like a seed he'd planted in my brain. It had grown all night long, sprouting branches and leaves.

I'd never even considered it before … the state of her relationship. Danika didn't strike me as the kind of girl who stayed in something for the sake of staying. She was too full of piss and vinegar for that, all New York attitude mixed with fire. But then again, I didn't really know the girl at all. Maybe she wasn't at all how she seemed. Now that we were *friends*, I guessed I could always find out.

A knock on my door before it opened had me annoyed. I must have forgotten to lock it after I'd gone into the kitchen for water in the middle of the night.

Mac popped his head in. "Good, you're awake."

"What do you want?" I sat up, propping my pillows up behind my back.

"How long until you have class?"

I grabbed my cell phone from the nightstand where it was charging and read the time. "Not for a few hours. Why?"

"Can you come with me to the cages? I need you to look at my swing."

I sat up in bed, leaning my back against the cold wall. "What's wrong with it?" I sincerely wondered because Mac's swing was just fine as far as I knew.

"I've been looking at videos, and I want to work on my power. Just need to make sure I do it right and don't get into any bad habits," he explained while I nodded along.

That made sense. Hitting for power gave you an advantage over other players. If you could prove that you could hit home runs, scouts looked a little harder in your direction when the time came.

"Give me ten minutes to shower, and I'll come get you."

"Thanks," he said before leaving, closing my door behind him.

I tossed off my covers, raked my fingers through my hair, and headed into the bathroom. My focus drifted the minute I stepped into the hot water and started running my soapy hands over my dick. Danika's eyes flashed in my mind. Her red lips parted. I imagined her on her knees in front of me, taking me into her mouth, moaning with delight at the control she had. She owned me, and she knew it. Reveled in it as she sucked and pulled at me, her hands working in unison with her lips.

"You like that?" she asked, and I couldn't even speak a response.

I worked faster, tossing my head back, still imagining that it was Danika's mouth sucking me off and not my hand doing all the work.

"Fuuuck," I said under my breath, and I knew I was close.

Her lips formed a small smile as she looked up at me, her hazel eyes filled with desire and the need to please me.

Faster. I worked my hand faster, jerking and pulling, and still, her face was all I saw. I quickened my pace until I exploded. The white liquid flying out, coating my fingertips, dripping down my dick as I slowed down and finally opened my eyes to survey my otherwise empty shower.

My breathing evened out, and my heart rate steadied as post-orgasm reality crashed down around me. Before I could berate myself for getting lost in a fantasy with someone else's girlfriend, I convinced myself that it was completely normal … that I hadn't done anything wrong because none of it was real. It was just pretend. But it still ate me up inside as I finished the rest of my shower.

After getting dressed, I tried to force it all from my head. I walked down the hall toward Mac's room and knocked on the door before opening it like he'd done to me.

"Ready?" I asked, and he perked up.

"Yep." He hopped off his bed and reached for his baseball bag.

"I'll drive," I said without thinking, my distracted mind obviously ruining my life.

"Well, that's good, considering I don't have a car." Mac laughed, and I knew I had been caught daydreaming or whatever. Thankfully, he didn't call me out on it.

I blasted the radio as we drove, hoping to drown out the possibility of any uncomfortable questions from Mac, but it was all for nothing because Mac wasn't even thinking about interrogating me. He had no idea the war that was raging in my own head. I was being paranoid and stupid.

When I parked the Beast, we hopped out and grabbed our bags before heading toward the cages. I saw the familiar shadow before he saw me.

"Hey, Dad," I said, and he turned around immediately, a grin on his face, his baseball cap pulled low.

"Son. Mac. You guys are here early."

"I need to work on my power swing, Coach," Mac jumped in.

My dad nodded. "That's good, Mac. Your swing is real pretty already, but it never hurts to add power. Show the scouts you can hit the long ball."

"Exactly," Mac said before hitting my shoulder. "That's exactly what I'm talking about!"

"I'll let you two get to it. But, Chance," he said, and I refocused my attention on him, "you'd better schedule a dinner with your mom before she shows up here and decides to eat at the baseball house."

"She wouldn't dare," I said jokingly with a little trepidation because that was something my mom would do.

He laughed. "She would, and you know it. She'd also bring your sister along just to torture you," he said before frowning. "And to make me crazy. Jesus, Chance, call your mother!"

"I will!" I shouted back.

I did not need my mom coming to the house and bringing my boy-crazy sister of all people with her. I'd never hear the end of it from either side. The guys on the team would tease me about both of them, and Jacey would never shut up about who she thought was hot.

"Tonight. Call her tonight," he added, and I knew we were both rattled.

"Promise," I said and watched as my dad started mumbling to himself, kicking the dirt as he walked away.

"That was fun," Mac added with a small laugh.

"Shut up and load the tee," I demanded with a frown as he leaned down for a baseball and placed it on top.

After an hour of hitting with Mac, we cleaned up all the stray baseballs, putting them back into various buckets before we headed for our classes. We walked away from the baseball diamond and toward the large buildings in the middle of campus in the distance.

"Do you have tutoring tomorrow?" Mac asked, and my body instantly tensed, like I'd been caught doing something wrong.

I kept walking, ignoring the looks and gestures from the handful of girls who passed us in the opposite direction.

"Yeah. Why are you going anyway? You pass all your classes with ease," I said, shooting him a look.

Mac always passed his classes with little to no effort. He was really book smart and great at memorizing concepts, which helped him pass tests. At least, that was what he'd told me once during our freshman year. I'd never forgotten it.

"I'm struggling already in Business Principles. Just reading the syllabus gave me hives. I just want to make sure I stay on track and don't slip up. If I get lost at the beginning of the semester, I'll be lost the whole time, you know?"

"Are you even taking Business Principles?" I teased as I pulled my baseball hat lower.

He scoffed at me, "Yes, I am. Why would I fake needing help? It's not like I have a hot-as-fuck tutor working with me like you do. Have you even seen my tutor? I don't think he even goes to this school."

I almost tripped over my own damn feet but said nothing

in response because, no, I hadn't seen his tutor.

"You're going to get drafted this year, Chance, but the rest of us need a backup plan, whether we want one or not."

I stopped moving and held my breath. I hated when anyone insinuated that my getting drafted was a done deal that could never be altered. Anything could happen before the draft next June. *Anything.*

"Mac, you remember Bubba Watkins?" I asked, my breath coming out in waves of frustration as we both stood still.

"Yeah, of course," he said, annoyed with my question. He continued, "He thought he was getting drafted and—"

"No, *everyone* thought he was getting drafted. The whole division assumed he was getting picked up. We all thought he was going," I interrupted, wanting to make my point crystal clear.

"Yeah, I know. *Everyone* thought he was getting drafted," Mac repeated, mimicking my tone.

"But what happened?" I asked, my jaw clenching so tight that I thought I might give myself a headache from the pressure.

"He didn't get the call," Mac said as he started walking again, and I followed suit.

"Right. He didn't get the call. And then what?" I baited, knowing exactly what came next in the story because I'd thought about it a hundred times before.

"Then, he couldn't play the next season because his grades were so bad that he wasn't eligible. There wasn't anything he could do to pull them up in time, and he lost a whole year of eligibility. His last year."

"Exactly." I never took baseball for granted. Nothing in life was a sure thing until it was actually happening and you were living it. Until then, fate could change her mind and completely fuck you over at any time. "Bubba thought he was getting drafted, so he stopped caring about his grades. Didn't make them a priority. And when that didn't pan out like it was supposed to, he lost his scholarship and his spot on the team. I will not be a story like Bubba Watkins. I refuse to be a life lesson whispered about for future Fullton athletes."

Mac blew out an annoyed sound. "Oh, come on, Chance. Bubba Watkins wasn't talked about on ESPN the way you are. He wasn't rated in the top ten national rankings or on every scouting leaderboard across the country."

"That doesn't mean anything." I shook my head, not wanting to sound like a dick because to guys like Mac, it did mean something. It meant everything to the players it wasn't happening to.

But that type of publicity was exactly the kind of thing I couldn't afford to pay attention to. If ESPN talked about me all the time, I didn't need to know about it. I couldn't care. That stuff made guys lose focus. It stopped being about the way you played and turned into being all about what the network was saying. Ego had a way of ruining things for not just athletes, but also people in general. Which was why I maintained strict focus on my game and pushed all the rest to the sidelines.

"Wonder if that means something," Mac said with a nod,

and I glanced in the direction he'd indicated before my stomach twisted at the sight.

Danika was walking hand in hand with some guy. Jared, I assumed. Her boyfriend. The girl wasn't mine. She didn't belong to me. Yet here I was, standing with my hands clenched into fists like Jared was touching something that didn't belong to him. I wanted to rip his hand from hers.

"I told you she had a boyfriend," I said, trying to sound unbothered, but holy hell, I was worked the fuck up.

Jared's hand moved to her lower back, inches from her ass, and I saw red like a madman. She smiled up at him, and they stopped walking as she pointed toward the entrance of a building. Nothing made any sense. Not my reaction to this, not the way I was feeling inside. Nothing. I was not this kind of guy. I didn't do things like this. I didn't feel these types of ways.

"You look really happy about that," Mac said with a laugh as he pointed at my fists. "Thought you weren't into her?"

"I'm not," I bit out before I unfurled my hands. "I barely even know her."

"Uh-huh. Let's go." He punched my arm before pulling on my shirtsleeve. "Carter. Walk."

I did as Mac had demanded, moving in slow strides, still torturing myself by watching as Jared pressed a quick kiss to Danika's lips. She walked away from him without looking back. He walked away from her like he had somewhere else to be. I squinted as I tried to focus in on his face.

Why the hell did he look so familiar?

Not Friends

Danika

CHANCE WAS BEING distant. He and I had been in this room for five minutes, and we'd barely spoken more than two words. He seemed angry. Or annoyed. No, he definitely seemed angry. It rolled off him like waves of energy, filling the room.

"Why are you being weird?" I asked because there was so much distance between the two of us that he might as well be in another room.

"I'm not being weird. Am I?" He looked up and batted his eyes at me.

I refused to be mesmerized by those green beauties.

"Yes, you are," I insisted.

He shrugged.

"What is it? What's the matter?" I pushed because that was what us girls did. We didn't always believe your words. Not when your body language, your tone of voice, and your mannerisms conflicted with the things you said. We pushed when we knew you were lying. So, that was what I did. I pushed.

"Are you always like this?"

"Like what?" I snarled.

"Bossy."

I snapped my gum. "I think you know the answer to that already."

He laughed, that small dimple appearing as he angled his body toward mine, but didn't move his chair.

"Listen, Hotshot, I just want to make sure you're not mad at me for some reason."

"Why would I be mad at you?" he asked, and I knew he meant it. His expression instantly shifted into one of confusion.

"I don't know. You're just"—I paused and sucked in a breath—"sitting really far away. And acting pissed off at the world."

A smirk appeared. "You want me to sit closer to you, Danika?" His tone was husky. Sexy. And I hated how much I liked it. "You like it better that way?"

I cleared my throat. "We obviously can't study if we're twenty feet apart."

"Would you rather sit in my lap?"

What the hell?

"Seriously, what is wrong with you?" I asked, feeling offended and disrespected.

Why was Chance talking to me like that? He was hot and cold, but it felt like something more. Like he was playing some sort of game, and I wanted no part of it.

His chair screeched against the floor as he pushed it back and stood to his feet. I watched him, my eyes wide as he started pacing back and forth in the tiny room.

"I can't be your friend, okay?" Chance said the words but refused to look at me.

My heart felt like it'd lodged itself in my throat. I hadn't expected him to end our barely begun bargain.

"Can't or won't?" I managed to ask through my shock.

"Does it make a difference?" He gave me a side-eye, still standing, his posture defensive, his jaw locked.

"It does to me," I said even though I had no idea what difference it made. Sometimes, I asked questions simply to be argumentative or to get more information out of people. I was definitely doing that now just to keep Chance talking.

"I can't," he said. "Today anyway," he breathed out like the admission physically pained him. "I just … can't be your friend today."

"So, you'll be my friend again tomorrow?" I asked, my tone filled with as much sarcasm because I didn't appreciate feeling like a fool, and whenever I did, sarcasm was my go-to defense mechanism.

He shrugged. "We'll see."

"Friendship isn't a game, Chance. You don't get to turn it off and on whenever you want."

"Fine. We won't be friends then. Problem solved."

I pushed out of my chair and stood before storming over to him and jamming my finger against his stupid rock-hard chest. "You don't get to decide for both of us." I continued my jabbing.

The distance between us was miniscule, but he closed it further, and our toes touched.

"I don't, huh?" He looked down at me, those green eyes flaming.

We were so close that I could feel his breath, feel the heat radiating off of his body into mine.

I swallowed hard and resisted the urge to close my eyes and lean in for a kiss. This guy was not my boyfriend. And even though I was ridiculously attracted to him, I didn't want to be. He pushed all of my buttons, riled me up without even trying, and made me feel too many things.

"No. It's not fair. And it's immature. Grow up, Chance," I spat and took a step back before I did something I'd never forgive myself for. I was not a cheater.

"Immature?" he asked.

"Extremely. The fact that you can't even handle being friends with me when I've given you no reason for it is stupid. And dumb. And moronic."

"You keep using words that all mean the same thing."

"So what?" I said, my tone completely flustered because he was right. And because my heart wouldn't stop racing. I was almost certain Chance could hear it reverberating off the walls around us. It felt that loud.

I gave my heart a silent pep talk, reminding it that there was nothing to see here, but it didn't listen. It had a mind of its own.

I let out a frustrated groan as I moved back to my chair and sat. "Let's get this over with."

Chance stared at me before he slowly moved toward his own chair and pulled off his hat. He ran his fingers through his dark hair before tossing his hat on top of the table. "I don't know how to be friends with you. I'm really not trying to be an asshole, Danika."

"Well, you could have fooled me." I reached for my book and opened it to some problems we needed to cover.

Then, I went to work, attempting to teach Chance Carter math that he would never in a million years even use. Not only because he was going to get drafted and play professional baseball, but also because no one used this crap in the real world and we both knew it.

I SLAMMED THE front door of my apartment as soon as I walked in and made an annoyed screaming sound. "I hate him, I hate him, I hate him!" I shouted, not knowing or caring if Sunny was home or not.

"Who do we hate?" Sunny appeared, a concerned look on her face.

That answered that question.

"Chance Carter. That's who!" I tossed my backpack on the table and dramatically flopped onto the couch, covering my eyes with the backs of my hands.

"Why? What did *Señor* Thick Thighs do?"

Pulling my hands away, I gave her a snarl, "*Señor* Thick Thighs? You've got to be kidding me."

"What?" she said innocently. "The guy's a catcher. He has delicious thighs. It's not my fault. I didn't make him."

"Please stop talking about Chance's thighs. I'm trying to be mad at him here."

She sat on the couch next to me and folded her legs up underneath her body. "What happened?"

"He's infuriating! Said that we couldn't be friends anymore."

"Were you friends in the first place?"

"We were! We made a deal. And he took it back," I said before realizing how stupid and juvenile I sounded. Great. Now, I was the immature one.

Sunny started laughing. "It's not funny. It just sounds funny. You're mad because Chance doesn't want to be your friend. So what? It's not in your tutor job description to be his buddy. Why do you care so much?"

That really was the million-dollar question. *Why the hell did I care so much?* "I don't know."

"Liar."

My eyes flew to meet hers. "Why would I lie?"

"Because you don't want to admit that you're attracted to him."

"Who isn't attracted to him?" I rolled my eyes and tried to play it off, avoiding the accusation.

"Exactly. But you think it makes you a bad person to be attracted to someone other than your boyfriend. News flash: it doesn't. It makes you human."

"That's not it. I mean, it's not like Chance is the only hot guy on campus," I said before I started searching my mind for other hot guys to add to my imaginary list. I came up empty and hoped Sunny didn't ask me to elaborate or start naming names.

"Then"—Sunny tilted her head—"why are you so mad that he doesn't want to be friends?"

"I already told you, I don't know!" I shouted, my temper flaring at Sunny for all the wrong reasons. I wasn't mad at her. I was mad at myself.

"I think you do know."

My teeth ground together with her accusation, and I tried not to think about why I was so worked up by Chance's flip-flopping behavior.

"Danika." Sunny's voice was soft, and I breathed out an exaggerated sigh before facing her.

"I really don't know why I'm so upset. I shouldn't care at all," I started to say before Sunny cut me off.

"But you do."

"But I do. I don't want to. But I do," I admitted before looking away and staring a hole in the carpet. It wasn't judging me the way I currently was. "And I really don't know why."

"Have you ever considered the fact that you might actually like him?"

I vehemently shook my head. "I don't even really know him. I can't like someone I don't know," I started to explain before adding, "I mean, I can't like someone at all. I have a boyfriend."

Sunny rolled her eyes and groaned at the same time. "Your boyfriend sucks, Danika."

"I don't know why you hate Jared so much," I said with a small shrug and watched as her entire body tensed.

"I just do," she said, and I wondered for the first time if she was hiding something from me. "I don't think he's the right guy for you, but it's not my life, so …"

A guttural laugh escaped from somewhere deep inside me. "And you think Chance is the right guy for me?"

"I didn't say that either. I just know Jared isn't," she said with confidence before looking somewhere over my shoulder.

Sunny was obviously feeling bold today. We'd talked about Jared before but never to this extent.

"I swear you used to like him. Then, one day, it just"—I paused as I snapped my fingers—"changed for some reason."

Sunny offered no further explanation. "Yeah, I don't know. You guys fight a lot. He's pretty controlling. And I'm not sure if that's just a New York thing or what, but I don't know if you even see it."

I started to feel a little defensive, like she had struck a chord or offended me somehow. Right when I was about to argue with her, I realized that she might be right. "I do see it. And I know that things between us have changed, but I just don't know what it means. I'm not sure that things won't go back to the way they used to be, you know? Like when we get back home after graduation, maybe things will get better. Do you think that's possible?"

"Are you actually asking *me*?" She started laughing, and I did too. Sunny had dated a handful of guys throughout the years, but they never lasted longer than six months. "Because you know I have no idea. You're the only person I know who is married to their high school sweetheart." She made a throwing-up face.

"We are not married," I argued. "We don't even live together."

"Thank God for small miracles," she breathed out, and I swatted her shoulder out of instinct more than anything else.

I was grateful, too, that Jared and I didn't live together. Again, another red flag wildly waving itself in front of my eyes that I refused to acknowledge or see.

"Can I ask you something?"

"Yeah."

"Are you still *in* love with Jared, or do you just love him?"

I swore she held her breath as she waited for my response, but her question honestly choked me up.

Of course I loved Jared. He had been there for me when my mom died. And we had been friends for years before we ever started dating. Loving Jared wasn't a question at all. I absolutely loved and cared and wanted the best for him.

But was I in love with him?

"Earth to Danika." Sunny snapped her fingers in front of my eyes. "It wasn't that hard of a question." She narrowed her eyes to study me. "Or was it?"

"I was just thinking."

"Thinking way too hard, if you ask me. You don't even have to tell me anymore. I have my answer."

"That's not fair. We've been together a long time, and it doesn't feel like it used to. Those all-consuming emotions fade away. I think if we burned that hot the whole time we were with someone, we'd all burn out eventually."

I remembered being madly in love with Jared, feeling the way it'd owned me every single time I took a breath, like I couldn't get enough of him. But I hadn't felt like that in years. *Do people always stay in a constant state of in love with their significant others, or does it change the longer you're together? Does love ebb and flow like the ocean, or is it supposed to stay solid at all times, never altering its course?*

"So, are you in love with him or not?"

I wanted to lie just to make her stop asking me these uncomfortable questions, but I couldn't. "I don't know. But I do *love him*," I emphasized the last words.

"I know you do." She sounded almost sad. Like she wished I didn't. "Let's talk about Chance again. It's way more fun." Sunny grinned, and I started shaking my head.

"Let's talk about Mac instead." I poked her shoulder, realizing that I'd never properly harassed her about hooking up with him at the party.

Her cheeks instantly turned red.

"Oh my gosh. Did you sleep with him and not tell me this whole time?"

"What? No! Mac doesn't sleep around." She looked at me like I was crazy for not knowing this.

"What do you mean, he doesn't sleep around? The guy's, like, the biggest player on the planet. How is that even possible?"

Her face pinched, her expression bewildered. "You really don't know?"

"Not unless you tell me," I said, equally as confused.

"Mac got his heart broken freshman year. I've only heard rumors about it, so I don't know how much of it is true, but from what I've heard, it was apparently pretty brutal. The point is that he doesn't let anyone get close to him now. Anything he does with a girl is on his terms."

"What does that mean, on his terms?" I hadn't heard the rumors about Mac's broken heart before, but I wasn't surprised.

"It means that he tells you up front what he wants from you and what you can expect from him in return."

I must have given her a dumbfounded look because she started laughing and held her hands up in the air before I could say anything.

"For example, at the party, he told me that, if I'd let him, he wanted to kiss me all night long, but he wasn't going to wine and dine me or call me the next day. Then, he asked me if I was okay with that and waited for my answer."

"He said all that? And you still let him put his tongue in your mouth?" I practically shouted between my disbelief and shock.

"I know it sounds insane, but it was actually kind of refreshing."

"Refreshing to know that you're going to be used up front, so you can lower your expectations to having absolutely none?"

"It was only kissing, Danika. And Mac was a great kisser, so I didn't mind."

"But what if you wanted to see him again? Or what if you wanted him to call you the next day?" I found myself as perplexed by this concept as I was fascinated.

"Um"—she shrugged both shoulders—"I did want all that. But I knew he wouldn't give it to me."

"And you were okay with that?"

"Well, I was until you started harassing me and making me overthink it all," she whined, and I apologized.

"He really didn't try to have sex with you?" I asked because I found that hard to believe.

She shook her head. "No. I mean, at least he didn't with me."

"Mac sounds even more bizarre than Chance."

"Probably why they're best friends," she said with a devilish grin, and I realized what I'd just done … I'd brought Chance back into the conversation when we hadn't even been talking about him.

I was so screwed.

Friends Eat Together

Chance

MY JEALOUSY TURNED me angry. And cold. And I was shit at hiding it from the one person I wanted to keep it all from. Danika read me like a fucking book, calling me out nonstop on my "attitude problem," as she liked to name it. The next tutoring session was painful as I tried my best to keep my distance, both physically and emotionally, from her, but she was like a damn magnet, pulling me closer in every way without even trying.

Anytime I broke protocol and asked her something even remotely personal, she'd chastise me and refuse to answer.

"That's a question for friends. And we're not friends, according to you, remember?"

I knew she wanted me to change my mind on that front, but I didn't know how to be her friend when all I wanted to do was bend her over the table and make her sorry for accepting this tutoring job in the first place. And I hated myself for it. All of this was new to me. Wanting her. Feeling this way about someone I shouldn't have any feelings for in the first place. I'd never been in a position where I didn't like the person I was becoming. I was a good guy who didn't fuck around and who rarely did anything he needed to apologize for.

Unlike most guys my age, I thought about the consequences of my actions. Whatever science said about our frontal lobes not being formed yet didn't matter in the Carter household. I had been raised to be aware of my choices and what could come from them. So, yeah, thinking about being inside Danika until we broke through the fucking wall didn't sit well in my mind. It sat perfectly fine in every other part of my body, but I needed to do my thinking with the right head, not the one in my pants.

I knew it was wrong, wanting her, but it wasn't going away. I thought that being cold and unfriendly would help me pull it together, but it only seemed to make it worse. The more I tried to avoid her, the more I found myself wanting her. Which was some pretty fucked up mental shit, if you asked me.

"Chance, are you even listening?" Her voice filled the space between us, and I shot my head up to look her dead in the eyes.

"I'm listening," I lied. My first test was coming up next week, and I felt seriously unprepared.

"Repeat what I just said then." She cocked her head and snapped her gum as I forced myself not to stare at her lips. "At least pay attention while we're in here, okay? You don't have to like me, but I really do want to help you pass the class."

She thought I didn't like her. If only she knew the truth. I rearranged some papers with questions and mock problems written all over them for me to figure out and attempt to understand. *Who had decided to make letters stand for numbers anyway, and more importantly, whyyyyyyyy?*

"You're right. I'm sorry," I said before sitting up straighter and grabbing my pencil. "What were you saying?"

"I was trying to explain about graphing linear equations," she said the words simply, like she wasn't speaking a completely foreign language.

My phone buzzed in my pocket, and instead of silencing it, I reached for it. I looked from the screen to Danika before saying, "It's my mom," and answering.

"Hey, Mom. Is everything okay?"

I listened as my mom informed me that I needed to come home for dinner and that she wasn't hanging up until I said that I'd be there. Then, she threatened to keep calling me back if I tried to hang up on her.

"I actually have an extra tutoring session that night," I tried to inform her, but she was relentless, refusing to take no for an answer.

"Um"—I looked at Danika, who was watching me intently as my mom continued dishing out commands that I knew I'd obey—"we'll see. I'm not sure. Listen, I've gotta go, Mom. I'll call you later, I promise. Okay. Bye. Love you too," I said before ending the call and pocketing my phone.

"You and your mom are close," Danika announced like it was a foregone conclusion instead of a question she was wondering the answer to.

"Yeah. She's the best. Harasses me like crazy, but all

moms do that, right?"

"Only if they like you." She offered a half-smile, but it felt like she was hiding something. "Is everything okay?" Danika asked, and I knew we were venturing back into friend-like territory.

I could have been a dick and reminded her that we were no longer friends, but it would have been bullshit. And my mom had put a solid crack in my armor when she insisted that I come home this weekend.

"She was threatening my life if I didn't come to dinner on Sunday night."

"But we have tutoring Sunday. You have your first test on Monday morning."

"I know. She told me to bring you."

Danika started choking. "She … what?"

"She said that you should come, too, and we could study there. I don't make the rules. I just have to follow hers."

"Chance, obviously, I can't come home with you." Danika fidgeted like crazy, her body restless.

"I tried to tell her the same thing, but she insisted."

"I have a boyfriend," she announced like I wasn't aware of that fact. "This isn't appropriate."

"You think I don't know that?" I adjusted the bill of my baseball cap before pressing back in my chair, lifting two of the legs into the air and balancing on the back two. "Look, I need the extra help before the test, but I promised my mom I'd come home. Just come with me, please. It will be painless, I assure you. My family is awesome, and my mom's a great cook." I gave her my best sales pitch because I honestly didn't see a way out of this. I could have blown off Danika and gone home without her, but I really needed the extra study session. Failing my test on Monday was not an option. I refused to start this semester off with an F.

She groaned and stared at her feet, her lips pressing together in a straight line. "This is a really bad idea. But fine."

"You'll do it?" I found myself getting a little more excited than I had any right to be.

She nodded. "I'll go … on one condition."

My jaw clenched, and I wondered what she was going to ask of me. I leaned forward, my chair hitting the floor with a screech. "What is it?"

"We have to be friends, Chance. This"—she waved a finger between us—"up-and-down, emotional craziness between us has to stop."

"I know," I admitted before apologizing, "I'm sorry."

"Don't be sorry. Just be normal."

"I'll try," I said, and I meant it.

I had no idea how to be normal around her. She made me question what normal even meant. She made me feel things I didn't want to feel.

"I'm going to need your number."

Her face went blank. "What?"

"Your phone number, Danika. Type it in," I said as I shoved my phone into her hands.

She frantically punched at the keys, adding her name and number in what seemed like record time before she handed it back to me like it was on fire.

"I'll call you when I'm on my way to pick you up on Sunday."

She looked nervous, and I knew that she was struggling internally the same way that I was. There was no way in hell these feelings were only one-sided. She felt them too.

"Okay."

"It's all good, Danika. Friends eat dinner together, right?"

"Sure." She shrugged with one arm. "They just don't usually do it at their parents' house."

"Why not?" I was being a smart-ass, but toying with her this way was fun. Seeing Danika flustered and knowing it was because of me gave me an ego boost I'd never known I needed.

She glared at me before answering, "Because meeting the parents is relationship material. Not friend material."

"Says who?" I pushed again.

"Society? Everyone? I don't know." She was rattled, and it was cute as hell.

"Let's break the rules then. Be different."

"I already said I'd go with you."

"Just don't want you backing out. Getting cold feet or anything."

Her back grew rigid, and I watched as her features steeled. I'd pushed her a little too far.

"This isn't a date, Chance. No cold feet required." She suddenly rose to her perfectly warm feet, and I followed suit, hovering over her frame.

"I'll see you Sunday," I said as I looked down at her, but

her eyes kept moving from my face to the door behind me. My eyes stayed focus on one thing—hers.

"Yep. See you then." She sounded unsure, and I couldn't have her changing her mind.

"I really need to pass that test."

"I know you do," she said before walking out the door, no doubt wanting to be the first one of us to leave the room.

I knew in my guts that it took everything in her not to turn around and look at me one last time before she disappeared out of view. *Little Spitfire.* I'd let her have this small victory, but Sunday was mine … whatever the hell that meant.

I MUST HAVE had a weird expression on my face because Mac called me out during dinner at the baseball house.

"Why do you look like a cartoon villain who just got away with something bad?"

My fork dropped to my plate with a clang. "Pretty sure I don't look like a cartoon anything, dick."

"You look"—Mac narrowed his eyes and tilted his head as he studied me, drawing way too much attention even if it was only from my teammates—"like you're up to something."

"He isn't wrong, Carter," Colin added from the other end of the table.

He was our starting shortstop, and before I could snap at him the same way I'd snapped at Mac, Dayton, one of our pitchers, chimed in as well.

"What *are* you up to, Chance?" he asked, dragging out the word *are*.

"You three are annoying. I'm not up to anything. What the hell would I be up to anyway?" I tried to argue, but Mac's face lit up like a damn kid on Christmas morning.

"Something happened with Tutor Girl," he said, looking at Colin and Dayton instead of at me.

Dayton let out a whistle. "I'd pay good money to have something happen with Tutor Girl," he teased. Or maybe he wasn't teasing because my blood started to boil in defense of his accusation.

"Don't start," I demanded, and he grinned.

"It's not our fault your tutor is fucking hot," Colin added, and I wondered if they all had death wishes. "But why the all black, all the time? Is she sad?"

"No, she's not sad," I bit out, defending her against his idiotic question. "And she's not available, so stay away from her."

"Because you're banging her?" Colin asked.

I actually fucking growled. It was embarrassing but too late to take it back.

"Because she has a boyfriend. And I don't need any of you guys messing with the one person who is going to help me stay eligible this season."

That shut them up. Momentarily.

"You do know that if I fail this class, I can't play this

year, right?"

They all nodded in unison.

"So, stay away from her," I instructed before tossing my dirty dish in the sink and stomping toward my room like a five-year-old.

I didn't get more than a few steps away before I heard them bust out laughing, saying I had it bad for Danika and how they'd never seen me this way before. The last thing I needed was to stay hanging around them and prove them all right. She was a problem. Hell, she'd been a problem, and now, I was going to bring her home to meet my damn parents.

What was I thinking?

Before I could psychoanalyze myself to death, someone knocked on my door. Without saying a word, it pushed open, and Mac's head poked through.

"Surprise, surprise." I grimaced as he walked into my room, uninvited, and closed the door behind him.

"What's up with you?"

"Why do you worry about me like you birthed me?" I asked because, sometimes, Mac acted like an overly concerned parent, and it was annoying. I mean, didn't he have enough of his own girl issues to be worried about without thinking about mine?

" 'Cause we're friends. That's what friends do." He moved toward the desk in my room and sat down in the chair.

Apparently, he planned on staying.

"Don't friends take a hint when you want to be alone

instead of interrogated?" I knew I was being a jerk, but I didn't want to talk about this anymore, and he wasn't going to leave until I did.

"Nope. They don't," Mac said, completely unfazed. "You really did look like shit at dinner. I just want to know what's up and make sure you're okay." I went to open my mouth in response, but he cut me off, waving a finger in the air. "And before you say anything else, you'd do the same for me if the roles were reversed, and you know it." He was right. And it shut me up. "So, are you going to tell me what happened?"

"She's coming to dinner at my parents' house on Sunday. And I thought it was a brilliant idea until I got away from her and started wondering what the hell I was thinking by pushing her into it. I mean"—I glanced up at Mac's amused expression—"I was not going to let her say no."

"Of course you weren't."

"And now, she's meeting my parents?" I said it like a question before shaking my head and rubbing at my eyes. "Girls don't meet my parents."

"I'm aware. How did this even happen?"

I filled him in on the phone call from my mom, and he smiled the whole time.

"Please stop smiling."

"It's cute." He started swiveling back and forth in my chair.

"Don't say shit like that."

"You like her."

"Mac." I was going to argue but knew it was useless.

"At least admit it. You're allowed to like a girl, Chance."

I blew out a long, annoyed breath as his swiveling came to a halt, and he pinned me with a stare.

"I can't like *her*," I emphasized.

"But you do."

"I might."

"So, what are we going to do about it?" he asked, his face lighting up with a grin.

"Nothing. Not while she has a boyfriend at least. That's a hard line I won't cross," I said the words and wondered who I was trying to convince because I knew that if Danika wanted anything from me, there was no way in hell I'd have the strength to say no.

Dinner with the Fam

Chance

I'D BEEN ON edge all weekend. Even going to the cages and taking extra hitting practice hadn't helped. I tried yoga, meditation, and even Pilates—that shit was awful—but nothing kept my mind from the upcoming dinner or the fact that I had Danika's number in my phone, but I felt like I wasn't allowed to use it.

I stared at her number at least a hundred times, tempted to send her a message but never did.

It. Was. Torture.

Knowing that Danika was only a simple text away but refusing to give in.

What if she was with her boyfriend when I reached out? I wouldn't be able to handle that. Knowing that he was with her when I wasn't. Touching her when I couldn't.

My dad didn't help matters when he cornered me after practice. "Heard you're bringing a girl home for dinner."

I glanced around, making sure none of my teammates were in a position to overhear our conversation. The only person who knew that Danika was going home with me was

Mac, and I knew he'd never tell anyone else.

"It's not a girl, Dad. It's my tutor."

"Your mom thinks it's more. She's got Jacey all riled up."

"What? Please make her stop, or I won't come." I dropped my catcher's helmet to the ground.

My dad stiffened. "You wouldn't dare disappoint your mom like that. Would you?"

I gave him a look before huffing out, "No."

"I'm just kidding about your mom and sister."

I punched his arm. "Why would you do that to me?"

He laughed. " 'Cause you should have seen the look on your face. I couldn't resist."

"Don't make this a thing."

"Is it a thing?"

"She has a boyfriend."

"Minor detail." My dad grinned, and I shook my head.

"Dad."

"What?" He shrugged before taking his ball cap off and putting it on backward. "Is her boyfriend on the team?"

I quickly spat out, "No," like the idea of poaching a teammate's girlfriend made me physically ill or something. "I'm not Logan," I said, referencing my ex-teammate who had tried to take another teammate's girl last season. It was a complete shitshow and could have torn us all apart. Thank God it hadn't.

"Like I said then"—he paused, and I had no idea if he was joking or not—"minor detail."

"That's not cool." I shook my head.

"I'm just messing around, Chance. It's the first time a girl's gotten under your skin."

"She's not under my ..." I started to argue, but he gave me a look that told me he knew better, and I shut up instead.

My dad turned to walk off the field when I realized that my entire body was locked up tight with tension.

"Dad, wait."

He stopped and turned to face me.

"No one else will be there, right? Mom's not having the whole family there or anything?" I asked because if my Uncle Dean, Aunt Melissa, Gran, and Gramps were there, it would be way too much. Danika would tell me to turn around and take her right back home the second we walked through the front door.

"No. It's just us, kid."

"Okay. See you Sunday."

I'D CONTINUED SPENDING my time staring at Danika's number in my cell phone, looking for an excuse to text her. I knew that once I opened that door, there would be no closing it, and I wanted to be better than that, so I held out. No matter how badly I'd wanted to shoot her a message, I had waited and sent my first text when I was heading over to pick her up.

She responded right away.

DANIKA: WHO IS THIS? I DON'T HAVE THIS NUMBER IN

MY PHONE.

CHANCE: VERY FUNNY.

DANIKA: I THOUGHT SO. <SMILEY FACE>

CHANCE: BE THERE IN 10.

DANIKA: I'LL BE OUT FRONT.

CHANCE: IN ALL BLACK, I BET.

DANIKA: I DO OWN OTHER COLORS, YOU KNOW.

CHANCE: ACTUALLY, I DON'T KNOW.

DANIKA: WELL, NOW, YOU DO.

I'd learned two things in that brief exchange. One: Danika owned something other than black, although I still doubted it. And two: she didn't want me to come inside her apartment. It was probably for the best, but it still somehow felt like a slap in the face. Even though I tried not to take it personally, when I navigated my dad's old Bronco into the parking lot and saw her waiting for me on the sidewalk—in all black, mind you—I felt a pang of disappointment rip through me.

This isn't a date, I reminded myself.

It was supposed to help, but it only seemed to make it worse. In this moment, I realized that I wanted this to be a date.

Pulling myself together, I slowed to a stop next to her. "Nice outfit," I said, looking at her off-the-shoulder black top, which revealed black bra straps underneath. Her black ripped jeans and dirty black combat boots finished off the ensemble.

This girl could never put on another color in her life, and I wouldn't give a shit.

"It's a New York thing, okay?" She shrugged as she hopped into my truck and tossed her bag to the floor.

"I've seen plenty of people in New York wear colors other than black," I argued, but honestly, I couldn't remember. I'd never paid attention to what people were wearing when I was there. I was too busy being caught up in the cool buildings and hanging out at the baseball stadium, meeting the players. New Yorkers' attire had been the last thing on my mind.

"They might. I don't." She was unapologetic. And she had nothing to be sorry for.

"Hey." I nudged her arm with my shoulder. "For the record, I always think you look beautiful."

"Don't say that," she said, her normally olive skin tone turning crimson. She liked the compliment, but it also made her uncomfortable.

"I mean it though. You really do," I pushed, and she squirmed as she buckled her seat belt. "Thanks for coming with me tonight," I said before putting the car in gear and pulling away.

She never responded, and I turned the radio up.

More than ten minutes passed before Danika reached for the volume control on my stereo and turned it down. Normally, I would slap anyone's hand who dared to touch my shit but not her. Never her. She could do whatever she wanted, and it didn't even bother me.

Why did this girl affect me so much? And why couldn't I

control the way I felt when it came to her?

"Is there anything I should know?" she asked, her attention completely focused on me.

"About?" I gave her a quick glance before I refocused on the freeway.

"Your family. Like a heads-up about anything? Are they going to try to embarrass you or me? And who all is going to be there?"

"It's just my mom, dad, and little sister, Jacey. I've never brought anyone home, so I have no idea how they'll act, but they aren't the embarrassing type," I said and prayed to God that it was true.

My dad had given me a lot of crap the other day, but that was the first time that had happened.

"You've never brought a girl home before?"

"I mean, once in high school, but I'd known her since I was five, so she wasn't a stranger."

"Were you dating?"

"Yeah," I answered, and Danika looked away. She stared out the passenger window for a little too long. "Did I say something wrong?" It felt like she was upset.

She turned back toward me. "No. How old is Jacey?"

"Fifteen, going on twenty. Her sole mission in life is to give me a heart attack, so if anyone is going to be embarrassing, it'll be her."

Danika laughed. "That's funny. I wish I had a sister."

"You can have mine."

"She might like me better than you, and then you'll be sorry," Danika said with a smile, and I could tell she was starting to relax, maybe even looking forward to tonight.

"Can I ask you something?" I said, knowing I was about to ruin the mood as I pulled off the freeway and took the exit.

"You know you can."

"Did you tell Jared you were coming home with me?"

Her relaxed demeanor instantly changed, and I watched as she swallowed hard. "No."

My hands gripped the steering wheel even tighter as I asked, "You didn't?"

"I didn't."

"So then, what happens if he texts or calls?" I started to get concerned because even though this wasn't a date, I wanted Danika peacefully to myself tonight, and the fact that Jared had no idea where she was could potentially cause a lot of drama. "Won't he want to see you? If I were your boyfriend, I'd want to see you," I added in a matter-of-fact tone.

"I'll just tell him that I had an extra session with you because you have your first test tomorrow. Which isn't a lie."

"Danika," I started to say.

"I know, okay?" She sounded flustered and upset with herself as she turned toward the passenger window again. "I know."

"Why didn't you tell him?" I asked, realizing that I had no idea what their relationship was like. I had always assumed she was happy. I'd refused to let myself think otherwise.

"Because he would have told me I couldn't come. We would have gotten into a huge fight, and it seemed easier not to tell him," she admitted before adding, "I know it's wrong. I know I should have let him know, but I didn't want to."

Even though I had very little experience with relationships, I knew that this was a slippery slope of sorts. Part of me loved the fact that she hadn't told him because if she had, he would have guilted her into not coming home with me, and I wanted her here. I was glad she had come. But the rest of me knew that this was dangerous ground we were on, and if we weren't careful, it could all come crashing down around us.

We pulled up to the privacy gates in my neighborhood, and I rolled down my window to punch in the code. The gates swung open, and Danika's eyes lit up.

"This is a beautiful neighborhood," she said, her head swiveling to each side of the street to look around. "Oh, I love the style and the landscaping. It's so green here."

"Yeah, it's really beautiful," I agreed because it was.

Growing up on the Newport Coast had been a dream.

I turned right, then left, and made another right before pulling into our driveway and shutting off the engine.

"Stay," I said before hopping out and going to the passenger side.

I opened her door and extended my hand as she reached for her bag that I knew were filled with torturous study materials for later.

"I can open my own door, Hotshot."

"I know you *can*, Spitfire. I just don't think you should." I helped her out before shutting the door behind her.

"Oh no. I didn't bring anything for your mom. My mom

would be horrified that I showed up empty-handed."

"Danika, it's okay. My mom won't be offended. She's going to love you." I offered her a smile, but she frowned in response.

"It's not about that, Chance. It's just basic manners. You don't show up for dinner at someone's house without flowers or a bottle of wine or dessert or something."

"Well, it's too late now. Come on."

I reached for her hand and pulled her without even thinking. She jerked her fingers from my grip, and I looked at her apologetically. I hadn't truly meant to do that. It had come so naturally. Instinctual, I guessed before mentally beating myself up for it.

"We're home," I yelled as we burst through the front door and into the oversize foyer.

"Chance!" my mom shouted from somewhere.

"We? I hope you brought me someone hot to look at." Jacey's voice filled the air.

Danika stifled a laugh while she looked around. Natural light filled every inch of the space, and I knew that all the blinds were up, so the ocean view would be on full display.

"That's my little sister. She'll be momentarily sad you aren't a guy."

"I'll win her over," Danika said with a smile, and I knew that she would.

I led us toward the kitchen. Danika followed a few steps behind, and I knew she was looking at the framed pictures that lined the walls. There were pictures of us as a family throughout the years, photographs my mom had taken of me playing baseball and Jacey dancing. There were pictures of my dad playing during his prime years on the Mets, coupled with ones of him coaching at Fullton State now. For as elaborate as our house was, it still felt homey, and I loved that the most. My mom could take anything and make it feel warm and welcoming.

"There you are," I said as we reached the kitchen.

My mom was bent over the cutting board, chopping at something.

"Hi, honey." She turned around, her green eyes bright and her long blonde hair up in a bun on top of her head.

I gave her a hug before she focused her attention on Danika.

"Mom, this is Danika. My tutor. Danika, this is my mom, Cassie."

Danika reached out her hand. "Mrs. Carter," she said, and my mom waved her away.

"Call me Cassie. And come here," she said before pulling Danika into a hug. "Sorry. I'm a hugger, not a hand-shaker."

"Well, I'm sorry I came empty-handed. I'm not usually so rude," Danika said, and my mom laughed.

"Oh, honey, that's not rude. You're fine. We invited you," my mom said sweetly.

"More like forced," I said with a choke, and my mom swatted my shoulder. "What? Tell me it's not true!" I argued.

"Well, can you blame me?" my mom asked.

Jacey strode into the kitchen, a sucker in her mouth.

"I can," she said before looking Danika up and down. "You're not a hot guy."

"Told you," I said, shaking my head.

"Nope. I'm better," Danika added, and Jacey giggled. "Guys are dumb. And nothing but trouble. And super bossy."

"So, you've met my brother then." She tossed the sucker in the trash can.

"Jacey," my mom tried to chastise, but she and my dad had raised us on sarcasm, so they couldn't get mad about it.

"Oh, Mom, you know I'm only kidding," Jacey defended before looking at me. "Kind of."

"Can we go now? We showed up, said hello. I really need to study," I joked, and my mom's face dropped.

"No. I'll lock Jacey in her room all night. Please stay."

"I'm standing right here," Jacey whined with an annoyed expression on her face.

"It's not always like this," my dad said as he stepped into the kitchen, looking larger than life. "Who am I kidding? Yeah, it is."

"Danika, this is my dad, Jack," I said as my dad walked immediately over to my mother and gave her a kiss before whispering something in her ear that made her blush.

Dammit. I had forgotten to warn Danika that my parents were still disgustingly in love and not afraid to show it. And I probably should have told her about their weird quarter fetish in case my dad started dropping fifty cents in my mom's hands all night.

Danika looked unfazed by my parents' affection but also seemed a little starstruck in a way. I hated it until I remembered that her dad was a huge fan.

"Didn't you say that your dad was a fan?"

Her expression shifted, and she looked slightly embarrassed that I'd called her out. "Yeah, he is. And I can't believe I'm even asking you this because it's so wildly inappropriate, but—" she started to ask, but my mom cut her off.

"Danika, what did you say your last name was?" My mom cocked her head to the side. "I didn't mean to interrupt you. It's just that you look so familiar, and you're obviously from New York, am I right?"

"I am, yes. And my last name is Marchetti."

My mom's jaw dropped open as she narrowed her eyes. "As in Ralph and Cecilia Marchetti?"

Danika's face lit up. I'd never seen her look so happy before. *How in the hell did my mom know Danika's parents?*

"You … you know my parents?"

"Actually, I do." My mom smiled. "How are they? How's your mother?"

Danika's face fell just as quickly. "She passed away a few years back."

"I didn't know that," I whispered toward Danika, and she turned to look at me.

"I know. It's okay," she whispered back, reaching for my hand and squeezing it before letting go.

My mom stepped out of my dad's arms and toward Danika. She reached for her and pulled her into another hug. "I'm so sorry. She was a really great woman."

"She was sick for a long time." Danika focused on the floor before looking back up and meeting my mom's watchful gaze.

"Jack, honey." My mom turned toward my dad, who was picking at whatever was in the bowl and tossing it in his mouth. "You remember Ralph and Cecilia? Real estate Ralph."

My dad grinned. "Ralph? Oh, man. That's your dad?"

Danika smiled as she pulled out one of the kitchen chairs and sat. "He is."

I moved to stand next to her, wanting to be there for support or needing to be near her—I wasn't sure which.

"Damn. He gave me so much shit about being on the Mets. Would always say, 'Why can't you be a Yankee, Carter? Why you gotta make me root for the Mets?' " my dad said, mimicking a really bad New York accent, but it made Danika laugh.

"I told you!" She instantly looked at me. "I told you that your dad was the only Met my dad liked."

"You did tell me that," I agreed, feeling a weird mixture of emotion and pride welling up inside of me.

"He really is a big fan of yours," she said, and my dad kept smiling. "Even still."

"We'll have to take some selfies and send them to him."

Jacey snorted, and I'd forgotten that she was there. "Dad, you sound so dumb when you say *selfie*."

"Why? That's what they're called, right? Your mom and I take selfies all the time."

"Stop!" Jacey pleaded as she covered her ears before yelling out loud, "I refuse to listen to this. I'll be back." She dismissed herself and left the kitchen.

"Can I ask how you knew my parents?" Danika's voice

was softer than usual, and the energy in the kitchen completely morphed into something I couldn't quite name.

My mom cleared her throat. "When we lived in New York, I used to work for a magazine, and we did feature spreads on the local entrepreneurs and their businesses. I'm pretty sure we featured your dad for his up-and-coming real estate company."

Danika nodded, like she knew exactly what my mom was referring to. "Did you write the article?"

"No, no. I took the pictures. I'm a photographer."

"Was my mom there that day?"

"She was."

"This is crazy, but did you take pictures of them together? Do you remember?" Danika's face was intense.

"I think I did. I remember your mom was staring out the window, and I think I took a couple of candid shots of her. She was so beautiful, and the light was so perfect."

"Oh my God. My dad has a framed picture of her alone and another one of them together from that day in his office at home. I never knew where they had come from, never even asked, but I think they came from you." Danika's voice broke and took a piece of my heart with it.

What are the odds that this girl would be connected to my family in this way? Hell, in any way? It was like a Christmas gift, and it was nowhere near December.

"This is incredible. Who would have ever thought?" My mom shook her head as she moved back toward the dish she had been working on and made my dad stop picking at it.

"Do you guys still have your place there? In New York?"

Danika asked.

My dad answered, "We do. It's in Sutton Place. We could never give it up. Too many memories."

He looked back at my mom, and she practically melted on the kitchen floor.

"And plus, I love that apartment," my mom added, clearly lost in memories.

"I forgot to warn you that my parents are super gross and in love," I groaned.

"Figured that one out all on my own, Hotshot, but thanks."

"Do you miss New York?" Jacey's voice asked.

I hadn't even heard her come back into the kitchen. Or knowing her supersonic hearing, which I'd also forgotten to warn Danika about, she'd probably overheard everything from a mile away.

"I do. But I know I'll be back there after graduation," she said, and my heart felt like it had been dropkicked.

Danika had her whole life planned out after she graduated. She was going to move back home. Most likely with her stupid boyfriend, Jared. A boyfriend who didn't know where she was right now.

"I've only been there a few times, but I really like it there. It's so cool." My little sister sounded wistful.

Danika agreed, "It is cool. There's nothing else like it. Just like there's nothing else like Southern California. I love it here, but it's completely different from the city."

"I think I'd like to live there," Jacey announced with certainty, and I choked, hitting my chest with my hand.

"Oh yeah?" I asked my little sister.

"Maybe I'll just go to college there. What do you think, Mom?"

My mom looked at her, no concern or worry in her expression at all. "We'll see how you feel when the time comes. You might change your mind."

"Why do you want to leave me, Jacey Bear? New York is so far away," my dad whined, and I coughed out an insult.

"Oh, Dad. Don't be so dramatic." Jacey rolled her eyes.

Danika glanced up at me, her eyes filled with emotion. It took all my willpower not to wrap her in my arms and hold on for dear life.

When Pasts Collide

Danika

CHANCE'S PARENTS HAD known my mom. My eyes welled up at this revelation, this unbelievable twist of fate.

How in the world could something like this even happen? How random.

Then again, maybe it wasn't random at all. Maybe every piece of my life had fallen together in this way because that was exactly what it was supposed to do. I was meant to come to Fullton State so that I could meet Chance and his parents. Because they had known my mom when she was alive. It was overwhelming. I was overwhelmed.

"Danika? Can I borrow you for a second?" Cassie asked.

I stood up from the chair I'd been sitting in and nodded. She reached for my hand. It was a simple gesture, motherly really, and I relished in it as I let her guide me down a long hallway. I noticed various jars filled with what looked like quarters all over the house before we walked into an office that I assumed was Cassie's. There were even more jars with quarters on the shelves and one sitting on top of the desk.

Only once we were inside the office did she let go of my hand.

Cassie Carter made me miss my mom even more, just by existing.

The room was well lit, but there were additional art lights hanging above framed black-and-white photographs, spotlighting each one along the walls. They were spectacular.

"Did you take all these?" I asked as she sat down at the desk and started frantically working at the mouse and keyboard.

"I did."

"They're really stunning," I said because they were.

The majority were landscapes of places I didn't recognize, but the ones that included people were heartbreaking, showcasing genuine emotion after what looked like some sort of loss. It was written all over their faces, and Cassie had captured it beautifully. Her pictures made you ache when you looked at them.

"Thank you. I have something to show you," she said as she waved me over.

I walked around, peered over her shoulder to the oversize monitor, and gasped. There, alive and in color, were pictures of my mother and my father together.

"Oh my God," I said before reaching out and touching the screen, my fingers resting on my mom's face. "I'm sorry," I said as I quickly pulled my hand back.

"It's okay," Cassie said, the warmth in her voice comforting. "I always keep copies of the pictures I shoot. Even the ones I did for the magazine. I wasn't sure if I could still find these so easily or not, but they were right where I thought they'd be on that external hard drive," she said, pointing to a bright red box that sounded like it was going to crap out at any moment.

"There are so many," I exhaled, still mesmerized as I stared at the screen, willing the pictures to come to life.

My parents looked so happy and so in love.

Cassie laughed. "Yeah. I always shoot way more than necessary. My motto was basically that it's better to have too many pictures than not enough."

Tears spilled down my cheeks. "My mom looks so beautiful."

Cassie turned to face me. "And you look just like her."

"You think so?" I wiped at my face, but it was no use.

"Yes, I do," she said as she stood up from her chair and hugged me before looking right in my eyes. "I'm going to make you copies of all of these, okay?"

I practically stuttered, "Really? Oh, yes. Please. That would be so amazing. Thank you."

"I'll email you a link to the files too. That way, you can share them with your dad if you think he'd be up to seeing them."

I wondered for a brief moment if the pictures would upset my dad or make him happy. "I think he'd love that."

"Good," Cassie said with a smile as she passed me a notepad and a pen.

I scribbled my email address down and pushed it back in her direction.

"Do you remember that day? I mean, I know it was a

long time ago, but what were they like?"

"I actually do remember parts of it. Your parents were a great team. Even back then. They were so different in the way they came across, but they complemented each other perfectly. Like true partners. Does that even make any sense?" she asked, her head shaking like she was speaking nonsense when she wasn't.

"More than you know," I said as I started thinking about my own relationship in comparison to what my parents had been like.

They'd fought for each other, not against. They had been a team, just like Cassie had said. But Jared and I … I wasn't sure we'd ever truly been on the same page. And we'd grown so far off course that I wasn't sure we could ever get back. More truthfully, I wasn't sure that I wanted to or not anymore.

Cassie started laughing softly as she pointed at a picture of my dad cracking up. Him laughing like that was rare. He was always inundated with work. Even when he tried to take time off, work stayed firmly rooted in the back of his mind, his phone never quiet, his wheels always turning. And that laughter had grown even rarer since my mom passed. I used to think that she had taken his smile with her when she left.

"I remember that your dad was trying to look tough for the photographs. He wanted to appear strong and smart. His goal was to attract big-money clients, and he said he couldn't look soft. But your mom kept making him laugh. I don't even know what she was doing half the time because I was too busy staring through my lens, but all of a sudden, your dad's eyes would wander over my shoulder, and a giant, toothy smile would break out of nowhere."

"That sounds like my mom," I said almost wistfully.

"It was a good day. Fun. Your dad never remarried, did he?"

A surprised sound escaped me. "No way. My mom was the love of his life. He always said he could never replace her, so why bother trying?"

"That's really sweet," Cassie said with a smile before turning serious. "Jack had better feel the same way about me."

"Are you joking? That man is so in love with you, it's sick. But not really because who doesn't want to be loved like that?" I added, feeling way too comfortable already.

"I love the way he loves me. I wouldn't trade it for the world. There's a bathroom around the corner if you want to go freshen up. I'll just copy these for you."

I nodded. "Thank you again. This is the best gift anyone could give me."

"What a small world, huh?"

"Yeah, small world," I said as I walked out of the office in search of the bathroom, but I ran into a rock-hard chest instead. "Oof, Hotshot. A little warning next time."

"I was just coming to make sure my mom hadn't kidnapped you or something. You've been gone too long," he said, sounding way too sweet and sincere for the current state of my heart. It was vulnerable. He reached for my chin and tilted my face up to look at him, those green eyes filled with concern. "You've been crying."

"Happy tears," I said, and his face relaxed only a little. He didn't like it when I cried.

"Promise? I mean, it's my mom and all, but I'll rough her up if she hurt you," he said.

Cassie yelled that she had heard that from the office, followed by Jacey saying the same thing from somewhere deeper in the house.

"Your sister really can hear everything. *That* was exactly the kind of thing you should have warned me about," I teased.

"I can still hear you," Jacey singsonged, clearly enjoying eavesdropping on us.

"Go away, troll," Chance yelled back in response.

I swatted his shoulder. "Don't call her names."

"She's fine. Bounces right off her hard head."

"Stop talking about me, or I'll come to all your games in crop tops and booty shorts and flirt with all your friends," Jacey shouted.

Chance visibly tensed. I made a mental note to make fun of him about it later when Cassie walked out of the office, holding a thumb drive between her fingers.

"Here you go, Danika," she said, handing it to me. "I also emailed you the link. You can just forward it to whoever you want to share the pictures with. I'll go finish getting dinner ready, but it's still about an hour away."

Chance looked at me. "We should probably study then."

I nodded in agreement. "You're right."

"Show her to the bathroom first," his mom said before she headed back toward the kitchen.

"This is crazy, right?" Chance shook his head, and a half-smile appeared along with his lone dimple.

"That your parents know mine?" I said in disbelief. "Crazy doesn't even begin to cover it," I said as Chance led me toward the guest bathroom.

He waited outside the door, refusing to leave me alone, even when I insisted that I could find my way back to the office by myself. His house wasn't that elaborate. It actually felt more comfortable than I would have expected, which was nice.

I thought he sensed more that I was teetering on an emotional seesaw that I might fall off of at any moment, and he wanted to make sure he was there to catch me if I fell. And to be honest, I found myself wishing that I could allow that, that Chance could be the rock I used to lean on, but I couldn't let myself go there. Depending on another guy while I had a steady boyfriend was beyond wrong. I needed to remember that, but Chance made it really fucking hard when he looked at me with those green eyes, all filled with concern and sympathy. He cared about my well-being, and I liked the way that made me feel.

Focusing on math was just the distraction I needed. It gave me a goal and a job to do. It was easier to focus than I'd expected, and we studied without stopping until Jacey let us know that dinner was ready. That hour had flown by.

"Think I'll ace it?" Chance whispered, clearly joking, as we made our way toward the kitchen.

I laughed. "I'm not sure about acing it, but you'll definitely pass. I know that much."

"I hope so," he said before adding, "Thank you for all the help. I still don't understand it, but you make it a little less complicated."

"Thanks"—a soft laugh escaped—"I think."

The Carters were easy, comfortable, and kind. And boy, did they love each other. It showed in everything that they did. The way they interacted and talked, in the things they said. I wasn't envious for what they had because I was lucky enough to have it, too, but it made me miss my dad and home. Chance must have sensed it at one point because he reached under the table for my leg and gave me a small squeeze before moving his hand.

I loved and hated how in tune he was with me. *How did a guy I barely even knew seem to understand me so well?* It was beyond all reason, but this night had already demonstrated that. The Carters and the Marchettis were connected, in more ways than one.

Dinner flew by too fast, and when I offered to help clean up, Cassie insisted that she had it handled and that we'd better get back to school. She wanted Chance to get a good night's sleep before his big test. She was a good mom.

"Thank you so much for coming and bringing my boy to see me. He wouldn't have come without you, so I'm grateful," Cassie said as she hugged me good-bye at the front door.

"I'm grateful. I can never thank you enough for what you've given me and my dad tonight. And for being so gracious and welcoming."

"Please come over anytime. With or without him." She

nodded toward Chance, who stood there, watching us with a joyful expression.

"Please come without him. You're so much cooler than he is," Jacey added from where she stood next to her dad.

"I know I am. Don't tell him though. We might hurt his precious ego," I said, and Jacey gave me a high five.

"Okay, okay. We're leaving, and when we don't come back, you'll have no one to blame but yourselves," Chance teased, and Jacey stuck out her tongue.

We headed outside with Chance leading the way, and I knew his family was still watching from the front door. I hadn't heard it close yet. When we got to his car, he unlocked the doors and opened mine for me … again. Damn Chance Carter and his chivalrous ways.

He got into the driver's seat and started the engine with one last wave toward his family. I watched as they closed the door, blocking all the light that had been spilling out from behind it. It was only then that I reached for my phone in my bag and checked it. I'd put it on silent before we walked in the house, afraid that Jared might text or call and start drama like Chance had mentioned. I was thankful I had as I looked at the string of texts from my boyfriend, each one more annoyed than the last.

"Jared?" Chance asked, his voice breaking the silence.

"Yeah. I didn't look at my phone once while we were there," I said, not sure why I'd offered up that extra bit of information.

"I noticed," Chance said, and I shouldn't have been surprised that he had been so observant. "Is he pissed?" he asked.

"A little, but I think it's because he's more worried than anything else. I just need to text him back really quick." I started typing on my phone, letting Jared know that I was sorry but that I'd been tutoring and I'd call him as soon as I got home.

My phone vibrated in my hand, and I hesitated before Chance suggested, "You should probably answer it."

I knew he was right, but answering it would lead to questions I wasn't in the right state of mind to get into. Plus, I wasn't comfortable with Chance hearing me on the phone with Jared, especially if he was upset.

"I'll wait until I'm home."

I could tell that Chance didn't agree and wanted to say something else, but he kept quiet instead.

"I'm really sorry about your mom. I can't imagine losing mine." Chance sounded choked up, just thinking about it.

"It was awful. I mean, one day, she was full of life, and the next, she was fighting for it. I know it wasn't that sudden in reality, but looking back, that's what it seemed like. Like everything changed in an instant."

"Was it cancer?"

"Yeah. Out of nowhere. She had this pain in her stomach, so they took an ultrasound, looking for a possible rupture, and they found tumors instead."

"I don't know what to say."

"When I first found out, I was so positive, you know? Telling her that she could fight this and we'd beat it. That kind of thing," I said, remembering exactly the level of denial

I'd felt back then. "But when reality started to sink in and I saw how fighting it only killed her differently, I stopped being so positive and optimistic."

"I'm really sorry."

My eyes started to water. "She stayed as long as she could. Held on for way too long because she knew I didn't want her to go."

"How old were you?"

"I was sixteen when she died. Thirteen when she was first diagnosed."

His hand moved from the steering wheel to the top of my leg, like it had at dinner. He squeezed, his thumb rubbing across my thigh almost absentmindedly. I looked down, and he jerked it away.

"I'm sorry. I seem to have this need to comfort you. I do it without thinking."

I swallowed hard and tried to blow it off. "It's okay."

"It's not. It's not my place. I keep trying to stay away from you, Danika, but you make it really hard."

Huffing out a choking sound, I argued, "I make it hard? I'm not even doing anything."

"You exist," he said, and I found myself struggling for anything to say after that. "Did *he* know your mom?" Chance's voice sounded strained.

"Who?"

"Your boyfriend."

I nodded even though I knew Chance couldn't see my head in the dark cab of the truck. "He did. Our families were old friends, and we went to school together. He was there for me when she died."

"Were you dating already when it happened?"

"Not really. Jared was around a lot, and after it happened, he just never really left," I said the words out loud and realized how odd they sounded.

"You needed him." Chance sounded almost defensive.

"I guess I did," I said because I'd never thought about it that way before. *Was it truly Jared that I needed, or did I just need someone, anyone?*

"He made you happy?" Chance asked without bitterness.

"He did." I nodded as I thought back to when we'd first gotten together. And even though I had been mourning the loss of my mom, Jared made me excited. "He was there for me. Without Jared, I would have felt really alone and been consumed in my sadness I think." He distracted me from my pain because everything with us had been brand-new.

"What about your dad?" Chance asked, and I couldn't help but smile.

My dad was my best friend. I not only loved him, but I also respected him. "My dad's really great. But he was always working. And once my mom died, he worked even more. I don't know how that was even possible, but even then, I knew that he was just doing anything he could to avoid his broken heart."

"Were you one of the things he avoided?"

The question sliced through me as I sucked in a steadying breath.

"No. It wasn't like that. I don't have daddy issues, if that's where you're headed," I said with a lighthearted laugh.

"I wasn't. I was genuinely curious." Chance's voice was calm.

"I know my dad loves me. I have never once in my life felt unloved. I think, at the time, I definitely could have used a little more of his attention, but I also understood that his heart was broken. And Jared helped fill that void."

Chance cleared his throat. "My dad would be devastated if he lost my mom. I think he'd turn into a shell of a person without her. I wouldn't even know how to help him."

"Yeah. It was really sad. I lost my mom, but my dad lost his partner and the person he'd thought he'd spend the rest of his life with. He had to distract himself with something. And making millions of dollars while doing it wasn't a bad side effect."

"Damn. So, your dad's like that, huh?" Chance laughed.

"Oh, you have no idea."

My dad was filthy rich. He had built his empire from scratch with no help from anyone, and everyone knew it. He was respected, looked up to, and connected. Things didn't go down in New York real estate without my dad knowing it was happening.

"Will you go work for him after you graduate then?"

"That's always been the plan."

"Your idea or his?" Chance asked, and I knew what he was getting at.

"Mine. My dad isn't the type to force me to do something I don't want to do."

Chance looked at me for only a second. "I can't imagine anyone forcing you to do something you don't want to do."

I swallowed hard. "You'd be surprised."

We pulled off the freeway and headed toward my apartment complex. Like everything else this evening, the drive had gone by too fast.

"Oh, hey, I almost forgot," I said before clearing my throat. "What was with all the quarters at the house? That's what they were, right? Quarters?"

"Please don't make me tell you what little I know about them," Chance said, wincing.

I laughed. "Well, now, you have to."

"It's just something my dad does. He gives my mom quarters, and then she saves them all. He started doing it in college, and I don't want to know the whole story because I know too much gross shit about them already."

"Okay, I'll give you a pass this time."

"Thanks," he said halfheartedly, and I realized that we were in my parking lot.

Chance pulled his Bronco to a stop, and I watched him hesitate before even looking at me. I knew that he was torn on how to handle this particular good-bye. Things between us seemed to only get more intense with time. I leaned toward him and pulled his body awkwardly into mine, thankful he was still wearing his seat belt. We hugged briefly before I pulled away, his green eyes boring into mine the way they always seemed to.

"Thanks for everything tonight. It was …" I struggled to find the right word as his lone dimple appeared.

"I still can't believe my mom had all those pictures."

"I can't wait to go look at every single one," I admitted

as excitement coursed through me. There were so many pictures of my parents that I'd never seen before. I couldn't wait to look at them and send them to my dad and tell him everything. I wished it weren't so late in New York, so I could call him right away.

Chance reached out and touched my hand. My entire body flooded with heat. "Go. Before I try and do something we'll both regret."

I swallowed hard, torn between wanting him to do it and absolutely knowing that we shouldn't. Reaching for the door handle, I pulled it open and hopped out. He waited until I got to the door of my building and went inside before he drove away. I grabbed my phone and typed out a text. I knew I was opening a door I'd struggle with closing again, but I did it anyway.

DANIKA: GOOD LUCK ON YOUR TEST TOMORROW. I KNOW YOU'LL DO GREAT!

His response was immediate, even though he was driving, and so Chance-like, teasing and torturous.

CHANCE: IS THIS WHAT FRIENDS DO?

Internal Conflict

Chance

THE DRIVE BACK to my place was brutal in a different kind of way. Danika's scent lingered in my truck, and I found myself inhaling deeply as I tried to breathe her in. Like it might make her a part of me or something stupid like that. I officially lost my damn mind as I replayed the night—how great my parents had been with her, coupled with the look on Danika's face when my mom had mentioned knowing hers. Her shock, disbelief, and sadness had all mixed together, and I would have done anything to take away her pain and anguish and replace it with something good. I hated knowing that she was hurting. My heart fucking ached, just thinking about it.

The fact that my parents had known hers felt like some sort of sick cosmic joke at first. Then, it felt like a connection that neither one of us could deny. Either the universe was making a giant-sized laughingstock out of us or it was trying its damnedest to bring us together. I honestly wasn't sure which.

I could tell that Danika was conflicted as well. That the

events of tonight had altered things between us. How could it not? It was too much to just be a coincidence. I was tempted to call my mom and ask her opinion, but I wasn't ready to have my own thoughts dissected when I was still trying to figure them out myself.

Before I could overthink any more, I was home. Killing the engine, I locked the car doors and headed inside, no idea who or what might be waiting for me. You never knew who might be sticking around at the baseball house. Thankfully, the house was empty, except for a couple of the guys hanging out in the kitchen. I gave them a head nod before going into my room, half-expecting to see Mac sitting there, waiting for me. He was the only one who knew that I'd brought Danika home tonight.

Clearing her from my mind, I thought about my test in the morning. I really needed to start this class off right, or I'd be making it harder on myself for the rest of the semester. Tossing my bag on top of the desk in my room, I heard him approaching before he even said a word.

"Hey," Mac said, and I waved him in without turning around, motioning for him to close the door behind him. "How was it? I've been dying here, waiting for you to get home."

I laughed because at least Mac was honest even if he did give me all the ammunition that I needed to bust his balls on a daily basis.

"It was nice," I answered, suddenly a little unsure of what to say or how much to confess. The night felt too personal. And not necessarily my story to tell.

"It was nice?" he mimicked my response.

"What the hell am I supposed to say? It wasn't a date or anything."

He groaned before reaching for a lone baseball on the floor and throwing it in the air before catching it. He repeated the motion. "I know it wasn't a date, but did your family like her?" he asked, still tossing the ball instead of looking at me.

"They did."

The ball landed in his hand with a loud pop. "That's it?" He looked at me, his eyes inquisitive. "They liked her? Nothing else? Your mom isn't picking out china patterns and planning the wedding or anything?"

I searched my mind for more memories of the night that I felt comfortable with sharing. "I think my sister likes her more than she likes me," I offered, hoping it would sustain him.

"That's 'cause game recognize game," he said with a howl, and I stopped short.

"Excuse me?"

"Your sister is going to be a tough little badass who has guys eating out of the palm of her hand," he started to explain, and my stomach twisted. I wanted to ban Jacey from even looking at another boy ever again. "And she knows it. She knows Danika has the same power. So"—he waved his hands in the air—"game recognize game."

"You're an idiot," I said, chucking one of my dirty shirts at his head.

I laughed as he battled to swat it away, but it kept getting caught on his fingers instead. He eventually won the war with my shirt. It currently lay on the floor at his feet, and I watched as he kicked at it, just to make sure.

"I think you killed it."

"It attacked me."

"I noticed."

"Did you talk to Cole?" Mac asked, and I remembered that I had missed a call from our old teammate earlier tonight.

"Shit. He called, but I didn't pick up. What's up? Is he okay?" I was suddenly worried.

What if Cole got released from his farm team? What if he got hurt?

"Yeah, he's fine. He and Christina are in town, and he wants to stop by. But he wants you to be here, too, so he can see us both. You know, 'cause we're his favorites." Mac smiled like he'd won a prize at a fair.

"How could we not be?" I asked with a grin of my own. "Will you set it all up?" I asked because everyone knew that if they left coordinating details to me, it would never get done. I was shit at planning that kind of stuff; I always forgot.

"I'm already on it. I know you have that big test tomorrow, so I'll let you go to sleep. I just wanted to see how the night went. And"—he snapped his fingers like he had remembered something—"I meant to ask about what her boyfriend said."

"What he said about what?" I thought back to all the things Danika had revealed in the car ride home. And even though I wanted to hate the guy, how could I, knowing that he'd been there for her so selflessly?

"Her going to your house tonight. Did she tell him? Was he pissed? I bet he was pissed," he started mumbling and saying things I couldn't understand.

I shrugged. "She didn't tell him."

"Whaaaaat?" he practically screamed. "How could she not tell him? You guys were gone for hours. No way that guy is anywhere close to that fucking chill."

I'd almost forgotten all about Jared's phone calls and text messages, and now, I was getting worked up, thinking that she might be in trouble with him because of it. I needed to reach out and make sure I hadn't caused waves. I wanted her to know that I cared.

"She had her phone on silent. She texted him from the car on the drive home, and then he called, but she didn't answer."

Mac started laughing. "This is great. She goes home with you. Doesn't tell her boyfriend. And then texts him before ignoring his call? Thank you for confirming the fact that she wants you just as badly as you want her."

"Shut up."

"Just saying." He started backing out of the room.

"Go away."

"Good luck on your test."

"Thanks."

"Good luck with the girl."

"Good night." I looked around for another article of clothing that I could have attack him on his way out of my room, but he slammed the door so hard in his attempt to escape that the pictures on the wall rattled.

Reaching for my phone, I sent Danika a text before I could stop myself. I wanted to make sure that she was okay and wasn't in any trouble because of me. She responded right away with a smiley face and instructions to go worry about the test and not her. Which, of course, only made me do the exact opposite. It was one thing when it was my idea, but when it came to her telling me what to do, my mind didn't work the same.

It rebelled.

And now, I couldn't stop thinking about her and Jared. Him being at her house flooded my thoughts. Of course he'd be there, holding her, touching her, kissing her, fucking her. Because she was his. She belonged to him. They had history, a past … and who was I? Just some guy who had come along out of nowhere and meant nothing.

Fuck. This depressed version of me sucked. I hated it and wasn't used to it.

I forced myself onto my bed, covered my face with my pillow, and tried my best to fall asleep.

I WOKE UP, actually feeling refreshed. My night hadn't been plagued with dreams or nightmares or anything that I could remember. When I reached for my phone, there was no text from Danika, wishing me good luck or anything. Not that she.

was even remotely required to do that kind of shit, but like an idiot, I'd assumed she would, and disappointment coursed through me because she hadn't.

After a cold shower to wake up my senses, I grabbed a protein bar and headed out the door to hopefully pass my first math test.

Here goes nothing, I thought to myself before the test began, but the truth was that this first test was everything. It would set the tone for the rest of the semester. This test would determine if I was going to be struggling for the next couple of months or not. Passing would relieve a little bit of the stress, but failing would only amplify it.

I refused to fail. Danika had been tutoring me well the past month, and I understood way more than I ever had before. I was as ready as I'd ever be.

When I finished the test, I smiled to myself. Walking to the front of the class, I put my booklet in the basket, and the professor dismissed me. Once outside of the door, I pulled out my phone. There was still no text from Danika, but that didn't stop me from texting her.

CHANCE: TEST 1 DONE.

Her response was quicker than I anticipated.

DANIKA: HOW DO YOU FEEL?

CHANCE: GOOD ACTUALLY.

DANIKA: DO YOU HAVE A BREAK NOW?

CHANCE: I HAVE ABOUT AN HOUR BEFORE I NEED TO BE AT THE FIELD.

DANIKA: MEET ME IN THE COMM?

CHANCE: SEE YOU IN 5.

Telling Danika I had a free hour was a bit of an exaggeration. I only had about thirty-five minutes to spare, but I didn't want her to feel rushed. If the girl was going to give me some of her time, I planned on taking it.

I spotted her standing outside of the glass doors, looking down at her phone. When she glanced back up, her entire expression changed, and even though I knew it was because she had seen me, I convinced myself that it wasn't about me at all. I had to stop myself from practically cuing up music and running to her like we were in a sappy romance movie. Instead, I tried to play it cool, taking a swig of my water bottle and walking slow, but inside, I couldn't get to her quick enough.

"Hey," I said before wrapping her in my arms and hugging her.

She felt so good there. She fit.

"Someone's excited," she said as she pulled away, her cheeks rosy. "You think you passed?"

"I know I passed," I answered with confidence before taking another drink.

"Do you think you aced it?" she asked seriously, and I almost spat out the water I'd been drinking.

"No." I laughed. "I didn't understand it that well. But I'll be really surprised if I failed."

Her face pulled together like she was in pain. "I'll be devastated."

"Are you hungry?" I asked because the commissary had all the food and I'd only downed one protein bar so far. I needed more protein before I worked out and hit the field.

"A little, yeah."

"Let's go feed you, Little Spitfire. My treat."

"I'm not even going to argue with you, Hotshot. I mean, the independent girl in me wants to tell you I don't need you to pay for my food, but I don't feel like fighting with you today."

"Good. You won't win."

It was still pretty early in the morning, so the commissary wasn't as busy as it was during lunch, but there were enough people that I noticed them paying attention. You'd think that I'd be used to being watched on campus, but there were times when it was a little unnerving. Like now.

"People are watching us," Danika whispered as we got in line.

"I noticed."

She scanned the area before she turned her back to the tables and faced me in line. "Are they taking pictures? Of us?"

I glanced over her shoulder to a table where a few girls sat, their phones aimed in our direction while they pretended like they weren't. "It's possible."

"I don't want random people to take pictures of me, Chance."

She looked so uncomfortable, and I didn't know what to do.

How could I fix this or stop people from doing what they

wanted to without creating a scene?

"I'm sorry," I said as I focused on the girls and shook my head.

They all put their phones down and looked away, embarrassed. That had worked—for now.

"It's just so weird. Don't you think it's weird that they act like that?"

I nodded in agreement as hard as I could. "Hell yes, I think it's weird. I'm supposed to be used to it, but how do you get used to that?" I started to say before overexplaining, "I mean, it would be one thing if I were playing in the majors. I'd understand it then. But this is college. We're all just a bunch of kids. I'm no different than anyone else."

Danika giggled as she moved forward in line. "Well, that's a lie."

I scoffed, "Come again?"

"You heard me. You're not like everyone else."

Smiling, I asked, "So, you think I'm special?"

"Stop trying to flirt with me in public," she said, completely calling me out.

Of course, it only made me want to do it that much more.

She took two steps forward and reached the counter, where she ordered before stepping to the side and letting me finish. And pay. I loved it—that alpha feeling of taking care of your woman. Only problem was that she wasn't mine, and she most likely never would be.

"Are you okay?" Danika asked, her hand resting on my shoulder.

"Yeah. Why?"

"You just had an odd look on your face for a second."

"Stop trying to flirt with me in public," I teased, hoping she'd drop the subject.

A tray of food popped on top of the glass counter, and I looked at the guy with a questioning expression. He gave me a nod, indicating that it was ours, and I grabbed it.

"I can get it," Danika said from behind me, and I looked down at her with a half-grin.

"No. You can find us a table," I said, and she agreed, no doubt searching for one that was the farthest away from prying eyes.

It might have been a difficult task, but it wasn't impossible. The commissary had some tables that were more private, hidden behind tall islands that were meant for studying.

"I see one," she said with a smile, and I happily trailed behind her, fully aware of the phones going off around us.

She pointed at the lone four-person table, where almost no one else was sitting nearby.

"Looks good," I said, and she tossed her bag into one of the empty chairs and sat down.

I placed the tray of food on top and watched as Danika removed the small plates and sorted them in front of each one of us.

"So, tell me about the test," she said, seemingly more relaxed as she sipped on her fresh juice smoothie.

"It wasn't easy, but I understood most of it." I grabbed for the bacon on my plate, breaking it into little pieces and sprinkling it over my eggs before taking a giant bite and practically moaning. I needed to eat every two hours, and I was starved.

"That's so good. How long until he posts grades?" she asked, her hands clasping together before she started picking at her muffin. I watched her cut the top of it off and eat it first. "What? It's the best part."

I laughed before answering, "I don't know. He didn't say, but I'll log in later tonight and check."

"Promise you'll text me as soon as you know?"

"I promise," I agreed.

"Text you as soon as you know what?" the unfamiliar male voice rang out.

I almost snarled in response until I saw Danika's face. She looked … conflicted and shocked. She pushed back from the table and stood up before launching herself into this guy's arms and giving him a peck on the mouth.

"Jared. Hi. What are you doing here?"

Jared shifted on his feet, his weight moving from one leg to the other as he removed her arms from around his neck. I watched as his hands balled in and out and as Danika deflated with the motion.

You really thinking about coming at me?

Danika looked crazy uncomfortable, and while I fucking hated it and wanted to make it stop, Jared seemed to almost enjoy it. He kept staring at her, his expression hard and unforgiving.

"Aren't you going to introduce me?" he sneered, and she swallowed hard.

What kind of guy got off on making his girlfriend feel

weak? An insecure one, I assumed.

"Sorry. Jared, this is Chance. Chance, this is my boyfriend, Jared," she said before sitting back down.

He extended his hand, and when I took it, he tried to squeeze me too hard, a silent show of strength that took everything in me to not start laughing in his face.

"You look familiar."

"I'm in a fraternity. I'm sure you've been to our parties," he responded before adding, "And I've been to a few of yours over the years." I nodded.

"Ahhh, that's probably it. Anyway, it's nice to meet you. You have a really great girlfriend," I said genuinely, not realizing that it would push his buttons even though I should have been more than aware.

"Yeah, I do." He grabbed her bag and threw it out of the chair before sitting down and wrapping a possessive arm around her. "She's been spending a little too much time away from me lately though. Wouldn't you agree?"

His words were like sour grapes in my mouth. He was a bit of an asshole, who seemed nothing like the kind of guy I thought he'd be after mine and Danika's conversation last night. He had been there for her after her mom died. He was in California with her now instead of staying back in New York. I assumed that she was a priority to him, not property.

"I wouldn't really know," I offered, and he scoffed.

"Jared, stop. We already talked about this. We were studying," Danika argued, but it was weak at best. Her eyes cut to me for only a second before looking away.

"You're right," Jared said, his agreement fake. "Babe,

can you go grab me a water?"

"Uh …" She stalled before agreeing, "Sure." She gave me an apologetic look before walking away.

Jared watched her round the corner before he turned to me, his face twisted, his expression angry. "You're not taking my spot. I haven't put in all this time to get benched in the last inning."

"What the hell are you talking about?"

"Figured if I put it in baseball terms, you might understand. Guess I was wrong. I've put in the work. You don't get to reap the rewards."

"Work for what?" I asked because I had no idea what the hell this guy was even remotely talking about.

"Don't play stupid, Carter. You know who her father is."

Was this douche bag actually telling me that he was using Danika for her money? For her dad's connections or company?

"You'd better not be insinuating what I think you're fucking insinuating."

He stood up from the table, slapped my shoulder, and plastered a fake-ass smile on his face. I wanted to hit him and knock it right off.

"You don't know anything about how Manhattan works. Whole different ball game in the city. Stay in your lane, California boy."

I shoved my chair back and rose to my feet, thankful that I had a couple of inches on the guy. "Get out of my face," I growled, and he laughed.

He fucking laughed.

"What's going on?" Danika's voice broke us apart.

"Nothing, babe. I was just giving Chance a geography lesson." When she didn't say anything in response, he continued, "You know, letting him know how different New Yorkers are from Californians."

She looked between us, not buying his lie. I willed her to suddenly have the ability to read minds, so she could read mine.

Please see through this charade, Danika.

"I need to go anyway. I have to get to the field," I said, only hesitating once her eyes met mine. "I'll text you when I get my grade," I added, hoping it would piss Jared off.

Danika knew something had happened while she was away, and no matter how badly I wanted to tell her, what was I supposed to say?

Oh, hey, I think your boyfriend is using you for your money?

Without any proof other than my own thoughts and his words, which I could have easily misinterpreted?

No way.

I'd learned my lesson this past summer about staying out of other people's relationships. That was one thing that was seared into my memory bank. Whatever the hell was going on between Danika and Jared wasn't my business, no matter how I felt about her, and I needed to remember that.

Don't Recognize Myself

Danika

"WHAT THE HELL was that?" I asked the second Chance stormed off.

I had no idea what Jared had said to him, but I knew it couldn't have been good. Chance had looked like he was seconds away from ripping Jared's head off when I walked up.

"Nothing." He unscrewed the cap off his water and took a drink.

"Sure didn't look like nothing to me," I snapped.

Jared walked me backward until I bumped the table with my lower back. His arms braced each side of my body, boxing me in. "I was just reminding Baseball Boy to keep his hands to himself."

My jaw tightened involuntarily, and it took everything in me not to fight back, but we were in public, and I was all too aware of the eyes watching. "I don't need you to do that."

"The guy wants you, Danika." He slammed one hand on the table out of frustration, and I swore it echoed throughout the whole commissary.

"Stop. You're causing a scene," I whispered, completely embarrassed before wiggling out of his arm shield and sitting down. I patted the chair next to me, hoping Jared would sit as well and was thankful when he did.

"I don't want you hanging out with him," he demanded, and I felt my defenses flare up inside of me.

"You have to stop doing that." My voice was weaker than I'd wanted, and I hated that I sounded so submissive instead of strong.

"Doing what?"

"Telling me what to do. You never used to be like this. *We* never used to be like this." I wanted to remind Jared that our relationship hadn't started out this way. He wasn't always so possessive and controlling.

I watched as his expression shifted. "No, we didn't. But then again, there weren't guys stalking you before, were there?"

And there it was yet again—the pretty justification for his ugly behavior.

"That was one time, Jared. And it's done now. You can't keep using that as an excuse to try to control my life."

"Excuse me for caring so much about you. For not wanting you to be in a situation where that could happen again. For wanting you to stay away from other guys who clearly want you and are not used to taking no for an answer. I'm just looking out for you, Danika. I want you to be safe. Protected. Why is that so hard to understand?"

When he said things like that, all my strength flew out the window, and guilt instantly replaced it. I felt bad for making him worry. And even though I hated how controlling he'd become, it felt like it was my fault somehow. Because of the situation I'd been in, I'd created this new reality between us. I had no one to blame but myself.

"Well, you don't need to worry about Chance." I tried to sound convincing. "Pretty sure he's not the type of guy to stalk a girl."

"Are you cheating on me?" Jared asked bluntly.

I started choking on the air in my lungs, slapping at my chest to make it stop. His question caught me completely off guard. Being jealous was one thing, but thinking I'd actually crossed the line and cheated was another.

"What? No. Never."

"I don't believe you." His eyes narrowed, and they looked almost … scary.

"Seriously?" I asked as I wondered what the hell had just happened. "Are you being serious right now? I've never given you any reason to—"

"You went to his house last night without telling me until you came back. You ignored my calls and texts while you were with him. Of course I think there's something going on."

I swallowed around the giant lump in my throat. *Has that always been there?* "I handled yesterday badly, and I'm sorry. But nothing happened," I told him as I apologized again.

I had already apologized to Jared a thousand times last night after confessing to him about where I'd really been. If the roles had been reversed and he had been at some girl's house without telling me, I'd have been beyond pissed, too, so I understood. But Jared was so angry that I never even got the chance to tell him about my mom or the pictures Cassie had gifted me of her. We got off the phone with him still pissed. I'd assumed he'd show up at my apartment to finish the conversation in person or to make up, but he never did. Not even after I'd asked him to.

"Jared," I said, reaching across the table for his hand and taking it in mine, "I messed up last night, and I really am sorry. I should have told you where I was going. I should have let you know."

He pulled his hand from mine and huffed out a disgusted sound. "No. That's just it, Danika. You shouldn't have told me. There should have been nothing to tell. You should have never agreed to go over there in the first place. You're my girlfriend, but you're running around like you're Chance Carter's whore."

"Excuse me?" I stood up, my pride finally making an appearance. "What did you just call me?" The derogatory names that some felt were okay to call girls were such hypocritical bullshit, and I wouldn't tolerate it.

"You need to start acting right." He pushed back his chair and stood as well. "And if I find out you're cheating on me—"

"You'll what? Call me another name?" I mocked.

"I'll make sure your little Baseball Boy knows whose girl he messed with. And I'll let him know where we come from and how we handle things like this back in the city," he threatened before walking away and leaving me alone at the table, strange eyes still on me, as I wondered what in the hell kind of reality television show my life had just turned into and how the heck I'd let it happen.

I sat down and put my head in my hands for only a moment before I heard Sunny's usually cheerful voice. "Well, that was fun to watch."

I glanced up to see her holding a tray of food and a book before setting it all down on the table and sitting next to me, where Jared had just been. "How much did you hear?"

She shook her head. "Not much really. It was more of the body language. He looked like he was yelling at you."

"He kinda was," I confirmed, and she bit into an apple, moaning as she chewed before swallowing.

"What is Jerk-Off mad about now?"

"He thinks I cheated with Chance."

She let out a sound, her head shaking. "He thinks *you* cheated? Oh, that's rich," she said before taking another bite.

"What does that mean?" I asked because her response was odd.

Is she insinuating that Jared's cheated on me? Does she know something that I don't?

"Nothing." She waved her arms around. "I just don't like him anymore; you know that," she admitted before swallowing. "Sorry. I know that sucks to hear, and it's not my place."

Her admission was hurtful, but it wasn't a surprise. I knew that she had stopped liking Jared. We'd already talked about it before.

"I know you don't like him."

"For you," she clarified like she had when we talked about this at home, and my phone buzzed. "I just think you can do better."

I reached for my cell, assuming it would be a text or something from Jared, but there was a simple message from Chance waiting instead, which read, *I passed.* I felt the smile break out on my face before I could stop it.

"Now, that's a smile I haven't seen in a while," Sunny said with a matching grin of her own. "Bet I know who the message is from."

"Stop," I said, trying to make my smile disappear but failing.

"It's not my fault Chance Carter makes you smile more than your own boyfriend does." The accuracy of her words made the breath catch in my throat. She shrugged, her blue eyes shining. "What? It's true, so I'm not sorry for saying it."

I knew that it was too. I just wasn't ready to admit it out loud and deal with the consequences of what exactly that meant.

Catching Up with Cole

Chance

MY PROFESSOR MUST have graded the tests right after we finished them or something because as I'd headed toward the field after breakfast, I'd pulled up my online account and seen that I'd gotten a B-minus. I was feeling pretty good for pulling that grade, and I knew Danika would be happy for me too.

I had texted her and was waiting for her to respond, but after about a minute, I needed to put my phone in my locker and get into the weight room. I was running behind. Having breakfast with her hadn't been the smartest idea, but when she asked, I couldn't say no. I didn't want to. And even though I thought Jared was a complete dick, it was a good thing that he had shown up when he did. I'd needed to leave, and without him ruining the morning, I wasn't sure I would have. I mean, of course I would have, but I would have been even later than I already was, consequences be damned.

Fall conditioning and workouts six days a week were mandatory. We only had one day off, and today wasn't it. So, when I stepped into the workout room three minutes after I was supposed to and saw Coach Jackson standing near the exit, I was pissed. Not because Coach was there, but because I was actually late for the first time in my college career, and I had no one to blame but myself. I watched as he looked up at the clock on the wall before walking out without saying a word.

"Dammit," I mumbled as Mac walked up, a towel around his shoulders.

"He was only in here for five minutes, man," he said, and I shook my head. "Five minutes. Swear."

"He's never here before we are," I said, still angry at myself because Coach usually showed up in the middle of weights and stayed until the end to make sure none of us skipped out.

"I know," Mac added. "Wonder why he was. Everyone's here," he said, and we both looked around at our team. "Except you."

Why did he pick today, of all days, to show up before us? And why the hell did I allow myself to be late? I was never late.

"Think he's pissed?" I asked, honestly wondering how much hell he'd be giving me later.

"Definitely." Mac shrugged. "By the way, why were you late?"

I considered lying for a second, telling Mac that my test had run over and the professor had given me extra time to finish, but that was just stupid. "I was at breakfast with Danika. Her boyfriend showed up."

He grinned. "I already knew that."

"What?" I punched him in the arm. "Why'd you ask me then?"

"Wanted to see if you'd lie or not." He gave me a look.

"And how the hell did you already know?"

"Snapchat. Instagram. Take your pick."

Before I could complain or groan, Coach reappeared near the door. "Carter. Now."

"Fuck," I mumbled before walking toward the exit, where he was waiting.

Once we were outside of the weight room, he shook his head.

"Don't come to the field today," he said with authority.

"What? Coach, I'm sorry I was—" I started to explain, but he cut me off.

"You know the rules, Carter. I expect a full commitment from you. Go home. You're done for the day," he said, and there would be no arguing. "If you show up at the field for practice later, everyone on the team will pay for your idiocy."

"Yes, Coach," I said before mentally beating myself up.

I couldn't believe that I'd allowed myself to get carried away this morning. My dad was going to be so mad, and he would have every right to be.

How did I let myself get kicked out of a practice?

Slinging my bag over my shoulder, I walked toward the parking lot, where I'd left my car earlier and debated my options. My gut instincts were to fight, to show up at the field anyway later so Coach knew how serious I was about the team and how sorry I was for being stupid. But I knew that would only backfire. Coach Jackson would send me right back home and tack on the rest of the week as well to make an example out of me. Then, he'd make my boys run until they threw up. All because I'd refused to listen.

I couldn't do that to my teammates, but sitting at home while they practiced today was going to damn near kill me. It didn't matter who you were; Coach's rules were meant to be followed. If you broke them, you paid the price. I'd always admired that about him. It felt good, being part of a team where no one received special treatment. It helped keep egos in check—mine included, apparently.

My phone buzzed as I sat in my Bronco, and I reached for it without looking. A text from Danika, congratulating me on passing my test with a million exclamation points, couldn't even bring me out of my bad mood. To be honest, I'd already forgotten about the test. I was too busy feeling sorry for myself to think about anything else.

A quick rap on my window made me jump. I turned to see my dad's face staring at me, his expression twisted in confusion. I rolled it down, and he placed a hand on my side mirror.

"Why are you sitting out here instead of lifting inside?"

I swallowed around the lump in my throat. "I was late."

My dad cocked his head back in surprise. "You were late?"

I nodded.

"Why?"

That was the one question I'd been dreading more than any other. "I was having breakfast with Danika in the comm."

He moved toward my window and leaned in, bracing himself on his forearms as I prepared myself for the lecture that I was sure would follow my answer. "Did you lose track of time?"

"No."

My dad started laughing. "No? Not even gonna lie to me, son?"

"Why would I lie to you?"

"Don't most kids lie to their parents to stay out of trouble?"

"Am I in trouble?" I asked with a little more arrogance in my tone than I had intended because what was he going to do, ground me?

"Looks like it to me," he said with a smug look on his face before pushing away.

"I'm sorry, Dad. I'm just pissed off."

"At who?"

"Myself," I breathed out in frustration. "Who else would I be pissed at?"

He shrugged both shoulders. "Never know. You could be mad at Danika. Or Coach Jackson. Or the commissary for being open."

I huffed out a quick laugh. "You and Mom raised me better than that. I don't really deflect."

"You can thank your mom for that one. Taking responsibility for your actions. Owning up to your mistakes and not blaming others. That's all her," he said with a smile, and I didn't say anything. "How long did Coach kick you off for?"

“Just today.”

“That’s good,” he said with a nod before snapping his fingers. “Oh, hey, how was your test?”

“I got a B minus.”

My dad’s grin grew even wider. “Nice. Guess the tutoring’s working then,” he said before taking a few steps away. “Hey, Chance. Don’t beat yourself up too much for today. Just don’t let it happen again.”

“Never,” I reassured him because I wouldn’t. What had happened this morning could never happen again, and I’d make sure of it.

“And don’t show up today. No matter how badly you want to, do not come to the field.”

“I know. I won’t.”

I SPENT THE rest of the morning damn near sulking in my room until well past noon. It was weird as fuck, being home alone while the rest of my teammates were at the field, practicing. I wanted to be there. I needed to be there. I was supposed to be there.

But I wasn’t.

Grabbing a bat, I walked into the backyard where a tee and a small net were already set up. I might not be able to hit with my boys at the moment, but I could still practice at home. It wasn’t quite the same, but it would have to do. I’d swing this bat until my fingers bled.

It might have looked extreme to someone from the outside, but when you loved something as much as I loved baseball, you fought for it. And when you fucked up and had no one else to blame for your mistakes, you punished yourself for it.

My phone buzzed and kept buzzing. I wondered who was actually calling me instead of texting as I pulled it from my pocket. Cole's name flashed across the screen.

"Hey," I answered.

"Hey. I thought I'd swing by later. You gonna be home?"

"Yeah. I'm here all day. Come by anytime."

"All right. That was easy. See you later," he said with a laugh before ending the call.

Most of us guys didn't tend to chitchat. We got straight to the point and then got on with our lives … with the exception of Mac. I was pretty sure that guy would talk on the phone for hours if you let him.

I kept hitting off the tee, even as sweat dripped down my forehead and burned my eyes. Only when my stomach growled and I felt a little dizzy on my feet did I stop. I needed food. And a shower.

By the time I got out of the shower, the house was loud, and I knew that my roommates were back. Toweling off my hair, I pulled on a pair of shorts and walked out of my room to find Cole sitting in the kitchen, drinking a beer with Mac, Colin, and Dayton.

"There he is." Mac gave a nod in my direction, and Cole swiveled in his chair to face me.

"Hey." He stood up and walked over, patting my back with both fists.

I hadn't realized how much I missed having him around until he was standing right in front of me.

"Hey, man. It's good to see you," I said.

"You too. Heard Coach kicked you out today. What happened?" he asked before sitting back down and reaching for his beer.

I eyeballed the rest of my roommates, who were waiting for me to answer. "I was late to weights." I tried to play it off like it was no big deal, but we all knew that being late during the off-season was as unacceptable as being late during the regular season.

Cole gave me a knowing look. "Coach Jackson doesn't fuck around, man."

"Tell me about it," I agreed, and he finished off his beer. "How's ball?" I asked, dying to know how playing professional baseball was from his perspective. He was already doing the one thing we were still striving for.

"It's good but hard." He looked me dead in the eye. "It's different than this was."

"How so?" Dayton asked.

We were all practically foaming at the mouths for this information. Every one of us wanted the chance to play professional baseball, and Cole was currently doing it. He was living the dream.

"Every player is good at what they do. Don't get me wrong; the guys here at Fullton are good, too, but it's just different," he started to explain, and we all seemed to lean closer toward him on instinct. "Everyone has the same goal. Every guy is getting paid to be there, and they all want to get to the next level. No one is there to stay in Single-A baseball for long, you know?"

I nodded my head and noticed that the guys were all doing the same. I'd had at least a million talks about this exact subject with my dad, but maybe things were different now. "What's the biggest change that you've noticed from college to pro?"

Cole stayed quiet for a minute, clearly weighing his answer. "It's twofold, I think. The hitting is one."

"What do you mean? How?" Colin asked, and I knew it was because hitting was the one area he was constantly trying to improve. He struggled on and off at the plate.

"Pretty much every guy can hit. Home runs, I mean. It doesn't matter if you can hit singles and doubles. As long as you rake in the homers consistently, you're golden to coaches."

Colin's face dropped. He almost looked like he was about to cry. "That's not even realistic."

"I know. It's not how I was taught to play either," Cole agreed.

"A home run every now and then is nice, but a three fifty batting average with a high number of RBIs sounds better to me," Mac said, and I knew that we were getting into the one thing that most players never thought about—the business aspect of baseball.

Thankfully, I had been well versed on the business side of the game because of my dad and uncle. "They don't care about that right now. They haven't for a few years. You can strike out ten times out of fifteen, but if those other five at bats are home runs, they'll practically throw you a parade," I said because it was true.

I'd been watching the game shift and bend and move since I started playing. It had basically evolved into a Home Run Derby of sorts, and it went against everything I'd ever thought about the sport.

"What's the second thing?" Dayton asked. "You said there were two things. The hitting was first. What's the second?"

"You'll like this one." Cole looked right at Dayton and grinned. "The pitching."

"What about it?" Dayton turned serious.

"The pitchers are all fucking on point. They have control. Speed. Accuracy."

Dayton nodded. "They should. Or else they shouldn't be there."

I laughed at the way Dayton had said it, but I completely understood what he was getting at. He was most likely going to be our Friday night starter this season, and you didn't earn that honor by being a half-assed pitcher who couldn't do his job well.

"You're right," Cole said. "But the big difference is, if they're struggling at all on the mound, they get yanked. There're just too many other pitchers waiting to take their place."

"Damn," Colin breathed out, and he still looked a little pale.

I clapped him on the back. "You all right, man?"

"Just feeling overwhelmed, and I'm not even there yet," he admitted, and I respected his ability to be so candid and vulnerable when the rest of us played tough all the time.

"You think it's hard now?" Cole asked Colin but didn't wait for a response. "Once you get drafted, the real work's just beginning. Every day, you have to get better. You can't slack. You can't ease up. You can't *not* improve."

I watched as Colin swallowed hard, his hands folding in, and I knew instantly in the pit of my stomach that he didn't have what it took to play professional baseball. This game required mental strength above all else. You could be a great player, but if you were easily rattled the minute something went wrong on the field, you were done for.

I figured I'd help Colin out and change the subject a little. "So, how's Christina?"

Cole's face lit up. If there was one thing he loved more than baseball, it was his girl.

"Great. Super busy with work and with me." He grinned before wagging his eyebrows. "She's amazing. So talented. So smart."

"Jeez. Marry the girl already," Mac deadpanned.

I was expecting Cole to have some kind of smart-ass response.

"I plan on it."

I jerked my head back. "Really? Already?"

"I mean, at some point, yeah. Of course. She's it for me, man." He sounded so sure of himself, which was a little surprising after all the drama he'd gone through to be with her. But that was probably why he felt the way he did. Maybe when you blew the world apart to be together, you ended up on solid ground.

"It's crazy to hear you say that when last year was such a shitshow," I said, merely meaning to point out the obvious.

"Last year was pure hell. But I'm grateful for it. We had to go through all that, you know? It was all worth it," Cole added confidently.

"You'd do it again?" Mac asked seriously.

"If it got us to where we are now? Abso-fucking-lutely. Plus, I can't imagine going through all of this without her. Having teammates is one thing, but they really only care about themselves. Everyone is trying to get to the next level, and that's a journey of one. Having someone who believes in you and supports you and is on your side?" He blew out a breath. "It's something else entirely. I'd be really lonely without her. I'd feel like I was doing all of this by myself."

"Damn," I said, unsure of why I sounded so shocked since I couldn't imagine Cole without Christina.

I guessed I'd never heard anyone describe getting drafted and getting the opportunity to play in that way before. No one had ever mentioned that it was lonely. Not even my dad.

"What about you knuckleheads? Mac still making out with every willing female on campus?" Cole looked around at the four of us and waited to be filled in.

"Hey, I'm right here," Mac practically whined.

"Well, are you?"

Mac shifted in his seat, like the topic made him uncomfortable when he was usually so overly cocky about it.

"Ask Chance about his love life instead."

Cole's face morphed into a look of instant amusement. "Carter, you have a love life?"

I smacked Mac's arm as Colin and Dayton all started talking at once.

"No," I practically shouted over the noise.

"Tell him about Tutor Girl," Mac pushed as Colin and Dayton oohed and aahed like a couple of fucking kids.

"Tutor Girl?" Cole looked at me expectantly, waiting for me to say more. "Are you actually dating someone?" Cole asked, totally confused, and Mac howled with laughter.

"That's the best part." Mac was still laughing. "She has a boyfriend!"

"Not sure why that's so fucking funny." I shot him a look that only made him laugh more.

Dayton and Colin both smiled, but so far, they weren't laughing, which I appreciated because I started to feel like a joke.

"It's not funny, per se. It's irony at its finest," Dayton said before adding, "Chance Carter finally likes a chick. And she has a fucking boyfriend."

Cole's hand gripped my shoulder. "Never thought I'd see the day."

"It's nothing. There is no day." I tried to play nonchalant, but everyone knew I was faking it. Or at least trying to.

Cole snapped his fingers. "Wait. You said she was a tutor? I totally know who you're talking about."

My entire body tensed with his words. "How could you possibly know who we're talking about?"

Cole looked me dead in the eyes. " 'Cause there's only one female in the athletic tutoring department who is fine as hell and hasn't graduated yet," he said before adding, "But I thought she quit after what happened to her last year."

I glanced at Mac, wondering if he knew what Cole was talking about, but he looked as confused as I felt. "What happened last year?" I asked.

"You guys never heard about the football player who stalked his tutor?" Cole asked, and the story vaguely rang a bell in the back of my mind but not really.

"I feel like I might have heard something about it, but I didn't pay it that much attention," I admitted before feeling like an asshole.

"I didn't hear anything about it," Mac said with a shrug.

"Me either," Dayton added.

Colin sat there, still sulking from the baseball conversation. I wasn't even sure he was listening anymore.

"What happened? You're sure it was Danika?" I asked.

Cole's head yanked back in recognition. "That's her name. From the East Coast, right?"

"Yeah, New York," I added, feeling defensive and angry.

"Mmhmm. It was definitely her."

"So, what happened? How many times do I have to fucking ask you that?" I practically bit his head off.

Cole huffed out a small laugh before pointing a finger at me. "You really do like this girl." He continued to grin, and I was about to lose my damn mind if he didn't tell me what the hell had happened to her. "So, I don't know much really. Just that the guy stalked her. Like, he showed up at her place a few times or something. It got pretty bad and she threatened to go to Compliance if he didn't stop.

"Who was it?" I ground out, wanting to tear the guy's throat out.

"I don't know for sure, but I always heard it was Kenny."

"That football douche who got drafted?" Mac asked with a snarl.

I didn't hang out with non-baseball players unless we shared a class, so I didn't know most of the other athletes on campus. But I remembered Kenny—not because he'd gotten drafted into the NFL last year, but because he was always acting like a fucking idiot whenever I saw him around. The guy did things like pound his chest, proclaiming to be Tarzan while he tossed girls over his shoulder and spanked their asses. It made me sick, thinking about a guy like him pursuing Danika. Her distaste for athletes made more sense now.

"Yeah. I don't know a hundred percent that it was him, but that's what I always heard."

"He seems like the type who wouldn't take no for an answer," Colin added out of nowhere, and I swore my blood started boiling inside my veins.

"Carter?"

I met Cole's watchful gaze.

"You good?" he asked.

"No," I admitted.

"Let it go. She handled it. He's long gone," Cole said, clearly trying to calm me down.

"The same way you'd let it go if it were Christina? The

same way you let it go last year with Logan?"

I was being kind of a dick, and I knew it, but this was Danika we were talking about. The thought of someone stalking her, showing up at her house and not taking no for an answer, was making me feel violent. I couldn't believe she never told me this had happened to her. But then again, when had I given her the chance? And why would she bring that up to me now? What would have been the point?

Something additional snapped inside me. Another piece of the Jared puzzle slid into place without warning. This was just another example of him being there for her when she needed someone. One more thing that had connected them, that bonded them together, that made their relationship stronger. One more thing that I could never compete with.

Maybe it wasn't about the money at all for Jared. I really didn't know, but I did know that it was none of my fucking business.

Secrets Brought to Light

Danika

I WAS NERVOUS for my next tutoring session with Chance. As I walked toward the library by myself, scanning my surroundings with each step, I felt those familiar butterflies come to life in the pit of my stomach. Maybe it wasn't nerves at all. Maybe I was just excited to see him.

Neither option was good, especially with the current state of my relationship. I hadn't talked to Jared since our fight in the commissary yesterday. I'd ignored all two of his calls and text messages. I knew that he felt like I was the one who was wrong, so I should be apologizing and chasing him, but I was tired of trying to fix the things that kept breaking between us. His controlling behavior was exhausting. And I was tired. Not to mention the fact that I was genuinely pissed at him. So, no, I wouldn't be doing the chasing this time regardless of my role.

Climbing up the stairs, I turned toward the private tutoring offices and spotted Chance already sitting in there, his back to me. He was gorgeous, all broad shoulders and strong arms. And don't get me started on that chest. Guys in college shouldn't look that good. They shouldn't be able to look like men who could slay dragons for their women, just to keep them safe.

But Chance Carter did. He'd looked like he wanted to kill Jared yesterday, and even if it made me a bad person, it'd turned me on. I'd never seen Chance look so angry, and I still had no idea why, but I assumed it had to have been about me.

I paused for a moment when I reached the door and inhaled a long breath before grabbing the knob. The moment my hand touched the cold metal, Chance turned around, his hard green eyes meeting mine and instantly softening. I tried to stop the smile from forming on my face but failed. It was official: Chance Carter made me giddy.

"Hey," I said as I closed the door behind me.

"Hey yourself," he said, his tone not as friendly as I had expected.

"You okay?" I asked because I hadn't thought for a second that things between Chance and me could go back to the way they had been at the beginning. Not after the other night at his house.

"Yeah, I'm fine," he said, sounding anything but.

I tossed my bag on top of the table with a loud thud and sat down. "Please don't turn into the old Chance," I practically pleaded, and he cocked his head to one side.

"The old Chance?"

"Yeah," I started to explain, "the one who goes back and forth, up and down. The one I can't read. I thought we were past all that. I thought we were"—I paused for a second—"friends."

He swallowed hard. I watched his throat bob. "We are."

"Friends tell each other what's wrong."

"Fine." He relented with a huff. "I heard something"—he shrugged one shoulder—"and it upset me."

Color me intrigued. I waved my hand to get him to continue talking. "Tell me more."

"Did something happen to you last year with a football player?" He tried to act composed, but the anger in his tone was undeniable.

I was caught off guard. Surprised. I hadn't even remotely expected this. I didn't want to lie to him, but I really didn't want to relive what I'd already put behind me either. "Yeah. How'd you hear?"

"One of my old teammates said something about it last night," he said casually, and every word stuck in my head.

He was talking about me to his friends?

"What did he say?"

"That a football player stalked you." His green eyes pinched together, and he looked like he was in physical pain.

It took everything in me not to reach out and comfort *him*. I wanted to grab his hand, kiss the top of it, and tell him that I was okay now. That he didn't need to worry.

"Is it true?" His voice cracked and I felt a piece of me crack as well.

Nodding, I answered, "It's true."

The pained expression on his face stayed put as he stared, and it damn near killed me.

"Are you okay?" He reached for my hand, took it in his, and held it, his thumb rubbing across the top.

I'd almost forgotten that he asked me anything. All I could feel was his skin on mine.

"I'm okay," I answered, but it came out in a whisper.

"Are you sure?"

"I am. He's gone now. And he stopped before it got really bad."

"He never should have started." Chance dropped my hand, and I focused on the empty feeling there instead of his words. "Danika." Chance's voice was strong, demanding that I give him my attention.

I looked up, unsure of what he needed from me. "What?"

"I'm going out of my fucking mind, okay? The thought of someone hurting you. Touching you when you don't want them to." His eyes closed, and his jaw clenched. His head shook one last time, like he was ridding it of all the bad thoughts and images that lived there. "I can't handle it. I literally can't fucking handle it when it comes to you."

This guy pushed every single emotional button I had inside of me. Jared made me feel stupid whenever he brought up the subject, but Chance made me feel protected and desired.

"I don't … I don't know what to say," I admitted honestly, stumbling over my own awareness.

"Is this a one-way thing?" He waved a finger between our two bodies, and I knew what he was asking.

What am I supposed to say? I had a boyfriend, and Chance was making me feel things I had no right to feel, asking me things I had no business answering.

"Please, Danika, I need to know at least that."

"It's never been a one-way thing," I said on a shaky breath. It was all out in the open now, and neither one of us could take it back. "But we can't do anything about it."

His face soured. "You plan on staying with Jared forever? You going to marry this guy? Is that what you're telling me?"

What? How have we gone from us having feelings for eachother to me marrying Jared?

Even though my gut response was to scream out, *NO*, at the top of my lungs, my body reacted defensively, as if it were being attacked. "I have no idea."

"Danika, listen to me." He turned in his chair, his body angling toward mine. "Your boyfriend's a dick. He was rude as hell to you and—"

"Stop," I demanded. "You don't get to tell me about my relationship. You don't get to have an opinion on something you know nothing about."

"I just never pegged you for that type of girl, is all," he sneered, and I had no idea what he meant.

"What type of girl?" I asked, repeating his words.

"The kind who gets off on being treated like shit. I thought you girls grew out of that phase after high school."

"That's it!" I yelled before pushing to my feet. "I can't do this with you."

He reached for my hand and pulled me back down to my chair, forcing me to sit. Our knees touched, and neither one of us moved to break the contact.

"I'm sorry," he apologized, but I still saw red.

"I can't keep doing this with you for the rest of the

semester," I said before taking back everything I'd worked so hard to make with him. "I know I'm the one who pushed us to be friends, but I can't be your friend, Chance."

I realized in that moment that my hand was still in his. He leaned forward, our faces inches from one another. His lips were close enough that if I closed the gap just a fraction, they'd touch, and I'd finally know what his felt like.

"I never wanted to just be your friend."

"I think you should find another tutor," I said quietly, my eyes focused directly on his mouth.

His tongue darted out to wet his bottom lip, and I swore I almost started drooling when he slowly pulled it between his teeth. I wanted to kiss him so bad, I could taste it. In all the time I'd dated Jared, I'd never been attracted to another guy. I'd never even considered the possibility. Until now.

"There is no one else, remember? I've already checked," he admitted, and I was mesmerized by the way his lips moved and pursed together.

"You checked?" I averted my gaze from his mouth and watched as he nodded before leaning back, giving us space but not too much. "Why?"

"Because of this. You distract me. You tempt me. I fucking want you, and I don't know how to stop." He sounded breathless, and my mind instantly went to the bedroom, wondering if that was how he sounded when he was having sex.

I imagined his large body hovering over mine, all of his hard muscles flexing, begging to be touched.

"I want to kiss you, Danika. I want to make you forget

that anyone else in the world exists, except you and me."

I held my breath as the weight of his words crashed down around me.

"But I won't. Because I'd hate myself for it after."

"I'd hate myself too," I conceded, "but that doesn't mean I don't want it as badly as you do."

"Then, break up with him," he said simply. "Break up with him, so I can finally know what you taste like. What you feel like. And so I can stop jerking off in the shower to make-believe bullshit images of you and have the real thing."

He thinks about me in the shower? Why do I find that so hot?

"It's not that easy," I said with a sigh.

Ending a relationship wasn't as simple as someone from the outside made it seem. Even with the drama and fights, it still wasn't easy to walk away from something you'd spent the last five years building.

"I know he's been there for you. But just because you have a past with someone doesn't mean that you owe them your future. If you want to be with Jared, tell me, and I'll back off. I'll never bring it up again. But if you're anywhere near as unhappy as I think you are, then do the right thing and end things with him. Just know that the second you do, I'm making you mine."

This was all too much. Everything that had lived in the dark between Chance and me was being tossed into the light, begging to be seen. I needed to get us back on track, focused. End the conversation that truly was none of his business and get him out of my relationship, where he didn't belong.

"We should really study."

He grinned, and his lone dimple appeared. "Okay, Danika, let's study."

He was giving in for me, and I took it without a fight.

Two Weeks Later

I'D BE LYING to myself if I said that knowing Chance wanted me didn't change things. It absolutely did. I started thinking more about what my life could look like without Jared. As a matter of fact, I couldn't stop thinking about it. My body, my mind, every part of me wanted to know what being with Chance would feel like.

Which was why, after our mutual admission and the fact that Chance had passed his next math test with ease, I'd taken his tutoring down to once a week. It was the right thing to do even though everything in me rebelled against the separation. I knew that Chance had hoped for a different decision from me as well, but I couldn't grant him that kind of power over me or my relationship.

He'd tried to text me a few times, but I'd put a stop to that, too, by either not responding at all or giving one-worded answers. He took the hint, choosing silence in return, which I both hated and desperately needed. It was the only way for me to figure things out on my end without Chance Carter clouding my judgment.

Whatever I decided to do about Jared, it couldn't be about Chance. But to be honest, it was really hard to separate the two of them in my head. Breaking up with Jared meant that I'd finally have a shot to be with Chance. And I knew that I wanted that, but I hated that I felt like a bad person because of it. I was not the type of girl to end one relationship for another. Or at least, I never had been before.

I hated that I felt like I was doing something wrong when everything about being with Chance felt so opposite of that. I wished my mom were here. It was one of those times when I longed to pick up the phone and call her for advice. I tried to think about what she'd tell me to do even though I knew she would insist that I follow my heart even if it broke someone else's.

Some of her last words echoed in my mind.

"Be happy. Be ridiculously happy, Nika. Don't let anyone else be responsible for your joy. That's up to you. So, chase it. Without abandon. Without guilt. Without fear. And never settle. Not in life. And especially not in love."

The front door slammed.

"Honey, I'm home," Sunny's voice rang out, and I giggled.

It was really damn hard to be sad around that girl. And even though she'd recently pushed me for information about Chance, I'd kept quiet. I kept our confessions to myself, locking them inside me, where I considered them safer. Sharing them with her would make them real.

"In the kitchen, where I belong," I teased, and Sunny

squealed in response.

"Baking, I hope!" she said as she bounced into view with a grin.

I held out a giant spoonful of homemade chocolate chip cookie dough, and she greedily grabbed it.

"Please tell me you sprinkled sea salt on top of the chocolate chips!" She leaned down toward the oven and tried to peer inside. "I can't see in there," she whined.

"Why the hell would I put sea salt on them?" I asked.

"You know nothing about culinary baking," she complained before grabbing the spoon filled with dough and licking it. "So, what's wrong? You only bake when you're thinking about things or trying to figure out a problem."

Damn. I'd figured I had at least a few more minutes before she called me out.

Looking at her with a frown, I relented. "I was thinking that Jared and I might need to take a break."

Her eyes looked like they were about to pop out of her head. "Is this a joke? Are you kidding? Seriously? Why? What happened? Tell me everything." She hopped on top of the counter and started swinging her feet.

"I just …" I paused, trying to remember all of her questions. "I haven't been happy in a while. And it's not getting better, you know?"

She nodded before tossing the spoon into the sink with a clang.

"I invited him over later to talk."

"Does he have any idea?"

"I don't know. I mean, there's no way he can truly be

happy. We've been fighting more than ever lately. It's like we can't even get along anymore. Everything I do makes him mad. And everything he does annoys me."

"Well, the Chance factor came into your equation," Sunny said, wiggling her eyebrows.

I found myself laughing. "The what?"

"I was trying to sound all math-y," she said with a giggle of her own as the timer buzzed.

Reaching inside the oven, I pulled out the freshly baked cookies and set them on top of the stove to cool.

"But you know what I mean. Chance came into your world and shook it all up."

"Yeah, but Jared and I weren't getting along way before Chance ever showed up. He just exacerbated the issue, I think."

"Ooh, big word."

I rolled my eyes. "Honestly, I just think he made it hard for me to ignore the fact that I haven't been happy in a really long time."

"Because, with Chance, you could be?" Sunny asked, her blonde hair falling over one eye, and I stayed quiet as her question rolled around in my head.

"I don't know," I said.

"Yes, you do. You just don't want to admit it. Still. Which is annoying because we both know the truth. Now, give me a cookie." She pursed her lips as I grabbed a paper towel and a spatula.

"What do you say?" I taunted with the cookie in front of her grabby hands.

"Pleeeeeeease," she said in a childlike voice, and I handed it over.

The thought of ending things with Jared was scary. It might sound dumb from the outside, but I was comfortable in our relationship, even when it sucked. And comfort was a key factor in staying somewhere you no longer belonged. Because it was easier. And because change was hard.

Jared and I both planned on working for my father's company once we graduated in May. We wanted to move back home to New York and start our successful careers and lives, side by side. We had planned out our futures since we had basically gotten together. Looking back, I could see how innocent we were, convinced that nothing could ever come between us if we didn't want it to.

But I wasn't sure I wanted that future anymore. When I looked forward, what used to be so clear was now blurry. Everything I'd promised Jared for years, I wanted to take back. I was mad at myself for being so naive, for assuming that nothing could ever change, especially my feelings for him.

"Just because you have a past with someone doesn't mean that you owe them your future."

Chance's words echoed in my mind, and I tried to force myself into believing them.

Take a Break

Danika

I PACED THE small space of my bedroom, trying to work up the courage or the nerve to have this conversation with Jared. He was on his way over and would be here any minute.

"Why is this so scary?" I screamed out, knowing that Sunny would hear me wherever she was in the apartment.

Instead of her answering, I heard the sound of her feet running toward me. "Because he's been a constant in your life for five years. That's a long time." I opened my mouth to respond when she sat on the edge of my bed and added, "Plus, you two have a lot of history. Like, *a lot* of history. That has to make it even harder. Or at least, feel like it makes it harder."

"I don't want to make a mistake. Is this a mistake?" I clasped my hands together and looked at her blue eyes.

"If you're not happy—and trust me, you're not, and you haven't been"—she looked almost sad—"then you're settling. And we are not the kind of people who settle!" she exclaimed as she stood up from my bed. "We don't settle in love when we could have so much better. Am I right, or am I right?"

I smiled, her words reminding me of the ones my mom had said to me all those years ago. "I don't want to settle. I just don't want to be wrong either."

"You aren't wrong. Take it from someone on the outside, looking in. Things between you two changed way before you ever realized it."

"What does that mean?" I asked in my go-to defensive tone, feeling like, once again, Sunny wasn't telling me something.

"I just meant that your heart's been unhappy for way longer than your brain has."

A knock on the door alerted us to Jared's arrival.

Sunny stepped closer to me and grabbed my hand. "Just remember one thing: how you're feeling about Jared and his suckiness has nothing to do with Chance and the fact that he's awesome."

I couldn't help but laugh. "I know that."

"But Jared will try to convince you otherwise. Don't believe him," she said before walking out of my bedroom and shutting her own door instead of answering the one Jared stood behind.

She really does hate him.

Walking to the front door, I sucked in a long breath before pulling it open. Jared stood there, a fist filled with roses and a smile on his face. I hadn't expected that.

"Hey, beautiful," he said as he walked in, giving me a heavy kiss on the lips instead of what had become our usual quick peck in greeting.

"Uh, hi." I tried to sound composed but couldn't.

"These are for you." He handed me the flowers, and I instinctively brought them to my nose, so I could inhale their scent. I didn't even like the way roses smelled, and here I was, breathing them in like they gave me life or something.

"Thank you. They're so pretty. What's the occasion?" I asked, realizing that he wasn't going to make this easy.

"No occasion. I just know that things haven't been great between us lately, and I wanted to fix that. I've been negligent. And jealous. I wanted to apologize and let you know that I'll be better."

Damn. I hadn't counted on that coming out of his mouth. I hadn't counted on any of this. His sudden change of heart. His willingness to see his faults and correct them. But they were just words, and he'd said them all before. I needed to remember that actions told the truth and that words could lie.

Walking into the kitchen, I reached for a vase and shoved the roses into it. I figured I'd deal with them later—cut the stems at an angle and trim the extra foliage, like my mom had taught me once before she died. When I turned around, Jared was right behind me, his body hovering as his arms wrapped around my middle and pulled me tight.

They were the wrong arms, and even though I knew them by heart, I struggled to get out of his grip.

"Hey, what's the matter?" he said as he set me free.

"Nothing. I just …" I hesitated, and it was in that second of silence that he continued.

"Danika, I really am sorry for how I've been lately. I've

been a jerk, and you deserve better." He leaned his weight against the counter, watching me.

I stood there, staring back, wondering what the hell the right thing to do was. Before he had walked through the door, I had worked up the courage to tell him that I thought we needed a break. But now, with all of his self-awareness and declarations, I wasn't sure that I could.

"Why'd you call me over here tonight? What did you want to talk about?" He actually sounded nervous, and I knew in that instant that he knew what I had planned on doing. "Danika?"

I swallowed hard before letting the words spill out, "I was going to tell you that we needed some time apart."

He instantly pushed away from the counter and reached for me. "No. Don't do this. We've been through too much together to just throw it away because we hit a rough patch."

"I know we have, but—"

He cut me off, "No buts. I've been a shit boyfriend, okay? It's all on me. I'll fix it. I'll fix us. Don't give up on us yet."

My eyes burned as I held back the tears. I felt like I was being torn in two. I wanted the break, but I owed Jared a chance to make things right, didn't I?

"We can be great again, Danika. I promise," he said as he stroked his fingers through my hair.

Jared said all the right things, but my stomach twisted in response. I knew in my gut that staying together wasn't what I really wanted, but I couldn't force my mouth to open and say the words.

"The jealousy has to stop. You were crazy with Chance the other day, and I was so embarrassed." I pulled away to look at him.

His jaw clenched. "I know." He breathed in and out three times before admitting, "I just love you so much that I get scared sometimes."

Jared wasn't the type of guy to open up emotionally and be vulnerable, no matter how hard I pushed, so hearing him talk like this was a little disarming.

"Scared of what?"

"Scared of losing you. I can't imagine life without you. We have so many plans," he said, zeroing in on the one thing that I wished we'd never talked about.

"I know we do," I said as my guilt soared. I wanted to say the words Chance had said to me out loud, but I lacked the strength.

"Just not yet, okay? Give me one more chance to make things right. I still want to be with you. I want the future we've always dreamed of having," he pleaded.

Even though I wanted to, I couldn't tell him no. He deserved more than that, and I found myself agreeing to his request, more out of obligation and guilt than anything else.

I wondered for a brief moment how disappointed my mom would be before I let Jared lead me into the bedroom.

Tried to Break Up

Chance

THINGS WITH DANIKA had gone from whatever the hell we had been to practically nonexistent. I'd done my best to put her out of my mind, but that never fucking worked. It hadn't worked since the first day I saw her, dressed in all black, full of attitude and that New York fire. I was a lost cause when it came to her. Especially after she told me that the spark between us wasn't just in my head. Her confirmation had damn near killed me, but I would take that torment any day of the week over the pain of not knowing.

She'd taken our tutoring meetings down to once a week, and it was absolute torture, going six days without seeing her face. Then again, it was absolute torture on the day I had to see her as well. I was a walking contradiction.

Why did no one warn me that having feelings for someone was such a fucking nightmare? Life had been so much easier before I fell for the one girl I couldn't have.

Feeling sorry for myself, I strolled through campus toward my upcoming class when I heard my name being called from somewhere behind me. I turned around to see a bouncy blonde speed-walking in my direction.

"Hi," she said once she reached me, sounding a little out of breath.

"Hiii," I drew out the word, a little unsure of who I was looking at before it all clicked. "You're Danika's friend right?"

How I'd pulled that information out of my memory bank, I'd never know, but her smile told me I was correct.

"Her roommate actually. And how'd you know that?"

"Would you be pissed if I said I remember you making out with Mac at our party?" I asked with a slight wince, and she laughed.

"Not even a little bit." She acted more proud than anything else about her make-out session with Mac, and that alone relaxed me.

"Cool. So, what's up?"

"I'm Sunny by the way," she reached out her hand and I shook it.

"Nice to meet you officially. I'm Chance," I said and she cracked up like I was the funniest person on the planet.

"Listen. Danika would kill me if she knew I was telling you this," she started to say, and I leaned in closer, my entire body begging to hear whatever was about to come out of her mouth next. "But I just …" She stalled before adding, "I just thought you should know."

"Sunny, you're killing me here. Know what?"

"She tried to break up with Jared last night."

I stumbled back a few steps, as if her words had physically forced me to. "What? She did? Wait, what happened?"

"Like I said, she *tried*, but he talked her out of it," Sunny snarled.

And the small sliver of hope that had popped up out of nowhere inside of me exploded into a million pieces before I could even think about latching on to it.

"You don't like him." It was more of an observation than a question, and I wasn't sure which surprised me more—Danika trying to dump the guy or the fact that her roommate didn't like him.

"I hate him," she said emphatically and with a frown that didn't match her otherwise cheerful demeanor.

"So, why are you telling me this? If she didn't actually break up with him, then nothing's changed." I found myself getting agitated and annoyed at the information. It wasn't really helpful.

She shifted her weight from side to side. "I know, technically, nothing's changed. But this is the first time she's ever tried to break up with him. It's the first time she's ever wanted to, Chance."

"I think he's using her." The statement stumbled from my brain and out of my mouth before I could stop it.

"Using her? For what?" Sunny asked, but the way she said it made me question myself and my read on the conversation I'd had with Jared in the commissary.

"Her dad's money?" I fumbled over my accusation.

"Why would you think that?"

"It was just something he said to me." I blew out a breath. "I can tell by the look on your face that I'm obviously wrong."

"It's just that Jared's family has their own money. I mean, it's not Marchetti kind of money, but still. Did you tell Danika?" She looked up at me, her blue eyes narrowing.

"No."

"Why not?" Her expression twisted and I suddenly felt like everything I was saying was the wrong thing.

"What am I supposed to say? I'm not trying to be the reason she leaves the guy. If they break up, I don't want it to be about me or because of something I said to her."

Sunny nodded her head before looking down at the watch on her wrist. "I get that. But just so you know, she likes you. She just doesn't think she's allowed to. Everything with Jared is…complicated. Look, I'm sorry, but I gotta go."

"Thanks for the info. I appreciate it."

She sped away as quickly as she'd arrived, leaving me alone without even glancing back.

I felt like I was walking on air as I headed toward my building, convinced that nothing could get me down until my eyes scanned the campus and landed right on her. Danika was up ahead in the distance, near my building. But she wasn't alone. Jared was at her side, his arm wrapped around her as they laughed at something.

She didn't look at all like someone who wanted out of her relationship. As a matter of fact, she looked like the exact opposite. I had to stop myself from throwing my fist through a wall as I kicked at the ground and sent bits of dirt and rocks flying everywhere.

Danika turned her head toward where I currently stood,

sulking, and even though we were still far enough away from one another, I knew the second her eyes landed on mine. Her body language shifted in that instant, and she actually seemed uncomfortable. I took it as a sign and sucked in my pride and walked straight at them. She saw me coming and locked her hazel eyes on to mine until I was mere feet away.

"Oh, hey, Chance," Danika said, her voice soft and surprised at my arrival.

"Hey." I tried to sound like seeing her with him didn't rip my guts out.

Jared gave me a head nod. "Bro," he started.

My entire body cringed. I wasn't this dude's fucking *bro*.

"Sorry about the other day. I was out of line. It won't happen again." His tone was convincing enough even though I could tell that he was full of shit and only saying it for Danika's benefit. He didn't mean a damn word.

When he extended his hand toward me, I stared at it a beat, wanting to break it instead of shake it. I stared at Danika, who clearly appreciated her boyfriend's bullshit gesture, and then I took his hand in mine and gripped it hard.

"It's all good," I lied and watched as he pulled her closer to him, kissing her cheek and then her mouth for my benefit.

His eyes stayed open and on me while he played the doting boyfriend. He knew exactly what he was doing, putting on a show for her, tormenting me.

"We were just about to grab some coffee. Do you want to come?" Jared asked.

Danika looked at him, then at me, and back again, her eyes wild.

"I gotta get to class," I said, and she grew visibly relieved.

Even though she was buying into the act her boyfriend dished out, being around both of us at the same time was making her uncomfortable, and I didn't like the way that made me feel.

"See you around," he said before pulling her away with little effort.

Danika gave me one last glance before leaving with him. I stood there for a minute, lost in my own head and all twisted up with the knowledge that Sunny had just dropped on me earlier. Danika had wanted out. Jared had convinced her to stay. He had her so well played, and she couldn't even see it. And I refused to be the one to tell her.

It went against everything I believed in to stay quiet and to play backup. As unnatural as it felt for me to sit back and wait, I knew it was the right thing to do. Being passive when it came to something I wanted had never been my strong suit, but fuck, I had no real experience when it came to long-term relationships. And like I'd said before, I'd learned my lesson about getting involved in other people's business the hard way. No matter how I felt about Danika or how badly I wanted to be with her, I couldn't do shit about it. If she was going to end things, she needed to do it on her own terms.

The second her relationship status changed, I would make that girl mine. But for now, I knew that I had to let her go and hope she'd eventually find her way to me. No matter how much it hurt to watch her walk away with him, I had to let her do it.

Grade Check

Danika

ASIDE FROM THE one day a week I had scheduled with Chance, I never saw him. That day on campus when I was with Jared had been a fluke or something because I hadn't seen Chance walking around or in the commissary since. I'd been tempted on more than one occasion to text him, but I stopped myself every time, determined not to send him mixed signals, no matter how mixed up my own heart felt.

Jared had been the model boyfriend, doing and saying all the right things. I could tell that he was trying so hard to make things right between us, but it all felt like too little, too late from my perspective. No matter what he did, I found myself wishing he wasn't doing it. The more he pushed, the more I felt pushed away. It was totally messed up, but it was the truth. We were still together, but I sensed that it wouldn't be long before that changed. I couldn't keep doing this to him, pretending like we were okay when we were anything but.

I got to our tutoring session first, making my way into the

office and attempting to get comfortable before Chance arrived. I scanned the area like a hawk, spotting him before he saw me. I noticed the way other girls reacted to him, their heads craning in his direction, phones up to sneak pics as they whispered to their friends. Chance gave it zero attention as he walked through the library, his eyes on the phone in his hand.

I looked forward to this singular day all week. And then dreaded the second it ended. God, I was so messed up.

"Hey," I said as the door pushed open, and he sauntered inside. It took everything in me to stay seated instead of standing up to greet him with a hug.

"Hey yourself."

I knew that he missed seeing me as much as I missed seeing him, and I should have hated myself for how good that made me feel.

"Has the professor updated your grade yet?"

"Not yet, but I keep hitting refresh," he said as he moved to sit down in the chair next to mine instead of our usual *as far apart as possible* routine.

We were waiting on his math grade to reflect his latest test results. Once we had that information, we could formulate a plan of attack for his final.

"How do you think you did?"

"Passed, but not sure by how much," he said, sounding a little less than confident.

"You've passed every other test this semester so far, so I'm sure you did better than you think," I attempted to reassure him.

"This one was harder though," he added, his green eyes sparkling under the fluorescent lights.

"I know, but hey, you're almost done." I smiled because this semester would be over in a few weeks. I'd go home to New York for break, and Chance would stay here.

He pressed a few buttons on his phone, and his face lit up. "It refreshed."

"And? What does it say?"

"C-plus." He grinned like he'd never been prouder, and it amazed me how excited he was for such an average grade. "Why are you looking at me like that?" he asked, his dimple in full effect. "I am totally passing this class!"

"Don't you want to get an A? Or at least a B?" I teased, and his smile turned into a full-fledged smirk.

"No. I just wanted to pass. And now, no matter what, I will. I'm eligible to play this year, and it's all because of you." He threw a fist in the air in triumph, his happiness infectious.

At this point, even if Chance failed his final, he'd still get a C in the class overall, which qualified as a passing grade.

"You did all the work."

"Yeah, but you made it easy to understand."

"I'm just glad I could help." I sucked in a breath and put my thoughts in order. "You don't need me anymore. Class is almost done, and like you said, you'll pass, no matter what now."

"What are you saying?" His smile dropped instantly.

"That we should probably stop the sessions altogether," I suggested, swallowing around the lump in my throat.

"If that's what you want," he said before adding, "But it's

not what I want. Just so we're clear."

"I know. That's why we need to."

He seemed conflicted, like he was stopping himself from saying whatever it was that he was thinking. Chance closed the space between us as he stood up, reached for my hand, and pulled me to my feet. He wrapped me in his arms and spun me around. I got dizzy from the contact, not from the spinning.

Just as quickly as it had begun, the spinning ceased. He put me down, but we were still standing close, our toes touching, and his eyes focused on my lips. I watched them intensely, wondering if he would dare cross that line in public, knowing instinctively that he wouldn't. Chance Carter was too composed, too in control.

"Let's go celebrate at The Bar," he suggested, and his breath fanned over me.

I felt myself stumble over my emotions. "Chance."

"I know, but listen, we're done tutoring for the semester. I'm passing the class, no matter what. That's a win in my book. We deserve to celebrate, don't you think?"

I hesitated for only a second, my better judgment creeping in before I slapped her back. "Let's go."

"Really?"

"Leave with me before I change my mind, Carter," I played and watched as he grinned.

"Carter, huh?"

"I could have called you Hotshot."

"Haven't heard that one in a while, Little Spitfire," he flirted.

And I knew that being alone with him and drinking

would be a potentially explosive combination, but for whatever reason, I felt like playing with fire.

CHANCE PULLED INTO the parking lot of The Bar, the local hangout for most of the students at Fullton State. I got momentarily nervous and questioned my decision before Chance called me out on it.

"Nervous?" he asked, and I let out a shaky breath before unbuckling my seat belt.

"A little bit," I admitted.

"About what? Seeing someone you know? Running into your boyfriend?"

Shaking my head, I responded, "No. Just that being in public with you means that my every move is tracked somehow. Someone is always watching."

"It's true. Did you tell Jared you were going out with me?" he asked, and I knew it was only because of how I'd handled things the last time we did something alone.

"I did."

I had sent Jared a text from the car to let him know I was going to grab a drink with Chance to celebrate him passing the class and that I'd text him as soon as I got back home. His jealousy seemed to have pretty much disappeared overnight, so I figured that my going would be a nonissue.

I had no way of knowing how wrong I was.

Her Boyfriend is Still a Dick

Chance

WE WALKED INSIDE, and I was thankful that The Bar wasn't packed like it had the potential to be, even during a weeknight. I'd checked online earlier to make sure that no live bands were scheduled to perform; otherwise, I would have taken her somewhere else. Yeah, I'd planned on asking Danika to go out with me tonight, even before I knew that we had a reason to celebrate. I'd assumed my passing grade would show up during our tutoring session at some point, and I had hoped to use it to my advantage.

Not that I was trying to do anything. I just … *fuck* … I missed her and wanted to spend time with her before she left for winter break. Plus, once my season started, I'd be way too busy to find excuses to hang out with her. And now that she had called off the rest of our tutoring sessions for the semester, who knew if I'd ever see her again? The thought crashed into me, and I swore my heart fucking sank lower inside my chest. The idea of never seeing Danika again after tonight sucked. But that was a very real possibility.

I headed toward the most secluded high-top table in the

back corner and planted myself there. Danika sat next to me instead of across from me, and the temptation to reach out and touch her was almost too much.

"I was just thinking about break," I started to say as she leaned closer toward me so that I wouldn't have to shout above the ruckus.

"What about it?"

"Do you go home the whole time?"

Our winter break was over a month long, and I was curious if she stayed here for any of it or spent the entire thing back in New York.

She nodded. "Yeah. I mean, my dad works most of the time, but if I didn't go home, he'd be all alone, and I hate thinking about him sitting there during Christmas and New Year's without me." A soft, sad smile played at her lips, and I wondered if I had been crazy, bringing her out tonight.

A cocktail waitress appeared out of thin air and asked for our drink orders.

"I'll take whatever IPA you have on draft."

"I'll have a cranberry and Belvedere," Danika said, and I shot her a surprised look.

"Belvedere, huh?" I teased because that wasn't some poor college student's vodka. Everyone usually drank whatever they could afford or whatever they could get the most of for the least amount of money.

"I hate shitty vodka. And I hate shitty vodka headaches even more." She smirked before lifting a shoulder.

"I can respect that."

"So, what do you do for break? Do you go home to

Newport or stay in the baseball house?" She wrinkled her nose, and I chuckled.

"What's the face for?"

"I just imagined you staying in that gross house the whole time and"—she visibly shuddered—"just … no."

I grimaced. "It's not gross," I started to defend the house before rolling my eyes and grinning instead. "Okay, it's a little gross. But we're guys. What do you expect?"

"Maid service," she said without skipping a beat.

"Sometimes, if one of the guys has a girlfriend, she'll clean the house for us. That's always nice," I said.

She snarled, "That's embarrassing."

"Nah, it's sweet."

"No, it's not."

"You wouldn't clean the house if you were my girlfriend?" I asked before realizing what I'd even said. "I mean, hypothetically speaking."

She put one finger in the air. "Hypothetically speaking, no." Her hazel eyes leveled me on the spot before she gave me a small smirk. "I might help pick up your room, but nothing outside of it."

I laughed loudly. "I knew it."

"I don't think we can help it," she started to explain. "We're nurturers, you know? Girls nurture. But it stops you guys from growing. And then we get mad at you because you rely on us to do things that you should be doing yourselves. But really, we created the mess in the first place. We just don't see it that way."

I felt totally lost and was thankful when the waitress

appeared with our drinks and placed them down before walking away.

"We're still talking about cleaning my room?"

"You're an idiot, Hotshot," she said as she reached for her glass and held it in the air.

Our glasses clinked together, and we both said, "Cheers," at the same time before taking a sip.

"You never answered my question, by the way."

I swallowed. "Which was?"

"Do you go home during break? You must, right? Your mom would kill you if you didn't," she said with a smile.

I loved that she had met my family and felt like she knew them enough to make assumptions. Anyone else, it would have pissed me off but not her.

"My sister would kill me more. But, yeah, I go home. It's just not for long. Usually for a couple weeks. The team has to be back right after New Year's. We have practice and preseason games before the spring semester even starts."

"Oh." She sounded caught off-guard. "I didn't realize that."

"Yep. We play a bunch of non-league games, so they don't count in our official record, but they still count overall."

"Are you excited?"

I shifted in my stool and straightened my back. "Very. I can't wait to play. You should come to a game. I can leave you tickets."

"Don't students get tickets for free?" she teased as she took another drink. Her glass was almost empty already.

"They do, but I could leave you better tickets. The student section is trash."

I thought back to giving Cole shit for leaving Christina tickets last season, but he had been right. The student section sucked, and he'd loved seeing his girl front and center, knowing that she was there to watch him. I knew that I'd love to look behind the plate and see Danika there. I'd love it even more if she were there *with* me.

"I'll think about it."

"Not sure if you've heard"—I crooked my finger at her, calling her closer—"but baseball's a real hot commodity at this school," I whispered.

"You don't say?" she whispered back, and goddamn, I wanted to grab her by the back of the neck and taste her lips.

I was so attracted to her. I wondered for a second how stupid I was to put us in this position, alone together and drinking. Maybe I enjoyed the torture.

Thankfully, we were interrupted by a commotion at the entrance doors. We both turned at the same time to see her boyfriend walking in with a group, who I assumed to be his frat brothers. Jared scanned the room, eyes landing on us for only a second before he started laughing at something.

"Shocking," I said sarcastically under my breath.

Danika looked at me. "I didn't know he was coming, I swear."

"I know," I said because I believed her.

I should have known that there was no way he'd be able to stay away from here tonight. Not when I was involved. It was in that exact moment that I realized that everything I had thought about Jared was spot-on.

I had ignored my gut reactions and my instincts because I wanted to be mistaken when it came to him. I'd tried to convince myself that every bad thought I had was either born out of jealousy, miscommunication, or the sheer fact that the guy had something I wanted—*her*.

But I wasn't wrong. And no amount of conversation now could convince me otherwise. He was scared to lose her. And he was threatened by me.

"Can I bring you two another round?" The waitress reached for Danika's empty glass.

I answered for both of us, "Yes, please."

"I was going to say no," Danika argued as the woman walked away.

"I know you were. Which is why I said yes."

Danika's head swiveled between me and her boyfriend. I'd assumed he'd come right over to our table and sit with us or at least say something, but he didn't. Instead, he and his bros sat down in a booth near us but never looked toward us again.

"Are you kidding me?" Danika said, her tone disgusted and annoyed. "He knows I'm here. He looked right at us when he walked in."

"Maybe he's just giving us space to do our own thing," I suggested with a shrug.

"No, he's not." She was agitated and perturbed.

"Then, what is he doing?"

Two fresh drinks were deposited on our table, and Danika reached for hers before answering me. She swirled it around with the tiny straw before taking a sip, not a gulp.

"He's …" She sounded flustered, like finding the right words were a struggle. "He's being possessive."

"And you don't like that?" I was genuinely asking because I had no fucking idea what girls liked, but I knew that my mom seemed to enjoy it whenever my dad got a little crazy over her.

"I do not like that," she said slowly, drawing out each word. "No one likes that."

I cocked my head in disagreement. "Hmm … I think some women like it."

She contemplated my statement, and I knew she was deciding between asking some smart-ass question or not. "Okay, sometimes, we like it. But not like this. Not all passive-aggressive." She waved a hand in Jared's direction without looking at him.

Nodding my head, as if that had made all the sense in the world and totally cleared things up, I asked, "So, you like it when it's aggressive-aggressive?"

Danika laughed, her lips toying with the tiny red straw. "I guess. No. I don't know." She put her drink on the table and rubbed her temples. "Sometimes, it's a turn-on. Other times, it's the opposite. I don't know how to explain it without sounding crazy."

"Too late." I took a long drink of my beer. "Incoming," I said because Jared was heading straight toward our table, flanked by two guys on each side.

"In what?" She shook her head, confused, before she looked behind her and saw exactly what I'd meant.

"My girlfriend and Baseball Boy, together again," Jared sneered.

I wondered why he was so riled up. The last time I'd seen him, he had faked being completely cordial, pretending like there were no issues between us. Maybe because he was in front of his boys, he felt like he had something to prove.

"I sent you a text."

"Why do you think I'm here?"

"That's why you're here? Because I told you I would be?"

"You're *my* girlfriend," he scoffed, emphasizing the word *my*. "Thought you might have forgotten that fact."

"Looks like she already has," one of his boys piped in.

I shot him a look that told him to shut the hell up. He pumped up his chest for only a second before taking a step back and snapping his jaw shut like a good little boy.

"You're making a fool out of me," Jared said, waving his hand in my direction. "Being seen in public with him when everyone knows we're together."

I pushed back from the stool and stood to my full height, muscles flexing. "What the hell is your problem, man?"

Danika stood up then and put her hand on my chest in an effort to keep me back. "I got this," she told me, but I refused to back down or leave her to deal with this asshole on her own.

"Mind your own business, Baseball Boy," he said before reaching for my beer and throwing it at me.

Motherfucker threw my own damn beer on me.

Looking down at my soaked-through shirt, I said with a

laugh, "Feel better now?" I acted perfectly calm, knowing that it would only piss Jared off more when, in reality, I wanted to rip his fucking head off and send his frat bros home with it.

"Are you kidding me? What the hell, Jared?" Danika yelled, and if everyone inside the bar hadn't been paying attention to us before, they were now.

"Maybe you'll stop embarrassing me," he growled toward her, referring to the fact that she was out in public with me, wet shirt and all.

"Yeah, maybe you'll stop embarrassing him," another frat bro shouted in response.

"What are you, a parrot?" Danika asked the frat dude, her voice laced with venom, and I couldn't stop the laugh that bubbled up and out of my mouth.

"Do you know how it feels to get DMs and texts of pictures of the two of you together? Everyone was asking me why my girlfriend was on a date with the hot baseball player." Jared's face turned red, and it looked like he was about to pop.

"But you knew it wasn't a date." Danika's response was so reasonable, and Jared was anything but.

"No one else did," he argued back.

"But you knew the truth, so who cares what other people think?"

He shifted. "I do. I fucking do. If we were back home, you'd never even think about pulling this sort of disrespect. It's like you've forgotten who you are. Who we are and where we come from."

This guy always brought up the fact that they were from New York like it came with a completely different set of rules for dating.

"Stop acting like we're from some sort of mob family."

"Stop acting like you're single!" he screamed before directing his anger at me and pointing. "And you, stay away from my girlfriend. How many times do I have to tell you?"

I shrugged, my T-shirt currently plastered to my chest with wet beer. I continued to play it off like it wasn't driving me absolutely insane, but it was. I wanted it off my body, and I wanted to strangle this fucker with it. "At least a hundred more since, apparently, I'm not a very good listener."

"Let's go, Danika. We're leaving," he insisted, and I wondered what she'd do.

"I'm not going anywhere with you."

That was the girl I adored—all feisty, headstrong, mouthy, and independent.

She looked around the bar at all the faces watching us like it was the first time she'd noticed the scene we'd created, and I could tell how uncomfortable it made her. Her entire demeanor shifted in that moment.

I watched as she swallowed hard, her eyes meeting Jared's before agreeing to leave.

"I'll leave. But not with you." And before I could offer her a ride home or say anything, she turned to me and added, "And not with you either."

Why the hell was I in trouble too?

Pre-Winter Break Party

Chance

THE REST OF the semester flew by, and I was honestly grateful for it. That night at The Bar was the last time I'd seen Danika in person—naturally, online stalking didn't count. And aside from the single text she'd sent me, replying to my fifty asking if she was all right, I hadn't heard from her since. She'd responded that she wasn't okay, but that she would be, and then she asked me to give her space.

So, I did.

And it fucking killed me.

I felt like it took every ounce of willpower for me not to text her or call her or show up at her door like that jackass stalker from last year. I didn't even let her know I'd passed my math final with flying colors. When I'd grabbed my phone to tell her because she was the first person I wanted to call, I'd remembered that she had asked me for space, and I forced myself to continue respecting her request.

I had no idea if her and Jared had broken up or not, but I figured that if they had, she would have at least told me that much.

Or shown up at my door.

Naked.

In a bow.

But since that never happened, I assumed that they were still fucking together and most likely always would be. I really needed to stop pining over someone who was choosing to stay in a crappy relationship with an even crappier guy, no matter their history or how disappointing it was. I was done chasing the girl who obviously wanted nothing to do with me.

"Still sulking?" Mac's voice shot through the ones in my head, and I looked up from my bed to see him walking in my room with a glint in his eyes.

"I'm not sulking."

"What do you call it then?"

I shrugged. "Fine. I might be sulking a little, but I was just telling myself to get over it."

"Well, you know what they say," he said as he plopped down on the edge of my bed, uninvited, per usual. "The best way to get over someone is to get under someone new."

"You're an idiot."

I reached for the shirt lying next to my pillow, rolled it up, and tossed it at his head. He caught it easily.

"But I'm not wrong."

"You are something else."

The smile on his face grew. "Yeah? Tell me more."

"I just mean that I've never seen anyone hook up with more chicks than you do. And there is never any drama. How the fuck do you pull that off?" I sucked in a breath before continuing my line of questioning, "Also, how do you never catch feelings for any of the girls you mess around with?"

His back stiffened, and the smile instantly dropped. "You remember what happened freshman year." Mac's voice was serious.

"Of course I remember. But that was two years ago, and you're still—" I started before he cut me off.

"Still what?"

"I just thought the hook-ups were a phase." I knew that his ex-girlfriend had done a number on him, but I'd figured he'd grow out of all the meaningless shit at some point. Get tired of it maybe or eventually want more.

"Nope."

"So, you're just going to do this forever?"

"I thought we were talking about you?" His eyes narrowed as his forehead creased. "But for the record, I'm not interested in getting my heart broken again."

"Well, for the record, your ex was a bitch."

"I know."

"Do you?" I asked because it was rare that Mac even approached this subject, let alone spoke about it. He usually got defensive and pissed off. Rightly so, if you asked me.

"What do you mean?"

"I just want to make sure you know that you did nothing wrong. That was all her."

His eyes roamed around my room, avoiding mine. "I know it was," he said before looking at me, the pain still obvious, even after all this time. "It still hurt though."

"I know," I said even though I didn't. Not exactly. Not

even remotely. I remembered, at the time, being grateful that it hadn't happened to me but feeling shitty that it had happened to Mac.

He clapped his hands together. "Enough depressing shit. You're finally over Danika?"

"I want to be. There's no point in wanting the girl who couldn't care less."

"Perfect! 'Cause I came in here to tell you, we're going to a party tonight."

"Ohhh—" I started to argue and make a face.

"Nope. You don't get to say no. It's the last party of the semester before everyone leaves for break. So, we're going."

"Will you leave me alone if I say yes?"

"*Only* if you say yes." He pushed off the bed and waited for my response.

"Fine, I'll go," I said, knowing I needed to get out of this house and do something other than feel sorry for myself. "Whose party is it?" I asked, praying he wasn't about to say that it was ours. I wasn't in the mood for a house filled with people who never left.

"Some fraternity. I don't know. You can be my wingman, and we'll steal all their girls."

"You don't need a wingman."

"I know. It's just fun to say. I'll be yours. You can channel your inner Mac tonight!" He sounded so excited that instead of arguing, I laughed, which I was sure he took as my agreeing as he walked out of my room.

Channeling my inner Mac … I played the idea out in my head before I found myself wondering what the possibility of it being Jared's fraternity might be? I had no idea which frat he was even in, so asking the name wouldn't have helped matters.

I wondered if Danika would be there or if she'd already left to go back home or not. I couldn't get over the girl if I kept running into her.

So, why do I want her to be there so badly?

THE MUSIC FROM the house was so loud, we heard it as we drove down the street, looking for a place to park. How fraternity houses existed in residential areas, I'd never know. I couldn't even imagine trying to live a normal life, surrounded by all that noise and shit.

Tucking my keys in my pocket, I glanced at Mac and my other two roommates, Dayton and Colin, as we piled out of my truck. I opened the front door and stepped to move inside as a wave of heat crashed into me. Sweaty bodies filled the dark room, and there was barely enough space to walk through them all.

"Chance!" I heard my name being shouted from somewhere inside, but I couldn't see for shit.

I hated strobe lights, all the bright flashing and disappearing. It fucked with my head and made me see things that weren't there.

"It's dark as fuck in here," I yelled toward Mac, who was

directly behind me.

"Just keep heading toward the back," he shouted and put a hand on my shoulder.

As I weaved my way through the gyrating bodies, a girl stepped in front of me, blocking my path.

"Hi," she said seductively before licking her lips.

I gave her a head nod in response but no words.

"Dance with me." She giggled and reached for my hand.

Mac gave me a small nudge from behind, but I braced myself instead, pulling my hand from her grip.

"I don't dance."

"Make an exception for me. I'll make it worth your while," she yelled into my ear.

I had to admit that I considered it. But only for a second or two before I snapped out of it. If I had even remotely thought that I could be like Mac tonight, I was mistaken. Randomly hooking up with girls wasn't me, and I couldn't fake it.

"Sorry, I can't," was all I said, and her expression fell.

She wasn't even mad about the dismissal, which was a relief. She genuinely looked disappointed. That was, until Mac whispered something in her ear, and her entire face lit back up, my rejection forgotten.

Mac to the rescue.

"You're welcome, brother," he said, and I shook my head before walking forward again.

When we finally broke through the plethora of bodies and made our way into the backyard, the night air felt like a reprieve even though it was still warm. I found myself wondering why we hadn't just gone in through the back fence in the first place.

"It's hot as hell in there," Dayton said as he wiped the sweat off his forehead.

"What'd you say to that chick?" Colin asked, directing his question at Mac and not me.

"Told her that I'd be back inside in a minute to finish whatever she'd offered Chance," Mac said, and I laughed.

"Of course you did," Dayton howled before clapping him on the back.

"Someone's gotta pick up Carter's leftovers," Colin added, and Mac scowled.

"I just didn't want her getting her feelings hurt, is all. Our season's almost here, guys. We need those stands full. If Chance goes around, breaking everyone's heart all the time, no one will show up. I consider it my civic duty to make sure the girls know we want them around," Mac said with the biggest grin I'd ever seen as the three of us busted up laughing.

"Speaking of girls," Colin said, and a mixture of dread and hope crept up my spine.

I figured he was about to point out Danika somewhere in the distance, no doubt wrapped in Jared's arms, but he pointed at a group of three skinny guys I didn't know heading our way. I almost laughed with relief.

"Baseballers," one of the guys said as he reached us. "Welcome." He opened his arms and waved them around like we were some sort of guests to his esteemed kingdom. "Keg's right over there, and hard alcohol's in the house. We always get a good card game going later if you want in. Cash only. Just let us know before eleven."

The four of us looked at each other, silent words passing between us before I spoke up, "Thanks for the welcome and the offer, but we're not allowed to gamble. Even for fun."

We all signed waivers and forms each season, acknowledging that we wouldn't, under any circumstances, participate in gambling of any kind. Getting caught meant that you not only got kicked off the team, but you were also banned from the league itself, which meant no transferring to a school of equal caliber.

"We wouldn't rat you out," the same guy said with a grin.

"Yeah, I don't think you would," I offered cordially, not wanting to start a fight. "But if anyone saw us or took pictures or anything, we'd get kicked off the team."

"It's not worth the risk," Mac added, and the three frat guys all nodded.

"All right. Well, have fun. Let me know if you need anything. Name's Jaden. These are my bros, Butch and Grady."

"Nice to meet you. Thanks again," I said before shaking Jaden's hand and watching them strut away, shouting some sort of theme song.

"Frat guys." Dayton made a face, and we all mumbled in agreement.

"I see someone over there I want to talk to," Colin said, looking at a group of girls surrounding a makeshift ping-pong table.

"I'll come with," Dayton said, and they took off, leaving Mac and me behind.

"They didn't even ask if we wanted to go with them," Mac whined, and I huffed.

"They knew I'd say no. And they knew you wouldn't leave my side," I teased even though it was one hundred percent the truth.

"Let's go inside. I'm in the mood for shots."

Grabbing Mac's bicep, I stopped his forward momentum. "I will leave your ass here if you disappear on me," I warned.

Mac had a tendency to vanish when it came to parties, shots, and females. One second, he was standing right there, and the next, he'd be gone. I'd spent hours looking for him one night last year, only to have him call me from home, asking where the hell I was.

"I won't disappear. Promise."

He held out his pinkie to me like we were in fifth grade, expecting me to take it with my own. I smacked it away instead.

"Let's go," I said, walking back inside the hellhole with Mac right on my heels.

The wave of heat smacked me in the face once more, and I stopped short, causing Mac to run straight into my back.

"What the …" he started before looking in the direction of my stare. "Is that …"

"Yeah, it is," I said before he even finished asking the question.

Jared was sitting on a chair in the kitchen with some girl who was not Danika on his lap, sticking her tongue down his throat. His hand was up her shirt for all to see.

"Shit, Chance. Don't." Mac tried to keep me from going over to him, but he knew it was no use.

No one could have stopped me from confronting this asshole. Stalking in Jared's direction, all I felt was the rage surging through me.

"What is this?" I shoved at him, breaking the sloppy kiss that had been happening moments before I arrived.

"What the hell?" Jared growled before throwing the girl off his lap and standing upright, causing red plastic cups to scatter to the floor. He looked around, his eyes searching wildly for whoever had just interrupted his public display of tongue-tangling. His face dawned with recognition the second that his eyes hit mine, and he realized it was me. "You're fucking joking."

"What are you doing?" I asked, my anger propelling me beyond all reason. Any and all rational thoughts flew out the proverbial window.

"What I'm doing is none of your business, Baseball Boy."

I wanted to break his jaw. "Does she know?"

"Does *who* know?" He sounded uninterested.

The girl he had just been kissing stood at his side, looking confused.

"Danika!" I screamed, creating even more of a scene. "Does Danika know?"

"Who's Danika?" the girl asked, but he ignored her and focused only on me.

"Like I said, it's none of your business." His tone was far

more controlled than mine was, and it only made me angrier.

How was he so calm and composed when I felt like I was losing my damn mind?

"It is my business," I shouted like a crazed maniac, taking a menacing step toward him.

I expected him to step back in response, but he didn't. He stood firm, and everything about his posture, his demeanor, his attitude baited me.

"How so? How is anything about Danika your business? Explain that one to me." He folded his arms across his chest and waited for my response.

I didn't have one. What was I supposed to say?

"What's going on here is none of your damn business, but you think it is. Because you care about Danika. Because you want her. You always have. And you hate the fact that she'll never be yours. Or that I can have her anytime I want."

I pulled my arm back, prepared to knock his fucking lights out, when Mac pounced. He steadied my arm, stopping me from moving as he created a blockade between myself and Jared.

"Stop, Chance. Chance!" Mac tried to get me to focus on him, but Jared's words kept replaying in my mind.

"Yeah, Chance, stop. Wouldn't want to hurt your arm and lose your season," Jared taunted, and Mac snapped to face him.

"Stop egging him on, or I'll let him go," Mac threatened, and Jared only blanched for a second before regaining his composure.

"You're telling her," I yelled over Mac's shoulder toward

a retreating Jared.

He turned around, his eyes slamming into mine. “Or what?”

“Or I will,” I deadpanned.

“No, you won’t.” He closed the distance between us enough so that he no longer needed to shout. “You didn’t tell her anything I’ve ever said to you before. And you won’t tell her about this either.”

He laughed as he walked away, but I didn’t find a damn thing funny. I needed to get the hell out of this frat house before I did something Coach couldn’t get me out of.

What Do I Do

Chance

PULLING MY KEYS from my front pocket, I stormed toward the front door, everyone making a path for me as I moved through them.

"Wait up," Mac shouted from somewhere behind me.

Only once I got outside of the house did I stop.

"Should we get Dayton and Colin?"

"Send them a text that I'm leaving. I'll pick them up later if they want, or they can come now," I directed with one destination in mind.

Mac typed on his phone and waited before it lit up the dark. "They're staying. Said they'll get home on their own."

"Good. You coming with?"

"Where we headed?"

"I need to see Danika."

"Chance"—Mac sounded dismayed, his voice filled with disapproval—"stay out of it."

I jerked my head toward him as I kept moving. "I can't." I sighed. "I can't, okay?"

I clicked the remote, and my truck unlocked with an

audible pop. Hopping in, I jammed the key into the ignition and revved the engine to life as Mac buckled his seat belt and rolled down his window.

"It isn't your place, man," he said, and I knew he was right.

I had a hard rule after this past summer to stay out of other people's relationships, but this felt too personal. *How am I supposed to ignore what I just saw? How can I justify Danika being cheated on and my knowing about it and saying nothing?*

"She doesn't deserve to be cheated on."

"No one 'deserves' to be cheated on." Mac air-quoted the word, and I cracked my neck as my anger lowered to a simmer.

"You know what I mean. She deserves better. Someone who can keep it in his fucking pants and not blatantly cheat where anyone could see him doing it."

"Maybe he wanted to get caught?" Mac suggested, and I practically laughed.

"Well, I caught him!"

"Okay, listen." Mac used his reasonable tone, and I knew he was about to suggest something I was either going to agree with or want to throttle him for saying. "Think about this for a second, okay?"

"I've thought about it," I argued as I made a right and headed toward Danika's apartment complex.

"Yeah, you've thought about it for all of two seconds," he huffed out like I was some kind of idiot. "Do you even know how this will go down?"

I glanced at him briefly. "What are you talking about?"

"Say you tell her. We go over there right now, you tell her, and she doesn't believe you. Wants proof. Thinks you're lying."

"I'm not a liar," I bit back. "And you saw him too."

"Yeah, I did," he agreed before rolling his window partway up. "But I'm playing devil's advocate here, Carter. People don't always like hearing the truth. Especially when it hurts. They fight back. They place blame. They get defensive and mad at the wrong people," he explained, and I groaned as I stopped at a red light.

"Yeah, yeah. They shoot the messenger. I get it."

"You just don't care?"

"I just don't care," I repeated, perfectly calm. "It's the right thing to do," I added before my own words felt like rocks in my throat.

The light turned green, and I pressed on the gas pedal as I started questioning myself. It was the right thing to do, but I thought I'd done the *right thing* last summer, too, and I'd gotten my ass handed to me instead.

I made one last right turn, and we were pulling into Danika's complex.

"Is she even home?" Mac asked.

"I'm not sure. But, hey," I started, wanting to give Mac a heads-up about Danika's roommate, "you hooked up with her roommate at the beginning of the semester."

"And?"

"Just reminding you, I guess," I said because I wasn't sure what the hell my point was. I just didn't want there to be any more awkwardness than there was already going to be.

"Okay. Thanks."

We walked toward the double doors, and I searched the box for Danika's last name before finding it and pressing the button.

It rang four times before someone answered, "Hello?"

"Danika?" I asked even though I knew it wasn't her. The voice lacked any kind of accent.

"Chance?" the female voice asked and I had no idea how she knew it was me from just my voice. "Hold on a sec," she said before the line crackled and went dead.

I looked through the doors and saw Sunny round a corner and come into view.

"Ah, I remember her," Mac said with a grin as Sunny reached us and popped one of the doors open.

If I didn't know any better, I would think he was interested in her.

"Hey, guys," she said before looking Mac up and down. "Figured it was easier if I came out. Just in case someone else needed the comm system to get in. What's up?" Sunny was playing it cool, and Mac noticed.

"Is Danika here?"

"No. She left this morning for New York." Sunny focused on me, finding something there as she asked, "Is everything okay?"

"Yeah. I just wanted to see her," I said, leaving out the rest of the reason why we'd stopped by so late, unannounced.

"At eleven thirty. On a Wednesday night? After you two haven't talked in weeks, you just wanted to see her?"

Damn. Sunny knew every detail about what was going on between Danika and me. It was a little unnerving even though it shouldn't have been surprising. Girls tended to tell each other everything. At least, that was what my little sister always said.

"I actually wanted to talk to her about some things," I added, hoping it would get Sunny to ease up a little.

"Well, like I said, she's already gone."

The way Sunny had said that she was *gone* caused nerves to race through me, and unwanted thoughts filled my head.

What if she moved back home for good and will be finishing up school there?

"She's coming back though, right?"

A soft giggle escaped. "Of course she's coming back. But not until the semester's about to start."

"I guess I'll see her next semester then," I said even though I had no idea if I would or not.

By the time she came back to campus, baseball would be in full swing, and my days and nights would be packed with little time for anything—or anyone—else.

"Maybe don't wait that long, eh?" she suggested, and before I could ask her to elaborate, she looked at Mac before walking through the door and disappearing out of view down the hall.

"Probably a good thing she wasn't here," Mac said as we turned and headed toward my truck.

"That's exactly what I was thinking," I agreed, to his surprise.

"Really?"

"Yeah. Sort of feels like a sign, her not being here."

I decided that there was a reason Danika was gone when I came to tell her the truth. Maybe it was divine intervention stopping me from making a mistake. Maybe fate knew something I didn't. Maybe Mac had been right in all the things he said on the drive over here.

All I knew was that if I was supposed to tell her, she would have been home to hear it. And she wasn't.

Back in New York

Danika

SUNNY CALLED TO let me know that Chance had come by the apartment. She practically burst my eardrums with her squealing, and I could barely make out what she was trying to say.

"He said he wanted to talk to you," she breathed into the phone.

"Anything else?" I asked because my interest was definitely piqued.

Chance and I hadn't talked since the night Jared showed up and ruined our celebration at The Bar. The most messed up part was that after that all happened, I had wanted Chance to chase me even though I was in no position to be chased. I hated myself for expecting him to do it. And then I hated myself even more for being disappointed when he never did.

Of course, Chance Carter would keep his distance; that was just the kind of guy he was. And I knew that it was on me to reach out to him. But the more days that passed, the harder that seemed to be. I couldn't figure out what to say or how to apologize without landing us right back to where we had always been—fighting off our mutual attraction with nowhere for it to go. Our relationship had been so complicated from the start as we tried to convince ourselves that we could be just friends when we both wanted more.

When I'd finally broken things off with Jared, I'd figured the smart thing to do would be to take a little time for myself and not jump into another relationship. I had to make sure that my feelings for Chance were real and not some sort of escape because I had been unhappy in my current situation. So, I stayed away from Chance, and in return, he stayed away from me. It was absolute misery.

"No, nothing else, but oh my God, Danika, tell him already. You're killing me here."

I sucked in a breath and leaned my head on one of the pillows on my bed. "I don't want to tell him over the phone."

"Yeah, well, you should have told him before you left," she chastised, as if we hadn't had this conversation ten times already.

"We've talked about this," I reminded her. "The last thing I wanted to do was to tell Chance I was single and ready to date him and then leave the next day for New York."

There was no point in spilling my guts to him when I was going to be gone for a month. Granted, we could have talked and gotten to know each other better over that time, but it just wasn't how I wanted things between us to go. I wanted to be with him in person when we started things up, not long distance. Maybe that was selfish of me. Maybe it was stupid. Maybe it also gave me a little more time to be alone, to be with my dad, and to deal with whatever hell Jared might try to inflict when he came back to the city over break.

"I know. It's just that"—she groaned—"do you know how hard it was to see him and not blurt it all out?"

"Tell me you didn't," I warned, and she was quiet for too long. "Sunny!"

She laughed. "I didn't."

"Thank God. And if you see him again, just stay quiet. I promise I'll tell him as soon as I get back to campus."

"Better hope he doesn't have a girlfriend by then," she teased, but I'd be lying if I said the thought hadn't crossed my mind.

Just because Chance hadn't dated so far in college didn't mean that it couldn't happen. Maybe realizing that he had feelings for me opened him up to having feelings for other girls. Anything was possible.

I shook my head to rid it of those thoughts. "I'll tell him. The second I land."

"You should tell him now. Or on Christmas! *I got you a present …*" She paused. *"Me!"*

She laughed, and I chuckled.

"I'll think about it," I promised, and we both hung up.

I THOUGHT ABOUT telling Chance every single day, but something always seemed to stop me. As excited as I was to be with him, it felt torturous to try to start something while being apart. Not to mention the fact that my mind was filled with unanswered questions. Like, *what if he didn't even want me anymore? Or what if he really never had? What if Chance only thought he wanted me because he couldn't have me, because I was unavailable?* That was the kind of thing your heart never realized until the opportunity was in your face, staring you down and begging for an answer.

No, I couldn't have this conversation with him over the phone. I needed to be able to look in his eyes and see his face when I told him that I was single.

Pulling up the Fullton State baseball schedule online, I took a screenshot with my phone and gave myself a quick pep talk. I knew what I wanted to do.

Walking into the dining room, where my dad sat at the table working on his laptop with a newspaper spread out next to him, I leaned over his back and hugged his strong shoulders.

"What's up, kiddo?" he said as he looked behind at me.

I sat down in the chair next to him. "I was thinking about leaving a little earlier than usual, if that's okay with you?"

His bushy, graying brows rose. "How early?"

"Just a couple weeks. But I can stay if you want," I said, knowing that my dad would never force me to stay if I wanted to go.

"Is this about that Carter boy?"

My cheeks warmed as I answered with a slight smile I couldn't stop, "Maybe."

I'd filled my dad in on my personal life the day after I got back. We were having dinner together at home when he asked how Jared was, and I spilled my guts about how I'd been feeling. I told him that Jared had changed. Or that maybe I was the one who had changed but that I hadn't been happy in a long time. I told him about the breakup and that I thought I might have feelings for Chance.

Part of me was scared that my dad might be disappointed in my decisions or not understand. I knew that he loved Jared like family, so I was nervous for his reaction, especially since we'd always talked about working for my dad after graduation. But he couldn't have been more accepting or gracious. He'd told me that he wanted me to be happy and that if Jared had stopped making me that, then I should move on.

"Life's too short to settle, Danika. Don't stay with someone who doesn't make you smile."

"I still can't believe you like Jack Carter's son," he said, sounding like a giddy schoolboy instead of the overprotective dad I'd come to know lately.

We'd talked about that as well over dinner. How I needed to be able to make my own decisions and he had to stop worrying about me so much. He'd told me that he'd never be able to do that since he was my dad and all but that he'd try.

I'd ended up saving the pictures that Cassie had taken of my parents all those years ago for Christmas. After I got back to New York, I took the flash drive to a local artist I knew, who turned three of my favorites into paintings. I framed them and gave them to my dad for Christmas. Then, we spent the rest of the morning looking at all the pictures Cassie had given me copies of. My dad told me stories about him and my mom that I'd never heard before. And he'd cried. Which, of course, made me cry.

Being in such an emotionally vulnerable state had made me want to reach out to Chance even more. I texted him, wishing him a merry Christmas, and he responded with the same right back. Then, he sent a string of Christmas emojis that made me wonder if Jacey had stolen his phone. When the dots appeared, I held my breath, waiting for him to say something else, anything else, but the dancing dots disappeared, and no new text ever came. I should have texted that I missed him. I should have texted that I couldn't wait to see him when I came back. But I hadn't.

My dad started asking me a million questions about Chance and what kind of guy he was and why I thought I liked him, and it made me realize how much I really did.

"Haven't seen you smile like that," my dad said before adding, "Ever."

"That can't be true," I countered because I was sure I'd smiled the same way when I first started dating Jared.

"I mean it, kiddo. The smile you get on your face when you talk about Chance, it's a new one," he said, giving me a half-grin. "I like it."

"Well, I hope Chance likes it too."

He closed his laptop. "What do you mean?"

"I'm just a little worried, is all," I admitted.

"About?"

"What if he doesn't like me back?"

My dad chuckled. "Then, he's an idiot, and I don't want you with him."

I smiled, and my dad cocked his head to one side, studying me.

"But seriously, why the hell would you even think that?"

"I'm just nervous. What if he only *thinks* he likes me?"

"Danika, stop speaking girl and just speak."

"I was with Jared the whole time. Maybe Chance is the kind of guy who wants what he can't have."

My dad made a face before nodding, and I hated that he was potentially agreeing with my assessment.

"I mean, I guess that is possible. But what does your gut say?"

"My gut?"

"Yes, Danika, your gut. If I were to say that Chance only liked you because you were with Jared, what does your stomach do?"

I swallowed hard, my head shaking. "It revolts. Fights against your words. They feel wrong."

My dad's face practically lit up, his eyes crinkling in the corner with his smile. "See? Your gut knows. He likes you."

My gut had better be right, I thought to myself.

"You're really okay with all of this?" I asked him again even though I'd already asked a handful of times since I'd been home.

He mussed with the newspaper at his side before folding it neatly, his eyes softening. "With what exactly? You living your life the way you want to? Following and trusting your heart? Not staying with someone you don't belong with? Making hard decisions because they're the right ones? With what, sweetheart?"

My eyes filled with moisture at his barrage of complimentary questions. "I know you love Jared like a son. And I've just cut him out of our lives."

His jaw tightened. "I like Jared just fine. As long as he's making you happy. He stops doing that, and I stop giving a shit about him. You're my daughter. My loyalty will always be with and for you. You understand that?"

"Yes."

"You don't seem so sure," he said, and I stayed quiet. "Sweetheart, you don't owe Jared your heart just because he had a piece of it for a while. Sometimes, relationships run their course. They have a time limit, and they run out. Not every relationship is meant to last forever. And that's okay. Your mother and I would never want you to stay with someone who didn't make you happy, no matter who it was, how long we'd known them, or how much we loved their family. Okay?"

I fought back tears and sniffed. I'd had no idea how desperately I needed to hear those words or how much I craved his approval for this life change. "Thank you, Dad."

He wrapped his arm around me and pulled me against him before kissing the top of my head. "My sweet girl. Now, bring that boy out here, so I can meet him."

"Dad!"

"What?"

"You just want me to date him, so you and his dad can become besties," I teased, laughing at his twisted facial expression as he tried to decipher what I meant.

"I don't know what a bestie is, but you know how much

this city still loves Jack. The only Mets player anyone likes."

"No, he's the only Mets player *you* like."

"True. Make sure you send me more selfies, okay? I made it my wallpaper on my phone. See?" He shoved his phone at me, unlocking it so I could see the wallpaper in the background behind all the apps and folders. It was the picture of me and Jack that I'd sent him from dinner at their house.

A smile played at my lips as a thought hit me. "You know, Dad, you should think about coming out and watching Chance play. I mean, after I convince him to date me. 'Cause if he says no, then I don't want you to come out. That'd be embarrassing."

"I'll come out to whack him if he says no," he said, his tone serious, and I wasn't a hundred percent sure if he was joking or not.

People always told me that my dad was scary. I rarely saw that side of him. The last thing he'd ever been to me was scary, but then again, I'd never crossed him or made him upset.

"So, you're okay with me leaving early to go watch Chance play?"

"That's what you're doing? Watching him play baseball?"

"Yeah, his season starts two weeks before the semester does. I want to go to a game before everyone's back in school. Plus, I really want to talk to him about everything in person. And sitting here, waiting to do that, is kind of killing me, to be honest."

My dad smiled like he couldn't have approved of what I

was saying more. “Go get your baseball player.” He reached for my hand and squeezed, and my mom’s face flashed in my mind.

“I miss Mom.”

“I do too. Every single day.” He released a breath, and even though I knew we both missed her, we didn’t bring up the subject often. It was still too painful, even after all these years. Life had continued after she left, but it was forever changed and not quite the same.

“I wish she were here,” I said, not trying to make my dad feel worse but it was true. I wanted to talk to her about Chance, and I wanted her to see how I was growing up.

“I’d give anything to have her back here with us and healthy. Everything I do is because of her and for you. I know you miss her, and I know I’m a piss-poor substitute.”

“No, Dad, you’re great,” I tried to interrupt, but he talked over me.

“No. Listen. Your mother was my best friend, but she was yours too. And I know there are things that a girl needs her mom for. A dad just isn’t the same. And I’m so sorry she got sick. I’m so sorry you’ve had to grow up without her. But I promise you this”—his hand squeezed mine again—“she’s with you even if you can’t see her.”

“You really believe that?” I asked because I’d never expected to hear that kind of spiritual talk from him. He was so logical.

“Absolutely.”

“Does she watch over you too?” I pressed, wanting to know more about this side of him.

"I know she does. I feel her sometimes. And I dream about her. Those are the best." A faraway look appeared in his eyes, and I felt his love for my mother even though she was no longer here.

"I used to dream about her too. But I haven't for a while now," I said, almost forgetting that she used to come to my dreams nightly when she first passed.

How did I forget that?

"Doesn't mean she isn't still around, okay?" His expression softened as he looked directly into my eyes, and I nodded.

"You'll think about coming out to visit?" I asked, hoping he'd say yes.

In all the time I'd lived in California, I'd never been bothered by him not coming to visit me there. He was always slammed with work and I understood. But now, I almost couldn't bear the thought of him staying in New York and not coming out at least once before I graduated. I really wanted him to meet Chance and watch a game with me.

"Depends on what little Carter's answer is."

His response made me smile.

"I love you, Dad."

"I love you too, sweetheart. And just so you know"—he pushed back from the table and stood tall—"we've never been prouder," he said, speaking for himself and my dead mother.

And I almost lost it. Again.

Surprise Visits

Danika

EVEN THOUGH I wasn't leaving until tomorrow evening, my bags were already packed and sitting by the front door.

I'd texted Sunny to let her know that I'd be home early, and she replied with, *Thank God. My parents are driving me nuts, and I need an excuse to leave them.*

Sunny hated staying in our apartment alone, so whenever I left to go home, she usually did too. It was just one more thing that we were completely opposite in. I relished in my alone time, and she'd do anything to avoid it.

I was in the kitchen, making a sandwich, when the bell dinged, indicating that someone had arrived on our floor from the elevator.

We lived on the Upper East Side in a historical building that had been built in the 1930s. A lot of incredibly rich and famous people had lived here throughout the years, but for the most part, it had been a quiet place, growing up.

The majority of the units had been in families for generations and were owned by people who refused to leave, but my dad had managed to snag one on the fourteenth floor when the previous owner lost everything in a stock market crash. He'd wanted to buy multiple units, but apparently, my mom told him that was "obnoxious," and he'd listened.

We had too many extra bedrooms as it was—for all the siblings I was supposed to have but never did. After having me, my mom's body couldn't hold on to any more babies, and eventually, they'd stopped trying. I knew they'd considered adoption at one point, but then my mom had gotten sick, and getting her better had become our sole focus.

The doorbell rang, and I walked slowly toward the front door, figuring that it was one of my dad's employees or associates.

When I pulled the door open, I almost dropped my sandwich. "Jared? What are you doing here?"

It wasn't the first time I'd heard from him during the break, but it was the first time he'd shown up at the house. He'd texted a few times since he'd gotten back to the city, and my responses had seemed to keep him at bay, so I'd figured I was in the clear.

He stepped over the threshold, inviting himself in. "Has it been long enough?" he asked.

I refused to move anywhere, except the foyer. "Long enough for what?"

"For you to see how stupid this is." He sounded bored before noticing my suitcases. He studied them before giving me an inquisitive glare.

"What are you talking about? How stupid what is?"

"Us breaking up. Us being apart. That's not what we do.

We go together, Danika. I thought being home would at least remind you of that."

I was caught off guard even though I probably shouldn't have been. It was just that Jared had taken my breaking up with him without so much as a fight. He'd practically sprinted out of my apartment, angry but agreeable, and I'd assumed he'd been as relieved as I had even though he never said so.

He took a step toward me, and I moved away in response.

"I've left you alone. I've given you time. I've given you space. Figured you'd come to your senses by now."

"I don't need time. Jared, nothing's changed," I said because we'd already gone over all of this back in California—how things had gotten so sideways between us, how we weren't the same couple we'd once been, and how neither one of us was truly happy.

But now, I was thinking that he hadn't listened to a single thing I said because he assumed I'd change my mind eventually or that I hadn't meant any of it in the first place.

"This is because of that baseball player, isn't it? Did he call you and tell you?" Jared's mouth twisted into a snarl.

I knew he hated Chance. He'd always felt threatened by him, and looking back, he had good reason to.

"Call and tell me what?"

"Nothing. Never mind." He tried to cover.

I wasn't buying it, but I also didn't care what he was referring to. I didn't want to talk to Jared about Chance.

"Fine, don't tell me. Is there anything else?" I asked, surprising myself at how badly I wanted him gone.

Jared and I had been friends for so long that I'd just expected we'd go back to that. I could see how naive that was now. You couldn't cross and uncross those kinds of lines that easily.

"You're making a mistake, Danika. You'd better really think this through," he warned, and I wanted to scream out in frustration.

"I have."

God, I'd thought this to death before I actually pulled the trigger and ended things. It had been a long time coming, and we both knew it. The fact that I'd felt nothing but relief after he left that night told me everything I needed to know. I'd made the right decision, and I'd done the right thing.

"When that baseball chump uses you up and tosses you aside like yesterday's garbage, I won't be there, waiting to pick up the pieces. I hope you know that. You can't come back from this."

"You need to leave," I said, pointing at the door.

We were done here.

He stepped toward the front door before stopping and turning around to face me. "He's getting drafted this year, and then what, Danika? He'll leave. And what are you going to do, follow him?" he asked with a sick laugh. "Yeah, right. Your whole life's already planned out, and it brings you *right back here*," he emphasized the last three words before continuing, "You're breaking up with me, so you can date this guy for the next five months? Why? So you can say you fucked a professional baseball player? Maybe he'll keep you on his roster. Call you every time he's in town for a series."

"My daughter asked you to leave." My dad's voice boomed throughout the entryway, echoing around us. He sounded pissed.

"Oh"—Jared cleared his throat—"Mr. Marchetti. I didn't see you there," he stumbled on his words.

"That's obvious. Now, leave before I throw you off the terrace." My dad moved to stand defensively in front of me, letting Jared know that he was no longer welcome in our home.

I couldn't see what happened beyond that, but I heard the front door open and then close again before my dad turned to face me, his fists clenched tight.

"That boy has changed. Has he always talked to you like that?"

"No. It started after the football-player thing. It's slowly gotten worse."

"Your boyfriend should never speak to you that way. It's not okay."

I felt like an idiot for putting up with Jared's behavior, for making excuses and justifying it instead of seeing it for what it was. "I know. It won't happen again."

He pulled me into a hard hug and told me he loved me and would kill anyone who talked to me like that.

"Thanks, Dad," I tried to say, but my face was smooshed against his chest, and I didn't think he'd heard me.

I GOT BACK to California a few hours before Chance's first preseason game. I'd taken the red-eye, which normally would have been awful, but flying first class had made everything bearable. Sunny picked me up from the airport before she had to head straight back home to her parents' house.

"I'm sorry I can't go to the game with you," she said for the millionth time.

"It's your mom's birthday. I'm pretty sure I can manage going to a game by myself." I was actually excited to be going alone. I needed to talk to Chance after the game, and I knew it would be awkward with an audience even if it was just Sunny. "I'll see you tomorrow. And thank you so much for picking me up. You didn't have to do that."

"I wanted to." She smiled as I closed the passenger door, and she popped the trunk, so I could grab my suitcase. "I can't wait to hear all the details," she squealed, and I suddenly got super nervous.

It was one thing to think about being with Chance when it wasn't a possibility, but it was another thing altogether when it was a real option.

"Wish me luck," I practically begged.

"You don't need it, but good luck! Go get your man! And tell Mac I still think he's hot and that I want to make out again!" She laughed as she pulled away, leaving me alone in our parking lot with a thousand thoughts racing through my head.

What the hell am I going to wear? I need a shower. And what am I even thinking, going to his game, unannounced, alone, and filled with hope when I haven't talked to him in weeks? Anything could have changed during that time. Heck, everything could have changed.

I convinced myself it would be okay as I unlocked the front door and stepped inside. The air felt stale from being closed up for too long. Walking toward the balcony, I opened the sliding glass door and closed the screen door instead, letting the warm air flow. Inside my bedroom, I tossed my suitcase on top of my bed and started to unpack my clothes and my thoughts. No matter how Chance felt about me, breaking up with Jared had been the right thing to do, and regardless of what happened later today, I knew I'd be okay.

Exhaling, I felt a calmness moving through me as I sent a text to my dad, letting him know I'd gotten home safe. He responded right back with a thumbs-up emoji and a heart, which basically meant he'd gotten my message but he was too busy to talk. I wasn't offended.

Hopping into the shower, I let the hot water wash over me before I scrubbed my body clean.

The baseball field was close enough that I could walk but far enough that I might be sweating through my shirt by the time I got there. I briefly considered calling for a ride before deciding that the walk would do me good. We walked everywhere in New York, and I could walk here too.

I got to the game a little early, and I made my way to the ticket booth, where I showed my student ID and picked up a free ticket.

"Danika?"

My name being called made me spin around.

"Hi, Mrs. Carter," I said with a smile as she pulled me

into a hug. I didn't know why I hadn't even considered the fact that she would be here, too, but it hadn't even crossed my mind.

"Please call me Cassie. Mrs. Carter is so weird," she insisted.

I looked around her for Jacey but didn't see her anywhere. "Are you here alone? Where's Jacey?"

"She didn't want to come. Said she's tired of watching baseball all the time. Can't say I blame her really. I'd be tired of it, too, if I didn't love it so much," she added with a proud smile. "Plus, seeing Jack in uniform is something I'll never get tired of."

I chuckled, loving that she still loved her husband that much. "I never thought about that. Jacey, I mean. Did she grow up, going to a lot of games?"

Cassie full-on laughed. "Her life revolved around the ball field. Sit with me, so I'm not alone? I have an extra ticket." She flashed two tickets in front of my face.

"Are you sure? Will Chance mind?"

Her face narrowed, her green eyes reminding me so much of her son's. "Why on earth would Chance mind?"

"I don't know. I just"—I paused for a second—"didn't tell him I was coming to the game today."

"So? He won't care." She waved off my concerns and looped her arm through mine.

I walked in step with her down, down, down and stopped right behind home plate.

"These are your seats?" I had to force the words out.

"Yep. Right behind home plate, so I can watch Chance

catch and see my hot husband."

"We're so close," I said, feeling super uncomfortable as I glanced to my left and noticed the clear view into the dugout. "We can see right in there," I practically stuttered.

"You'll get used to it." She tried to comfort me. "Here, I'll sit in the seat closest to the dugout, so you aren't in full view, okay?"

"Thank you," I breathed out with relief.

Sure, I'd only moved one seat over, but it was one seat farther away from the team, and I could shield myself with Cassie's body if I needed to.

I could feel her eyes on me, studying me before I turned to look at her.

"I forgot how nerve-racking it can be," she said, sounding almost sympathetic.

"Being here, you mean?"

She nodded. "Yes, being here. I used to get nervous, watching Jack play."

"I can't imagine you ever being nervous about anything," I said because Cassie handled herself with such confidence that it radiated throughout her very being.

"The girls were pretty mean back then."

"It's funny how little we change. As females, I mean. When it comes to other females," I said, but I wasn't sure that I'd made any sense.

"Our competitive nature against each other runs deep. Are they mean to you for dating my son?"

"Well"—I laughed—"we're not dating, so I don't know."

"That's right. You have a boyfriend." She closed her

mouth and stared out at the field, where the other team was taking infield.

"Not anymore," I said.

She faced me with a giant smile. "Does Chance know that?"

"Not yet."

"Oh, this is going to be fun." She clapped her hands together right as her husband stepped onto the field, and I swore I heard her gasp. "That is one fine specimen of a man," she said as Jack walked up to the fence separating the field from the stands.

"Hey, beautiful. Can I take you out after the game?" he said, looking directly at Cassie.

"Depends," she said in response.

He grinned, looking confident and cocky, and I wondered if this was how he had been when he was Chance's age.

"On what?"

"Will you be wearing that?"

His smile grew lopsided as he asked, "Do you want me to wear this?"

"Definitely." Her head nodded.

Their flirting was adorable—and a little uncomfortable to be in the middle of.

"Then, I wouldn't change for the world," he said. "So, is that a yes?"

"Hell yes."

"Good. Hey, Danika." He waved before walking away.

"Hi," I mumbled under my breath.

Cassie giggled. "Sorry about that. I can't help myself

sometimes."

Watching Jack and Cassie together made me realize that true love really could exist. It was easy to forget sometimes, especially when real life crept in and smacked you to your knees. What they had was special and rare, but it was possible. And I wanted it. I wondered if I could be that lucky.

First-Game Nerves

Chance

"NOT TO FREAK you out or anything, but I need you to look at your mom, dude," Mac said, and I wondered what the fuck he was talking about.

I rarely looked in the stands. Maybe a quick glance at my little sister when she screamed my name like a banshee but never any other time. Especially not when Mac suggested I did it. That usually meant he was scoping out chicks.

My mom was not a chick. Well, not one for Mac to be checking out anyway, if he wanted to continue living.

I turned and searched the stands for her usual seat. "Whoa," I said out loud, my heart leaping into my throat as I noticed that my sister was not the person sitting next to my mom, like I had expected.

Danika sat on the other side of her instead.

"Did you know she was coming?" Mac asked, keeping his voice low.

"I didn't even know she was back in town," I responded in the same quiet tone, not wanting to draw attention or have any of my teammates overhear.

"And she's sitting with your mom?"

"Apparently."

"Did you start dating Tutor Girl and not tell me?" Mac whined. "I'm hurt, man. I'm supposed to be your best friend."

"You are my best friend, idiot. We're not dating. I haven't talked to her in weeks, and she has a—" I started to say before he cut me off.

"Boyfriend. I know. But we both know he cheated on her, and I'd bet it wasn't the first time. Maybe she found out and dumped his ass?" He sounded excited at the prospect, and I had to admit that the idea excited me too.

"Maybe."

I hated not telling Danika what I had seen at the party, but I always fell back on the fact that if I was supposed to be the one to tell her, she would have been home that night. And she wasn't. So, nothing had changed.

"Chance! Mac! Get your asses over here," Coach Jackson yelled.

We scrambled down to where he stood in the dugout. The rest of my teammates watched, and I was embarrassed for being so blatantly called out.

"Coach," we both addressed him at the same time.

"What the hell is so interesting in the stands?" he asked, craning his head to look out toward the half-filled stadium.

"Nothing," I said, shaking my head, and Mac responded in kind.

"Then, keep your eyes on the field. Heads in the game," he demanded even though the game hadn't started.

The visiting team was still taking infield, but we didn't dare argue.

"Yes, Coach," I said before punching Mac in the arm as we headed away.

We stopped about halfway, leaning our arms against the bars that separated the dugout from the field, and watched the opposing team finish up.

"Sorry," Mac apologized for drawing my attention to the stands in the first place and getting us yelled at by Coach.

"It's fine," I said as I moved to grab my catcher's helmet and glove.

It was our turn to take infield and show these guys who they were up against.

I HATED TO admit that we were a little rusty. We'd racked up three errors in six innings, and that was something we never did. Our team was typically flawless. It was what we were known for. Coach Jackson was pissed, his face as red as a tomato even though we were still winning by two runs. Our pitchers were off, missing my calls and missing their marks. I had to work extra hard behind the plate to catch their shitty pitches and frame them as strikes, which was fine, but I was keenly aware that Danika was two rows behind my back, watching my every move.

I'd never dealt with that kind of mental distraction

before. Girls always looked at me, waited for me after games, yelled out my name, and shit like that, but I never cared before. I cared now. I cared way too much for my own good.

"Let's go, Chance!" My mom's cheerful voice met my ears, and I fought back a smile that no one could see behind my mask anyway.

The runner at first base—where Mac stood, waiting for my throw—taunted me after each pitch snapped into my glove. He kept taking two skitter steps toward second before he moved back, looking like an idiot because I knew he wasn't running. At least, not yet. His body language gave him away. His legs might have been moving toward second base, but nothing else on his body was. When a runner tried to steal, their entire being was aimed in the same direction. He had to get there faster than I could throw the ball, which was hard to accomplish—and I wasn't being cocky.

The pitch flew across home plate. The batter swung and missed as the runner at first base took off. But he was too slow, and we both knew it. I threw the ball hard, watching as it flew directly into the shortstop's glove, waiting at second base.

He tagged the runner, and the umpire screamed, "Out!" before making a hand gesture, signaling the same.

Cheers erupted from the crowd in the stands, but only two voices stood out from the rest—my mom's and Danika's. Her accent was undeniable, and again, I wondered to myself what she was doing here.

The rest of the game sailed by without much fanfare. We kept our lead and won by two runs, which made Coach

Jackson happy, but he was still pissed about the errors, reminding us that we'd be working extra on fielding since we apparently didn't remember how to do it right.

My dad was pretty mad, too, which didn't happen all that often. He reminded the pitchers that they were there to do a job, and if they couldn't do it, there were plenty of other guys who would kill for the chance to try.

That was how Division One baseball went. If you fucked up, you got replaced. There was no shortage of guys waiting in the dugout for their shot to steal your position. It wasn't theirs to win; it was yours to lose.

I always remembered that line.

Mac and I headed toward the locker room. Considering the fact that I was the only one on the team who wore equipment while playing, I was an absolute sweat show by the end of each game. Showering could not wait until I got home like it could for some of the other guys.

"I'll be five minutes," I said to Mac before adding, "But you don't have to wait."

Usually, I gave Mac a ride home, but sometimes, he went with our other roommates instead.

"I'll be outside," he said as he slung a bag over his shoulder before dumping his dirty uniform into the bin.

Our equipment manager washed all of our clothes, which was a perk that I was grateful for. I couldn't imagine washing my shit and not shrinking it or screwing it up somehow. The school probably knew that, hence the organized guy who handled all of that stuff for each team.

After toweling off and changing into some clean clothes,

I headed out to look for my parents. I wondered if Danika would still be around, but I had no idea what she was doing at the game and not in New York in the first place. School didn't start for a couple more weeks.

Before I exited the locker room, Mac rounded the corner and almost ran straight into me. "Hey, man, Danika's still here, so I'm gonna catch a ride with Dayton."

"Oh," I said through my surprise. "Okay. I'll see you back at the house. Thanks for the heads-up."

"I expect a full report."

"I know you do." I faked a groan before following him outside.

"Hey, honey," my mom said with a big smile as soon as I came into view.

Danika stood at her side, talking to my dad, but I noticed the quick look she threw my way. My mom hugged me and then congratulated me on the win and my game.

"Thanks, Mom."

"Look who I found," my dad announced, his arm wrapped around Danika like he had picked her out special just for me.

"Hey, Little Spitfire," I said without thinking as the nickname slipped out, and she grinned.

"Hey, Hotshot," she said back before moving to give me an awkward hug.

Or at least, I was awkward, not knowing where she stood with Jared, seeing her for the first time in months in front of my parents. It was all a little too weird.

"What are you doing here?" I hadn't meant to sound so

confrontational, so I tried to recover. "I mean, I thought you'd be in New York until the semester started."

"I know, but I came back early," she said before looking between me and my parents, who now stood, holding each other.

"I can see that. But why?"

"Jesus, Chance, give the girl a break. Be happy she's here," my dad said, reminding me that we were having this conversation with an audience. One who wouldn't keep their opinions to themselves.

"No, he's right, Mr. Carter," she said, defending me. "I was supposed to be gone still. But I broke up with Jared, so I came back."

Excitement and shock tore through me at once.

Did she come back for me? Did Jared admit what he did?

"He actually told you?" I asked.

She shifted on her feet, her facial expression completely changing into something unreadable. "Told me what?"

"Oh." I looked at my parents. "Nothing."

"Chance, I don't care that your parents are right here. What do you think he told me?"

I cleared my throat. "That I saw him over break at a party. He was with some other girl. We had words."

Her face changed again into an expression I wished I didn't recognize. Danika was pissed.

"Okay, wait a second. You thought Jared had cheated on me?" she questioned and waited for my answer.

"Yeah." I kicked the dirt because I felt like a schmuck.

"And you didn't tell me?" Her eyes searched mine, and

the utter disappointment shining in them nearly broke me in two.

"I tried." I started to tell her about the night I went over to her place, but she wasn't having it.

"You tried? What'd you do, Chance? Call me and tell me? Send me an email? Text me, so we could talk about it?"

I swallowed around the rock in my throat. "No."

"Then, you didn't try to tell me shit," she barked, completely calling me out.

"Danika, I went to your apartment," I tried to defend my silence on the matter, but I knew that I'd made the wrong decision when it came to her. No matter what I'd been told last summer, this situation was different.

Danika faced my parents and stunned us all. "Excuse me, Mr. and Mrs. Carter, but I'm really pissed off at your son right now, and I need to go," she said before turning to me. "Don't follow me, Chance. Leave me alone."

"Shit," I breathed out before apologizing to my mom for the bad language even though I knew she didn't really care.

Danika stormed away, her black top and jean shorts fading away quicker than I liked.

Squeezing my eyes closed, I sucked in a breath before looking directly at my mom. "I messed up, huh?"

"Her boyfriend cheated on her, and you didn't tell her?"

I blew out a breath. "Yeah. I mean, I saw him at a party with another chick."

"You should have told her. Why didn't you?" My mom sounded genuinely confused and interested in my answer.

"You should *not* have told her," my dad interjected,

emphasizing the word *not*.

My mom unwrapped herself from him and pinned him with a look. "Excuse me, Jack? Of course he should have said something."

My dad made a weird sound. "It's not Chance's business. As guys, we don't get involved in other people's shit like that. It's not our place."

"Not your place? Oh, really? Doing the *right thing* isn't your place?" she argued, and I felt like there was some double meaning behind her words that I wasn't quite aware of.

"Kitten," he said, calling my mom by her nickname that always made her roll her eyes but also made her melt. "We don't think the same way that you ladies do. We mind our own business. How would it have looked if Chance had told Danika and she didn't believe him? What if she'd thought Chance was lying or just trying to cause trouble because he liked her and wanted her for himself? What if it had backfired on him when he was just trying to tell her what he saw?"

My dad made some very valid points. They were exactly what I'd thought and how I'd convinced myself that I had done the right thing by staying quiet after I tried to tell her once.

"But now, she feels stupid," my mom started to explain. "Do you know how embarrassing it is to be the last one to find out something like that? And she thought you liked her."

"I do like her."

"Then, you should have told her. Even as a friend. She

would have wanted to know what you saw." My mom inhaled before putting her hand on my shoulder. "Turn the situation around. If you were dating someone and Danika had seen that girl with another guy at a party, would you want to know about it, or would you want her to keep the information to herself?"

My stomach dropped as I imagined the scenario. "Of course I'd want to know."

"Exactly."

"Shit. Shit. Shit." I kicked the ground some more. "I need to fix this."

"You will." My mom was encouraging, and it made me feel marginally better.

"You don't think she'll hate me forever?" I asked her since she spoke girl and my dad and I obviously did not.

"She doesn't hate you now. Like I said, she's embarrassed. And disappointed that you didn't say anything to her. She doesn't understand why."

"Your mom's probably right," my dad added.

"Probably?" My mom shot him a look.

"Fine." He reached for her and pulled her hard against him. "She's always right. Listen to the woman."

"Thanks, you guys. I'll call you later," I said as I took off jogging toward The Beast, a few thoughts in my head.

Danika was single. She had come back early from New York. And I'd almost blown it between us.

I refused to let that happen.

Cheated in Silence

Danika

TEARS SPILLED DOWN my face as I hopped into the car I'd called to pick me up. Anger, frustration, and embarrassment fueled my silence on the ride back to my apartment. The news of Jared being with someone else already stung, but that was pretty hypocritical of me, considering the fact that I'd wanted to be with Chance already too. What hurt the most was Chance thinking that Jared had cheated and keeping it from me. For whatever reason, that felt like more of a betrayal.

I pulled out my keys and went to put them in the lock, but the doorknob turned. I knew I'd locked it before I left for the game.

Opening the door slowly, I yelled out, "Sunny?"

"I'm here!" she shouted before running out of her room. "We celebrated early, and my parents told me they couldn't take any more of my moping. They forced me to leave. I just got back ten minutes ago."

I managed a slight laugh, imagining her family asking her to go.

"Wait. Have you been crying? What happened at the game?"

"Um, Jared hooked up with some other girl over break."

Sunny didn't look that surprised. "So? You two were already broken up by then."

"But Chance didn't know that. And he saw Jared."

She moved to the couch and practically fell onto it. "What? How do you know that?"

I sat down on top of the coffee table across from her. "Chance thought that was why we broke up. Because Jared had cheated on me and I'd found out."

"Okay. Let me get this straight." She held a hand in the air. "Chance thought Jared had cheated on you, but he didn't tell you?"

"No! I mean, yes, he thought that. And, no, he didn't tell me."

"And you're mad because …" She dragged out the word, and I couldn't believe I had to explain this to my best friend.

"I'm mad because how can I trust him to have my best interests at heart? How can I trust him to protect me and look out for me? And why wouldn't he have told me something as important as that?"

She nodded as she processed my words. "I get what you're saying. I mean, it's not like Chance is bound to any kind of guy code to Jared. He's not one of his teammates or anything."

I hadn't even considered the guy code. I knew that most guys stayed quiet when it came to this kind of thing. At least, most guys in New York did. They never ratted on each other, no matter how much dirt they had. But I'd figured that Chance was different. Or maybe I'd figured that how he felt about me made things different.

"I thought he liked me. If he knew something that would end my relationship, why wouldn't he be dying to tell me?"

Sunny's face lit up like a realization had struck her on the top of the head. "Maybe he did."

"What do you mean?"

"When he came over that night I called you, he was flustered. Desperate to see you. And crazy upset when I told him you'd already left for home."

I remembered then what Chance had said back at the field. I had been too upset at the time to process all of his words. "Oh my gosh. He did say he came over to the apartment. He must have wanted to tell me then."

She leaned back and grabbed a pillow. "It does sort of make sense though. That he wouldn't want to be the one to tell you that kind of thing."

"Why does that make sense? How does that make sense?"

We girls told each other things. Especially hard things. If we found out that someone's man was cheating, we'd let our girlfriend know. Even if she didn't believe us. Even if it backfired and ruined the friendship—because, sometimes, it did. But we never let our friends walk around, looking like fools.

"I think that Chance wouldn't want to be the guy you chose to be with out of default. Does that make any sense?"

"No. Explain."

"Hypothetically speaking, if Chance had told you he saw Jared cheating, you most likely would have broken up with him and then given Chance a chance. Ha-ha. Chance a chance," she said, laughing at her own pun. "There's no way he'd want you to date him just because Jared had messed up."

It was like a lightbulb went off inside my brain. "He wants me to date him because I want to be with him over anyone else."

"Yep," she said, sounding excited.

"But that's exactly what I did."

"But he doesn't know that. He doesn't know anything yet."

I felt super annoyed with myself. Somehow, I had turned this situation into a complicated mess when all I meant to do was make it easy. Breaking up with Jared first without additional complications, strings, or judgment. Taking the time to make sure my feelings for Chance were real without the pressure of Chance knowing I was single. Coming back early to tell him that I had chosen him and wanted to be with him, if he still wanted me. Everything I'd done was supposed to be the right thing, but it felt like I'd messed it all up instead.

"I still want to know why he didn't tell me." For whatever reason, I couldn't let that part go without hearing it from him.

"I'll take you over there," Sunny said, pushing herself up from the couch without me even asking. It was like she'd read my mind.

"Thank you." I grabbed my purse and my cell phone, and we bolted out the front door.

I couldn't get to him fast enough.

We drove in relative silence the short distance to the baseball house until Sunny started peppering me with questions. The house was around the next turn, and she asked, "Are you nervous?"

"Not really. I just want to hear everything from his point of view. You and I can make excuses and try to figure him out, but none of it matters if it isn't true."

"You're right. You guys have a lot to talk about." Sunny looked around as she pulled into the driveway and stopped her car. "I don't see his truck anywhere."

I looked around, too, like I might be able to prove her wrong. "Me either."

"What do you want to do?"

"I'll just wait. He has to come home eventually," I said with a shrug before opening the passenger door and sliding out.

With my luck, Chance would go stay the night at his parents', and I'd be waiting out here for him for a week.

Sunny rolled down the window. "Work it out with him. You've waited too long not to," she said before adding, "And call me if you need me to come get you. But I'm hoping you won't." She wagged her eyebrows as she drove off, leaving me standing outside the baseball house, looking like a damn groupie.

Talk It Out

Chance

I PARKED MY truck, and my head was all over the place as I walked toward the front door, staring at the ground. I'd rushed over to Danika's apartment after leaving my parents, but no one had answered. She didn't have a car, so I'd had no idea if she was home and avoiding me or if she genuinely wasn't there. I kind of figured she was ignoring me. While I didn't blame her for it, I really wanted to make things right, and we couldn't do that if we weren't talking.

I noticed the black shoes against the white pavement first, and my eyes roamed up, taking her in. "Danika."

She was sitting on the stoop of my house, all alone. Maybe my mom was right, and she really didn't hate me.

"Hey." She sounded sad, and it made my chest ache.

"I was just looking for you," I said, hoping we were on the same page.

"You were?" Her tone turned skeptical, and I hated it.

Things seemed so shaky between us, and I wanted them to be rock solid.

"Of course I was." I reached out my hand to help pull her

up. "I want to talk to you. I want to fix this. I want to explain."

She inhaled softly before her eyes turned glassy. "I really need to know why you didn't tell me," she said, her voice breaking slightly, and I realized that I'd hurt her. My keeping this information from her had hurt her.

"Let's talk inside." I opened the front door and held it for her to walk through.

She looked fucking beautiful, walking into my house as I directed her toward my bedroom. Knowing she was here for me and not some party we were throwing fired me up.

"Hey, Chance, how'd it go with Tutor Girrr—" Mac started to yell before stopping short. "Oh. Uh … never mind. Hey, Danika," he said before giving me a look that screamed, *Oh shit*, and disappearing.

She giggled, and I took it as a good sign. Ushering her through my door, I closed and locked it behind her.

"For privacy," I said when she shot me a look after hearing the door latch. "If you're uncomfortable, I can unlock it."

Her head shook. "I'm not uncomfortable."

Danika looked around my room, and I had no idea where to tell her to sit. She basically had three options: the chair at my desk, my bed, or the floor. I'd be lying if I said I hoped she didn't choose the bed. She moved to one side of my mattress and sat down before propping her feet up. I sat on the opposite side of her. Far enough away but still close enough to reach out and touch her if she let me.

We both stayed silent, staring, not knowing where or how

to start, so I took the initiative.

"I want to hear everything that happened with you and Jared," I said because I was damn curious.

She was single now, and I was dying to know exactly how it had happened.

"I'll tell you anything you want to know. But can you tell me about the cheating thing first?"

I nodded in agreement because whether we started with this topic or ended with it, it still had to be discussed. "Um, I was at a party before break, and he was with some girl. I told him he'd better tell you about her or that I would."

"We were already broken up by then," she said in almost a whisper, and surprise ripped through me.

"Really? He sure didn't act like it." I remembered what I'd said to Jared and how he'd reacted, the way he'd insinuated that they were still together and I had, of course, assumed that they were.

"So, you definitely thought he'd cheated on me?" It was a question and not a statement, like she was looking for clarification or needed me to say it out loud again.

"I did."

"And you came over to my apartment to tell me?" Another question.

"I did. But you were already gone. And I took it as a sign," I tried to explain, feeling foolish.

She shifted on my bed, pulling her legs in front of her and crossing them over. "A sign for what? To never tell me?"

I swallowed hard. This was one hell of an uncomfortable conversation, and I'd never had one like it before. "Pretty much. I convinced myself that if you were supposed to hear it from me, you would have been home for me to tell you. Plus, everyone told me to stay out of it."

"Well, everyone's a fucking idiot, Chance!" Her voice rose.

"I know that now." I wanted her to understand where I was coming from, but the only way was to tell her what had happened last summer. I sucked in a long breath. "Can I tell you a story?"

"A story?" Her eyes narrowed like she wasn't sure if I was joking or not.

"I played baseball this past summer. It was a really prestigious league. Invite only," I described, and she nodded along, her eyes softening. "Okay, well, there was this guy on my team, Tanner. He had a girlfriend back home, but he was hooking up with the local girls almost every night."

Danika made a sound, and I swore she'd mumbled, "Pig," under her breath.

"He was an egotistical asshole. Typical dirtbag guy, thinking he could get away with anything he wanted and never get caught. His girlfriend was coming out to visit, and when she got there, one of the local girls didn't see her." I stopped for a second and thought a littler harder. "Or maybe she did. Anyway, she wrapped her arms around Tanner and started kissing him."

"She did not." Danika's eyes grew wide. "What did the girlfriend do?"

"Flipped out. She wanted to leave. Tanner tried to calm her down, but another guy on the team and I ended up taking her back to the airport," I said, filling her in on what had happened that night.

"Was it just that one girl, or were there others? He's been so distant," Beth asked through her tears.

I hated lying to her, but I wasn't sure what to say. I looked at Cayden for help, but he was driving and ignoring her questions as he pretended to need directions to the airport even though he was from the area. I felt caught in the middle, torn between right and wrong, defending a shitty teammate or telling his girlfriend the truth.

Turning around to look at her in the backseat, I asked, "What did Tanner tell you?" I wondered how exactly he'd tried to talk his way out of the shitshow he'd created.

"He said it was only one time and that she turned into some psycho stalker he couldn't get away from."

I let out a disgusted sound before I could stop myself, and Cayden punched my leg, telling her everything she needed to know. Tanner Michaels was not only an asshole, but also a slandering liar.

"So, it was more than once then? I knew it," she practically whispered as she continued to cry, wiping her eyes with the sleeve of her hoodie.

"If you really thought that it was only one time, then you wouldn't be in the car with us, heading back to the airport," I said because it needed to be said.

If Beth had truly believed Tanner, she would still be sitting at the Waterfront right now without a care in the world. Hell, we all would.

"I know. That girl told me in the restroom that it wasn't just once. And that it wasn't just her. Did you see him with other girls? I can't believe he'd do this to me. We've been together for four years."

Beth was asking all the right questions but to all the wrong people. Then again, if she had asked Tanner, he'd have lied to her, and she'd never know the truth. Neither Cayden or I answered her question.

"Oh my God, come on, you guys. I've already been made a fool of, just tell me how big of one I've been."

I imagined my mom and how hurt she must have felt when she found out what my dad had done to her all those years ago. At least he'd been the one to tell her even though I knew it had torn him apart to do it.

"He's been cheating on you all summer, Beth. With every chick who's willing."

Cayden reached across the car and punched me in the arm. "Dude," he started to say, but I fought back.

"What? It's the truth."

"But it's not our story to tell, man. Beth, you can't ask us anything else. You're putting us in a really bad position."

"I won't. Thank you, Chance ..." Beth paused before adding, "For telling me."

We arrived at the airport, and Beth got out of the car with her small duffel bag.

She leaned in the passenger window. "Thanks for the ride. Tell Tanner I hope he breaks his arm."

Cayden and I both laughed uncomfortably. We never wished broken bones on people. It was bad luck.

"Are you sure you'll be okay?" I realized that it was already late, and we were leaving her alone to fend for herself in a strange airport.

She wiped at her face and sucked in a deep, loud breath. "I'll be fine. Thanks for getting me here," she said before turning and disappearing inside the terminal.

"Dude," Cayden said again as he pulled away. "You know that Tanner's going to find out you told her, and it's going to come back on you. And not in a good way," he warned.

I shrugged, not really feeling all that concerned. I figured that I could deal with a pissed off Tanner. "But I didn't do anything wrong."

"You told his girl the truth. It wasn't your place. We don't get involved in our teammates' shit, man. Come on. You gotta know that."

I stopped recanting the memory and looked at Danika's face. She didn't look pleased.

"Are you mad?"

"All I've learned is that you told some perfect stranger the truth about her cheating boyfriend, but you wouldn't tell me."

"I'm not finished."

"Then, finish."

Who knew that doing the right thing could have such bullshit consequences? To say I'd learned my lesson was a massive understatement. Half of the team refused to talk to me after that night, let alone make eye contact with me. If they had the option to choose their catcher, they chose to work with anyone other than me. They no longer trusted me off the field, and that spilled onto it as well.

I'd never been in trouble on a team before. Then again, I'd never thrown one of my teammates under the bus before.

Coach pulled me aside before warm-ups one afternoon. "What the hell did you do to my team, Carter?"

"Coach?" I looked at him questioningly and tried to play dumb.

"My team? They're all pissed at you. Act like you have the fucking plague. What the hell did you do?" His accent grew stronger with each question he asked.

I sucked in a breath before admitting, "Ratted out Tanner to his girl, sir."

Coach let out a sound that was more like a holler than a laugh. "You're fucking joking."

"Wish I were, Coach," I said, but I struggled. I honestly thought I'd done the right thing, but if everyone's attitudes were any indication, all I'd done was royally screw up.

Coach gripped me by the shoulder and turned me away from the rest of the team, walking me down the chalk outline at third base. "Why the hell would you go and do something as stupid as that?"

" 'Cause we were driving her to the airport and she asked."

"Haven't you ever heard of lying, son? Taking one for the team? Protecting your boy at all costs, no matter what? Where's your damn loyalty?"

"I don't owe Tanner shit. Least of all my loyalty," I

argued before I had a chance to think about the words forming in my head and stopping them from coming out of my mouth. I'd never talked to a coach like that before. "Sorry, Coach. I didn't mean—"

"No, you listen here. Tanner's your teammate. You don't have to like him, but you do have to have his back. That's the only way this works. Apologize. Tell him you fucked up and that you're sorry. Tell him it won't happen again. Fix my damn team, Carter, or I'll send your ass home. I don't care how good you are."

"For real, Coach?" I asked, unsure if he was pulling my chain or not.

Would he really send me home because I'd meddled in someone's personal life?

"Do I look like I'm joking?" He pointed at his face, which held a scowl and no hint of humor.

"You do not."

"Because I am not. We don't meddle, son. We don't get involved. We don't get in the middle. And we sure as hell don't throw our teammate to the wolves just because a girl asked you a question. She isn't your problem. His relationship with her isn't your problem. Stay out of people's shit, Carter. Learn that lesson now. Ingrain it in your pea brain." He stabbed my head with his finger. "Take it home with you to California and don't ever fucking forget it," he said as a ball of spit formed in the corner of his mouth. He looked like a rabid dog about to attack, and I was the only one in range.

"Yes, Coach."

"Now, go fix my damn team," he said before stalking off, pulling his baseball cap off, and running his fingers through what little was left of his hair.

I turned around to see the guys huddled in the outfield, the majority of them watching me with glee in their eyes. They were happy I had gotten my ass handed to me. Tucking my tail between my legs, I jogged over and shoved myself between two teammates who did not make room for me. I couldn't believe I had to apologize to this cheating, egotistical prick.

"Hey, man. I fucked up," I said, looking right at Tanner. "I'm really sorry I said that stuff to your girl. It wasn't my business, and I shouldn't have said anything."

"What the hell, Carter? I mean, who does that?" one of my teammates asked from inside the huddle.

I shrugged before answering, "I don't know. I messed up. It won't happen again. You guys can trust me."

Murmurs broke out, and I wasn't sure who was saying what exactly.

"Apology accepted," Tanner spoke up as he stuck his hand out, and I gripped it hard, giving him a firm shake. "You did me a favor actually," he added with a grin.

"Did I now?" I asked, wondering how on earth I'd done that.

"I was looking for a way to get rid of Beth before I got drafted. Now, I don't have to, so thanks for that." He turned to give someone a high five. "It was still a dick move though. Don't pull that shit again. The next guy might not be so forgiving," he said before clapping me on the back.

I wanted him nowhere near me, but I had to play like I did.

"I won't. Lesson learned," I said, and I meant that part. I would not be getting involved in anyone's love life again, no matter what I knew about it.

Danika sat on my bed, staring at me, and I had no idea what she was thinking, so I said, "The end." I wanted her to know that the story was over.

I sat there, waiting, hoping she'd see my point of view, but the longer she stayed quiet, the more nervous I grew.

"I can see how you'd be confused," she finally spoke, and I felt my entire body relax. I wanted to melt into the comforter on my bed with relief.

"Really?" I asked because it seemed too good to be true that she'd understand or forgive me so easily.

"Really. And just so you know, you did do the right thing. Telling Beth was noble," she said, sounding proud of me, and I hadn't felt proud about that moment one time since it happened. "And your summer coach was a dick. That whole way of thinking is just wrong."

"It made me really confused, to be honest," I admitted because I'd been raised by Cassie Carter. And that woman was all about owning up to your mistakes, being honest, and telling the truth, no matter what. Having it blow back on me in such an extreme way had puzzled me and made me question myself. I also felt like I'd done something really wrong, so I never talked to anyone about it.

"It makes sense. Why you wouldn't know what to do.

Why you took me being gone as a sign not to tell me." She stared at her hands. "But for the record, I always want to know things. Okay?"

"What kinds of things?" I asked for clarification of my own.

"All of it. I don't want you to keep stuff from me. You have to let me in. You have to tell me the truth. You can't keep quiet to protect me or because you think you might get in trouble. Always tell me. No matter what."

I pushed up from my side of the bed and walked over to where she sat. Kneeling in front of her, I reached for her hands and held them, looking deep into her hazel eyes so she knew I meant the words that were coming next. "I'll never lie to you or keep anything from you again. I never meant to hurt you. And I'm so sorry that I did. I didn't know any better, and this is all new to me."

"I know," she said before leaning closer toward me, her lips daring me to claim them, practically begging me to.

Talking is Overrated

Danika

SEEING CHANCE CARTER in front of me, on his knees, was a sight to behold. This guy was something else. And my heart ached for him after I'd heard what he'd gone through last summer. No wonder he'd been so twisted up about telling me or not. Everything that I'd assumed about why he hadn't was wrong. I'd been so far off-base.

"Thank you for telling me all that." I pulled my hand from his and ran it down the side of his face, the stubble on his cheek prickling my fingers but I welcomed it. I'd never been able to touch him like this before. I wanted more of him. Hell, I wanted all of him.

"Danika," he breathed out before grabbing the back of my neck and pulling me to him.

Our lips crashed against each other's, our mouths opening before his tongue found mine, and I swore I moaned, my body radiating with desire. Chance continued kissing me, his fingers splayed at the back of my head, and it felt like I was drowning in lust. The feel of his lips and the taste of his tongue sent me reeling.

"I've wanted this for so long," his breath was hot against me, his tongue swiping across my bottom lip before he nibbled at it, and the room spun.

People talked about chemistry and fireworks and that kind of stuff all the time, but I'd never believed in it before this moment. My skin felt like it was alive, tingling with awareness wherever he touched me. And that kiss … that was the kind of kiss that set rooms on fire; it was so electric.

Pulling away, I palmed his cheeks with my hands, trying to steady my breath as I looked into his green eyes. They were so beautiful, so alive with passion, and it was all for me. That knowledge alone was more than exhilarating.

"I want this. I want you. But I want to clear the air about everything before we cross that line," I said, and he bit down on his lip, his head cocking to one side as he stared at my lips. He was lost in them, as I was in his eyes. "Chance? Did you hear me?" I asked with a grin.

"I heard you," he said before hopping up on the bed and sitting next to me. "Here, let's move back." He scooted to the wall, propping up pillows for us to lean against. "But I have to say something first." He wiped the corners of his mouth. "That was one hell of a first kiss."

"There are no words," I said in agreement, and his solo dimple appeared. "And put that dimple away," I teased, and it only deepened.

"This dimple?" He poked his finger there.

"Yes, that dimple." I leaned toward him and pressed my lips there, my eyes closing with the contact.

"Don't start something you can't finish, Danika," he said

in a whisper, sounding out of control, and I loved the thrill that rushed through me.

"Oh, I can finish it all right," I whispered against his ear before biting it gently and sucking it into my mouth. "And I plan to," I added, and his whole body tensed under my touch. Glancing down, I noticed the bulge coming from his shorts, and I resisted the urge to reach out and wrap my fingers around it.

"You're testing my self-control. I have very little when it comes to you as it is, but you're pushing it right now." His chest rose up and down as his breathing escalated, and I knew that he had seen me looking.

"Maybe I should go get us some water." I started to move, and he reached for my wrist and held me firm.

"Don't you dare leave this bed," he growled, and I knew I'd never been more turned on before in my life. "Whatever we need to talk about, let's get it over with. Quickly."

I broke all contact and scooted away from his heat. I couldn't concentrate with Chance touching me or being that close. I was trying to start our relationship off on the right foot, but he made the idea of talking seem extremely overrated. Who wanted to talk with words when we could be talking with our bodies?

Shaking my head, I tried to focus. "I know you have questions about me and Jared."

His expression soured for a second. "I did an hour ago. Now, I just want to know what you look like naked. The sounds you make when you come. The way your body moves when I'm inside you. And how you taste when I'm eating you."

"Jesus, Chance," I breathed out, resisting the urge to reach down and touch myself at his dirty mouth.

"Sorry. I was not thinking about Jared right now."

His admission broke the trance, reminding me how important it was that we discuss this and get it all out in the open so that nothing lingered between us.

"I know, and I promise this will be the one and only time he's in the bedroom with us," I said before wincing because that sentence was awful. "Where should I start?"

Chance blew out a long, cleansing breath. I could tell he was trying to refocus and calm himself down. He needed the blood to flow from his pants back up to his brain even though I liked it where it was.

He cleared his throat and said, "I guess at the beginning. When did you guys break up?"

"About a week after you and I went to The Bar," I said and watched as Chance looked a little shocked.

"Seriously? That long ago? Why didn't you say anything?"

"I know," I began to explain as I searched for the words. "I just wanted to make sure that the breakup would stick," I said before shaking my head. "No, that doesn't sound right. That isn't what I mean. I just wanted to make sure that I was doing the right thing."

"You could have told me." He looked so disappointed and sad. "All this time, I thought you two were still together. I figured that's why you stayed away from me."

"I know that it might not make sense from your

perspective, but after I ended things with Jared, I needed the time to figure out my heart. I wanted clarification. I couldn't do that if I jumped straight from him to you."

Chance nodded. "That makes sense. I hate it, but it makes sense."

I smiled softly before continuing, "I wanted to tell you. So many times, I wanted to tell you, but then the semester was ending, and I was going home. And I didn't want to start something when I was leaving for New York."

"Danika, I would have started something with you if you were going to the moon. I just want to be with you." Chance's voice was so honest and vulnerable that it took everything in me not to crawl into his lap and kiss him again.

"I want to be with you too," I admitted, and he reached out, his hand gripping one of mine.

"How did Jared take you breaking up with him? He doesn't seem like the kind of guy to just let you go without a fight," he asked like there was something he wasn't saying.

"He was surprisingly okay with it at the time. At least, that's how he acted. Like he had known it was coming. Like he'd half-expected it. I don't know. I'd thought he'd be pissed, but it seemed like he couldn't have cared less," I said, remembering that the biggest fight he'd put up about our breakup was just the other day. "He didn't act that way in New York though."

Chance removed his hand from mine as he sat up a little straighter. "What do you mean?"

"He came to my house, unannounced, and basically said he'd given me enough time."

"Enough time for what?"

"To come to my senses," I said, hopefully sounding as disgusted as Jared's words had made me feel.

"What'd you say?"

"I told him that I still meant what I'd said and that I didn't want to be with him."

"Is that true? You don't have any lingering feelings for him? You guys were together a long time. I'm sure it's not that easy," Chance asked, and I understood why he did. They were the same questions I'd asked myself over and over again.

It had honestly caught me off-guard, the way I felt after the breakup. Part of what had kept me holding on for so long was the fear that I might be making a mistake or that maybe this was just a phase our relationship was going through and it wouldn't always be this way. Jared had been by my side for so many years, and I was used to him being there, felt like I owed him loyalty. What if I ended things and regretted it? That question had haunted me.

"I don't regret breaking up with him. I'd thought I might before I actually did it, but once I did, I felt relieved. I don't want him back. And it's extremely fucked up, but I don't even miss him," I added because it was the truth.

"You're sure?"

"I've never been surer about anything." I wanted Chance to know that there was no competition here and that Jared was not a threat to our future.

The second he had walked out of my apartment, I felt the weight of the world lift off my shoulders. My soul felt free and happy. The earth felt like she had opened all of her doors for me to do and be anything I wanted. I had known then that I'd made the right decision even if it had taken me way too long to make it. Better late than never.

"I can't be a rebound, Danika. Not with you. This can't be something you want to do to get it out of your system, and then you'll go back to him after."

Has he even been listening? I wondered before realizing something. "Are you feeling vulnerable right now?"

"I think so." His eyes narrowed, and his expression shifted.

This was all new to him, and labeling his emotions wasn't something he'd ever had to do before.

"It's kind of sexy."

"It doesn't feel very sexy." He shook his head, disagreeing with me, but he was wrong.

He looked so incredibly hot, sitting there with his heart in his hands, basically asking me not to break it without saying those exact words. I knew I needed to reassure him more, to let him know that I wanted to do this with him and only him.

"You could never be a fling. And this is not a rebound. Jared and I have been over for a long time, and we both knew it."

"Then, why'd you stay?"

"Because it's easy to stay when you're comfortable and it's familiar."

"So then, why'd you break up with him?"

That was the question I'd been waiting for. "There were a lot of reasons. We stopped being good together. We fought all the time. That was all we seemed to do anymore."

"Yeah, I saw some of that."

"But I mostly broke up with him because I couldn't stop thinking about you," I said before adding, "But I didn't tell Jared that part."

I watched as Chance swallowed hard, his throat bobbing with the action. "Well, he obviously knows about me."

"And he assumes you had something to do with it. But I waited. I didn't jump from him to you. I took my time," I said, trying to rationalize my decisions even though I knew I didn't need to.

"You took too damn long," Chance growled, his confidence back. "And I don't care what Jared thinks. Or says. You did the right thing by anyone's standards. And Jesus, Danika, I don't give a fuck. I just want you."

"I want you too."

"It's about damn time," he said before moving quicker than I'd anticipated. His hands were suddenly on my back, pulling me lower on the bed as he hovered over me, his muscles flexing, hair flopping over his green eyes.

"Don't stop," I pleaded because I'd waited too long for this moment, fantasized about what it would be like to touch him and have him touch me. I'd dreamed about it for months, even when I had no business doing it.

"I've wanted you since the first moment I saw you." He leaned down to kiss me, taking my mouth like he owned it. And he did. He always had, even when it didn't belong to him. "But there's no way I can have you once and never have you again."

"What do you mean?" I asked as I licked my lips, hoping to tease him.

"This. Sex. Us," he said, still hovering over me, those broad shoulders just begging to be bit. "I want all of you. And not just for tonight."

"What do you need from me, Chance?" I asked, forcing him to say the words out loud. "Tell me what you need."

"I need us to be together. I need this to be real." He wagged a finger between our two bodies. "I need you to be mine. My girlfriend."

"Then, ask me." I couldn't stop grinning because I wanted this too.

"You want me to ask you?" He leaned back on his heels, taking his gorgeous body away from mine.

"Uh-huh," I all but mumbled around my smile, missing his nearness.

"No," he said, his face serious, and I got nervous. "If we do this, we're together. We're not seeing other people. We're not casually dating. We're not friends with benefits. We're a couple. You're my girl. And I'm your guy. Any questions?"

"Just one," I breathed out, so turned on that I could barely stand it. "Why aren't you inside me yet?"

No More Talking

Chance

"W*HY AREN'T YOU inside me yet?"*

The tone of her voice, all breathless and sexy, lit a fire in my bones and made my dick instantly ten times harder. I'd never wanted anyone the way I wanted Danika. My body craved her. Everything about her called to me and pulled me near. Staying away from her last semester had been a form of torture I never wanted to experience again.

And I knew I'd never have to. She was here, lying on my bed, waiting for me to make her mine. I'd meant what I said. Once we crossed this line, there was no going back. I wasn't the kind of guy to fuck and leave. To be honest, I rarely fucked at all, but that was out of necessity for protecting my future.

I knew firsthand how the wrong girl could really screw that all up. The only way to make sure that there weren't any problems of the female variety was to control who was in and out of my bed. It may it have seemed like a drastic measure to take, but growing up as Jack Carter's son could do that to you.

"God, you're beautiful. You know that?" I said as I leaned down, taking her mouth with mine.

Her lips were as perfect as I'd always dreamed they'd be. She tasted like spearmint and some kind of fruit. I had no idea which, but I couldn't get enough of it as I ran my tongue along her lip before diving inside her mouth. She moaned, and I had to stop myself from coming in my pants.

"I want to feel you," she said around our kiss as she tugged at my shirt. "Take it off," she demanded, and I reached behind my head, grabbed the fabric, and pulled it free. "Oh my God, that was sexy. Put it back on and do that again!" She grabbed for my shirt and threw it back at me.

"Seriously?" I asked through a laugh, and she nodded, her eyes bulging wide.

"Yes. How did you do that? We don't take off our shirts like that. Do. It. Again!" She was so happy that I did as she'd asked. Her jaw dropped. "Always take your shirts off like that. Every time. Okay? Promise me."

"I promise," I said before touching the bottom of her shirt and lifting it slightly, exposing her tanned skin. I pressed my mouth there, licking and nibbling my way across her stomach, as her hips lifted and started gyrating in small circles. "You begging for me without words, baby?" I asked, staring at the lower half of her body, and she stopped moving completely.

"I'm just"—she lifted her head to look at me—"so turned on. I want you inside me."

I shook my head. "Not yet. I've waited too long for this moment to not enjoy it."

"Who says you won't enjoy being in me?" She pretended to be offended, and I stopped myself from grinning.

"I'm going to enjoy every inch of you first. Now, stop talking, Danika. Unless you're screaming my name, I don't want to hear any more words."

"Damn. You're bossy," she said, and I shot her a look before she added, "I like it though."

I liked it too. There was something about feeling strong around an already-strong woman that was an absolute turn-on. It was like she empowered me and added to my strength instead of doing the opposite that so many guys warned about.

Kissing her stomach, I inched my mouth lower at the same time as my hands worked on the button of her jeans. It came undone with a pop, and I moved to the zipper, dragging it down. Her hips wiggled as she tried to help me get her out of them.

Leaning back on my legs, I used both hands to tug and pull the fabric around her hip bones, which were currently my favorite things. They stood out, begging to be noticed, so I leaned forward, kissing each one before going back to her jeans. When I had shoved them down enough, she started kicking, turning them inside out before casting them away. My breath hitched as I took her in. Seeing her almost naked for the first time was overwhelming. I lost all my words.

My hands moved instinctively to her ankles before my fingertips brushed up the length of her calves to her knees. I wanted to touch every inch of her naturally bronzed skin. She was so damn soft, and I was nothing but rough edges and callous hands. I thought I breathed out a curse as I looked at her, but I had no idea what my mouth had said. I ran my hands up her thighs, skimming around the hem of her underwear but not going inside. She sucked in a breath.

"You like that?" I asked, feeling like a damn superhero at how my touch was causing her to react. It only made me want to do it more. I wanted to own her body, her movements, her pleasure.

"I'm not allowed to talk," she said, and I let out a soft huff.

"Who knew you were so obedient?" I teased.

"I can stop," she said, but it wasn't believable. Danika was pliable under my touch, willing to do whatever I asked.

I responded with a resounding, "No," and her eyes rolled back into her head as she closed them, her hips moving to grind against my hand.

I'd never imagined Danika being submissive in any way, but having her like this for our first time in bed was perfect. I guessed a part of me needed her to listen and not fight back for once.

My fingers skated over her panties, across her pussy, and her entire body clenched as the heels of her feet dug into the bed.

"Chance," she breathed out, and I smiled, knowing what she craved.

Lowering my head between her thighs, I licked at the fabric of her panties. The sound that escaped her lips made me want to fuck my own mattress; it was so hot. I kept licking her, panties still in place, knowing that it was driving her as crazy as it was driving me. I knew she was dying for me to slide them over or off, so I could taste the real thing.

I couldn't wait a second longer. Pulling the fabric to one side, her bare pussy exposed, I practically dived in headfirst. My tongue went in, barely touching her flesh, just so I could torment her a little longer. She grabbed for my head and pulled my hair hard.

"Chance. Do it already," she begged.

"Do what?" I asked against her, my breath hot and teasing, my lips talking to hers.

"Eat my pussy. Please."

I had no idea how I hadn't lost it right there in my pants. There was zero chance I'd ever been more turned on in my entire life. My dick was so fucking hard; it throbbed and ached with each beat of my heart.

I started feasting on her. Licking with long, flat strokes of my tongue before fucking her with it. My tongue darted in and out of her hole, making her squirm and buck against me before I eventually replaced it with a finger. Pushing it all the way in, I fucked her with it as I licked her clit, the taste of her driving me wild.

"Oh fuck, Chance. Just like that," she moaned as I finger-fucked her and licked her like I had been born to do it. "Don't stop."

Not a chance, I thought to myself.

"Come for me, baby," I said, hoping she would.

I'd never had a girl come in my mouth before, and I prayed to the pussy-eating gods that I was doing it well enough that she would. If the way she moved was any indication, she liked exactly what I was giving her.

"I'm going to come," she moaned, and I kept doing what I had been doing, too cautious to change a thing and ruin it all.

My hand kept fucking her, harder and faster as I licked her, alternating between flicking and sucking her clit into my mouth. She practically screamed as her hips lifted all the way off the bed, and her fingernails dug into my skull. Her body shuddered as it pressed back onto the mattress, her breaths coming out in rapid but uneven pants.

"Holy shit," she said, her eyes closed, and I wiped at my mouth with the back of my hand.

"That was the hottest thing I've ever seen," I said, hoping she knew how much I meant it.

Watching her come apart, knowing that it was because I was making her feel good, was beyond sexy.

She pushed up onto her elbows and looked down at me, her breaths still erratic. "Oh yeah? Well, that was pretty hot on my end too." Her mouth was still open as she dropped back onto the bed with a thump. "I just need a second," she said, holding one finger in the air.

I chuckled before getting up off of my knees and standing upright. "I'm just going to take these—" I declared, but her body was instantly at mine, her hands grasping for the waist of my jeans.

"That's my job," she said before unbuttoning each one.

My arms fell to the sides and I let her do whatever she wanted to me.

Danika pulled at my jeans, forcing them down my thighs

with a little bit of a struggle. "Damn thick thighs," she cursed, and my hands cupped her cheeks.

She looked up at me, so sweet and innocent.

"You don't like my thighs?" I asked with a grin, stopping myself from laughing.

"Everyone likes your thighs. I think they have their own fan page." She licked her lips before leaning forward and planting a soft kiss on each one.

Hooking my boxer briefs with both hands, she tugged them down next to my feet, and I stepped out of them.

I realized then that I was standing buck naked in front of Danika, her eyes wide as she took me in. I would have felt more vulnerable, if she wasn't currently looking at me like I was a god in a human form. This woman made me feel invincible.

"Talk about being beautiful," she said as her hand reached for my dick and wrapped around it.

"You don't have to." I wanted her to know that she didn't have to do anything she wasn't comfortable with, but it was too late.

Her hot, wet lips wrapped around the head of my cock as her tongue joined in somewhere underneath it. She started sucking, moving her head back and forth, and I needed something to hold on to or else I was going to fall to the floor. Looking around quickly, I realized that there was nothing within reach.

"Danika," I said, wrapping my fingers in her hair to get her to at least slow down. "Oh God, Danika," I moaned again, but she wasn't stopping.

She sucked harder, moved faster, gripped my balls with her hand, and I knew I was about to lose it.

"Stop, baby."

She pulled out with a pop, dropped her hand just as quick, and eyed me with a mixture of fear and curiosity. "Stop? Did I hurt you?"

"No. It felt so good. I was just going to fall if I didn't brace myself on something," I said before pulling her up to her feet.

I pressed my body against hers as we stood face-to-face, my hard dick hitting her, begging to be let in.

"You were going to fall?"

"More like collapse," I said, and she giggled, feeling proud of herself, I guessed. "I'm not sure I'll last very long if you keep doing that anyway. I need to be inside you."

"Yes, please." She tore herself away from my grasp and moved back to the bed, still in her bra and panties.

"You have way too many clothes on," I mentioned, and she nodded in agreement. "Why don't you take them off while I try and find a condom?"

"I'm on the pill," Danika said.

Somehow, I had known that she was. Probably because she'd had a long-term, serious boyfriend before me, but the last thing I wanted to think about right now was some other guy being inside her. Ever.

My mom had raised me to always use protection.

Even though I hadn't needed it since my last girlfriend in high school, the message always stuck in my head.

"*No matter* what," my mom had always warned. "Girls

lie. They can be wrong. And accidents happen."

Regardless of how I felt about Danika, I knew I wasn't ready to be a father.

"Can never be too safe, right?" I said.

I dug around in my nightstand for the pack of condoms I kept in there and prayed they wouldn't be expired or that the guys hadn't used them all. They came into my room sometimes and stole them from me, teasing that I didn't need them anyway, asking why I even had them in the first place.

They weren't wrong, and before right now, I'd honestly never cared that they took them. As I pulled out my drawer as far as it would go, trying to find one, I was immensely thankful that there was at least one left. The last thing I wanted to do was go ask one of my roommates for one and ruin the whole moment. I searched to read the expiration date, and once I realized that we were in the clear, I ripped open the foil and pulled the condom out.

Moving toward the bed, I sat down, rolling it onto my length before turning to face Danika, who was watching me, her eyes hooded and filled with lust. My breath got stuck in my chest. She was completely naked and perfect. And waiting there for me.

Girls, if you ever wonder what guys are thinking about once we finally get to see you with no clothes on, trust me, it isn't whatever imperfections you think you have.

You're naked.

We're excited.

We can't believe you let us see you with no clothes on.

And we want inside you.

Because you're fucking gorgeous. And naked.

I positioned myself over her waiting body and leaned down to take each breast into my mouth, sucking on the nipple and teasing it with my tongue. Danika moaned and pulled at my hair, once again making me feel like a superhero with sex powers. Before I could grab for my dick and take it in my hand, her hand was on me, guiding me home.

She put the head of my dick right at her opening and lifted her hips slightly as I pushed slowly inside. If I moved any faster, I was going to blow it already. The only thing I'd had sex with lately was my hand, and being inside Danika felt nothing like that. Her body wrapped around me, clenching and pulsing as I pressed all the way in as deep as I could go.

"Danika," I breathed against her neck as I moved to kiss her. My tongue entered her mouth, matching the pace of the rest of my body—gradual and precise.

People talked about making love, as opposed to having sex, and I was pretty sure this was what that felt like. Pieces of my body seemed like they were suspended in air while the rest of me was completely connected to her.

"You feel so good." Her eyes rolled in the back of her head.

I kissed her neck again before quickening my pace. Hearing her words had excited me.

"I don't want to come already," I warned, and her eyes popped open, meeting mine and holding before she gripped the back of my head and pulled me to her.

Her lips attacked mine, and her tongue was frantic inside

my mouth, working me up even further. We kissed like that for a minute, all hot and bothered, each one of us frenzied for the other, all the previous slow movements gone. It was like we couldn't get enough of each other.

"You can. Come for me, Chance," she begged, rolling and grinding her hips against my pelvis, and I knew I couldn't hold out much longer.

I moved faster than I wanted to. I was at the point where I no longer had control. My dick wanted the release, and I was going to give in. I pounded into her, and the sounds she made let me know that she liked it, so I kept doing it.

"I'm coming," I said, my eyes closed before rolling in the back of my head as I held my breath.

"Yes. Yes, Chance," she practically sang, her nails digging into my ass as I gave one last thrust and lost myself inside of her.

Stick a Fork in Me

Danika

HOLY SHIT. IF sex with Chance was always going to be that good, I was in for a world of trouble. That was unlike anything I'd ever experienced before, but I didn't want to tell him that and potentially scare him away. Or bring up the fact that other guys had been inside me after just having the best sex of my life so far. I couldn't help but wonder if he felt the connection between us the same way I did.

There had always been something pulling Chance and me to one another, but this was a whole other level. I didn't have the words to explain the way I currently felt in the afterglow. My skin had always prickled whenever Chance was near, but having him touch me and be inside me, my entire being felt like it was vibrating with life.

I lay there on his bed, Chance breathing heavily next to me as he grabbed me and pulled me onto his chest. His heart was racing.

"That was incredible," he said, his voice breathy and exhausted.

"It was," I agreed, and he leaned up, his stomach muscles

tightening with the movement as he strained to look at me.

"Right? It was …" he started to say before pausing. "I don't know what it was, but it was something."

"Yes, it was that."

"I'll be right back. Gotta get this thing off." He motioned toward the condom still covering him.

I had been surprised when I told him I was on the pill and he still insisted on wearing one. I'd just always heard that if you gave a guy a reason not to, they'd take it. But then again, Chance Carter wasn't like other guys.

His head poked out of the bathroom. "You hungry?"

"Starved actually."

"Wanna get a pizza?" he suggested, and my stomach growled.

"Only if you get the right kind," I said playfully even though I was not playing.

Pizza was a serious topic for New Yorkers, and I'd learned that Californians had no idea what they were doing when it came to it. Barbeque sauce? Chicken? Wood-fired crust? No, no, and no.

"I know. Deep dish. Extra-thick crust. Absolutely cannot fold it in half. Eat it with a fork," he said matter-of-factly, and my jaw dropped open.

"You'd better be joking." I narrowed my eyes at him, and he busted up laughing.

"My parents raised me on New York pizza. It's a travesty, trying to find it anywhere else, but I know a place. You'll be impressed."

"You were joking about the deep dish and the fork

though, right?" Until he answered me, I couldn't be sure.

"Yes, babe, that was a joke."

"Couldn't believe I was going to have to break up with you already," I huffed out before adding, "And just after the best sex of my life."

That got him to move all the way out of the bathroom. He was still naked. And good God, naked Chance Carter was a sight to see. His thigh muscles were ridiculous, but his shoulders and arms matched. He was thick in all the right places.

"Did you just say"—he moved back to the bed, his giant body covering mine—"best sex of your life?"

I bit my bottom lip so hard; I thought it might bleed. "Mmhmm."

"Good to know." He dipped down, his tongue sweeping in, and my body wanted him all over again. "Now, get dressed." He gave me one last kiss before moving away and digging in his dresser.

"HOW HAVE I never heard of this place?" I looked around at the small mom-and-pop pizza shop Chance had driven us to.

We were sitting in barstools at a high-top table while families filled the booths around us.

" 'Cause you're not local." He shrugged before squeezing my hand, which he never seemed to let go of. "Kidding. It's because they don't advertise."

"It smells like home in here," I said, breathing in the smell of garlic and baking pizza crust.

"Do you miss it?"

"New York?"

"Yeah."

I spun a little on my chair, wiggling my ass back and forth while I thought about how to answer. "I was just there."

"I know, but maybe you miss it all the time? I think when I leave California, I'll always miss it, no matter where else in the world I am."

"I miss parts of it. But I like it here too. And I really like my new boyfriend," I said with a smile as I studied his green eyes and wished I could read his mind. "I mean," I started to stutter, wondering if I'd labeled us too quickly, even with his pre-sex declaration earlier.

"Don't take it back."

"Take what back?" I pretended to be clueless, but I knew exactly what he meant.

"Calling me your boyfriend." He grinned, and that dimple appeared. "That's what I am."

It was my turn to smile. "Okay, boyfriend. So, would you ever leave California permanently?" This conversation was a little serious, but I felt okay with having it. I assumed that we'd have to talk about our futures at some point.

"I'll go wherever I'm drafted. But honestly, I'd always like to have a place here."

That was my opening to ask baseball-related questions. "How does that work anyway? Like, I understand the draft process, but isn't baseball split up into a bunch of different levels or something like that?"

"Yeah. They're called farm teams. Whoever drafts me has a farm team that I'll go play for. They typically start at what's called Single-A. Then, there's Double-A, Triple-A, and then the major leagues."

"So, you work your way up in order?"

"Chance!" His name was shouted, and we both turned toward the woman behind the counter. "Pizza's ready, dear."

"Be right back." He hopped off his stool, and I swore she winked at him as he grabbed the pizza and brought it to our table, but I couldn't be sure.

He opened the box slowly, where only he could see. It was like he was inspecting it before he opened it wide and presented it to me with a, "Ta-da," and a wave of his hand.

I grinned from ear to ear because it looked just like pizza from back home. But I'd been fooled before, and I knew that just because it looked like home didn't mean that it tasted like it.

"I hope this tastes as good as it looks," I commented before pulling apart a slice and tossing it onto one of the paper plates he'd brought over. "Damn, that's hot." I waved my fingers back and forth as I blew on them at the same time.

"Give it a sec," he instructed before looking at me over the box. "You asked if we went in order after the draft."

"Yeah. Like, do you start at Single-A, then go to Double, and then Triple?"

"Not always. Some guys go straight into Double-A. Or some guys go from Double-A right to the bigs."

"Bigs?" I asked, not knowing what he meant.

"Big leagues. Majors. The show," he said as it dawned on me. Those were all different names for playing in the major leagues.

"Sorry. Yeah. Gotcha. The bigs. But you just go wherever the farm team is?"

"Yep. Wherever they send me, that's where I'll go play."

"And who do you live with?" I never realized how many questions I had about this profession, but once we started talking, they kept popping into my head.

"Sometimes, the teams set up host families that you can stay with. Other times, a bunch of the guys end up sharing an apartment. You get paid to play, but it's not much. My buddy Cole lives with his girlfriend. But he got a signing bonus, so …" he said, like that explained everything.

I watched as he grabbed his slice of pepperoni and folded it in half before taking a big bite. "Chance, I am so turned on right now."

He stopped chewing and looked around, as if debating what to do about the situation he'd created. "Yeah? You like that?"

"You folded the slice in half! Hell yes, I like that."

"That's how you eat it." He shrugged, and I wanted to climb across the table and kiss him square on the mouth.

I grabbed my slice, watching the oil from the cheese drip out as I did the same.

"Oh. This is good." I shouldn't have talked with my mouth full, but it needed to be said. It definitely tasted as good as it looked.

"Told you," he said, taking another bite and practically finishing it off. "What about you?"

"What about me what?" I grabbed a napkin and dabbed at the corners of my mouth.

"You told me once that the plan was to work for your dad after college. But I never asked what you were going to do."

I shrugged, wondering what exactly to say and how. "My dad would love it if I took over the company eventually, but like I told you before, he'd never force me to do it."

"Is that what you want to do? Take over the company?"

It was funny, hearing Chance ask me that question. With Jared, things had been so different. In the beginning we seemed to share a vision, but when my mind started to shift and I talked about other options, Jared always dragged me back on course. He refused to let me change or alter our future plans, regardless of how I felt about them.

"I always thought so," I said without adding the parts about Jared.

"But not anymore?" Chance folded another slice with a smirk before taking a giant bite.

"I don't know." I absolutely wanted to be involved in my dad's company in some capacity, but as far as running the entire empire, I wasn't sure my heart was in it that deep. I saw how hard my dad worked, rarely taking days off and never going on an actual vacation. I had no desire to be owned by my career. I craved that elusive work-life balance everyone yearned for. "I don't want to disappoint my dad, but I'm not sure it's the right move for me."

"How come?"

"Having a career is really important to me. But I don't want my entire life to revolve around work."

"You have that luxury," he said as he swallowed the last bite of his latest slice, and my hackles instantly rose.

"What does that mean?" I asked a little too defensively.

He held up a hand. "Calm down, Little Spitfire. I only meant that it won't be that way for me. I will be whatever baseball needs me to be. I'll go where it tells me to go. And I'll do what it tells me to do. I'll rarely get days off. I'll miss holidays, birthdays, and important dates. And even in the off-season, I'll be working toward the next season. Baseball will own me. And I'll let it."

I wasn't sure exactly why Chance had felt the need to tell me all of those things, but it seemed like some sort of warning. Like he was giving me an out if I thought I couldn't handle all the things he'd just explained.

"When you put it that way, it doesn't sound too fun."

He grinned. "Oh, it's fun. I'll get paid to play baseball, Danika." His grin grew even wider, if that was possible. "You know how many guys want that opportunity? Almost every single one who's ever played at some point. But I'm not under any illusions either. I'm realistic about what it means for my life and the people in it. I will miss important things. I will disappoint people. I will push my body to the brink of exhaustion and whatever else because I love this game and there's nothing else I'd rather do than play it."

"See," I breathed out, completely in awe for the level of passion he had. "I've never loved anything the way you love baseball."

"You will." He winked before grabbing my hand.

"Will I?"

"Yeah. You're gonna love me like that," he said before bringing my knuckles to his lips and pressing a kiss there.

My heart raced. My body melted. I knew that we were still in the honeymoon phase of our relationship, but I found myself wondering … *Is this thing with Chance forever?*

I Have a Girlfriend

Chance

THE NEXT FEW weeks were cake. I'd gone on my first road trip with the team, and it was easier than I'd ever imagined it could be. I wasn't sure why I'd thought there'd be issues between my girl and me, but there were none, and I was extremely thankful for it. The last thing I needed was any kind of drama when I was on the road. Maybe it was because everyone else on the team always seemed to get into fights with their girlfriends during away games, so I'd expected Danika and I would too. That we would have some sort of adjustment period, lack of trust, or something my parents had always half-warned me about. But she was trusting while I was away, and I called her every night from the bed of my hotel room while Mac made fun of us in the background.

Back home, we spent a lot of our nights together but not every single one. I thought it was important that Danika and I were able to be apart, although I had no fucking idea why or what exactly I was trying to prove by enforcing that. So, even though it was usually my idea to sleep alone, I hated whenever we did. Danika was easy to get used to, all curled and tucked up against my body. I missed holding her, kissing her lips, and being inside her.

Sometimes, she defied me and showed up at the house anyway.

"I like sleeping with you," she'd say, knowing I'd never ask her to leave.

But mostly, I went to her place to sleep over. The girls took care of me like I belonged to both of them but not in some sort of creepy, sharing way. Danika would never go for anything like that, and to be honest, I had zero interest in anyone but her. The girls kept me fed, and I liked food.

But whenever I'd been gone for too many nights in a row, Mac would call me, whining, asking when I'd be home and complaining about how I'd let a girl replace him. I always told him that he could come over, too, but he never said yes.

"Just come. The girls cook and bake, and they'd love to take care of you the way they take care of me," I tried to convince him one afternoon.

He shook his head. Whatever thoughts he had inside of it, he kept to himself. "Nah. Can't do that."

" 'Cause you might actually start liking Sunny?" I asked, wondering if my instincts were right or not.

"She's too cute and sweet for her own good," he said.

"How can a girl be too cute and too sweet? She's cool as fuck," I pushed, wondering if I could get him to break.

"Gotta keep my distance *from that one," he said.*

And my suspicions were confirmed. He was purposefully staying away from her. Ever since his ex-girlfriend had dumped him, he'd never been the same, and he never wanted to talk about it.

My eyes opened as my phone alarm blared, and I reached over Danika's sleeping, naked body to grab it and shut it up. She moved her hips against my hard dick, and I wasn't sure if she had done it on purpose or subconsciously. Her dark hair was splayed out across her pillow, and I moved it in order to touch her neck with my lips. I started softly kissing her, and she giggled, tucking her chin into her chest.

"So, you are awake?" I whispered against her as her naked hip-grinding continued.

"I mean"—she tilted her head in my direction—"your alarm did go off." Her hand suddenly cupped my dick, surprising me before she started moving it up and down.

"Danika," I growled. The way she held me felt amazing.

"Mmhmm?" she asked, her hand job continuing.

I threw my head back in pleasure and blew out a long breath. "If you don't stop," I warned, "you'll be sorry."

"Will I?"

"I'll come all over your hand instead of inside you, where I belong."

Her hand stopped moving just as quickly as it had started. "Can't have that," she said before I heard the sound of her nightstand drawer opening. She tossed me a condom. "Here you go, Hotshot."

"I should make you put this on me," I teased, and her

eyes widened.

“You wouldn’t dare. Not after last time.” She sounded so mortified, and I couldn’t help but laugh.

Danika had mentioned wanting to see what it was like to put one on me, but it kept getting stuck or wouldn’t unroll, and then she ripped it with her fingernail. Everything that could have gone wrong did. It was hilarious, but my girl didn’t agree.

I carefully rolled the condom down my length, taking my time as she watched, shifting over onto her back. I had never had an issue with condoms before, but I was tempted to stop wearing one with her. I wanted nothing between us, not even a thin layer, but I never gave in to the temptation, and she never asked me to.

“Ready?” I placed the tip of my covered dick at her entrance, wondering how different it might feel without the condom.

Her hazel eyes closed as she answered, “Yes,” before lifting her hips up, and I pushed inside, feeling her warmth and tightness surround me, even through the condom I wore.

I didn’t last nearly as long as I’d wanted to, but morning sex always seemed to go that way. I woke up hard, needed to pee, and lasted about three whole minutes before I came.

“I’ll make it up to you later.” I kissed her lush lips as she squirmed under me.

“Chance”—she rolled her eyes because we’d had this conversation before—“you know I don’t care,” she said, and I honestly believed that she didn’t.

“But I do.” I kissed her one last time before hopping out

of bed to flush the condom and get dressed for class.

She whistled as I walked away from her, completely naked, and made some comment about my ass that I couldn't quite hear. Turning around, I gave her a wink and a head nod before shutting the bathroom door. Some things needed to be private. Like pissing.

When I walked out again, she was already out of bed and dressed. In all black, of course.

"Do you own anything white?" I teased, knowing exactly how many pieces of white clothing she owned.

One of the first things I'd done when I came over was go through her closet and look at her clothes like a psycho. She had them sorted in an order that only seemed to make sense to her. Something about sleeve length, she had mentioned, and all I knew was that in a sea of black, there were about twelve tops in other colors. Three of them were white. But she never wore them.

"I do, but I'm about to set them on fire, so I don't," she said, sticking out her tongue.

I grabbed her, claiming that tongue as my own. "You've got a sassy mouth."

"Guess that's why my boyfriend calls me Spitfire," she bit back, and I shook my head. The girl had a comeback for everything.

I watched as she opened her bedroom door and waited for me to join her.

We stepped into the short hallway, and Sunny was already up, making coffee.

"Morning," she said with her signature grin.

"Is she ever not smiley?" I nudged Danika's shoulder.

"I can hear you," Sunny said, and it reminded me so much of my little sister that all I wanted to do was tease her more. "And since when is it a crime to be happy? Huh?" She cast me a fake glare.

"She reminds me of Jacey," Danika said, and I smiled.

"That's exactly what I was just thinking."

"Jacey? Your fifteen-year-old sister?" Sunny said, sounding almost offended.

"Yeah, but she's cool," Danika defended, and I groaned. "Is she coming to the game today?"

"I have no idea," I said because my sister used to come to every single game of mine, but lately, she'd seemed to stop, and my mom had let her. "Maybe if she knows you'll be there, she'll come?"

"She knows we're together, right?" Danika leaned against the counter as Sunny handed her a mug.

"I assume so. I mean, my parents know, so I'm sure they either told her or she overheard it with her supersonic ears."

"I'm gonna text her."

I shot Danika a look. "You have her number?"

"I'll get it from your mom," she responded, and my look only intensified.

"You have my mom's phone number?"

"Yep," was all she said.

She didn't elaborate, tell me when they had exchanged numbers, or add any more information other than her answer. My girlfriend had my mom's phone number. That was normal, right?

I glanced at my cell phone. "Shit. I gotta go. You'll both be at the game?" I asked even though I didn't need to.

Of course they would be there. But I liked asking anyway. I never wanted to assume that Danika's life revolved around my schedule, no matter how much I wanted it to.

"Of course," Danika said with a smile before sending me off with a kiss and a smack on my ass that made Sunny howl with laughter.

WALKING ACROSS CAMPUS, I heard Mac shouting my name, and I gave him a nod even though I had no idea if he could see it from where he was or not.

"Baseball Boy."

The words hit my ears, causing my feet to stop moving.

I turned to my right and faced Jared, a slew of his fraternity brothers lagging behind in the distance. I had known in the beginning of my and Danika's relationship that it would only be a matter of time before I ran into him. But seeing him now, all these weeks later, caught me a little off guard. I guessed, somewhere along the way, I'd started assuming that I'd never see him at all or that he wouldn't talk to me if he happened to spot me on campus.

I'd been wrong.

"You do know you're just temporary, right?" His voice was arrogant, confident, and annoying.

"What are you piping off about?" I tried to sound unfazed, but something about the guy always seemed to get to me.

Maybe it was because he had history that I could never compete with, and for whatever reason, it made me feel like I'd never know Danika the way that he did. And I really fucking hated even thinking that because I wanted all of her, in every way, and it felt like parts of her would forever belong to him.

"It's always been me and her. Once the two of us go back to New York and you get drafted and you're wherever the hell you are"—he waved his hand in the air as if dismissing me—"we're going to get back together. You're not in this picture, Baseball Boy. And we both know it."

"You're the only one who sees it that way," I said with confidence even though I considered how much of what he'd said could be true.

He'd sounded so sure of himself, so resolute in his thought process, that it immediately filled my head with doubts.

"Am I?"

"Danika's no longer your concern," I said, throwing his words from last semester back at him.

He laughed. It sounded fucking sinister, and it made me bristle, wondering if he knew something I didn't.

His frat brothers had almost gotten to us, and Jared took a single step closer to me before throwing the final verbal dagger. "You'll ruin her life."

I scoffed before giving him a look, indicating that I was

growing bored. "And how will I do that?"

"You'll let her follow you around the country, chasing your dreams instead of hers," he said point-blank, and I felt the lump form in my throat. "You'll take away everything she's ever worked for. Everything her dad has built for her. You'll let her throw it all away for you. And that's the very definition of selfish."

"Let me get this straight." I scratched the back of my head. "Now, you're concerned for Danika's well-being? It wasn't that long ago when you basically told me you wanted what her dad had built, and that's why you were with her in the first place. Money."

"Hey," he growled, moving to poke a finger at my chest, and I glared at it, basically fucking daring him to touch me. He put his hand down instead. "I put in the work. For years, I've stayed by her side and picked up the pieces every time she fell apart. I deserve to get something for all of that. I deserve a place in that company. I've earned it."

"You're such an asshole." I'd never met anyone who was this motivated by money. I'd thought it was something that only happened in ridiculous movie plots.

"I might be an asshole, but you're the one who's going to break her heart," he said right as his buddies caught up to us, all of them posturing and puffing up their chests like they were prepared to take me on. "And when that happens, I'll be there for her, like always. It will be me by her side, running half of Manhattan, like it was supposed to be. And we'll forget you ever existed."

"Sounds like you have it all worked out then," I offered

with a nod.

"It's only a matter of time. You can't see it clearly, but I can," he sneered before looking at his bros for approval and then down at some fancy watch on his wrist. "You get drafted in what, a few months? I can wait it out until then."

"Good luck with that," I said before walking away.

I was done. But Jared obviously wasn't. He shouted something at my back, but I was too in my own head to make it out clearly. I had to get away from him. I couldn't handle hearing another word come out of his mouth about Danika or her future or my lack of a place in it.

"Sorry it took me so long. I didn't come over until I saw all his frat dickheads show up." Mac suddenly appeared next to me. "What the hell was that about?"

I'd forgotten that he had been waiting for me.

"Nothing." I tried to blow him off. I didn't want to talk to Mac about it. I didn't even want to think about it for one second longer, but I was rattled.

Fucking. Rattled.

I couldn't get Jared's toxic words out of my head or the one question that kept repeating itself in my mind.

Is he right?

IT WAS HOT as hell out already, and my catcher's gear made it five times hotter. The second I stepped out of the locker room and onto the field, I knew I was fucked. My mind was still filled with all the things Jared had said. I spent the rest of the afternoon overthinking my relationship with Danika, worried to death that I was ruining her life by wanting her to be with me. *How selfish was I?*

No matter what I did, I couldn't clear my mind. And that was bad business for any ball player. Baseball was a mental sport, and if you fucked with your ability to get your head on straight, you might as well sit it out. The worst part was that every other player on the opposing team knew it too. Being rattled on the ball field was like wearing a giant neon sign that read, *FUCK WITH ME*.

I was having my worst game in years. I'd made two throwing errors from home plate on guys who tried to steal on me. Normally, they knew better. Running against my arm was a test that most guys failed, much to their coach's ire. Was the runner on base faster than the ball? The answer to that question was usually a resounding no. But not today.

Today, the answer was maybe. I'd basically invited them to take their chances on me. And twice, I'd overthrown the ball to third base, allowing runners to score and almost tie the game.

My dad walked up to me after the inning and pulled me aside. "What's the matter with you?"

"Nothing. I'm just in my head," I said, shaking it back and forth, like that might make the words Jared had planted there spill out of my ears instead of taking root.

"I can see that. Get out of it," he said, like it was that easy. Like he'd never been in this position before.

We all had bad games. Even the great Jack Carter.

"I'm trying," I ground out.

He was pissing me off. No one wanted to stay in their head on the field, and he damn well knew it.

"You're making it worse."

"Well, you're not making it any better."

"Is it Danika?" he said, and the mere mention of her name made my stomach twist.

"I can't talk about this right now, Dad."

We couldn't get into a discussion about a girl in the middle of a game. That was unacceptable, and we both knew it.

"Yeah, well, I'm here if you need me," he said before adding, "After the game. Try to pull it together." He slapped my shoulder before jogging away.

Great pep talk, I thought to myself as I reached for my helmet and bat.

My next at bat, I struck out at the plate, looking. I'd watched the last strike sail right down the pipe and didn't even attempt to swing. It was my third strike out of the game.

Coach Jackson swore, his disappointment in me obvious for everyone to see and hear. "Carter," he said through clenched teeth as I stalked toward the dugout.

"Coach," I said, sounding as dejected as I felt.

"Sit it out."

"What?"

"You heard me."

He was pulling me from the game. In the seventh inning while we were down by one run.

I never got pulled.

I never sat out a game.

Guessed there was a first time for everything.

I resisted the urge to throw shit, specifically my helmet, as I moved down the length of the bench in the dugout to sit alone and sulk. This was my own fault, and I had no one else to blame but myself. My sheer inability to get out of my head and be the leader I was expected to be on the field was baffling. I'd never struggled with focusing my mind before. But then again, I'd never had a girlfriend in my college career before. Compartmentalizing wasn't as easy as I'd always thought it should be. I had harshly judged my teammates in the past, wondering why they couldn't seem to put their love life on the shelf for nine fucking innings and focus on the game. Now, I actually understood.

Leaning forward, I glanced in the stands before leaning back just as quick. *Fuck.*

Not only were Danika, Sunny, and my mom here, but so were Uncle Dean and Aunt Melissa. Uncle Dean must have been dying inside, watching me play so shitty. He was my unofficial sports agent until I was legally allowed to sign with him. I wondered how frustrated he was and if he'd have to do any kind of damage control after I played a game like this. I knew I was being a bit dramatic, but there were aspects of the baseball business that I didn't know yet. Maybe one bad game was all it took to make scouts doubt a player and lose interest.

To make matters worse, Gran and Gramps were here, too, watching this travesty. They rarely came to my games anymore, which I understood and was perfectly okay with. The stadium seats were far too uncomfortable for them to sit in for three hours straight, and the weather was usually either too hot or too cold. Plus, they didn't drive much on their own anymore, complaining that people were always in too much of a rush and that their eyesight wasn't what it used to be. Uncle Dean must have picked them up and brought them.

The only saving grace was that my sister and cousins didn't seem to be around. It was bad enough to play this kind of game in front of everyone I cared about, but having it in front of three annoying teenage girls who would never shut up about it after would have been even more of a nightmare for me.

I leaned forward again, catching a glimpse of Danika and my mom laughing at something. The sight of them together should have made me happy, and it would have before this morning, but right now, it only made me confused.

When I looked at Danika, I didn't see an end date to our relationship. I saw a future. A future that I wanted her to be a part of. Did wanting that make me selfish, like Jared had said? Because if Danika chose to be with me, that meant she was choosing this crazy baseball lifestyle too. A world where everything could change in the span of a single day and anything could happen. She would never have a predictable, stable, normal life, like most other people.

That just wasn't how being a professional athlete worked. And I'd had years to adjust to the idea of what playing baseball professionally meant for me as a person and future husband and father. Danika had no clue, not really. Having her own career would be a struggle, and after the other night, I knew that she wanted one. She wasn't the kind of girl to be satisfied with following me around the country. She needed something of her own.

I had no idea how to give that to her and still keep her. I wondered if it was even possible at all.

Not Himself

Danika

I WAS SURROUNDED by Chance's family, and I couldn't have been happier even though Chance was having what appeared to be a pretty bad game.

When I'd shown up today, I'd had no idea that I'd be meeting his aunt Melissa and uncle Dean or his grandparents—Gran and Gramps, as they'd insisted I call them. They were all so welcoming and kind. I wondered briefly if Chance knew how lucky he was to have so many people care about him before thinking that he most likely did. Chance wasn't the type of guy who took things for granted.

Being surrounded by all this Carter love reminded me of growing up in New York with all my friends' families. My own extended family had been spread out for most of my life. My mom's parents lived in France, and I had rarely seen them as a kid and hadn't seen them since the funeral. And my dad's parents lived in Italy on some sprawling estate that grew grapes for wine. They used to visit a few times a year but never since my two aunts, my dad's sisters, had moved there to help them oversee operations. I wasn't sure if they ever planned on coming back to the States or not.

I'd basically grown up being the only Italian girl from the city with no siblings and only her mom and dad. Everyone else seemed to have generations of family living within a three-block radius, who got together every Sunday for barbeques and homemade dinners. I used to feel sort of left out, like I was missing something, until my friends started including me in their family rituals.

"I've never seen Chance play so bad before," Cassie whispered before eyeing me. "Did you two have a fight?"

"What? No. I mean, not that I know of." I laughed uncomfortably.

"They don't fight, Mrs. Carter," Sunny interjected, and I gave her a look before she snapped her lips shut and pressed them together dramatically.

"I'm just teasing, but he's definitely not himself. Something has him unfocused."

"You can tell that just by watching him?" I asked, fascinated.

"Oh, absolutely. You will, too, eventually." She smiled, and I hoped she was right. I wanted to know that Chance was *off* just by looking at him.

"Any idea what's gotten into him?" his uncle leaned forward and asked.

Both Cassie and I shook our heads.

"Weird," he said before typing out furiously on his phone.

I hated how concerned everyone sounded. I started wondering if I was the reason Chance was so unlike himself.

Did I do something and not realize it? I had no idea what was wrong, but something clearly was.

"What was it like, dating *the* Jack Carter when you guys were here?" Sunny asked with a giant grin, and I practically groaned, a little embarrassed.

Cassie looked over her shoulder at Melissa. "How do I even answer that question?" she asked before Melissa shook her head.

"I'll answer it," Melissa said before Cassie shushed her.

"Jack was a piece of work. He was a mess," she said before looking at Gran and Gramps and apologizing.

"Oh, honey, you know that I'm well aware of what a mess he was," Gran said.

Cassie continued, "I was a mess too. We were two immature and hurt people. We took our pain out on each other. But we also saved each other."

"They mostly saved each other," Melissa said before adding, "Of course, that was after putting each other and everyone who ever cared about them through hell."

"She's one to talk." Cassie thumbed toward her. "Remind me to tell you the nightmare story of how those two finally got together."

"Hey, it's not a nightmare story." Melissa mocked offense, and we all laughed. "Fine. I was a little bit of a nightmare."

"But you're my nightmare." Dean wrapped an arm around his wife and kissed the side of her head. "I honestly wouldn't change a moment of our story."

"You wouldn't?" Melissa asked, like this was the first

time he'd ever said something like that to her before.

"Nope. I think it worked out all right in the end. Don't you?" He grinned, clearly still head over heels for his wife, and she leaned over to kiss him.

If this was how all the Carter men loved their women, I wanted to keep mine. I used to think that finding a love like my parents had was a fantasy, but now, looking around at this family, I knew it could be real. It was rare but still possible.

"Chance just got pulled." Cassie's green eyes tugged together as she watched her son walk into the dugout.

I'd never seen him look so angry before.

"What does that mean?" I asked.

"That he's not playing for the rest of the game."

"Do they do that sometimes? Considering it's really hot out, and he's got all that gear on." I hoped that I sounded reasonable, but I ended up just sounding stupid and uninformed instead.

"Not usually. Unless they're ahead by a lot," Cassie said.

I glanced at the scoreboard even though I already knew the score. We were still down by one run.

"So, this isn't normal then?"

"This is definitely anything but normal."

The mood instantly shifted once the family realized that Chance was out for the rest of the game. Uncle Dean suggested that Gran and Gramps go home and get out of the heat, and they agreed.

"Tell my grandson I was here," Gramps said, his voice gruff and husky.

"I will. I'm sure he already knows," Cassie reassured him before giving him a giant hug.

"Make sure my grandson brings you over for dinner," Gran said to me before leaving.

"Aw, I will. Thank you." I smiled, and just like that, our group shrank from seven to three.

The rest of the game sucked because Chance wasn't in it. I didn't care what the team did if I couldn't watch him play. I found myself bored and uninterested. Thankfully, I wasn't the only one. Cassie felt the exact same way.

"I always lose interest in the game if Chance is out of it. That's shitty, I know. But it's the truth."

The game finally ended, and Sunny headed for home, leaving me and Cassie alone to wait for Chance. Looking around, I kept shifting my weight from foot to foot.

"Are you nervous?" Cassie asked, and I realized that I was.

"I think I am. Is that dumb?"

"No. I was a wreck anytime after Jack had a bad game. I never knew what kind of mood he'd be in."

"How'd you handle it?"

"With a lot of patience." She laughed. "And yelling."

"Yelling?"

"Sometimes, I didn't want to be understanding. Just because he had a bad game, that didn't mean I wanted to be his emotional punching bag, you know? So, sometimes, I yelled at him. But he liked it," she said, rolling her eyes.

Her response made me even more nervous.

"Do you think Chance will be mean?"

"No," she attempted to reassure me. "But he might be quiet. And if he is, it's not personal, I promise. Just give him a little time to process the game. He'll come out of his head and be normal again."

I swallowed hard. "Okay. Time to process. I can do that."

"Dating an athlete is a different beast than dating a normal guy, isn't it?"

"There are so many more things to think about. Like, it isn't just about you and him. It's about you, him, and—"

"Baseball," we both said at the same time.

"Here he comes."

I looked up, watching Chance head toward us, his dad next to him.

"Hey." He leaned down and gave me a quick peck before hugging his mom. "Where'd everyone go?"

"It was too hot for Gran and Gramps to stay if you weren't playing, so Uncle Dean took them home early," Cassie explained, and Chance nodded.

"Was Uncle pissed?" he asked.

"At what?"

"The way I played?"

"Of course not. He was just wondering what was wrong. I'm sure he'll call you later," Cassie said.

"Okay. You ready?" He turned to me, and I smiled, but he didn't return it.

My nerves reappeared as we said good-bye to his parents and headed toward the parking lot, our hands at our sides and not on each other.

He opened the passenger door for me and helped me

inside the Beast, but his eyes never met mine. I wasn't sure if something was wrong or if this was how he acted after having a bad game. I had no idea what to do or say, so I stayed quiet, letting him take the lead. I wished I had asked his mom for more advice on how to handle an athlete's mental state.

Because this was awful.

Chance stayed as muted as I was being, and the silence was so loud, it hurt my ears.

"Chance?" I finally said as we neared my apartment complex. "This is all new to me," I started to explain.

"What is?"

"Learning how to deal with your state of mind after a game." I wanted to be careful with my words. "So, I don't know if this is normal or if there's something else going on."

He seemed almost uncomfortable. "I don't usually play like that," he said, his voice quiet but strong.

"I know. Your mom said the same thing. So did your uncle. They were all asking me what had happened," I said as he pulled to a stop in a visitor parking spot and cut off the engine.

He blew out a quick breath. "What'd you say?"

"That I didn't know. Did something happen?" I took off my seat belt and angled my body toward him.

He looked at me and hesitated, like there was something he wanted to tell me but wasn't sure if he should. "Your ex got in my head."

"My ex?" *Jared did this?* "When?" That was the last thing I'd expected to hear Chance say. I'd had no idea that he'd even seen Jared or that they'd had words.

"This morning." His response was clipped, and I wanted every single detail that he was choosing to leave out.

I realized that I was going to have to pull the information out of him by asking all the right questions. "What did he say?"

Chance swallowed, his eyes looking over my shoulder before landing back to mine. "He said that if we stayed together, I'd ruin your life."

"What?" That was the only word I managed to muster as my anger soared. How the hell Jared thought he had any right to interfere in my relationship was beyond me. "That's ridiculous. He's just mad that I broke up with him. He's even madder that we're together. Chance, he'd say anything to get inside your head. And look, it worked." I was shocked. I'd never thought that Jared could say something that Chance would take seriously or listen to without talking to me about it first.

"But is he right?"

"What do you mean, is he right? How would you ruin my life? You're the best thing to ever happen to me. I've never been this happy before." My emotions came spilling out. I meant every word, but this wasn't how I wanted to tell him all of those things, in the middle of a disagreement filled with miscommunication and hurt feelings.

"He said that you'd throw away all your future plans to chase mine."

I reared my head back like I'd been slapped. "And how does he know that?" I was getting more and more pissed off by the second.

I really hated it when people made assumptions and decisions for me without asking. If Chance wanted to know what exactly I'd do for him and his dreams, he could have asked me.

"How does he know that, Chance? Did he ever ask me? Have you?"

His green eyes flashed with pain as he winced so slightly that anyone else would have missed it. But I didn't. "He made some good points. You're supposed to work for your dad, and I'm hopefully still getting drafted. Our lives are headed in two very different directions. How are we going to make that work?"

The way he'd asked the last question made my anger evaporate as fear and insecurity took its place. I knew exactly what he was doing.

"What are you saying?"

Chance fucking Carter was trying to break up with me.

And I was not having any of it. Not now. Not ever.

Stubborn Little Spitfire

Chance

"JUST SAY IT," Danika pushed from the passenger seat.

She knew. She knew exactly what I was trying to do, but I was too afraid to admit it. Once I said the words out loud, I could never take them back. I'd never been in this position before—having a girlfriend I was in love with and didn't want to lose but wouldn't dream of taking anything away from her.

"I don't want you to throw away your dreams for mine."

"You already said that," she snapped.

Oh, she was pissed, and it caught me off guard. I honestly hadn't expected her to put up a fight.

"I just don't see any other way. I'm going to keep falling for you, and I'm going to want you with me twenty-four/seven, Danika. I'll have to move, and I'll want you to come with me. I can't ask you to give up your career and follow me around the country. And I also can't live long distance forever. Take your emotions out of it, and you'll see that what I'm saying is true."

"I'm a girl. I can't do that. I'm built on emotions." She

sounded so defeated, and I hated that I was the reason for it.

"But you know I'm right."

"No," she said, still being stubborn as her eyes met mine and held, like she was begging me to challenge her.

I swallowed, carefully measuring my next words. "My career doesn't really breed partnership. It breeds sacrifice … from you."

She exhaled long and loud. "Why do we have to figure this all out right now?"

"Because every day that you're a part of my life, I'm finding it really damn hard to see the rest of it without you in it."

"That's usually a good thing." Her hand reached for mine, and she intertwined our fingers.

I knew that, yes, finding your forever person was typically a positive, but this didn't feel like that. This felt selfish on my end. And I didn't want to be that for her.

"Chance," she said quietly, and I looked at her, my heart aching inside my chest, "I know that having a relationship with someone in your situation is possible. People do it all the time."

I nodded in agreement. "They do. But the girls don't usually have their own careers," I said before thinking about Cole and Christina. Christina seemed like an exception, running her own social media management company that could be done from anywhere. "I mean, mostly, they do charitable work with the team and social media influencing, but you have a family business to think of. A business that's only in New York. It's a little different."

"Well, how did your parents do it? Your mom had a successful career of her own."

I'd known that was coming. That she would bring up my parents and the fact that they were still together and in love and my mom had done well for herself.

"Yeah, but she freelanced and called her own shots. And when she did work for someone else, she gave it up because being with my dad was more important to her than being away from him all the time."

She sucked in a breath. "I didn't know that. I'd just assumed they'd made it work."

"They did. But it took a lot to get there. My mom fought for her independence. And then she gave it up. But she got it back again after my dad retired. Their relationship was a lot of give and take, but it was scheduled around my dad's career. You get what I'm saying?" I was trying to let her know that baseball always came first, and there was really no way around that without quitting the game.

Danika closed her eyes and rubbed them. "Look, I know you're trying to break up with me right now. But I'm not going to let you," she said with some kind of mustered confidence, and I couldn't help but laugh.

"You're not going to let me?"

"No. And I'm not getting out of this car until we've worked this out." She folded her arms across her chest to amplify her stubbornness.

"What do you suggest? How the hell do we 'work this out'?" I asked, using finger quotes around the last part.

She stayed quiet, and I assumed she was thinking. I really

didn't know what to do. I'd thought that letting her go was doing the right thing by her, but now, I wasn't so sure.

Did I jump to conclusions and decide too fast, all because of what Jared said to me?

No, I knew it wasn't only because of him and his words. My mom had raised me to respect the fact that the girl in my life would want independence and something to call her own. She'd told me that I couldn't expect anyone to support my dreams if I wasn't willing to support theirs in return. And that true partnership was built on mutual respect and communication.

"What are you thinking about?" she asked, breaking my inner monologue.

"I was just convincing myself that this was the right thing to do."

"Which part?"

I gave her a soft smile. "The part where we deal with this now instead of putting it off until later when it would be a million times harder to try and figure out."

"Yeah. I hate that you're right, but here's what I'm thinking." Her voice settled and grew steady, and I knew she was moving out of an emotional state of mind and into a more logical one. "I can't make any decisions about this without all the facts. But the one thing I will say is that you don't get to decide for me. Do you hear me?" She reached across the truck and poked me in the shoulder. "You don't get to choose what I do with my life. It's not only up to you, and it's not fair."

I pulled my eyes together, noticing the way that she

looked at me, so serious and determined. Damn, she was beautiful. And smart. I wanted to take it all back, pull her from the passenger seat and onto my lap, where she belonged, and kiss her until she saw stars.

Nodding, I apologized because she was right. In trying to do the right thing, I had taken her choice from her, figuring that I knew what was best.

"So … first question," she started. "Do you even want to be with me? I mean, do you want this to work, or are you just looking for a way out?"

Jesus. She thinks I don't want to be with her?

I scoffed, practically choking on the air around me, "I want you so damn much that I can't bear the thought of doing anything to hurt you. Thinking about you resenting me somewhere down the line because of my job fucking kills me. I want you. But I don't want you to give up everything in order to be with me."

Her eyes started to well up, and I watched as she sucked in a breath and looked away, trying to regain her composure.

"Good answer," she turned to face me, her voice cracking as a single tear fell.

"Don't cry." I wiped away the lone tear from her cheek, and she closed her eyes the second my hand touched her skin.

"I'm not." She breathed in and out a few more times, her eyes still closed, and I wondered what kind of pep talk she was giving herself and not sharing with me. "I don't want us to end," she admitted before adjusting her position and scooting up straighter, her long, dark hair spilling all around her shoulders.

"I don't either."

"It shouldn't be this hard to stay together."

"I know," I agreed because it seemed really fucking unfair. Instead of focusing on that, I nudged her back on topic. "You said you wanted all the facts before you decided. So, what do you want to know?"

"Everything." She shrugged.

I nodded and let out a short chuckle. "Okay. It might be easier if you asked questions."

"I'm not really sure what to ask. I mean, you're the one who's so convinced we can't stay together. Why don't you tell me why?"

Damn. She'd put me on the spot, and I deserved it.

"It's like I said that one night at dinner. My entire life will revolve around the game. We basically play nine months out of the year. Longer, if we make it into the playoffs. And pitchers and catchers report before everyone else for spring training. Baseball will be my priority. It'll be my job. I'll have three to four days off a month. A month, Danika. And sometimes, we'll spend that day traveling, so it's not really a day off at all."

Her mouth had fallen open by this point, and she looked at me like everything I had said sounded crazy. "When does the season start?"

"For me, in February."

"Right, 'cause you're a catcher. And you report first," she said, repeating facts back to me and storing them in her head for later, I assumed. "And when does it end?"

"October, depending on playoffs."

I watched as she counted the months on her fingers, stopping at nine, just like I'd said. "What happens between October and February? You have all those months off to do whatever you want?"

"Technically, yes. It's called the off-season. But I still have to stay in shape and work out and hit during that time. My head will still be in baseball mode even though I'm not playing."

She swallowed. "But you can go on vacation during those months? And you would be around for Thanksgiving and Christmas?"

"Vacations, yes. And I would be around for those holidays. New Year's too. But that's it. I'd miss the rest. Your birthday. Our anniversary. Any celebrations with friends."

"And what about when you travel during the season? How many games are away?"

"Anywhere from ten to seventeen usually."

"So, almost half the month." She sounded sad, and it killed me. But she needed to know the reality of what I was signing up for.

"Yeah."

"What else?" she said point-blank. "What else is there? Groupies? Girls hitting on you?"

"Always. But you'd never have to worry about that," I tried to reassure her, knowing that I was not the kind of guy to fuck around, and that wasn't changing anytime soon.

I'd learned a lot from my parents' relationship, and that was one thing I never wanted to go through. They had told me how devastating it was, from both of their perspectives, and it had always stuck with me.

She smiled, and it lit up the whole fucking truck. "I don't even worry about that now, and I probably should."

I reached out and touched her hand. "No, you shouldn't. After everything my parents went through, I'd never put you through that."

Her face pulled together in confusion. "Your dad cheated on your mom?"

I nodded. "It's a long story."

"I would have never guessed that. Not ever. They're so in love."

"I know. They recovered nicely," I said with a grin.

"They did. Okay, so one, you'll never be home." She put up a single finger before adding another. "Two, you'll miss a bunch of shit. And three, girls will hit on you constantly. What else am I missing?"

"This is serious, Danika. You can list things off like they're not a big deal, but when it's your life every single day, it's not the same. Shit gets old. Your life will revolve around my schedule. You'll get sick of it. Me always being gone. And if I have a bad game or I'm in a hitting slump, I might be a dick to you. I won't mean to be, but my performance on the field will affect everything else. And if I get traded, I'll have to leave immediately. There are no guarantees or stability. My life will not be my own. And yours wouldn't be either." I hadn't meant to raise my voice, but it was essential that Danika understood the magnitude of what I was telling her.

Being with a professional athlete definitely had its perks, but it still wasn't easy. My mom had always reminded me, growing up, that it took a certain kind of girl to handle that lifestyle. Danika could, I knew that, but that didn't mean she wanted to.

She brushed her hair behind her ear and pulled on the lobe.

"It's a lot to take in," she finally admitted, and I was both relieved and irritated.

She was giving me exactly what I'd pushed her for—understanding. But now that I'd dumped all the facts into her lap, I realized that I wanted to hear her say that they didn't matter, that nothing mattered more than us figuring it out and being together. I was being a complete fucking hypocrite, and I knew it. But knowing that still didn't change the way I felt.

"It is. I know. You should take some time to think about if it's what you want or not," I told her even though I hated thinking about giving her up.

Each time my instincts to fight for her flared to life, I tamped them down, reminding myself that having her hate me somewhere down the road wouldn't be worth it. If she chose me and chose us, it had to be her decision, and she had to be okay, knowing all that she'd be giving up for it. I was basically asking her to choose this lifestyle or walk away from us altogether.

"For someone who's never had a girlfriend before, you're pretty good at being a boyfriend."

I coughed and slapped my chest. "I didn't say I'd never

had a girlfriend before." Her head reared back in surprise, and I answered before she could ask, "It was in high school. I haven't had one since."

"Oh. Yeah, of course. Anyway …" She waved it off like we didn't need to even discuss that again. "I need you to know that I do want to be with you, but you've given me a lot to think about and consider. I think taking some time to figure it all out would be best," she said, and I felt my heart deflate inside my chest like a balloon losing its air.

"No matter what you decide, I'll understand," I said even though I wanted to fucking puke after saying the words.

Thinking about my life without her now that I had her in it felt impossible. How that shit worked, I'd never understand. I'd been perfectly fine without Danika for years, never feeling incomplete or like I was missing any part of me. But after having her, all that had changed. If she left me, I'd understand, of course, but I'd never fully be okay again. Parts of me would always be missing. And she'd walk around, holding them and not even know.

"Thank you. And thank you for being up front and honest about all of this even though it totally sucks and I hate it." She was thanking me for basically handing her the scissors to sever the ties between us. One cut was all it would take, and she held all the power.

"Yep. Take all the time you need, by the way. I'm not going anywhere." I didn't want her to feel rushed or worried. Like there was some sort of time limit on this decision. While she was weighing all of her options, I'd be one hundred percent focused on baseball and making sure a game like I'd played today never happened again. "But before you get out of my truck …" I leaned toward her, reached for the back of her neck, and pulled her against me like it might be the last time I ever got to.

My tongue entered her mouth, and she breathed into me, a moan combined with a whimper. My dick instantly hardened. This girl affected me like no other ever had. I wanted to tell her that I was falling in love with her … hell, that I loved her already, but I refused to fuck with her head like that. I focused on the taste of her tongue instead, sucking and nipping at it as her fingernails dug into my shoulders like she was afraid to let go. We were two people, frenzied, unsure of what tomorrow would bring and choosing to live for the moment, taking everything that the other gave. And I gave her my all.

I'd give her anything she wanted, today, tomorrow, and forever, if she'd let me. I wondered if she knew that, and somewhere deep down, I knew that she did, even without me saying it. I really fucking hoped that my girl would choose me in the end because knowing that she would eventually move on and end up with someone else would be like breathing in dirt instead of oxygen for the rest of my life. A constant reminder of my loss, filled with pain and grit, all while slowly suffocating me. It sounded like a shit way to go.

Realizations

Danika

MY HEART ACHED with each step I took away from Chance's truck and toward my apartment. I hadn't felt anywhere close to this level of hurt when Jared and I broke up. I had felt relieved. But right now, the last thing I felt was an ounce of relief even though I knew that what Chance and I were doing was an incredibly mature and smart thing to do. I'd felt so grown-up that we were able to talk about things calmly instead of fighting over them the way I used to do with Jared.

I understood why Chance felt the way that he did and why he was concerned even if my heart hated it. It made sense to me, and even though it sucked that he could be so logical when it came to his emotions, I realized that I was trying to be logical too. Being a girl, I wanted Chance's feelings for me to override every other thought in his head. But I knew that even if they did, he'd never admit it. Not while he was asking this of me.

What I hadn't told Chance was that I was determined to figure out a solution for us. When he'd mentioned ending things, my heart had felt like it had cracked in two as I struggled to catch my breath. Every time he encouraged me to think about my future, I saw him standing there with me. There wasn't one time when I pictured my life later on and he wasn't included in it. As shocking as that had initially been to me, it was also extremely telling. I knew what I needed to do; I just wasn't sure how.

Pulling open my front door, I stepped inside. The smell of chocolate chip cookies instantly hit my nose, and I swore I started to drool.

"Cookies?" I asked out loud, and Sunny peeked around the cabinets with a grin.

She looked all around me, clearly assuming that Chance would be with me, like usual. "I thought he'd want some sweets since he had such a bad game, but he's not with you?" she asked, sounding utterly confused.

"No. He went home." I rounded the corner and stood in the kitchen, watching her.

"Oh. I didn't peg Chance for one of those guys," she said, scooping out more batter and setting it onto the pan.

"One of what kind of guys?"

"The kind of baseball player who got super pissed after a bad game and wanted to be alone to sulk in his misery instead of carrying on with his life," she stated like she was some sort of expert on athletes.

I decided to be frank. "He tried to break up with me," I said the words super fast, unable to hold them in a second longer.

The spoon clanged against the countertop as it dropped,

and I stared, watching it bounce and twirl before falling to the floor with an even louder sound.

"Because of his game? Whoa, he's really over the top." She bent down to pick up the spoon, tossing it into the sink before pulling open the drawer and grabbing a clean one.

"It wasn't because of the game. He saw Jared this morning."

Sunny snarled, "So what? Who cares?"

"Jared said some things, and they didn't sit well with Chance," I tried to explain before wondering if I was oversharing things that should have stayed between him and me. But Sunny was my best friend, and girls needed to talk about things with each other. It was how we survived.

She popped out her hip—her annoyed stance. "What kind of things?"

"He told him that I'd give up my future for him. And shit like that. He made Chance worry."

Sunny focused back on the tray, filling the last empty space with dough. "Chance is a good guy."

"I know. He basically laid out what life would be like for me if we stayed together. He told me to take some time and think if it was the kind of life I wanted or not." I hopped up onto the counter and reached for one of the already-baked cookies on a plate. I wasn't sure why, but I half-expected Sunny to swat my hand or something, so I was relieved when she didn't. When I took a bite, the chocolate dripped out and hit me on the chin. I wiped it away. "These are so good. Why are your cookies always so delicious?"

"It's the sea salt," she said with a shrug as she put the last batch into the oven. "You know this already. I tell you this everytime."

"The sea salt," I parroted like it was new information even though it wasn't.

"I sprinkle sea salt chunks on top of the dough before I cook it. It changes everything," she explained, and suddenly, I couldn't taste anything other than the salty flavor combined with the sweet dark chocolate. "That's why I tell you to do it too. But you never listen."

"I'll start listening. I promise," I said, taking another bite. "You should sell these."

"Maybe someday. Anyway, what kind of life? What did he mean?"

I chewed first, savoring every bite before swallowing. "He meant if we stayed together when he got drafted. He explained what being with a professional baseball player would mean for *me*."

Her mouth pursed, making her lips look huge. "That's actually kind of nice. And you'd never thought about it before?"

"Not like that. Not the way he explained it," I said, feeling a little naive.

"I've heard it's not easy. I have a couple of friends who are with professional football players. The perks are great, but the rest of it takes a toll."

"Yeah. Chance was very realistic about it all. Did you know his dad had cheated on his mom?" I asked, just remembering that he had mentioned that.

She shot me a weird look. "Everyone knows the story of

Jack and Cassie Carter."

"I don't."

"Maybe I should rephrase," she said. "Everyone who's from this area knows their story. You can look online. I'm pretty sure it's all on there. I think there might even be a book about it."

As much as I wanted to satisfy my growing curiosity, I decided against it at the moment. I knew that I was only distracting myself from what I really needed to do. "What do your friends say?" I asked, and she looked confused. "The ones dating the football players. What do they say about it?"

"Oh. They say that the females are one thing, but the grueling schedule and the fact that it has to be their number one priority is another." Sunny offered me a shrug, like, *What did they expect?*

The buzzer dinged, and she reached for an oven mitt.

"Could you do it?"

She glanced at me while she pulled out the baking sheet and shut the oven door. "Could I do what? Date an athlete?"

"Yeah. Seriously. Do you think you could do it?" I had never even considered or thought about this kind of thing before tonight. I'd stupidly assumed that anyone could date a ball player, but I was starting to realize that maybe that wasn't the case at all. It seemed like it would take a certain kind of girl to handle the pressure and stress that went along with it.

"I mean, you know how much I love the players at this school." She winked, and I laughed, thinking about her and Mac. "But I don't know. I want to say yes, but I'm kind of insecure and jealous. I think the other girls alone might drive me insane. I'm not sure I could handle it."

I swallowed and blew out a long, slow breath as I thought about myself and Chance. Other females wanted him, and they made that fact known, but I'd never really paid them much attention. And I knew that was because Chance didn't either. No matter what any other girl said or did, he couldn't care less, and it made me react in the same manner. I couldn't even think of a time when some other girl had caused chaos between us.

"I think it would depend on the guy," Sunny said, breaking my train of thought as she hopped up onto the counter across from me, a cookie in her hand.

"Huh?"

"About the girls and my jealousy. I think it would depend on the guy. Like Mac, for example. I'd be going out of my mind anytime I couldn't reach him on the phone or if he was out of town for away games. I wouldn't want to live like that day in and day out. Always wondering. Always worried. Always insecure," she elaborated as she took a bite.

"I wouldn't either," I agreed because if Chance had made me feel that way when we were together, I wouldn't have entertained being with him in the first place.

"So, what are you going to do?"

That was the million-dollar question. "I don't know yet."

"Are you going to talk to Jared about what he said to Chance?"

It was funny how little Jared's opinion seemed to matter to me anymore. When we'd first started dating, I couldn't have imagined not caring about what he thought. But I wasn't that girl anymore. I felt more like my own person than I had in years.

"Honestly? I don't want to give him the satisfaction." I knew that if I reached out, Jared would pat himself on the back after realizing that he had come between me and Chance. "I don't want him to think he has that kind of power over my relationship. Or me," I added before pushing off the counter.

Sunny's face turned serious, and it looked so odd to see her so expressionless when she always seemed to be smiling. "He hit on me once," she spat out, and my jaw dropped, her eyes focusing on her hands in her lap.

"What? When?" I asked as I took a step toward her.

Months ago, I would have been furious, hearing this. But now, I just felt shocked more than anything else.

She looked up at me, concern written all over her face. "It was last year. Around the football-player incident. He tried to kiss me one night while you were in your room," she said.

All the pieces started clicking together. The way Sunny had stopped liking me and Jared being together, calling us names, and encouraging me to break up with him. And how her face always soured whenever I brought him up. Or how she'd disappear into her room on the rare occasion that he actually came over. Which, now that I thought about it, he had stopped coming over here, always insisting that I go to the frat house instead for whatever reason.

"Are you mad at me? I'm sorry I never told you. I was

afraid you wouldn't believe me. You two had so much history, and you're from the same place. And I didn't want to be the reason you broke up." She was babbling, but it didn't stop. "I don't know … it was a crappy position for me to be in, but I should have said something."

I reached for her hands and held them. "I should have known." I glanced up at the ceiling before focusing back at my best friend. "You changed around him, and he stopped wanting to come over here. I should have put two and two together, but it never occurred to me."

"Why would it?"

"I'm sorry you felt like you couldn't tell me," I said because I understood that she must have felt so shitty this whole time, keeping this information from me. It must have been eating her up inside. "Chance has never hit on you, right?" I asked with a small chuckle, and her smile returned.

"No way. He'd never do that."

"You'll tell me if he does?" I asked.

"Promise," she said, pulling her hands from mine and extending her pinkie.

I wrapped my pinkie around hers, and we shook, the pinkie promise made even though I hoped we'd never have to use it.

Propositions

Two Weeks Later

Danika

I HADN'T MEANT for so much time to go by without seeing or talking to Chance, but it was just the way things ended up being. In my defense, Chance had been out of town for half of those days, traveling with the team, so it wasn't entirely my fault. We had texted a couple times, basically saying how much we missed each other, but that was it. He gave me the space I needed, and I took it begrudgingly, knowing that it was for the best.

I kept my distance, wanting to make sure that my decision—when I finally arrived at one—wasn't one I'd change my mind about one day down the road. I needed to be certain—about everything. And it took me some time to figure out exactly how I could make this work between us and still have something of my own.

Because at this point, that was what I wanted—both Chance and a career.

Which was why I was currently pacing a hole in the

carpet of my living room, waiting for my dad to call me back, thankful that Sunny was still at class for the next hour. Nerves raced through my body. Even though my dad had never been anything other than supportive of me, this was a very serious topic, potentially life-changing for us both. It involved his company, and that wasn't something my dad took lightly, no matter who was propositioning him.

If I was being honest with myself, this idea had been percolating in my mind for well over a year, but I'd never given it much thought because I always knew that Jared wanted to stay in the city after graduation. Since I assumed that he and I would be together and working for my dad, my idea didn't make that much sense to pursue at the time. But ending things with Jared gave my life a new beginning. The idea had immediately sprung back into my head after talking to Chance the other night. Ever since then, I couldn't stop trying to work out the details so that they'd make sense for both myself and my dad's company.

I wasn't sure my dad would even agree to it, but I had to at least try. If he said no, I wasn't sure what I would do. I'd be back at square one, but I decided to cross that bridge once I got to it. My phone rang in my hand, and I stared at my dad's name flashing on the screen. I almost didn't answer; that was how nervous I suddenly became.

"Hey, Dad," I answered before forcing myself to sit down at the round kitchen table. Reaching for the pen and pad of paper I'd put there, I looked over my notes.

"Hey, kiddo. Everything okay?"

"Yeah, it's good."

"That Carter boy staying in line?" he asked, pretending to sound threatening even though there was humor in his tone.

"He is," I said, not wanting to get into the fact that we were on a break or taking time apart or whatever you wanted to call it.

"Good. So, what's going on? I can tell by your voice that you need to talk."

How did everyone seem to read me so easily? I never felt like the kind of person who was that transparent, but lately, I must have been.

"I wanted to talk to you about my future with the company," I said, clearing my throat as my words caught.

"Okay. What about it?" His voice turned more curious than anything else, but I was relieved that he didn't sound concerned.

"I've been thinking about the role I want to take in it," I started to say, and he interrupted me.

"You still want to work here, right?" He sounded so sad.

"Yes. Of course, I do. Just in a different capacity, if it makes sense."

"I'm listening." He said. "What were you thinking?"

I blew out a long breath and started to explain my vision, hoping that I didn't sound stupid or naive. "I've heard you talk about your high-end clients and how they want multiple properties in various locations. But you only sell them in New York. You basically give the rest of their portfolio away to other people without earning a commission or a finder's fee."

My dad laughed into the phone. "You're not wrong. I do

give away millions in potential profit because I simply don't have the time to take on anything outside of the city. I'm just way too busy."

"I know. Which is why I was wondering if we could open a division for those clients. We could be really hands-on and offer them a sort of white-glove experience, if that makes any sense. We would provide all the initial research for wherever they wanted to buy property and present them with a portfolio of options based on their preferences and needs. And then we'd work with the seller's agent to negotiate the deal. Is that possible? I mean, can we legally do that?"

"Honey, anything is possible with the right amount of money."

"What about international properties? I know it's different than in the States, but I'm not sure how."

"International doesn't have agents like we do, where they split the commissions. It's all based on negotiations."

I hadn't known that. "Okay." I scribbled some notes. "What do you think?" I nervously tapped the pen against the pad, the thumping matching my heartbeat.

"And you would run that division?"

"I mean, eventually, yes. Once I have more experience and people trust me. I still have a lot to learn when it comes to that. Especially in the international market. But in the meantime, I was thinking of implementing a questionnaire for potential clients to fill out. The more clients we had, the better the questionnaire would become. It would be intuitive and create a report that would tell me exactly what they were looking for, as long as they knew. I'd go over it with them to make sure we didn't miss any details, but that'd be something that I could do from anywhere."

"I see." My dad's voice turned almost animated. "Does this have anything to do with your new boyfriend? Am I to understand that you won't be coming home after graduation?"

"I didn't say that, Dad," I stumbled on the words, and we both knew I wasn't telling the whole truth. "I just want options," I admitted.

"The *working from anywhere* kind of option?"

"I mean"—I practically snorted from trying not to giggle—"kind of. Yes. Is that bad? I do think the division is a great idea, and I'd thought about it way before Chance was in the picture. And I could have an office in New York, so I could fly there to meet with our clients in person if they preferred that. Otherwise, we could do online meetings. But I know that a lot of your high-end clientele are traveling the majority of the time and aren't in one place, so just coordinating time zones would be the biggest challenge."

"You've done your research. I'm impressed."

I smiled super big even though he couldn't see it. "I've also created a mock questionnaire that I want to send you, so you can see how it works. And then I'll send you a link to the report that it makes. I'll also create a database as well, specifically for this division, which will be extremely detailed."

"You've given this a lot of thought then?" It was definitely a question and not a statement.

"I have. I'd really like to do it if you think it makes sense and is a smart direction for the company to head in. But I understand if it isn't something you're interested in. I just wanted to ask."

"Sweetheart, I'd give you the world if you wanted it. And this is something I've mulled over at least a thousand times over the years. I just never had the time to pursue it, and at some point, I stopped caring about trying to expand my market."

A defeated sigh escaped me as I interpreted what my dad was trying to tell me.

"Maybe I let the idea go because it was never the right moment. Life always seemed to get in the way," he said, and I knew he was talking about Mom. "It seems like it might be the right time now."

"Really?" I felt my blood pressure rise because this was something I was genuinely interested in and wanted to do. The idea of finding beautiful properties for people excited me, and I knew I'd be good at it.

"Really. If this is something you want to do, we should do it. We have nothing to lose."

"Dad, thank you so much. I won't let you down."

He chuckled lightly into the phone, and I heard the sound of ice clanging in a glass through the line. "I know you won't. But we'll work it out. I really want to see the mock questionnaire you compiled, so send me that as soon as we hang up. And, honey?" He waited for me to acknowledge him before he continued, "It's okay that you want to be with this Carter kid."

The tears instantly welled up in my eyes, and I tried to

fight the emotions back. "It's not too soon? I was with Jared for years." Once again, I found myself wanting my dad's approval.

"When it's the right person, you just know. And if you lose them, you never get over it," he said, sounding a little emotional, and I ached with his pain. "But I'll tell you something, honey. If your mother were still alive, she would have started the division you're talking about. She mentioned it to me more than once."

"She did? Really?" My heart swelled inside my chest. I loved having anything in common with my mom, but this was something else entirely. It felt so bonding to be of the same mindset even though she was no longer physically here.

"Really. She had this gypsy, entrepreneurial spirit. She loved New York, but she loved traveling and trying new things. You're just like her in that sense. Manhattan is a big city, but even it's not big enough to keep you."

I'd never thought about it like that before. I never even considered myself to be a gypsy spirit. I thought that I'd be perfectly content to stay in one place eventually, but maybe somewhere deep down, I always knew that I needed to get out. Which was why I had picked a college as far away as I could when it was time to go.

"It would have been so much fun to work with her." The thought came into my head, and instead of holding it back, I shared it, hoping it wouldn't make him upset.

"I know. I can see the two of you now"—he laughed—"running the damn world and selling a piece of it to everyone who crossed your path."

I smiled, too, as I pictured it. My mom and I would have made an incredible team. Life was so unfair sometimes. Right now, I felt like grieving her loss all over again.

My dad sniffed before forcing out a cough. "I need to go, honey. Unless there's anything else?"

"No, that's it."

"Don't forget to email me."

"I won't. Thank you, Dad. Thank you so much."

"I'm really looking forward to this," he said, and my pain shifted back into excitement as well.

"Me too."

We hung up, and I grabbed my laptop, checking over the mock questionnaire that I'd set up one last time before emailing him a link to it. I also told him to play around with the options, that depending on the answer, certain additional fields would appear. I sat there, staring at my sent folder as the front door swung open, and Sunny walked in.

"Hey," she said before tossing her bag onto one of the chairs. "It's hot as balls out there."

I glanced toward the balcony window. "I haven't been out yet."

"Did the call go well?"

I'd told Sunny all about my idea as I tried to flush it out in my head. She'd loved it so much that she suggested I hire her as well. It wasn't the worst idea, but picturing happy Sunny in Manhattan made me laugh every time I tried to imagine it. She'd stand out like a neon painting against a jet-black sky. But maybe that kind of change would be good for her, the way coming out here had been good for me.

"He loved it," I said with a grin, closing my laptop. "I just sent him an email with all the details."

"I knew it. It's brilliant. You got me all crazy about it. So, I'll just wait for my job offer." She grinned as I considered the prospect of her being in the New York office permanently while I traveled with Chance.

The only downside in my perspective was our combined lack of real-world experience. The people we'd be dealing with wouldn't want "kids" handling their investment properties, and I wouldn't blame them.

"I'll be in touch. Your interview went well," I teased.

"When will you tell Chance?"

Sunny had been badgering me daily since Chance and I parted ways. Sometimes, it felt like she wanted us back together more than anyone else.

"I'll go over there tonight after his practice."

"Thank God. Thought you might torture us all and make him wait longer." She shook her head in disapproval. "I could not stand another winter-break scenario. My heart couldn't take it again," she said, referencing the time when I'd kept my distance from Chance to make sure that I had done the right thing by breaking up with Jared.

"I'd go see him right now if he wasn't in class."

"Go anyway. Take him out of class. Go sit on his lap during practice. Straddle him like a spider monkey."

"It's not the worst idea you've ever had." I laughed as I pictured trying to straddle Chance while he squatted in his catcher's gear. "Great. Now, I'm turned on with nowhere to go."

"Go to his classroom!" she yelled, and I grabbed my bag, pretending to run out the door before stopping short. "Tease!"

I was tempted to go to his building and wait outside for him, but I didn't want this conversation to be cut short, and that was exactly what would happen. There was so much I needed to tell him, and I refused to do it with a time limit.

Tonight, I'd go over to Chance's and pray like hell he still wanted me the same way that I wanted him—for forever.

I Have My Answer

Chance

I SAT IN the kitchen of my parents' house, just like I'd been doing every night we didn't have a game. I'd been avoiding going home to the baseball house, trying to escape what being alone with my thoughts did to me. It wasn't pretty. I tended to spin out pretty badly, creating a narrative that ended with Danika and Jared together and me alone for the rest of my life with only baseball to love. Not to mention the fact that it was too tempting to want to head over to Danika's apartment and sit in the parking lot like a fucking psycho.

"So, I gave her space. Told her to take her time and figure out if she could do this or not," I said finally, explaining what was going on between Danika and me to my parents.

Danika hadn't been at a home game since the day of my worst game ever, so my mom knew something was up between us even though I hadn't wanted to talk about it. Until now.

"That was smart," my mom said. "It must have been

hard, but it really was the right thing to do."

"But it's been two weeks. I haven't heard from her in two weeks," I said, grabbing my hair and pulling at it.

"Chance, your mom has always told you that this lifestyle isn't for everyone," my dad chimed in. "You asked her to think it all over, and she obviously is. You can't be mad at her for doing what you asked her to."

"Your dad's right. Plus, it's better that you know it now instead of when it's too late," my mom added, and it was exactly what I'd said to Danika.

"Do you guys think that she couldn't handle it?" I asked, suddenly worried about their answer.

If my parents thought that Danika wasn't cut out for this life, I knew that it would subconsciously affect the way I felt about her. I would still want to be with her, but something would always linger in the deep recesses of my mind and hold me back.

"I actually think she'd be great. She's so unaffected by the girls in the stands. She seems very confident and trusting. Those things are really important because they come into play," my mom said.

I hadn't even thought about what it must be like for her during the games. Danika had never mentioned other girls being mean to her or anyone confronting her.

"Are the girls mean to her? Do they talk shit to her?" I said before apologizing for swearing even though I knew they didn't care.

"Put a dollar in the swear jar," Jacey piped up from the living room, and I pointed in her direction, my mouth wide open.

"We have a swear jar?" I asked, annoyed that she could hear me in the first place.

"We do now," Jacey shouted back. "Double for you."

"Oh my God, stop listening," I shouted.

"I can't help it, loudmouth!"

I snarled, "Go to bed!"

"You go to bed!"

"Do something," I complained to my parents, who sat there, shaking their heads. "Doesn't she have an off button?"

"You could always go to your own house. You know, the one where you live," Jacey said.

I snapped my mouth shut instead of fighting back as my dad laughed. That girl always had to have the last word.

"Mom," I said, directing the conversation back to the topic at hand, "are the girls mean to Danika?"

She shook her head. "I haven't heard anything, but she doesn't even pay attention. I mean, she doesn't even look around or try to listen in. She's completely focused on you and chatting with me. I was not like that when I was her age." My mom gave both me and my dad an uncomfortable grin. "I was constantly on guard."

"To be fair, the girls were pretty awful to you, Kitten," my dad added, defending my mom.

"Well, you did sleep with half the school," she said before wincing as she looked at me. "Sorry, Chance."

"I already knew all of this," I groaned, not wanting to think about my dad screwing his way through Fullton State.

Thankfully, my phone buzzed, and I looked at it. A text message from Danika sat there, asking if we could talk.

"Look." I turned the phone toward my mom. "I gotta go."

I instantly hated that I was at my parents', so far away from the baseball house. I texted her back, asking her to give me thirty minutes before texting again and asking her if she needed a ride. She told me that she'd meet me at my place, and I had no idea if that was a good sign or not.

"Good luck," my mom said before giving me a hug.

"It has to be good news, right? If it were bad, she'd just call me. Right?" I looked between my parents, who both shrugged their shoulders, which was not reassuring. "You guys are not helping."

"Drive safe," was all my dad said before clasping my shoulder and telling me it would be okay.

"Let us know what happens. I'm invested," my mom reminded me as I walked toward the front door.

"You like her, right?" I asked point-blank.

"I like her a lot." My mom smiled.

"Thanks. Bye, Squirt," I yelled toward my little sister, who sat on the living room couch, watching some show that looked like an absolute nightmare.

She gave me a wave without even turning around, and I was half-tempted to go tackle her and turn off the TV just to annoy her, but I needed to get home.

I MADE IT back to the baseball house fast. And not because I had been speeding. The freeways had been empty, and every light had seemed to turn green as I neared it. There was still time before Danika was supposed to be here, and I considered taking a quick shower, but I didn't want to be in there if she came over early.

Mac was in the kitchen when I walked through the front door. He always waited up for me, no matter what he said.

"You're back early." He knew that I'd been staying at my parents' at night until pretty late.

"Danika's coming over," I said as a lump formed in my throat.

"Shit. Right now?"

"Yeah."

"What do you think she's going to say?" Mac asked.

He knew everything that had happened between us, and he was the one person I talked to when I wanted to talk. Which wasn't often. I tended to keep a lot of my feelings inside—at least while they were still up in the air.

"I don't know. But she wouldn't come here just to call it off in person, would she?" I asked him basically the same question that I'd asked my parents, hoping he'd have a better answer.

"I wouldn't think so. But then again, Danika would probably want to tell you whatever it was face-to-face. Good or bad."

I'd thought the same thing, which was why I was nervous. The doorbell rang, and I locked eyes with Mac, the lump taking up all the space in my throat.

"Do you want me to get it?" he asked since I wasn't moving.

I shook my head. "I got it," I said before forcing my legs

to move toward the door and pulling it open.

Danika stood there, wearing jean shorts and a white tank top.

"You're not wearing black," I said, and she peered down at her clothes.

"Nope. Can I come in?" She looked up at me, her hazel eyes full of whatever she was hiding behind them.

I hated when I couldn't read her, but right now, I was at a loss. I stepped aside and watched as she walked through the front door, hoping it wasn't for the last time.

"Hey, Mac." She gave him a smile and a wave, which he returned, before she focused her attention back on me. "Can we go to your room and talk?"

I nodded. It was like all words had seemed to disappear from my vocabulary before I pulled my fucking shit together. "Yeah. Let's go. See you later, Mac," I said as I led us toward my room and closed the door behind her.

Waving toward the chair at my desk, I watched as she sat before moving toward the edge of my bed and doing the same. We sat far enough away from each other that we couldn't touch but close enough to read facial expressions and eye contact.

"It's been hell, staying away from you these past two weeks," she said as she blew out a breath, and I noticed that she was emotional.

"It hasn't been easy for me either," I said back, wanting her to know that I'd hated every moment that we were apart, but I wasn't mad at her for it.

"I'm sorry it took me so long but—" she started to say,

and I cut her off.

"It doesn't matter. What matters is whatever you've decided. Not how long it took you to reach the decision."

"I've been doing a lot of thinking. About everything you said," she added, and I was grateful.

It was exactly what I'd wanted her to do, although every day that she had been away from me felt like I was being sucker-punched in the gut. I'd tried to block the feelings out, focused on baseball like my life literally depended on it, but she always found a way in.

"I'm glad."

"So, basically, you weren't wrong about me eventually resenting you," she said, and I had a bad feeling about the direction this conversation was heading. "I agree with you. I think if I didn't have something of my own, I'd get mad at you one day because of it. Even though it wouldn't be your fault. And it would have been my decision. I would feel like I'd compromised everything and you didn't have to compromise anything in order for us to be together."

"I know. And that's absolutely correct," I agreed because it fucking was. Like I'd told her, baseball demanded sacrifice … and not just from me.

"I took our time apart seriously. I considered all the options. I even looked online about what dating a professional athlete was really like," she said with a sheepish grin before frowning. "That wasn't fun reading."

I had no idea what she was talking about, but I assumed the worst. The internet was probably filled with stories about being cheated on, lied to, and left behind. Not that those things weren't true, but I wasn't a typical athlete. Hell, I wasn't even a typical guy when it came to all of those things, and I hoped she knew that.

"Did it make you not want to be with me?"

"It had very little impact on my decision," she said, and I felt marginally relieved. "But I talked to my dad earlier."

I perked up a little but only because her voice had lifted. "Okay. And? What did he say? Does he want you to come home? Get back together with Jared?"

"What? No." She giggled. "My dad does not want me and Jared together."

That was news to me. "He doesn't?"

"No." She waved me off. "Listen to me. I suggested something for his company that I'd like to be a part of." She smiled so big, and I found myself smiling back at her, mostly because she seemed so cheerful, just talking about this. "And he agreed."

"Is it a good thing? What is it? You look so happy right now."

"It would be a whole new division for property purchases outside of New York for high-end clients. I'd still have an office in New York that I'd need to be at sometimes. And I'd also have to travel, depending on the client and the location of the property, but the majority of the work would be done online and via video-conferencing."

"And your dad said yes?"

"He did."

I sat there for a minute as everything she'd said processed in slow motion inside my brain. *Is she saying what I think she's saying?*

"So, wait," I stumbled, making sure I got it right before I got too excited. "Are you saying that you can work from anywhere?"

"I can work from anywhere," she reinforced the point.

"And you want to do this?" I asked again, still not wanting to believe that she was saying she was mine.

"I can't wait to start doing this."

"Does this mean what I think it means?" Clearly, I needed her to spell it out for me, and I wasn't even sorry about it. I was vulnerable, and even though I hated feeling weak, she also made me feel safe.

"If it means that you can't get rid of me ever again, then yes." She grinned before jumping off the chair and landing in my lap, straddling me.

My arms wrapped around her waist as my skin buzzed with the contact. "I'm in love with you, Danika," I said, no longer able to hold back the words due to pride, ego, or fear. I'd been scared that it was too soon, that we had gotten too serious, too fast, or that I didn't know what real love was, but saying the words brought me peace and calm that I'd never experienced before, and I knew it was right.

"I'm in love with you too," she said, and my heart had never felt so full in my entire life.

I'd had no idea that hearing those words could make a guy feel like he could do anything. Walk on water. Save the world. Stop global warming. I was invincible as long as this girl chose me.

And all night long, I showed her how much I appreciated

her choosing us.

Parental Advice

Danika

WE FELL BACK into our routine like we'd never been out of it. Chance never made me feel bad for taking time away to decide if I could handle things or not. There was no guilt, no pressure, no constant bringing it back up and throwing it in my face. I wasn't sure why I'd expected a side of asshole behavior to accompany us getting back together, but then I reminded myself that this was Chance and not Jared, and everything made sense.

It was interesting to become aware of the dysfunctional things I had put up with once they had become a part of my life. I'd stopped seeing the behavior as crazy because it had slowly become the norm, and it had been easy to make excuses for it. Life had a funny way of showing you things but only once you were free of it. Hindsight truly was twenty-twenty.

Sunny had a paper she was struggling with finishing and wanted to get done before it ruined her entire weekend, so I was on my own for tonight's game. Grabbing a bottle of water from the commissary and stuffing it into my bag, I headed toward the baseball field. From the looks of everyone around me, mostly girls clad in various baseball jerseys—Chance's included—I wasn't the only one going to the game.

"Isn't she with Chance now?" I heard someone ask, and I couldn't help but start listening in.

"I think so. If he's anything like his dad, that won't last long," another female voice said from behind me, and I heard giggling.

"I heard his whole avoiding girls' thing is just an act, and she's just one of many," another voice said.

I refused to put up with this bullshit the entire walk.

I stopped and turned to face them, the look of surprise on their faces fueling me on. Of course, they hadn't thought that I'd say anything. "You have something you want to say to me? Something you'd like to ask about my boyfriend? I'd be happy to fill you in."

"Uh, no," they stuttered, completely caught off guard.

"Well, if you do, say it to my face next time and not my back." I was not afraid of confrontation and had no issues with standing up for myself.

The girls stayed quiet the rest of the walk to the field, where I had tickets waiting for me and they didn't. I knew they would be sitting in the shitty student section, and I silently hoped their makeup would melt off. Petty, party of one.

By the time I walked down to my seat, Jacey and Cassie were already sitting there, their blonde hair pulled back into ponytails with a baseball cap covering their heads. I got super excited to see them both, but I hadn't seen Jacey since the dinner at her house, and that was months ago.

"It's about time you came to a game," I said as I pulled her into a hug.

She was a beautiful teenager, who was going to turn into an even more beautiful twenty-something-year-old. Chance and Jack were going to lose their minds with her.

"Me? You're the one who hasn't been here!" Jacey spouted back, and I realized that she was right. "Please tell me this means you and my dopey brother are back together." She rolled her eyes the same way that Chance did, and the gesture was so familiar that I found myself staring at her face like a weirdo before pulling out of it.

"How did you know we weren't together?" I asked her before looking around her shoulder at Cassie, who was grinning at our exchange.

"Because he was so annoying. I couldn't take it anymore. If it lasted any longer, I was going to have to call you and demand you take him back."

I looked at her, confused. "He was at your house?"

"Oh my God, he came over, like, every night, moping and whining and asking Mom and Dad for advice. I pretended to be in the other room, but I heard everything."

Shaking my head, I couldn't help but laugh. "You're dangerous, you know that?"

"Yeah, I do."

And I believed that she did. The girl was going to be a terror when she grew up, but as long as she was on my side, I was all for it.

Cassie laughed at her daughter's admission before

standing up to give me a hug. "I'm so glad you two worked things out," she said quietly in my ear before sliding over one seat, so I could sit between her and Jacey.

"Me too."

"I really hoped that you would," she offered with a smile, and it made me feel so good.

Knowing that Chance's mom liked us together was a big deal to me. I'd be lying if I said I didn't want her approval. I absolutely did.

"I almost called you," I admitted as she sat down, and I followed suit while Jacey still stood, looking around.

"You should have!" she practically shouted before slapping a hand over her mouth. "But really, you can call me anytime. Especially about that kind of stuff."

"I wanted to, but I didn't want to put you in the middle or make it weird."

I really had thought about calling her multiple times. She knew what it was like to date and eventually marry a professional athlete, and after searching online, I learned way more about her and Jack's relationship than I had ever meant to. Sunny had been right; there was a book written about them, but it seemed wrong, reading it, so I refused to order it or give in to my curiosity. I'd promised myself that if there was anything I wanted to know about their relationship, I'd ask them myself. Going about it any other way didn't feel right, like I'd be going behind their backs somehow.

"It wouldn't have been weird. You were looking for answers, and I could have given you some. But I understand why you didn't. Maybe it felt like I wouldn't be able to be unbiased?" She was genuinely asking.

I shook my head. "No, it wasn't that. The baseball part was just for information purposes mostly. I was more concerned with figuring out a good work situation. And no one could help me with that part until I knew exactly what I wanted to do."

"I heard. Congratulations, by the way," she said, and I realized that Chance must have reached out after we worked things out to give her an update.

I loved that they were so close. Some girls hated having boyfriends who were mama's boys, but in Chance's case, I thought it was sweet. Cassie wasn't competitive, so she never made me feel like I was less than or beneath her. I was grateful for the way she had raised him and for how she treated me—like family.

"Are you two going to talk about this the whole game?" Jacey asked.

"Probably not the whole time," I teased, and she groaned. *Oh, to be a teenager again and bored with everything around you.*

"Maybe I'll go walk around campus and check it out. Can I, Mom?"

Cassie contemplated the question, like she was unsure if she should let Jacey out of her sight or not.

She must have waited too long because Jacey said, "Never mind. I'll just stay here," and Cassie visibly relaxed before her eyes widened.

"I almost forgot. Your cousins are coming," Cassie said, and Jacey perked up.

"Yay! We can walk around campus together then, right? So, I won't be alone?"

"I'll ask your aunt when they get here," she said, and Jacey moped only momentarily before sucking it up.

That was one more thing I loved about Chance's family—that they all came to watch him play. I enjoyed being a part of it.

"Ask me what?" Aunt Melissa suddenly appeared behind us, and I stood up to tell her hello. She pulled me into a hug across the stadium seats, her wavy, dark hair sticking to my eyelashes. "It's good to see you again."

"Thank you. You too."

"Your cousins are in line at the snack bar," she informed Jacey.

"Already?" Jacey asked before standing up and running over to find them.

"Where's Dean?" Cassie asked, and I had just wondered the same thing.

"He's watching some kid play in *Alabama*." She stuck her finger down her throat and made a puking face before looking at me. "Sorry. Inside joke from a hundred years ago."

"You two hate Alabama. Noted," I said, pretending to check it off an imaginary list. "Does your husband travel often to watch guys play?"

"Yeah. Dean always wants to meet any kid he's thinking about signing first. He doesn't believe in doing everything online. He wants face-to-face meetings. And he wants to see what kind of person they are."

"I think that's smart," I said. There was something different about talking to a client in person, as opposed to online. It was more personal, and I believed it led to a better relationship, one that was more trusting.

"It is smart. But I miss him when he's gone," Melissa said, and Cassie pretended to throw up. "Oh, please, you're one to talk."

"I know; I know." Cassie waved Melissa away as the announcer's voice broke through the hum of the crowd and our conversation.

He ran through the lineup for the visiting team before music started blaring, and he introduced our players. The crowd went wild. I'd been to a few games before, but I swore that it was louder today than it had ever been.

As each name was announced, the high-pitched squealing and shouts from girls filled the air. But none compared to the sound of the screaming and cheers that could be heard when they announced Chance's name in the lineup. The entire stadium erupted, and I added to it, cupping my hands around my mouth as I yelled for my man. I felt nothing but pride as I watched him strut out onto the field in his catcher's gear with his helmet in his hand. He stood behind home plate, and looking at him from behind was a sight to behold. I couldn't stop staring. He must have sensed it because he glanced behind himself and gave me a grin that made my entire body melt. At least, I hoped that smile was for me; otherwise, I was about to feel like the world's biggest idiot.

"He never looks in the stands," his mom said with a wicked grin. "He likes you," she teased, and I felt giddy inside.

We stopped talking as the national anthem played, and the crowd sang along. And just like that, the game started, and the three teenage girls reappeared, carrying more food than I knew they could eat.

"Did you buy one of everything?" I asked Jacey as she sat down next to me.

"Pretty much." She shrugged before shoving a cheese-covered chip into her mouth. "Want one?"

"Hell yes, I want one," I said before taking the chip with the most cheese on it and eating it. "Thank you," I tried to say, and she laughed.

Everyone seemed to be invested in the game while I was solely invested in Chance. He was the only one on the field I cared about, so my eyes stayed firmly glued to his body and actions. Every once in a while, I'd get lost in a fantasy, remembering what those hands could do to me and how they made me feel. I wanted to be the baseball every time he gripped it, his fingers rolling and moving it around like it was an extension of him. He commanded that ball the same way he commanded my body. Knowing what he looked like underneath all that gear was a blessing, and I was definitely blessed. I couldn't wait to get him home later.

"Right, Danika?"

Shaking my head, I looked at Cassie, completely flustered and embarrassed. "I'm sorry, what?"

She laughed. "I said the girls should be fine, walking around campus right now, don't you think?"

"Oh yeah. It's still light out. I'd just make sure they came back here before it got dark."

"That's what I was thinking too," she said before leaning over me and giving Jacey instructions and demands.

The three teenagers stood up and practically skipped away, and Melissa jumped down and took Jacey's seat.

"Do you want to switch with me?" I asked, assuming that she'd want to be next to Cassie.

"No, you're fine. I'll have to move once Jacey gets back anyway. Heaven forbid she be far away from her brother," Melissa said.

I looked at Cassie. "Is that true? I feel like she doesn't want to be here."

"She doesn't," Cassie said. "But when she is here, she has to be closest to him. I don't know why. It's just her thing. She's always been that way."

"That's kinda sweet."

"I heard that you and my nephew broke up. What happened?" Melissa asked, and I was a little taken aback.

"Melissa! Don't listen to her, Danika. She's nosy," Cassie pretended to chastise her.

Melissa threw her hands up. "What? I can't ask her what happened, but I can ask you? That doesn't seem fair." I opened my mouth to respond, but Melissa stopped me. "I already know anyway. Sorry. But I didn't know you two had worked it out. Are you happy?"

I nodded. "Yes. Very. I think we'll be okay," I said as I blew out a small breath.

She threw her arm around me and pulled me close. "I think you will be too. I like you for him. And I don't like anyone for my nephew."

"That means a lot. Thank you," I said, and I hoped she knew how genuinely I meant it.

Melissa grinned, her eyes practically closing. "Oh, you have so much fun stuff to look forward to." Her words were positive, but the way she'd said them were disconcerting.

"Don't scare her off," Cassie said quickly, and I got a little nervous. "We just got her back."

The crowd erupted once more, and we all looked toward the field just in time to see the ball fly over the center field fence. Mac had hit a home run, and all the guys were running toward home plate, waiting for him to get there. I watched as Mac pulled off his helmet once his foot touched home and high-fived his teammates with it before sprinting back into the dugout. Chance looked so excited, and I watched him slap Mac on the back and then the ass before picking him up in a back-breaking hug. Boys were really adorable sometimes.

"Can I ask you something?" I addressed the question toward Cassie, but I made sure Melissa heard me as well.

"Of course. You can ask me anything," Cassie said as she waited for what I might say next.

"How did you get through it with Jack? I mean, was it hard for you when he played professional baseball, or was it easy?" I figured that I might as well ask so that I was more prepared for what my potential future entailed.

"It definitely had its challenges," she said, her face twisting for a moment, "but it's nothing you can't get through. As long as you guys are honest with each other and communicate about everything."

I nodded in understanding because everyone always said that the key to a healthy relationship was communication. "It's so easy to let things spin out of control if you don't talk about them," I said, realizing just how sideways Chance and I could have become these past few months if one of us hadn't pushed the other to stop running and talk it out.

"It's extremely easy to keep things to yourself. To assume that your partner should just know when you're upset and about what. But that isn't fair," she started to explain, and I found myself hanging on to each and every word. I wanted her advice. "None of us are mind readers. We have to talk. It usually fixes everything anyway."

"Eventually," Melissa added, and they both laughed while I felt a little left out, not knowing exactly what they were referring to.

"It's not always easy to talk about the hard things. But you have to. If you're starting to feel resentful. Or angry. Or like you aren't getting enough time and support for you," Cassie explained, "you have to tell him. He won't know anything's wrong unless you let him know."

That was a good point. I knew that, in the past, I'd expected Jared to sense that I was upset about things and instinctively know how to fix them. Not only did he not fix the things that bothered me, but he also carried on like everything was fine. Because in his mind, it was. And that had only made me angrier and more annoyed.

"She's right. Guys are pretty simple. They will want to fix what's wrong. But they have to know what it is first,"

Melissa said.

I was grateful to have the two of them to talk to. They filled a void I'd tried to pretend I wasn't living without.

My brain reeled as it fought with itself about the next question I wanted to ask. I knew it was none of my damn business, but a part of me wanted to know how Cassie had done it. It seemed so impossible from the outside.

"I read some stuff about you online. I didn't mean to, but I was researching, and it came up."

"What kind of stuff? We went through a lot," Cassie said with an awkward laugh.

"That's putting it mildly." Melissa made a silly face.

"The cheating?" I whispered before looking around. I didn't want anyone to overhear our conversation and start judging or eavesdropping. I felt protective over Cassie and Jack for whatever reason.

"Ooh," Melissa made a sound like she'd been sucker-punched. "Straight for the jugular."

"I'm sorry. It's not my place. I shouldn't have even brought it up," I said, feeling awful for instigating such a touchy topic and what was most likely still a sore subject.

"Don't listen to Fun Size over there." She thumbed toward Melissa, and I started grinning at the nickname. "That was a long time ago. A lifetime. What did you want to know?" Cassie seemed completely unfazed by my asking, almost like she had expected the question.

"How did you forgive him?" I couldn't imagine.

Her smile softened. "It wasn't easy. Forgiveness for something that devastating is really hard. It eats you up day in and day out if you let it. And people said a lot of horrible things about me online. They called me a doormat. They said I was weak," she admitted with sadness, but I still heard the strength in her voice. I knew all the things she had accomplished in her life, and Cassie Carter was the opposite of weak. "The thing is, it's really easy to judge a relationship from the outside when you're not the one in it."

I nodded in agreement because that was exactly what I had done when I first read about it online. I judged. I made assumptions. I'd put myself in her position and convinced myself that I'd never be able to forgive that kind of indiscretion. I assumed that once a guy did something like that, he could never fix things. Once trust had been obliterated, it would never rebuild the same way. I had no idea how someone could forgive a cheater, but here I was, looking at a woman I completely respected, unable to imagine her married to anyone else.

"But other people have no idea what goes on behind closed doors. They think they know everything, especially when a celebrity is involved. So, maybe from the version of my and Jack's relationship they had in their heads, I appeared weak to them. I know that I wasn't. I know that there's strength in forgiveness." She looked past me as she said those words, and I thought she was looking for her husband.

I glanced at the field but didn't see him when Cassie continued, "To be honest, Danika, no one else saw how sorry Jack was. They have no idea how hard we worked to rebuild the trust we'd lost. They didn't know the things Jack did to make sure that I was okay or how he made sure to never put me in a position where I felt vulnerable or unloved again. He worked to prove to me that I was the only woman for him. And he's proven it every day since."

I listened as she talked, unsure of what to say in response. My words felt inadequate, like I didn't have the life experience to even attempt to contribute.

"He made a mistake," I said, finding some words after all.

"Yes. He made a mistake, and people make those. He was sorry. I didn't have to forgive him. It would have been really easy to walk away with my pride, but I would have missed out on all this love." She closed her eyes for a moment before reopening them. "I can't imagine going through this life with anyone else."

"There was no way you were ever going to end up with someone who wasn't Jack Carter," Melissa added before wiping at her eyes. "Sorry, but your story always makes me a little emotional. And as someone who watched the whole thing unfold, Jack deserved to be forgiven, and you can never convince me otherwise."

"She's only saying that because if I never forgave Jack, she wouldn't have ended up with his brother."

"That is not true." Melissa got animated. "Okay, okay. It's totally true."

Cassie laughed before sucking in a long breath. "You know, people have strong opinions about cheating. They take it so personally that they lose the ability to be rational, or see things from different angles. The whole thing becomes very black and white to most people." She chopped the air with her fist.

"But you didn't see it like that?"

"It wasn't black and white. Situations rarely are. And look, I'm not saying that everyone deserves to be forgiven because they don't. And some people don't deserve second chances. But Jack did. And I don't subscribe to the theory of *once a cheater, always a cheater* or else I wouldn't have taken him back and we wouldn't still be together."

"I always thought that cheating was just in someone's nature," I admitted, feeling a little naive. "That if they did it once, they'd do it again."

"I think most people thing that. Jack's the prime example of that not being true," Cassie said matter-of-factly, like there was no question.

"You never worried that he might cheat again?"

"Of course I worried. But that's what I'm trying to tell you. Jack showed me every single day that I had nothing to worry about. I asked him to prove it, and he did. The other girls didn't go away, but the way he interacted with them did. He owned up to his mistake, knew he'd made one, and never wanted to make it again. Jack made me feel like the most important person in his life. Even more important than baseball. He gave me exactly what I needed to be able to move past it and truly forgive."

"Is this seat taken?" The familiar voice hit my ears, and I turned to look.

"Dad?" I practically jumped into his arms. "Oh my gosh, what are you doing here?"

Family Meeting

Chance

MY TEAMMATES FANNED out around me, and I stopped in my tracks, noticing a strange man standing next to my mom and Danika. It made me curious, and for whatever reason, I couldn't stop watching them.

"Who is that with our girls?" my dad snuck up behind me and asked over my shoulder.

"Girls? Mom is not a girl," I argued.

"I'll tell her you said that." He grinned.

I stuttered on my response, "You know what I mean!"

"Do we know who that is or not?" My dad's voice turned serious. He did not like strange men talking to my mother.

"No clue." I shrugged. "Give me five, and we'll go see."

"Make it four," he said, sounding uncomfortable—and Jack Carter was rarely uncomfortable.

Leaving my dad alone for too long might have disastrous results, so I decided to forgo the shower altogether and quickly changed into some street clothes, tossing my dirty uniform in the oversize bin and putting on extra deodorant. When I walked out of the locker room, my dad was already changed and waiting for me. I had no idea how he'd gotten there before me, but then I looked down and noticed he was still in his coaching uniform, minus the jersey. He'd basically thrown a T-shirt on over his coaching pants, and he still had on his turf cleats.

I peered around him. "He still there?" I asked, and my dad let out some gruff-sounding response. "Let's go then," I said before I started walking.

We headed up the cement ramp toward the main aisle, where Danika, my mom, and this strange man still stood, talking. They hadn't even moved from their seats, and our women were always waiting for us at the gate near left field.

Dad and I strode down the stairs toward the three of them, none of them even noticing we were coming.

"Hey," I said as I reached Danika and bent down to give her a kiss, assuming that my dad was probably doing the same thing.

"You're done already?" she said before pulling her head back. "Oh, you didn't shower?"

"Do I stink?" I asked, suddenly mortified, and she laughed instead of answering. Of course I stunk. I'd just played nine innings, covered from head to toe in catcher's gear.

"Chance," she said before focusing her attention on the man at her side, "this is my dad, Ralph Marchetti."

"Oh. Sir"—I extended my hand toward him before shooting my own dad an embarrassed look—"it's so nice to meet you."

"Ralph Marchetti," my dad's voice boomed in the

almost-empty stadium, his demeanor instantly relaxed. "Fly all the way out here to give me shit about the Mets in person?"

"I came out here to make sure your son was good enough for my daughter," he said with a wink, and they both started howling with laughter, but I almost pissed my pants.

Ralph wasn't kidding, wink or not, so I wasn't sure what the hell they both found so funny.

"I should, um"—I thumbed toward the locker room—"I should go shower. I'll be, like, five minutes."

Danika leaned up on her toes. "Why didn't you shower in the first place?"

"I'll tell you later," I whispered before kissing the top of her head. If I kissed her on the lips again, her dad might chop off my head and mount it on a wall.

"Where's Jacey? I saw her earlier," I asked my mom.

"She left with your aunt. She's spending the night there."

"We have the house to ourselves?" my dad piped up, his eyebrows wagging, and there were some things I just wished I could unsee.

"Well, I invited Ralph to stay with us."

"And I told her no," Ralph interjected quickly, clearly not wanting to overstep any bounds.

"Of course you're staying with us! I have so much cool shit to show you," my dad countered, suddenly excited to catch up with an old friend.

Danika and I both cast each other a weird look.

"Only if you're sure it's not an inconvenience," Ralph pushed, and my dad insisted again until he agreed.

"Go shower." Danika smacked my ass, and I could have died right then and there. Her dad was definitely going to murder me.

I heard my mom sniff the air. "You too. Why didn't either of you shower?" she asked, and I had no idea what my dad said to her because I was already too far away.

The sound of my dad jogging to catch up had me pause and wait.

"Oh, man, Danika's old man is here. You'll like him. He's a great guy from what I remember. Funny. Ambitious. Motivated and smart as hell."

"And probably going to kill me as soon as any of you turn your backs," I mentioned matter-of-factly.

"You really like this girl." It was a statement, but he sounded almost wistful as he said it. "I found the love of my life my junior year too."

I wanted to argue, just to do it, but there was no point. We both knew I'd be lying.

WE MET UP with our "girls" and Ralph at the left-field fence, like usual. I felt a million times better after showering, but I was still nervous. I wanted Danika's dad to like me. Actually, I wanted him to like me a hell of a lot more than he had ever liked Jared, if I was being honest.

"We thought we could go to Newport, and I'd pick up

some food on the way. We know how hungry you both are after a game," my mom suggested, and my stomach growled in response. "And I thought it would be more comfortable, being home instead of at some restaurant."

"I like food," I said as Danika reached for my hand and intertwined our fingers. My eyes instantly went to her father's as he watched our interaction, his eyes zeroing in on our locked hands. I almost pulled mine away, but Danika would wonder what the hell was wrong with me.

"Are you tired, Dad?" she asked, her concern for him sweet. "I just meant because of the time difference."

"I'm a bit wiped, yeah. But I think Jack and I are hanging out tonight, so I'll rally," he said, and Danika laughed.

"You'll rally?" she teased, and he wrapped an arm around her shoulders and pulled her out of my grip. "Did you rent a car?"

"No. I can't imagine trying to drive out here," Ralph said, and I remembered that most New Yorkers didn't drive at all if they could avoid it. That was what happened when you had a functioning and well-planned-out public transportation system, unlike whatever we called ours in Southern California.

"We can give you a ride," I offered, wanting to be polite but secretly hoping he'd want to ride with my parents instead.

"No way. Ralph's coming with me," my dad interjected. I shot him a grateful look, and he gave me a quick head nod. "We'll see you all at home."

I looked at Danika and reached for her hand again.

"Guess that settles that," I said, and she smiled.

"I can't believe my dad's here."

We reached the Beast, and I pulled open her door for her and helped her inside.

Hopping into the driver's seat, I clicked my seat belt and started the engine before leaning over and taking my girl's mouth with mine. It had been way too long since I'd kissed her. Her fingers dug into the back of my neck, holding me tight as our tongues touched, and I got way too turned on. This girl had changed my whole world.

Pulling away slowly, I asked, "Did you know your dad was coming out?"

"No. Not at all. He just showed up at your game!" She sounded so excited and happy. "I think after our conversation about the company and what I wanted to do with it, he realized how serious we were," she said before snapping her lips closed.

"Go on," I urged as I put my truck in drive. "We are serious, Danika. I've always told you that. This was never a fling or a one-night stand. I warned you from the beginning."

She grinned again, her cheeks flushing with her emotions. "I think he just wanted to meet you …" She paused and added, "Or he wanted to hang out with your dad."

I laughed. Personally, I thought he wanted to hang out with my dad and potentially murder me for taking away his only baby girl. We drove on the freeway with the radio playing in the background, and before I knew it, I was exiting and almost home.

Stopping at a red light, I leaned toward Danika and

pressed my forehead against hers. "I love you," I said, certain that I'd never get tired of telling her that or hearing it in return.

Her face broke out into a huge smile as she closed her eyes for a moment before reopening them. "I love you too."

"What was that?"

"The eyes thing?"

"Yeah."

"Just making sure this wasn't a dream and that you were real," she said, and I laughed.

"I feel the same way about you, baby," I said as the light turned green.

"You know, Chance, just for the record, I don't care about baseball," she said, and I almost slammed on the brakes as I shot her a questionable look. "I just meant that baseball isn't why I like you. I like who you are as a person and the kind of guy you are. The way you treat me and make me feel. The baseball stuff is just a bonus but only because it makes you so happy and you're so passionate about it. But if you never played another game again, I'd still want you just the same."

I glanced over my shoulder to check for oncoming traffic before pulling my truck to the side of the road and turning on the hazard lights. Placing the car in park, I initiated the emergency brake and sat there, staring straight ahead. I'd never expected to hear something like that from Danika. Mostly because I hadn't thought I needed it. I'd never once thought that she liked me for the wrong reasons, but having her say it out loud had me overcome with emotion.

Swallowing hard, I blew out a few quick breaths and focused on maintaining my cool instead of completely breaking down.

"Are you okay? Did I say something wrong?" she asked, suddenly concerned, her hand on my shoulder. "I meant all that in a good way." She sounded so nervous, as if she'd messed us up somehow when it was the furthest thing from the truth.

I couldn't look at her. Not yet. I was going to fucking lose it if I did, and I really did not want to cry in front of my girl. Hell, I couldn't remember the last time I'd cried at all, but I wasn't about to do it now.

"Chance? Look at me," she pleaded, and I put a finger in the air, asking her to give me a minute.

I'd had no idea that someone like her existed or that I would ever find her. A female who honestly didn't care if I played baseball or not. She loved me for who I was, not what I could be or what I could offer her.

"I never thought I'd find someone like you," I said as I finally worked up the courage to look at her without bawling. "I really thought I'd be alone forever. I mean, I hoped that maybe I'd find a girl someday, but I never knew how it would happen. It just didn't seem possible. She'd always want Chance Carter, the baseball player, and never just Chance Carter, the guy." I reached out and cupped her cheek in my hand. "Then, I met you. And you changed everything. You made me feel something I'd never felt before, and at first, I hated myself for it because you weren't mine to want. You weren't mine to have, and it tore me up inside."

Her eyes started to water, and mine did the same.

"Girls always say they have walls that guys need to climb, but I had armor. And you cracked it the first day I met you, and you've been slicing through it ever since."

She started crying and didn't even try to stop, and I felt my own tears start to fall before quickly wiping them away. I remembered what Cole had said when he came over that day, about having a partner and feeling really alone if Christina hadn't been there to experience it all with him. I couldn't have understood what he was saying at the time, but I felt like I completely understood it now.

"This thing between us isn't temporary, baby."

"I know it's not," she said as she wiped away her tears, and my heart expanded, just hearing her say those words.

"Can we go to my parents' now? I'm starving." I tried to lighten the mood, and it worked.

Danika giggled and leaned over to kiss me and tell me she loved me. Then, I pulled back onto the road and headed toward home.

When we pulled into my parents' driveway, my dad's car was already in the garage, but my mom's wasn't, so I parked my truck so that my mom would have enough room to get in. I unclicked my seat belt and leaned toward my girl once more, giving her another kiss before we went inside and I'd be too scared to make out with her in front of her dad.

"Is there anything I should know?" I asked, throwing her own question back at her from when we'd visited my parents for the first time together.

She smiled in recognition. "Nah. My dad's a softy. Even

if he pretends to be super tough, it's all an act."

"That doesn't really help," I complained, and she grabbed my hand and pulled me toward my own front door like she was the one who had grown up there and not me.

We walked through the front door to the sounds of yelling and laughter coming from somewhere in the house.

"Oh my God. I think they're in the pool." I looked at Danika, and she shook her head like there was no way that was possible.

"Not a chance. My dad is not in the pool with yours."

"Why not?"

"I don't think I've ever seen my dad swim before?" she said it like a question before continuing, "Whenever we go to the Hamptons, he always lounges around the pool but never gets in it. And my memories of swimming as a kid were always with my mom."

"Okay. Maybe they're in my dad's office," I suggested with a shrug. "Also known as his sports memorabilia room."

"That's more likely," she agreed as the front door swung open behind us, and we turned to see my mom struggling with a handful of bags.

"Help," she said, and we raced to her and took some of the bags from her hands.

"Is this all food?" I asked, wondering if she'd invited fifty other people over without telling us.

"I wanted Ralph to try real Mexican. I might have gone a little overboard," she explained, but I understood completely.

Mexican food tasted different depending on which state you were in. And there was nothing that tasted like

California's. It was the best, hands down, no matter what anyone else tried to say or sell you.

"I'll take some home to Mac. He'll be so happy," I offered, and my mom's expression turned pouty.

"We should have invited him over. You're always leaving Mac out. Poor Mac," she said.

I shook my head. "Do not feel sorry for him. He's probably making out with some girl as we speak," I said, and Danika busted out laughing.

"It's true. He probably is," she said, having my back, and my mom quieted as we all started pulling the containers of food out of the bags and setting them on the counter.

She truly had gone overboard, but I wasn't complaining. That just meant leftovers, and I was all about that.

"Boys," she shouted.

I looked at her, half-expecting my cousin, Coby, to come running in. That was what she always said for the two of us, but now, she meant my dad and Danika's.

"Boys?" I teased.

"What was I supposed to say? I don't know. It was just easier. Leave me alone." She pulled out plates from the cupboard and set them down near the plethora of food.

Ralph and my dad came in, both of them sniffing the air.

"Mexican? You got me Mexican?" My dad reached for my mom and spun her around, kissing her neck and hair.

"I got it for Ralph," she teased before giving Ralph a sweet look, and my dad cocked his head back in mock defense.

"I might send you home with the kids," he said, and I

almost started coughing.

The food was amazing, and Ralph commented on how they didn't have Mexican food like this in New York.

We all shouted, "I know," in unison, and his accent grew so thick in response that it made me laugh.

I looked around at our blended family and couldn't believe that this was my life. *How did things chang so quickly and without warning?* I'd never known that my life was missing anything before, but if you removed Danika from it now, I'd have a hard time breathing without her.

With a full stomach, I realized just how exhausted I was.

"You two had better get home. Unless you want to stay the night here?" my mom offered, and I honestly didn't care either way, deciding to leave it up to Danika.

"We should probably go home and be closer to the field since your game is early tomorrow," she said, and I knew I had a keeper.

"See? You're a good baseball girlfriend, and you don't even realize it," my dad said, meaning it as a compliment.

"I'll see you tomorrow, Dad?" Danika asked her father.

"Of course," he said before giving her a hug and reaching for my hand. "Can I talk to you for a minute?" he asked me.

I suddenly wanted to throw up everything I'd just eaten. I wasn't sure I even responded to him, but I followed him blindly, knowing that I'd do whatever he asked.

Why didn't anyone ever warn me how nerve-racking it is to meet your girlfriend's dad? I wanted to pummel every guy friend I'd ever had who had never told me this part about dating.

"I wanted to meet you before you got drafted and took my little girl away from me," he started.

I had to stop myself from shouting, *I knew it*, before bracing myself for the pummeling that I was sure was about to come.

"I love your daughter, sir," I said, hoping he would let me live a little longer so I could keep doing it.

He chuckled deep. "Call me Ralph. And I know you do. I can tell," he said, and I wondered if parents just knew these kinds of things.

"This might be awkward or inappropriate, but I need to ask it, sir," I said, shifting my weight and wondering how to word this.

"Ralph," he repeated before giving me a wave.

"It's about Jared. Is he going to be a problem for us? He keeps alluding—" I started to clarify, but he cut me right off.

"Jared will not be anything to either of you. I've talked with the boy. He really did love my daughter, but then something changed for him, and he became more focused on working for me and taking over the company. I'm not sure exactly what happened, but he will not interfere in your lives. And if he does, you make sure to let me know." His tone was forceful and direct.

"Thank you. I hope you didn't take that like I couldn't take care of your daughter. It's just that Jared seemed a little unhinged." The last thing I wanted was this man to think he was leaving his daughter in weak hands. "I would never let anything happen to her."

"I'm not worried, Chance. You're a great kid. Heck of a

ball player, and I only saw the last three innings. You remind me of your dad."

"Really?" I perked up because that was one hell of a compliment, and maybe he wasn't going to murder me after all.

"Even though he was a lefty, you guys have some of the same movements and mannerisms," he said, and I grinned because I'd heard that before, but I hadn't always believed it.

"I'm really glad you came out. It was nice to get the chance to meet you. I've never seen Danika so happy," I said, hoping he knew that I was being genuine.

"Neither have I," he said, and I felt the shock rip through me.

I wanted to make Danika happier than anyone else ever had, but I didn't know if I was.

"Really?"

"Really. You have my approval to steal my daughter away and make her happy for as long as she lets you." He grinned before wrapping a hefty arm around my shoulders and slapping my back.

I fought back a cough as I thanked him and walked out to get my girl and take her home.

Dreams Come True

Two Months Later

Chance

THE REGULAR BASEBALL season had ended, but we'd made it to regionals and were currently up in Northern California for the next game. If we won tonight, we'd advance to Super Regionals, and if we won those games too, we'd be off to the College World Series in Nebraska. I really wanted to go to Omaha and play baseball there.

But right now, I was sitting in my parents' hotel suite, surrounded by my family.

I'd thought about having some of the guys watch the draft with me, but it felt like it might be in poor taste. What if none of them got drafted and only I did? The last thing I wanted was for any of them to feel like I was throwing my success in their faces. I knew how badly each and every player on my team wanted their shot at playing pro ball, so I talked to my dad about it, and he thought I was right to keep it limited to family only. He'd said there'd be enough celebrating with friends after.

I'd felt bad about leaving Mac out, considering that he was my closest friend, so after asking him a million times if he was sure he wanted to watch it with us, I'd invited him over.

He was currently sitting at one of the tables with the twins, eating something my mom had ordered, I wasn't sure what. The only people missing were Gran and Gramps. Since they couldn't travel the way that they used to and hated flying, my mom had them on video chat on her phone. The best part was that I could only see Gran's eyeballs and Gramps's mouth. Neither one of their full faces was in frame, and Danika couldn't stop giggling about it as she sat next to me on the couch, her hand in mine.

Speaking of Danika, she'd graduated from Fullton State two weeks ago, and instead of heading back home to New York after, she stayed with me and came to all of my post-season games. I'd tried to encourage her to go home and get things figured out before draft day—mostly, I meant for her to pack everything she owned and get ready to move with me—but she'd refused to leave while I still had games to play. She was amazing, and I was grateful.

Even more amazing was her dad. He had flown out to watch the regional games in person and to be here for the draft. Ralph and I had grown pretty close in the last couple of months. He followed all of my games online and sent me text messages regularly, and I kept him updated on his daughter and sent him a lot of selfies. He liked that, and I liked keeping him happy.

Everyone was sitting on couches and chairs, pretending

not to notice the camera filming us, as we waited for the Major League Baseball Draft to begin. The only thing I couldn't stand was how my sister was currently dressed. It wasn't so much her clothes as it was the full face of makeup. She looked like a damn twenty-year-old movie star, and I hated it.

"Remind me to put on my social media later that my sister is only fifteen," I growled toward Danika, who laughed at me and called me crazy.

But I knew how guys would react to seeing her on TV, and I wanted to stop that shit before it started. My little twin cousins weren't much better in the makeup department, and I'd almost insisted that the three of them go hide in the bathroom when the filming started, so they wouldn't be seen.

Uncle Dean walked up and asked to pull me aside. He let me know that I was going to get drafted in the first round, but he wouldn't tell me which team was interested, no matter how many times I asked. He just got a funny look on his face and shrugged like it didn't matter. And honestly, it didn't. We all knew that I'd go play for whoever wanted me. I'd passed up this opportunity after high school, but I wasn't going to do that now. It was time.

"How certain are you?" I asked my uncle, referring to the first-round part.

Going in the first round was a big deal, and I hated getting my hopes up if they were only going to come crashing down around me. I'd seen it happen before. I'd been with guys who thought they were going early in the draft, only to end up going late or not at all. It was absolutely crushing to watch. There was nothing comparable to watching your dreams explode all around you, knowing that you couldn't do a damn thing to stop it from happening.

"I'd say, ninety-eight percent," he said. "Don't worry. You're getting drafted today. Even though you can't accept the offer until you're done playing all of your college games," he informed me, as if I needed the reminder. "And I'm not your agent until after then either."

"I know, Uncle."

If I got drafted today, I couldn't officially accept; otherwise, I wouldn't be eligible to play the rest of Fullton's season. I would be considered a professional athlete at that point, and professionals couldn't play in the NCAA. We had to hold off on making a decision until the last college game was over and done. But in the meantime, that would give my uncle time to work on negotiating the signing bonus and other details, like an injury clause, when it came time. And I could focus on winning the College World Series.

"It's time," someone announced. Maybe it was the guy behind the camera or the one with the notepad—I couldn't be sure.

My eyes roamed the room and met Mac's, and he gave me a supportive nod. I nodded back before heading toward the couch.

I sat down between the two most important women in my life. Danika was on my left, and my mom was on my right. I knew that everyone else in the room was rotating between staring at me and the TV, but all I could do was stare straight ahead.

Looking at the television screen, I willed it to say my name while trying to pretend that I wasn't nervous as hell as the baseball commissioner appeared. Out of the corner of my eye, I saw the red light come on the camera, and I knew that they were filming. There had been talk that I was a top ten contender, but no one had ever claimed that I'd go in the number one spot, so I wasn't expecting it. That had been deemed for some kid from Florida, and just like the experts had said, they were right. His name was called first, and I imagined how excited he must be as his family suddenly appeared on the TV. They were jumping up and down, screaming and yelling, and I couldn't help but be happy for the guy.

We didn't have to wait much longer as my imagination turned to reality at the sound of my own name coming out of the TV speakers. Our hotel room erupted. So did the rooms around us, where I knew my teammates were.

"Holy shit," I said to no one in particular, but Danika was at my side, kissing my face and telling me, "Congratulations," at the same time as my mom was hugging me, shoving her phone in my face so I could see Gran's and Gramps's partial faces.

"Congratulations, Chance!" they both said.

I told them, "Thank you," even though I was pretty sure they couldn't hear me.

"I love you. I'm so proud of you," Danika said into my ear, and I turned to kiss her like no one else was in the room, not even her dad. I'd gotten past thinking that he might murder me at any point just for existing … at least for the most part.

"I love you too," I said, the grin feeling like it took up my entire face.

No matter what anyone had said to me in the past, this hadn't been a sure thing until it actually happened. And it was a much different experience from when it had happened in high school. I'd gotten drafted then, too, but it hadn't felt anywhere close to this. It wasn't in the first round, and no one was filming my reaction to the news. To be honest, I wasn't even watching the draft in the first place. I'd heard the news from one of my teammates on my summer ball team, and I'd been totally caught off guard.

This couldn't have been more opposite.

"Son." My dad was suddenly standing in front of me, his hand extended. I reached for it, and he pulled me up. "I couldn't be prouder. I'm so happy for you. You deserve this."

"Dad"—I felt myself getting emotional—"I'm going to be a fucking Met," I said as it all started to sink in.

The New York Mets had drafted me. Getting the chance to play on the same team that my old man had made this even more fulfilling. I would have played anywhere, of course, but this made all the dreams I'd had as a little boy who worshipped his father come true.

"Ain't that something?" Ralph said, and I looked at him before taking his hand and shaking it as well. "Can't believe I have to root for the Mets again. I'll never live it down," he pretended to grumble with a grin.

"Another Carter jersey to hang on your wall," I said

hopefully. I wasn't in the Major Leagues yet.

"Proudly, son."

Shit. Ralph had called me son. This day could not get any better.

"I can't believe you're going to be on the same team as Dad was." Jacey threw her arms around me and hugged me tight.

"Pretty cool, huh?" I asked, hugging her back.

"You're happy, right?"

"So happy."

"I can't believe you'll be in New York before me. I'm definitely coming to college there now," she said, her tone more excited than I'd ever heard it before.

"You're only fifteen. You might change your mind by then," I said, not meaning anything by it, but I could tell that I had offended her.

My little sister was strong-minded and determined, and no one told her what to do with her life, least of all me.

"I'm not a little kid, you know."

"I know. Guess I'll see you in New York then," I said, if only to appease her, but the smile on her face told me that I should know better.

She'd already made up her mind about where she wanted to go to college, and I would definitely be seeing her in the city at some point.

God help Manhattan.

"Can I interrupt?" Uncle Dean stood between Jacey and me, and I gave him a nod.

"What's up?" I asked as Jacey walked away from us and

back toward our parents.

"Obviously, we can talk about the specifics later, but they're offering a five-point-two-five million dollar bonus," he said, and I wanted to laugh at how unbelievable that was.

The fact that I'd not only get to play baseball for a living, but they also wanted to give me millions of dollars on top of it just to sign with them was insanity. So many other people in different jobs deserved that kind of money more than I did, but that didn't mean I wasn't going to take it. I wanted to live a comfortable life. I wasn't interested in struggling, but maybe Danika and I could start a charity.

"You good with that?" my uncle asked, and I wondered if he'd been talking to me that whole time while I'd been talking to myself. "It's more than your dad got," he added.

I'd already known that. My dad had gotten a five-million-dollar signing bonus.

"Not by much, but it's still over the top," I said.

"Welcome to the world of being a professional athlete in America." He slapped my shoulder before giving me a hug. "Congratulations, Chance. You've worked hard for this. And you'll continue working hard every single day for as long as you play. You deserve to be paid well for it. This isn't a normal nine-to-five job."

I knew all of that. It was just a weird feeling, was all—to have this money being basically tossed at me when, yesterday, I'd had none of it.

My uncle threw me a hat, and I caught it easily. Looking at it, I noted the Mets logo and smiled.

"Don't put that on yet," he directed, and I firmly placed it on my head. "Rebel. Just like your sister."

"Chance." It was Mac.

I had no idea why I was so anxious to look at him. We'd both been with Cole last year when he got drafted, and there were no hard feelings. But then again, neither one of us had been eligible to get drafted yet.

"Holy shit, man. You did it! I told you!" He seemed genuinely excited.

"Thanks." I gave him a hug and felt like I'd hugged more people in the last ten minutes than I had in my entire life. "You good?"

He blew out an uncomfortable sounding breath. "Yeah. Totally. Draft's not over yet," he said.

I knew that he was still holding out hope for himself. And I did the same.

"No, it's not," I agreed before reminding myself to ask my uncle if Mac was on anyone's radar or not.

"Chance, we need you," the camera guy shouted over the chaos, and I looked toward the wall where they'd set up a white sheet for filming.

"I'll be back," I said.

As I headed toward the film crew, I watched as Mac quietly slipped out of the room. He thought that no one had noticed, but I had.

After filming a handful of various video clips and taking pictures that wouldn't be shown or aired until after my last college game, I pulled Danika into one of the bedrooms so that I could talk to her privately. The room, even though it was filled with family, was still celebrating. The film crew was packing up to leave, and my phone was blowing up with text messages and internet notifications.

"So," Danika said with a smile as she pulled at the collar of my T-shirt, so she could reach my mouth, "I'm dating a New York Met?"

"Not yet," I said because I still couldn't say yes to them officially. "But soon. How's it feel?"

"Feels like it did yesterday. And the day before that." She pressed a kiss against my lips after each sentence. "Like I'm dating a hotshot," she said, and I bit out a laugh as I wrapped my arms around her and pulled her tighter.

"Do you know where their farm teams are located?" I teased because I knew she had zero idea.

Her expression grew serious. "Where? They're not actually in New York, are they?"

I looked at her, watching her grow distressed with each second that ticked by. "They're in some city in Florida; Binghamton, New York; and Syracuse, New York."

She slapped my shoulder. "Shut up, babe. Seriously?"

"Seriously. So, what do you say? Will you come with me?" I asked because I had to. Even though we'd already decided to move together, I still wanted to ask.

"I'd go anywhere with you," she answered before giving me another kiss.

And she would.

Epilogue

Mac Davies

IT WAS STUPID, and I was being an idiot. Here I was, back in my and Chance's shared hotel room, feeling sorry for myself. I was happy for him. I'd always be happy for him because he'd deserved to get drafted, but I wanted it too. That was why I'd left when he sat down with the reporters. I was afraid that he'd be able to see my jealousy. And I hadn't wanted to ruin that moment for him.

When the days came and went and my name was never called in the draft, I couldn't help but feel that pang of disappointment in my guts. I wondered if that was how Cole had felt when he didn't get drafted his junior year. I thought about calling him and asking. I needed someone to talk to, but I didn't want to sound like a pussy.

I had one more year left. One more year to show the scouts that I was worth drafting. That I was good enough to play professional baseball for them. But honestly, I wasn't sure that I was. I was good enough to play for one of the best college baseball teams in the country, but that didn't mean that I had what the scouts were looking for to go beyond that.

So far, not a single one had approached me. There were no agents banging down my door, hoping to represent me when the time came. No emails, no phone calls, no messages through Coach Jackson. No nothing.

And as much as I hated to admit it, there was a pretty damn good possibility that I'd be going back home to Arizona after my senior year and taking a job with my dad's company. It had always been the backup plan. One I hoped I'd never need. One my dad had assumed I always would. The thought alone made me want to get on a plane and disappear. Having my failure thrown in my face daily wasn't something I was looking forward to. I really fucking wanted to prove my dad wrong. But so far, all I was doing was proving him right.

FULLTON STATE HAD ended up making it to the College World Series. We didn't win though. A bad call by the umpire at home lost the game for us. Chance had clearly tagged the guy out at home plate, but the umpire had called him safe. The thing about bad calls was, they couldn't be taken back. So, even though we reviewed the tape a hundred times after the game was over and saw that the runner really was out, it was too late. It'd changed nothing. In our minds, we knew we'd won, but on paper, we'd lost. And to everyone else, we weren't the champions.

Chance and Danika had left for Florida soon after we got back from Omaha. The Mets had sent him to Class A-Advanced instead of regular Single-A. I knew he wouldn't be there long either, so I hoped Danika liked packing up and moving. They seemed really happy though.

And that was when I realized that playing professional baseball wasn't the only thing I wanted for my life.

I wanted the one other thing that had kept eluding me—a real girlfriend. I knew I came off as the team's biggest player, but it was all a front. A defense mechanism. As long as I called all the shots, I couldn't get hurt like I had freshman year. All that needed to change. And I had no idea how to do it. Especially when all the girls only wanted to hook up with me because I was a baseball player.

What happened if I no longer was one?

THE END

Other Books by J. Sterling

Bitter Rivals—an enemies to lovers romance
Dear Heart, I Hate You
10 Years Later—A Second Chance Romance
In Dreams—a new adult college romance
Chance Encounters—a coming of age story

The Game Series:
The Perfect Game—Book One
The Game Changer—Book Two
The Sweetest Game—Book Three
The Other Game (Dean Carter)—Book Four

The Playboy Serial:
Avoiding the Playboy—Episode #1
Resisting the Playboy—Episode #2
Wanting the Playboy—Episode #3

The Celebrity Series:
Seeing Stars—Madison & Walker
Breaking Stars—Paige & Tatum
Losing Stars—Quinn & Ryson

The Fisher Brothers Series:
No Bad Days—a New Adult, Second Chance Romance
Guy Hater—an Emotional Love Story
Adios Pantalones—a Single Mom Romance
Happy Ending

THE BOYS OF BASEBALL
(THE NEXT GENERATION OF FULLTON STATE BASEBALL PLAYERS):

The Ninth Inning—Cole Anders

Behind the Plate—Chance Carter

Safe at First—Mac Davies

About the Author

Jenn Sterling is a Southern California native who loves writing stories from the heart. Every story she tells has pieces of her truth as well as her life experience. She has her bachelor's degree in radio/TV/film and has worked in the entertainment industry the majority of her life.

Jenn loves hearing from her readers and can be found online at:

Blog & Website:
www.j-sterling.com

Twitter:
twitter.com/AuthorJSterling

Facebook:
facebook.com/AuthorJSterling

Instagram:
instagram.com/AuthorJSterling

If you enjoyed this book, please consider writing a spoiler-free review on the site from which you purchased it. And thank you so much for helping me spread the word about my books and for allowing me to continue telling the stories I love to tell. I appreciate you so much. :)

Follow Me on These Book Loving Sites:

Amazon

BookBub

Goodreads

Thank you for purchasing this book.

Please join my mailing list to get updates on new and upcoming releases, deals, bonus content, personal appearances, and other fun news!

tinyurl.com/pf6al6u

TEXT: JACK

TO: 77948

Made in the USA
Middletown, DE
28 April 2022

64827140R00248